FEARLESS

SOMERTON SECURITY, BOOK 3

ELIZABETH DYER

PRAISE FOR ELIZABETH DYER

"An excellent blend of suspense and romance—I was sucked into the story from page one!"

—Susan Stoker, *New York Times, Wall Street Journal,* and *USA Today* bestselling author

"Funny, clever, and suspenseful—I couldn't put this book down! The world needs more nerdy-hot heroes and fierce-hot heroines."

—Penny Reid, *USA Today* bestselling author

"Sexy, suspenseful, and downright hilarious in places. *Defenseless* had me gripped with the perfect balance of romance and intrigue. A tightly crafted plot combined with a beautifully told story as well as characters I was rooting for meant I couldn't put it down."

—Louise Bay, *USA Today* bestselling author

"*Defenseless* from Elizabeth Dyer is my favorite romantic suspense debut of 2017. Fast-paced action, heart-pounding passion, and a cat that rides a Roomba! I love it when the tension in a book is tempered with humor, and this author delivers in spades. Georgia Bennett and Parker Livingston are meant for each other. She's the type of woman you'd want to be friends with. And he's '. . . lazy Sunday mornings after sex-against-the-wall Saturday nights.' Love it!"

—Dana Marton, *New York Times* bestselling author

"*Relentless* is a fast-paced, action-packed romantic suspense that had me turning the pages late into the night. Ethan Somerton is determined to rescue his friend, taken prisoner by the Columbian cartel. To do that he must infiltrate the Vega family, and he zeroes in on the mafia boss's niece, Natalia Vega, as a way to find the information he needs. Sparks fly as these two dance around each other. *Relentless* is a sexy, edge of your seat story with a complex hero and a woman trained to kill. I highly recommend it."

—Sandra Owens, author of the bestselling K2 Team and Aces & Eights series

"Edgy, passionate, and laced with unexpected humor, Relentless is this summer's romantic suspense must-read. From their first meeting, I rooted for Ethan to break through Natalia's well-earned walls and show her a love worth fighting for—even if it might cost them everything."

—Jessica Hawkins, USA Today bestselling author

PRAISE FOR ELIZABETH DYER

"An excellent blend of suspense and romance—I was sucked into the story from page one!"

—Susan Stoker, *New York Times, Wall Street Journal*, and *USA Today* bestselling author

"Funny, clever, and suspenseful—I couldn't put this book down! The world needs more nerdy-hot heroes and fierce-hot heroines."

—Penny Reid, *USA Today* bestselling author

"Sexy, suspenseful, and downright hilarious in places. *Defenseless* had me gripped with the perfect balance of romance and intrigue. A tightly crafted plot combined with a beautifully told story as well as characters I was rooting for meant I couldn't put it down."

—Louise Bay, *USA Today* bestselling author

"*Defenseless* from Elizabeth Dyer is my favorite romantic suspense debut of 2017. Fast-paced action, heart-pounding passion, and a cat that rides a Roomba! I love it when the tension in a book is tempered with humor, and this author delivers in spades. Georgia Bennett and Parker Livingston are meant for each other. She's the type of woman you'd want to be friends with. And he's '. . . lazy Sunday mornings after sex-against-the-wall Saturday nights.' Love it!"

—Dana Marton, *New York Times* bestselling author

"*Relentless* is a fast-paced, action-packed romantic suspense that had me turning the pages late into the night. Ethan Somerton is determined to rescue his friend, taken prisoner by the Columbian cartel. To do that he must infiltrate the Vega family, and he zeroes in on the mafia boss's niece, Natalia Vega, as a way to find the information he needs. Sparks fly as these two dance around each other. *Relentless* is a sexy, edge of your seat story with a complex hero and a woman trained to kill. I highly recommend it."

—Sandra Owens, author of the bestselling K2 Team and Aces & Eights series

"Edgy, passionate, and laced with unexpected humor, Relentless is this summer's romantic suspense must-read. From their first meeting, I rooted for Ethan to break through Natalia's well-earned walls and show her a love worth fighting for—even if it might cost them everything."

—Jessica Hawkins, USA Today bestselling author

ALSO BY ELIZABETH DYER

Somerton Security

Defenseless

Relentless

For every single reader who asked: What about Will?
This one is for you.

CHAPTER ONE

São Paulo, Brazil

She was being followed.

For Cooper Reed, it was an experience as uncomfortable as it was depressingly familiar.

Disavowed by the CIA. Forgotten by the army. Buried by her family.

From predator to prey—if nothing else, she could appreciate the irony.

That was her life now.

The constant threat of discovery. Sleeping with a gun by her side, a knife in easy reach, burning through countries and jobs and identities.

Alone.

Under the best of circumstances, it was an exhausting race without a finish line.

But nights like tonight, as a misting rain soaked her jacket then gathered and slid beneath her clothes in tiny, determined rivers, life was an endless nightmare and the cost of waking too damn high.

She slipped across the street and around a corner.

Shadows followed her.

Eyes burned through her.

Paranoia rose like a shiver across her skin.

Living with a price on her head—modest but growing—had hollowed her out until the only thing that filled her was a desperate rage.

That she'd been used.

That she couldn't go home.

That sometimes, in the early hours of the morning, when memories and hard realizations kept her from sleep, she didn't believe she deserved to.

The things she'd done to try to make things right. To save her best friend, her partner. . . She'd made compromises and crossed lines—so many lines she wasn't sure she'd ever be able to find her way back.

A problem for another day, she reminded herself. And only one of many.

For now, she had to focus on moving forward. And tonight, she had to deal with her shadow, before he dealt with her.

Permanently.

She tugged the hood of her coat down, hiding her features: blonde hair that still clung to a muddy brown dye job, fair skin that had seen layer upon layer of sun, but remained far lighter than the bronzed hues that surrounded her in South America. She stood out, drew stares, commanded attention.

But she could disappear when she wanted to. Long enough, at least, to turn the tables and grab the advantage.

Not that she needed it. She'd seen this one coming. He wasn't skilled at the hunt, something she'd been born to. So she'd lingered near windows, stepped slowly through crowds, and strolled through streets and around corners. He thought himself a predator, but she led him like a lamb. In a city of twenty million, anyone could go missing—there one minute and gone the next—and in the South American *favelas*, tinderboxes of redbrick stacked and sprawled, alive and dying, pulsing with the primal beat of survival, anyone could be wiped from the playing board.

It wouldn't be her.

She knew the neighborhood too well. Had walked the endless turns and paths and alleys that led to secret doors and private ventures and abrupt dead ends. She'd made deals and greased palms, brought kind conversation to some and quiet threats to others until the locals recognized her for who and what she was: someone desperate for a way out, but without the means to leave.

A foreigner, but one of them, too.

They wouldn't bother her.

She turned again, doubled her pace, whispered a hello to the little boy, his cheeks sunken and his eyes bright—a mural splashed against crumbling mortar that always left her with a strange sense of hope.

Two more turns and she took the half-dozen stairs up to a darkened doorway, careful to avoid the spill of rain off the gutter-less roof.

She stilled and waited. He didn't disappoint.

It took ninety seconds—she counted, timing his progress—and he appeared, his pace a cautious prowl forward. Barely out of his teens and a local, but one who'd left the *favelas* for the lure of the cartels and the money they offered. It was there in his clothes, wet and clinging to his skin, but new and clean. In the chain, gold and glinting, around his neck. And in the pistol tucked against the small of his back. It wasn't fancy, and the serial number would be missing but it'd shoot straight all the same.

If he lived to see thirty, he'd reach what passed for old age in his profession.

He might have had a chance—life out here was capricious at best—but he'd come for her.

A fatal mistake.

How had he found her? He wasn't agency. Wasn't even the sort of contractor they sometimes employed. It didn't matter. He was green and sloppy, and Cooper had been in this life long enough to know that a true threat would be one she never saw coming.

No. Whoever this guy was—mercenary, opportunist, or something else altogether—he wasn't her end.

But she would be his.

She let him pass, started her count again. Factored in the way the rain would muffle her steps and dampen his senses. Recalculated the distance she needed to maintain surprise. He was still new enough at this to be cautious, to keep his movements slow and quiet. It did him credit, but the learning curve in this business was brutal, and his job didn't promote the careless.

Cooper slipped down the steps, hugged the deep shadow of the buildings, and fell into his wake.

Gunshot? Too loud.

Knife? Too messy.

Stranglehold? Not with their height disparity—she wouldn't have the leverage.

A blow to the outside of his knee would take him down and her training would do the rest.

She'd snap his neck.

Fast. Effective. Silent.

By the time his body made its way to the morgue, he'd become just another statistic in a city rife with them.

And she'd be gone.

He turned, heading toward what Cooper knew to be a dead end.

She quickened her pace; there'd be no better opportunity.

A hand reached out of the dark, grabbed her bicep, and jerked her through a door she hadn't realized was open.

Bait and switch? God *damn* it.

She went for her gun, a last, desperate resort, but pressure to her wrist encouraged her to let go. No-fucking-way. She brought her knee up, clipped the heavy muscle of a thigh and elicited a laugh instead of a grunt.

"Now, now, love," a deep voice scolded, "it's not sporting to kill the young ones."

Cooper stilled, murder on her mind, but not in her heart.

Pierce. Because sure, why *wouldn't* he be here? The man was like a bad penny.

"Sporting?" she asked on a huff. "He'd have shot me, snapped a photo, and collected the two hundred thousand on my head."

"Three-fifty, last I checked." Pierce shrugged as if she hadn't just leveled up in a big way. He released her, but stayed close, crowding her against the wall. "It'd be like shooting Bambi."

"You expect me to believe you have a weakness for green mercenaries and baby animals?"

"Chicks dig baby animals," he said, his accent muted and generically European, as if it had been worn down beneath the grind of time and constant travel.

As always, it made Cooper wonder where the man had come from.

"But I couldn't care less about the kid." He braced his hand above her head and stared down at her. "By all means, kill him, but before you do, you should know he wasn't sent to murder you."

"The gun he had tucked in his pants implied otherwise," she said with a roll of her eyes.

"Think it through—he's young. Local and inexperienced—"

"And dumb enough to think that just because I'm a woman, I'm helpless." She tilted her chin up. "An easy payday."

"Perhaps," he agreed. "Though the people who want you dead aren't stupid enough to waste an opportunity on a cartel kid who won't live to see his next birthday."

"Then why?" she asked, her thoughts racing to put together the puzzle Pierce had clearly already solved.

"When you picked up a shadow, you entered the *favelas*—why?" Pierce asked.

Cooper shrugged. "I know them. Most people get lost—"

"And you can disappear. A neat trick and a distinct advantage."

Yes, except the kid was a local. And though the cartel had provided the means to escape the slums, he'd been born here. This was his backyard, and Cooper, no matter how many paths she explored and how many routes she memorized, was a visitor in this maze.

Which meant . . .

"Ah, realization dawns," Pierce gloated.

"He was herding me toward something," she said, her skin going cold, then flushing hot with embarrassment and anger. She'd made it so easy for him.

"Not something," Pierce corrected. "*Someone.*"

Cole. Jesus, he'd found her. Again.

Exhaustion doused her rage.

"Thanks," she told Pierce, her annoyance with him smothered beneath the weight of what might have happened if he hadn't stepped in.

"Don't thank me," he said, his voice a rough whisper of regret. "I'm not doing you any favors, Cooper. Avoiding this . . . it's only putting off the inevitable. The man wants you dead. If you had any sense at all, you'd kill him first."

She ducked beneath his arm and paced away. "You know I can't do that."

"Can't?" he asked. "Or won't."

She shrugged. "Pick one. Cole's my partner." For a long time, he'd been so much more than that. Her best friend, her spotter. Her work husband and her brother-in-arms.

"He *was* your partner. Now he's just a guy who wants you dead. I'd find that hard to forgive."

"It's not his fault." Which was the truth and the only thing that mattered. Someone in the CIA had taken everything about Cole that was good and decent and *human* and corrupted it with a cocktail of drugs and illegal experiments. And for what?

To create nameless, faceless men and women willing to kill on command, without question or remorse?

Familiar anger rose on a heavy wave, but Cooper forced it back. The why didn't matter. Not right now.

She wanted to know who had ordered it . . . and how to fix it. Everything else could wait.

"Such loyalty," Pierce murmured. "I do hope he earned it."

He had. Ten times over, Cole had earned it. She couldn't, wouldn't abandon him.

"So what is this?" She stowed her gun then tugged at her rumpled field jacket. "I save your life, you save mine?"

Pierce cracked a grin, white teeth flashing, single dimple high on his right cheek winking. That smile, half rueful honesty and half crafted lie had probably charmed a number of women into regrettable life choices. It had certainly worked on Cooper.

Once.

Oh, she hadn't done anything so stupid or self-indulgent as fall into bed with him. No, she'd done much, much worse.

"If this makes us square, you place far too little value on what you did for me," he said, all humor bleeding from his voice until it dropped like a curtain of rain. The truth, on the rare occasion it fell from his mouth, always came in a stark, heavy deluge. Cleansing and fierce and with the power to drown her beneath the weight of reality. "When you cash in on the favor I owe you—

and we both know you will—*then* we'll be even." He stepped
toward her, a potent presence in the dark, but friend or fiend she
was never sure.

"You've got a rare and valuable chip in your pocket, Cooper."
He brushed a thumb across her cheek and wore conceit with the
surety of experience. "A golden ticket. Do spend it on something
more interesting than a chocolate factory."

She scowled. But mostly because he was right. For now, at
least, Cooper held Pierce in her debt. She wasn't about to
squander the advantage. Besides, keeping him on the hook was an
amusement in and of itself.

"So, what's this then?" she asked, the muscle in her jaw flexing. "A gesture from the goodness of your heart?"

"You insult me—we both know I don't have one."

She snorted. Oh, Pierce would love for her to believe that.
And his reputation did precede him—cold, calm, calculating.
Disinterested at best, vengeful at worst. It all depended on who
you asked.

Though everyone said the same thing eventually: Pierce
didn't do *anything* he didn't want to. But always did *exactly* what
he said he would.

He wasn't a man you wanted to screw over.

But he wasn't a man she feared, either.

"What are you doing here, Pierce?"

He studied her for a moment, his gaze guarded but weighted
with raw, open honesty he so rarely shared. "You don't belong in
this life, Cooper."

"And you do?" She shoved him away as if such a simple
action could push aside words she didn't want to hear. What
good did they do? He was right, but after over a year on the run
she was no closer to answers, to proof, to a cure. She was chasing
ghosts . . . and becoming one herself.

Pierce grimaced, then reached out to tuck a rain-soaked

strand of hair behind her ear, his touch gentle and his fingers calloused.

"Can't go home when there's no home left," he admitted, dropping his hand. "But that's not true for you, is it?"

No, it wasn't. She had a family. A hometown. Old friends with changing lives. A surly cat that probably didn't miss her but would ignore her in punishment all the same. Homesickness had long ago become her faithful shadow. But she couldn't go home. The second she crossed the US border the target on her back would double in size and glow like the Vegas strip. The CIA had sent Cole, but in the end, they just wanted her dead. They wouldn't be picky about the method. Not if they thought she could expose them.

"Having a home isn't the same as having a way to get there. Even if I wanted to, even if Cole didn't need me, there's too much in the way, too many who want me dead."

"Then let's clear a path."

She shoved her fists into her pockets. She'd tried, damn it. But there was just an endless series of questions and every time she got close to answers, the price on her head climbed and the questions multiplied. She needed *proof*. Names. Documents. Witnesses. She had to find someone who'd been part of the experiments who was still capable of exposing them.

"Just like that, huh?" She snapped her fingers. "Easy peasy?"

"You know better than anyone that searching for something is never as simple as we want it to be."

A truth that had been drummed into her head over and over and over again in sniper school. She could study the same landscape day after day, and still miss the target. It wasn't enough to look for the man hidden in the weeds—he was as adept at hiding as she was at stalking. No, she had to look to the weeds themselves. Learn to see the way they moved or bent around an object they'd been used to conceal in the first place.

"Sometimes the smallest detail reveals the game."

"And you have that?" she asked. It wouldn't be the first time. Pierce had been a light in a life that so often left her cold and alone in the dark. He'd brought her rumors. Names. Leads.

A few had even led to answers. One had led her to Curtis Strauss, a program director within the agency. They'd met for an exchange. Cooper had walked away with a thumb drive and her life.

Thanks to the CIA, Strauss hadn't been so lucky.

But his files had explained enough that she'd stopped running from Cole long enough to try to figure out how to save him. But she needed so much more than a few redacted files.

"No," Pierce said slowly, his pale green eyes glinting like sea glass. "But William Bennett might."

Cooper froze, a rush of heat across her skin clashing with the blade of ice between her ribs.

Will.

"You *do* know him," Pierce said as if she'd verified something he'd long suspected. "Professionally?" he asked before his smile turned amused and a little bit wicked. "Intimately? Both?"

She didn't respond. Partly because Pierce wanted her to, and partly because she didn't have an answer he'd understand. Hell, *she* didn't understand it. She and Will had never met—not really. And yet, she knew him. Liked him. Respected him, which frankly to her mind was more important.

And though she rarely allowed it, she still thought about him.

Recalled his awful sense of humor.

Remembered his rumbled laugh in her ear.

Relived the stone-cold calm in his voice as he'd followed her instructions and let her lead his team through narrow streets and blind turns and out of a city desperate to kill them.

And later, when he'd somehow magicked her contact details

out of thin air, he'd used that same damn voice to make her laugh . . . and make her moan.

So many dirty promises.

So many casual conversations.

But they'd never met. Certainly hadn't slept together.

And yet . . . she knew him. Professionally. Personally. Intimately.

And she didn't like hearing his name in Pierce's mouth.

"The blush suits you, love. Though it does give a man pause. Makes him wonder what it takes to put it there."

"Keep wondering." She brushed him off with a roll of her eyes. "And anyway, I supplied some last-minute support to his team." She shrugged. "I was already there, and they were desperate. I coached Bennett through the city, took out a few obstacles, but that was it."

"If you say so."

"Why is his name coming up now?" she asked and realized with a certain sense of sadness that she wasn't all that surprised. The last time she'd seen Will—through a scope and at a distance —had been the same day Cole had done his damnedest to kill her. Cooper had never been one for coincidences, but it had taken months before she'd understood how closely those two events were related.

And realized just how much Will would hate her.

"A little over a year ago, Bennett was killed after an operation went bad in the jungles of Colombia . . ."

She sucked a breath, absorbed another blow she hadn't anticipated, but didn't say anything.

Pierce didn't comment, but that damn mouth twitched. "Or so the story goes."

Relief, heady and addictive, rushed through her before she could quash it.

"Sound familiar?" Pierce stepped back and pulled a pack of cigarettes from the inside pocket of his coat.

Cooper had never deluded herself into believing her situation was somehow special. That she'd been the first person the US government had found it easier to kill or forget about entirely. Hell, the CIA had *told* her how easily they'd disavow her if she were ever caught working in a foreign country.

But then, she hadn't been caught at all, had she? And she hadn't been abandoned. She'd been marked for death.

"He was left behind?" She forced the next question past a clogged throat. "Accident? Or something else?"

"Initially?" he said with a shrug. "Looks like it was just plain bad luck." He withdrew a silver-plated lighter with a weathered monogram Cooper had never been able to read. "Intel says Bennett was seriously injured and another man died. His team had reason to believe him gone."

"But?" And oh, there was definitely a but. Judging by the way Pierce was drawing this out, it was one she'd probably love and hate in equal measure.

"*But* dear William lived . . . and someone high up in the Department of Defense looked the other way."

"Why?"

"Best guess based on my intel? Bennett's life was traded to cover up dirty deals and a large payday." He shrugged. "War profiteering of one sort or another."

"Charming." She snorted, wrinkling her nose as the scent of burning paper and cheap tobacco hit her. "But I fail to see what this has to do with me."

"You and Bennett have more in common than you realize," he explained, exhaling a steady stream of smoke through his nostrils. It curled on the eddies of his breath and disappeared into the dark. "Smart. Driven. Distinguished military careers. Both hand selected for Special Forces training. Never did make it as far as sniper school, but—"

"Nobody's perfect." These were all things she knew already, so where was he going with this? "Get to the part that's relevant, Pierce." And quickly, because all of her energy was going into blocking out the thought of everything Will had no doubt suffered over the last year.

Pierce grinned, then puffed out a practiced ring of smoke. "Bennett has some interesting friends, present company included, of course." He took another drag, the tip of his cigarette a glowing ember in the gloom. "Including one Felix Harrigan. Know the name?"

She shook her head.

"I'll give you a hint—he died one sunny afternoon in Afghanistan. Seems a sniper permanently interrupted treasonous plans."

Blood drained from her face to pool slick and churning and rancid in her stomach.

"Now you remember."

Of course, she did. She'd never forget it. The heat of the sun. The bite of wind-tossed sand. The punch of the rifle and the *clink* of the shell.

That was the job. Scope the scene. Sight the shot. Pull the trigger.

"What does that have to do with Will?"

"Harrigan made a deposit in his name."

"Money? How much?"

"Don't be common," Pierce scolded her on a sigh. "You know full well it's never that simple."

"Currency, then," she argued. Because if she'd learned anything, it was that everything had a price.

It was why the CIA employed people like Cooper, and why they recruited men like Pierce—people with fewer scruples, extensive contacts, and the ability to go where other assets could not.

He dipped his chin, the tilt of his neck a silent touché. "True enough. But in this case, no money changed hands."

"What then?" she asked on a ragged, frustrated breath.

"Don't know for sure," he said with a shrug and a long exhale of smoke. "What I can tell you is that Felix Harrigan has a safe deposit box in Panama City . . . one in Will Bennett's name."

Evidence? A thrill, illicit and hungry and with the teeth of a starving predator, rushed through her.

Pierce pushed something into her hand. When he pulled away, Cooper opened her palm to find an old receipt, a string of numbers scribbled on the back. "Coordinates?"

He nodded. "Damnedest thing—the second chatter surfaced that Bennett might not be dead after all, a contract hit the net. Someone doesn't want Bennett anywhere near that box, and they're willing to kill to make sure he never gets close. If that doesn't make it priceless, not much will."

Cooper swallowed. Oh, but there was a price. She'd paid it— as had the men she'd killed on the CIA's orders.

"What's the contract value?" she asked, worry and excitement fighting a bitter war in her stomach.

"A hundred and fifty—but it'll climb fast. Be careful, Cooper. Combined, the two of you are a lucrative day's work."

Half a million dollars. That was what her life would be worth the second she was so much as rumored to be near Will.

"But not enough to tempt you?" she asked, mostly because she knew it would annoy him.

Pierce sniffed. "Take more than money for me to kill a friend."

"Is that what we are?" She didn't believe it for a second. Pierce wasn't the sort of man to allow himself friends, no matter what they'd done for him.

He let his gaze slide from her face, down her body, then back up again. He cocked his head to the side and pulled that damn charming grin to his mouth. "Why? You have something else in mind?"

Not in this lifetime, and he knew it. There was affection there. Loyalty, of one shade or another. But nothing between them could ever be casual and neither of them could ever afford to trust the person they took to their bed. A criminally stupid mistake for anyone in their position.

"How do you know all this?" she asked, clutching Bennett's location in her hand and fighting back a shiver.

"Because I'm the best," Pierce said with a flippant shrug. "And I still have friends. Some of them have done well for themselves—"

"And some of them owe you favors."

Pierce grinned. "It is a truth universally acknowledged that I'm not a man you want to be in debt to."

"Handy, then, that you're in mine."

"A reality I'm not at all comfortable with." He dipped his head toward the piece of paper he'd pressed into her palm. "See what you can do to rectify that, would you?" He flipped up the collar of his jacket and stepped through the doorway, the patter of rain *tap tap tapping* against his shoulders.

When she didn't say anything, Pierce turned back as if the soak of the evening shower didn't even register. "Move fast. I wasn't the only one asking questions. South America is about to get very, very hot."

"How much time do I have?"

He shrugged. "Bennett might have a week, if he's lucky. You don't have near that much time. Cole tracked you here—you need to get Bennett and go dark as fast as possible. You have a way out of Colombia?" he asked casually.

She nodded, already putting the pieces into place.

"Care to share?" he asked, the smile in his voice if not on his face.

"I'm not nearly stupid enough to tell you that."

"You don't trust me?" he asked, palm to his heart.

She just stared at him.

"You're learning." He dropped his hand, caught her gaze, and skewered her with approval. "Good luck, Cooper." He disappeared into the night, his voice floating back to her. "You're going to need it."

She lingered, giving Pierce plenty of time to slip into the maze of the *favelas*. By the time she left the darkened alleys and hidden turns, making her way back to streets crowded with the micro-economy the slums supported, night had truly fallen, and she'd memorized the coordinates.

She paid for a quick meal from a hot grill and fed the paper to the open flames as she ate.

She knew exactly where to find William Bennett, though she couldn't be sure who she'd find waiting for her. Captive, traitor, soldier, or the man she'd tried so hard to forget—it didn't matter.

She didn't care.

Couldn't afford to.

Will was her path forward, and God help any man who stood in her way.

CHAPTER TWO

The Mountains of Colombia

"You hit like my sister."

Will Bennett wheezed as he took a vicious jab to the ribs, then a second blow to the kidneys strong enough to ensure he pissed blood for days. He stumbled sideways, six inches of mud pulling at his bare feet, sucking him in and weighing him down. Fever and dehydration made him slow but fuck it. What did he have to lose?

Worst case scenario: this time, they killed him.

He chuckled and forced his feet to hold him. Hell, *best* case scenario was that this time they killed him.

Win-win, as far as he was concerned. Just so long as he could stop fighting, stop dying, stop existing in this hellish limbo between life and death.

He spat blood and brought his fists back up. "Actually, I take it back. My sister would have made that combination her bitch."

He grinned, tongued the edge of a tooth that wobbled, and tossed out, "Guess that means she'd make *you* her bitch, too."

Matías studied him, his face a ragged and scarred; curdled by a life spent in the pursuit of malicious amusement.

"You know 'bitch'?" Will asked. Matías, like most of the men surrounding him, spoke little to no English, and the few who did speak English knew better than to use it to communicate with Will. But then, they didn't know that thanks to his Delta training, Will was conversational in a half-dozen languages—including Spanish.

He didn't intend to educate them.

Much.

"*Puto?*"

Matías went stiff, the insult carving canyons of rage across his face.

"He knows," Will said, tossing Diego a wink. The ham-fisted bastard was as violent as he was stupid, which in this hell hole passed for overachieving. But the combination had earned him a spot as Matías's second.

Diego glanced between them, confusion lining his brow.

Apparently, Will would have to spell it out.

"*Eres su puta, sí?*"

Rage slid over Diego's confusion like a tide over sand. He charged, but Matías stopped him with a barked command. Pity. Diego was an easy mark and an easier win.

And Will really, really wanted a win today. Wanted the pleasure of breaking someone else's bones. The vicious joy of splitting someone else's skin.

Instead, Matías stepped forward. Of all the men in camp, he was the most measured, the hardest to manipulate. Dangerous, where the others were just mean. He wasn't here by happenstance, wasn't a victim of a shitty economy or a rough start. This life suited him as if it had been custom cut and tailored, and every morning, as the sun bled across the horizon, Will watched him slip into the role he'd chosen.

Cold, calculating, and cruel, Matías was a devil among men pretending to be demons.

In a fair fight, it'd be no contest.

But what in the last year had been fair?

Matías wanted Will to break.

Will wanted him to die.

Neither would win.

But Will *would* lose, just as he had every time he'd been dragged from his cell and forced to fight for his life . . . and for the enjoyment of those who'd imprisoned him.

Violence for the sake of it. For the sick pleasure of others who'd enjoyed it. It went against everything he believed about himself, about his training, about his job.

He'd hated it, hated them.

At first.

But as months had dragged on, his hatred, like home-brewed moonshine, had aged. Become more potent, more layered . . . and burned away nearly everything else. Hate kept him on his feet. Hate kept him fighting. Hate and the heavy blanket of anger that they'd *done* this to him kept him going.

But there would be no victory, not for him. The half-dozen assholes surrounding him, cheering, betting, spitting, would step up if Matías fell—an endless cycle of men ready to test themselves against the American. The prisoner. The Special Forces soldier.

He dodged a kick to his knee and blocked a punch to the face.

But no one said he had to make it easy. *Or painless*, he thought, throwing a combination that sent Matías reeling on a curse.

Will would make them work for a win. But he couldn't refuse. Then they brought out the ants, the knives, the pliers.

Torment was inevitable, but the choice of tormentor was still his.

So he persisted.

It was just what he did. What he'd always done.

He'd fought through the grief of losing his parents. Brawled his way through tumultuous years in foster care. Worked himself to the bone to raise a kid sister with a smart mouth and a give-no-shits attitude. Fearless persistence had led him through boot camp and eventually carved a path that led straight to Q Course.

He'd tested himself against everything life and the army could throw at him and, in the end, earned a place on Delta Force.

His colleagues called him a determined son of a bitch.

His sister called him a stubborn ass.

For so long, Will had simply considered failure beneath him. Something other, weaker people did. People who didn't know how to keep getting up.

But one failed mission and endless months of captivity had changed all that.

Now he stared failure in the face every single day. Watched as Matías's grin grew colder, meaner, *triumphant*.

Will was fading and they both knew it.

Death, like a predator in the night, lurked just out of sight.

God, he'd been arrogant. Had simply assumed that whatever life threw at him, he'd find the strength to deal with the mess, pull himself together, and start the climb again.

It was what men like him did.

Overcome.

Survive.

Conquer.

But that wasn't his life anymore, and he was ready to meet his end. So fuck it all to hell.

He shifted his weight, kept his hands up, and spat blood and saliva at Matías's feet.

To the sound of cheers, Matías struck, moving through the trampled grass and mud as if it were friend rather than foe. Probably was—seemed like the whole damn country, from insects to weather to the gripping, cloying earth, hated Will.

He blocked a punch. Dodged another. Torqued his body and put all the force, all the frustration, all the helpless rage into a right hook that clipped Matías's chin and snapped his head back on a wicked clack of teeth.

The bastard hit the dirt as Will staggered, trying to pull out of the momentum of his swing.

He slid to his knees, panting and breathless, the taste of victory a sweet, fleeting burst against his tongue as Diego grabbed his hair, drove a knee to his face, and spat curses at his feet.

The pain of a broken nose and the brutal clutch of gravity pulled Will to the soaked ground.

Flat on his back, each breath a misery, Will stared up at a foreign sky obscured by the heavy roil of an angry storm.

He set his nose, tasted blood, and wondered why he bothered.

"Levántate."

As mud slipped and squished through his hair, his clothes, his fingers, Will searched for the strength to stand, to fight, to goad Matías or Diego or any of the other bastards into going too far. After so many months at the mercy of men he considered beneath him, that tasted like a goddamned win to Will.

Even if it killed him, he was going to find a way to get the last laugh.

He chuckled. *Even if it killed him.*

He rolled to his hands and knees, his muscles burning, his arms shaking, his skin unnaturally hot against the cold fall of rain.

Stand. Fight. Force them to make a mistake.

Or quit. Give in to fear and apathy and a darkness that had burrowed deep and taken root.

"*Levántate.*" A heavy boot to the ribs accompanied another demand to rise.

Rock bottom wasn't a foundation on which to build. It was soaked earth, cold mountain air, and the greedy swallow of a far-flung hellhole determined to consume him, until nothing, no matter how frail or pathetic or weak, remained of him to find.

Little by little, piece by piece, he'd lost himself. His body to bullet ants. To a machete. To fever and rot and a starvation that ate at him until his cheeks went hollow and his body consumed muscle, leaving behind long limbs, aching joints, and an over-grown beard.

He clenched his fists, let the mud slide through his fingers.

But he'd lost much more and much worse.

He'd run out of "fuck yous" and "go to hells." Forgotten the man who'd once worn scars like flesh-struck trophies.

There was no freedom or release or heady rush of victory for him.

Just death, and his inability to embrace it.

"*Rogar por la muerte.*"

Will let out a ragged laugh. What a bunch of pricks.

They wanted him to *beg* for the privilege of dying. Thought they could pry that from him with fists and boots.

Not in this life or the next.

They'd given it their best shot—pushed him to his limits until he'd snapped, done things he couldn't take back and didn't know how to live with—but still, they'd come up empty.

Delta and a ballbuster of a sister had seen to that.

He may be beaten, but he wasn't broken. Not here. Not today.

Looked like he had a few "fuck yous" left in him after all.

"*Levántate!*"

One last mission. One last fight.

Then he could finally rest.

He pushed to his feet. Turned to stare at the man who'd wreaked so much torment upon his body and lifted his chin on a snarl.

With deliberate strokes and casual cruelty, they'd carved away everything that made Will the man he was.

Time to take something from them.

"*Bueno.*" Matías smiled as lightning cleaved the horizon, the roll of thunder a deep, trembling herald of what came next.

Will let his arms and legs go loose, dragged in a breath, released it, then did it again as the circle of men grew interested, drew closer.

He couldn't take them all—not in his condition—but he could make them regret every indignity they'd visited upon him.

And when they killed him, because that's what it would take to bring him down, he'd have his revenge.

They never should have touched him. Never should have pushed him. And they *never* should have forgotten just who they were dealing with.

Now, they'd pay.

The rain eased off, the wind died down, and the air grew thick as if the world itself waited with baited breath for what came next.

Matías gripped the handle of the knife he'd taken from Will upon his capture, turned his body, and lunged forward on a yell— only to stop when mere feet away, Diego's head burst like a melon at a Gallagher show.

Lightning struck, and another man fell on a crack of sound, sharp and short, caught somewhere between the tip of a whip and the boom of a jet.

Sniper.

On instinct, Will dropped as the whip cracked again, once, twice, the explosion on the heels of the *zing* of a large caliber bullet traveling three thousand feet per second past his head.

Two more men fell, dead before they hit the dirt.

Three down. Four to go.

Ethan?

Will glanced toward where Diego lay sprawled in the grass like a Rorschach test. No. Couldn't be. Nothing short of a high-powered sniper rifle was going to create that kind of damage. An accomplished shot his best friend might be, but Ethan was no sniper. From the tree line, on a clear day, with no wind, the man was deadly. Under pressure, but with a weapon he knew? Will wouldn't bet against him. But in foreign terrain, working against a thick, turbulent atmosphere, and firing a rifle about as subtle as his sister's flirting?

Ethan's ego could suck it, the man couldn't make that shot.

So who then?

Ortiz? He was in a committed relationship with his MK-13.

The sky splintered with the sonic boom of a fifth shot that missed the mark and sucker punched an old SUV but was closely followed by a sixth that sure as fuck did not.

Whoever it was had a pair of cannon balls between their legs —or didn't give a shit about collateral damage.

A seventh shot rent the night and a sixth man died at a run.

Silence settled, the quiet thicker, darker, as if hell itself had come to collect.

Will looked up. Found Matías staring back at him from mere yards away, blood spatter covering the side of his face. He was fucked, and his expression said he knew it.

Will waited for the shot. For freedom. For Matías's head to split and this nightmare to finally, finally end.

Nothing.

Just the distant rumble of thunder, the pale flash of lightning, and the screaming silence left by people who'd died violent deaths.

Will clenched his fists, inhaled wet, metallic air that smelled like blood but tasted like righteousness. Like vindication. Like justice meted out for his approval if not at his hand . . .

Oh.

His breath left him in a rush, adrenaline sliding in to take its place.

Oh, *fuck* yes.

He didn't know who was just over the horizon. Didn't care.

They'd seen enough. They understood.

And they were giving him the opportunity to take back what was his.

He wouldn't waste it.

"You gave me a choice once. Do you remember?" he asked, letting Matías rise from the mud and the muck, a courtesy he'd never granted Will. "Slow. *Lento,*" he translated. "Painful. *Doloroso.*" He widened his stance. "Or quick. *Rápido.*" Will smiled, his dry lips cracking and bleeding beneath the strain. "Either way, you die. *Tú mueres.*"

Matías glanced over his shoulder, gauging the distance from the roughed-out clearing to the fall of a hill that led straight into the dense Colombian foliage.

"You'll never make it," Will said in clean, clear Spanish rather than the halting word or two he'd pretended to pick up over the last year. He'd concealed his ability to speak their language, clutched tight to one of the few advantages he'd had. But no more. "Yeah, I speak Spanish, asshole. Always have." He brought his hands up, kept his muscles loose. "Let's finish this."

Matías took a step back, then another, his pace quickening as his gaze landed on the bodies sprawled around the camp.

Coward.

He'd been the first to pull Will from the pit. The one to order his ear cleaved from his head. The one who'd denied food and water and basic human decency.

And the one who'd ordered Will to kill an innocent or watch him be tortured to death.

It shouldn't have surprised him that the moment the winds shifted, the second karma arrived, that Matías's first thought went to retreat, but it did.

His pace quickened, and the *zing-crack-boom* of a shot followed Matias's steps. He stopped as the bullet dug dirt at his feet. That message didn't need an interpreter.

Stand. Fight. Pay for what you've done.

Matías raised the knife he'd stolen. The one he'd used to pull screams from Will's throat, to carve scars on Will's skin. But it wasn't his. Didn't belong in his hand.

And Will wanted it back.

On a scream of desperate rage, Matías attacked, and this time, *this time*, Will welcomed it.

Had he been healthy, hydrated, free of the weight of a fever that pulled sweat from his pores like blood from a stone, Will would have taken the thrust of knife on the outside, and had Matías on his back in seconds. Instead, he had to work against illness and injury, starvation and weakness, and a fever that burned hot even as his hate burned cold. It slowed his reaction by a mere second, not even two, and forced Will to confront the thrust of knife on the inside. It caught him, a vicious slice of red-hot agony, along his ribs.

But not good enough. Not by half.

This was a maneuver Will could perform in his sleep.

A skill he'd developed under similar, unforgiving circumstances.

Not for the first time, he was grateful for the uncompromising demands of his instructors in Q Course. For the sheer perfection his teammates had demanded of him through every deployment and each special assignment.

Injured, but unstoppable, Will caught Matías by the inside of the elbow; spread his fingers and drove his hand into the bastard's face, catching the lips, gouging the eyes, and taking him to the ground.

Control the head and you control the body.

Like the flash of memories before the last gasp of life, his training came back to him in a rush, and he realized it had always been there. Waiting, like a snake hibernating beneath a rock, dormant but deadly.

In seconds, the world changed. Will was back on top, trapping Matías's wrist and his knife with a knee. Even in his emaciated state, Will still had enough strength to keep the man pinned.

He wrapped his hands around the bastard's throat, tightened his grip, felt his own fingertips brush behind his skull.

Satisfaction strengthened him, and hate hardened him against the last, panicked gasp of an animal fighting to live.

"You had me at your mercy once." He squeezed. Watched as Matías's eyes bulged. "Never again, asshole."

Not ever. Not for anyone or anything. He was through being at the mercy of others.

Matías choked, his face turning red, saliva pooling at the corner of his mouth.

It was a better death than he deserved. Cleaner. Faster. But Will wanted it over more than he wanted to go ounce for ounce in suffering.

"*Lento?*" Will asked. "*O rápido?*"

Matías gurgled, his left hand coming to Will's face, his fingers scrabbling for Will's eyes, his hair—anything he could use to draw Will off—but this wasn't a fight he could win. His stocky, five-foot-seven frame no match for Will's emaciated six-foot-two.

Matías grasped Will's wrist. Tugged at the arm Will kept wedged with his knee.

His eyes bulged.

Blood vessels burst.

Matías scrabbled for the last thread of a cold, malicious life.

And Will pressed him to the dirt, relaxing his grip just enough to draw it out, just enough to make it hurt, just enough to let the sadistic prick wonder if he might relent. If he might let him go.

Just enough to let Matías wonder if Will were the better man. If he held forgiveness, as well as contempt, in his heart.

He didn't.

Matías had carved it away as surely as he'd cleaved Will's ear from his head.

Matías deserved to die, and Will deserved to be the one to kill him—he knew no simpler truth than that.

A minute passed in an eternity and a life bled away.

Will let go.

He struggled to rise, his hands shaking, his shoulders burning, his skin on fire.

He stumbled, nearly tripped over Diego, kept going, then ended up back on his hands and knees, puking into the grass as the wind kicked up and the rain came down.

The rain would fall, and the jungle would grow, and all of this would be lost to time and the hungry teeth of a living mountain.

But it had left its mark, a deeply struck scar that he couldn't see but knew would never fade.

He'd killed a man with his bare hands—an eventuality he'd trained for, but still a first. He'd taken lives, but not like this. Not up close and personal.

And not with hate-fueled satisfaction in his heart.

He didn't regret it. Couldn't.

Worse, he'd enjoyed it. And that scared the shit out of him.

He crawled away, collapsed to the cold, muddy earth, then forced himself to turn, to stare up at a sky that seemed determined to drown his fever and cleanse his conscience.

Maybe this goddamned country didn't hate him after all.

The rain turned wind-driven and thin, stinging like a swarm of angry insects against his skin.

He shivered. Maybe not.

He had to find the energy to get up. To work his way down the mountain. Try to make his way home and back to the man he'd thought he was.

He didn't recognize himself anymore. And as he closed his eyes, let rain and heat and agony wash over him, he wondered if, after everything, anyone else would recognize him, welcome him, or forgive him, either.

CHAPTER THREE

"You can sleep when you're dead, Bennett."

The voice, feminine and tinged with a deep southern drawl, slipped through Will's blood like honeyed bourbon, warm and rich, and with just a hint of a playful bite.

It promised a wickedly memorable night and a brutal morning of well-earned regrets.

And though it had been over a year, Will would know that voice anywhere.

Cooper.

Though he'd once spent endless hours wondering just what she looked like, he didn't have to open his eyes to know she'd be beautiful. Of course, she was—she sounded like home.

Still, the temptation tugged at him. How many years had he wondered about the face that belonged to the voice he'd grown so fond of? The one that had called him an arrogant asshole, then saved his life in the same damn conversation. The one that stubbornly refused to laugh at his jokes. The one that went thick and soft and slow as a summer afternoon when he'd told her just what he wanted to do to her. Where he wanted to put his hands, his mouth, his tongue.

So no, he didn't *need* to look to know Cooper Reed would be beautiful. He'd known that for years.

But because he'd wondered what form that beauty would take for just as long, he swallowed hard, opened his eyes, and drank his fill.

Cooper stared down at him, her expression curious, her frame rangy but her body hidden behind gear and rain-soaked clothes. Her hair was a forgettable brown that, plastered to her neck and side of her face by sweat and weather, probably looked darker than it was. Will couldn't quite make out the curve of her cheek or the cut of her jaw beneath the grime she'd smeared across her face, but her eyes shone the same clear, deep blue of the steady waters of Lake Champlain.

He let go of a breath, loosened something taut and angry and helpless that had coiled tighter and tighter within him, and took his first real breath of freedom.

And because he'd stared too long and been struck dumb in a way he was not at all familiar with, he blurted out the first thing that came to mind.

"Little short for a storm trooper, aren't you?" He wheezed at her startled expression.

"I see captivity hasn't improved your sense of humor." Cooper huffed, sounding for all the world as if she'd trekked up half a mountain in search of enlightenment, but found the number for 1-900-Psychics instead. "But still, *Star Wars?* Either you're feverish or worse, a nerd."

"You got the reference," he offered from the flat of his back.

She cocked her head to the side, a full smile gracing a mouth that had whispered everything from instructions to assurances, and later, when he was no longer in the field or under fire, that same mouth had gone quiet and stumbled right up to the edge of a moan as he'd made all sorts of illicit promises.

"Nice shots," he grunted through the pain that seared his side as he sat up.

Amusement tugged at the side of her face, as if she'd decided to indulge in a joke she knew well, spoke often, and always enjoyed. "You can say it now—my balls are bigger than yours."

Will tasted a laugh, his first real one in months, and responded to the familiar joke as he had a dozen times before. "We can compare later."

God, how many times had he imagined this moment? Pictured Coop standing over him, staring down at him, her mouth satisfied and her eyes dancing. He'd had different, more intimate circumstances in mind, imagined *her* laid bare before *him*, rather than the other way around. Circumstances where pleasure trumped gratitude and clothes were optional.

Still, this wasn't the first time he'd had her at his back, and the sense of security in that wasn't new, but it was the first time he'd felt so damn vulnerable beneath her watch. The first time he'd wondered if life and the cost of living had gotten the better of him, if there was anything left of the man he'd been when they met.

"Wanna get out of here?" She extended her hand and helped pull him to his feet, gripping his elbow when the Earth tilted slightly to the left.

She ran her gaze from the top of his head to the bottom of his feet, then up again, which made him feel both exposed and also very aware of the difference in their heights. From the flat of his back she'd looked tall and lean, but on his feet and face-to-face he realized she couldn't be an inch over five-eight with her boots on.

"You're bleeding," she said, nodding toward where Matías, may the bastard rot in hell, had caught him with the knife.

Will tugged at the hem of his shirt, pulling the fabric away from a ragged gash that still hadn't clotted.

Cooper whistled through her teeth. "You're supposed to *zag*, Bennett."

"Always preferred to zig." He dropped his shirt and tried to ignore the heartbeat beneath his ribs and the hot slide of blood down his side.

"Keep pressure on that. I've got a med kit in my pack, but you're going to need stitches." She smiled sweetly at him. "I'll try to keep them neat."

"Straight scars are for pussies," he said through gritted teeth. "I want a lightning bolt."

"My initials it is."

Will suppressed a laugh as he followed her toward the ancient SUV that had been cobbled together with random parts, copious duct tape, and ran on a steady diet of diesel and dreams. Coop opened the door and popped the hood, then bent at the waist, her shirt riding up to reveal a gun holstered at the small of her back. "Well, this thing is a piece of junk, but at least it doesn't look like I cracked the engine block."

He scanned the clearing, looking for backup, for support, for someone monitoring the perimeter. Instead he found her discarded pack and the rifle she'd used to clean the scene. It wasn't military issue, and it sure as fuck wasn't a weapon a well-supported field asset would carry. That thing was Frankenstein's monster. At a quick glance, Will counted six parts, none of which were original, and none designed to work together. That was black market and homemade, put together will skill, knowledge and, if he had to guess, a bit of MacGyver magic.

"What are you doing here, Coop?" he asked.

"Well," she said, snapping the hood closed and rolling her neck. "I'm not Luke Skywalker but I *am* here to rescue you."

A grin that wasn't stretched and brittle and brought to life by some morbid thought or self-deprecating acknowledgement eased across his face.

"Wait." He drew up short. "Does that make me Princess Leia?"

"You're doing a better impression of Chewbacca at the moment," she said, tugging lightly at the end of his beard.

He caught her hand, held her eyes. "Thank you." He squeezed her fingers but because she went still and wary, as if she expected him to use proximity and size to his advantage, he let go. She unzipped the top of her pack, pulled out a wad of clean, plastic-wrapped socks, and tossed them over. "Dry your feet and grab a pair of boots from someone who no longer needs them. We're leaving."

He did as she said, watching as she broke down the rifle as if she'd done it a thousand times before.

That wasn't a last-minute weapon choice. It was hers. Something she knew as intimately as an old friend or dedicated lover. Which meant if she was still with the CIA, she was way, way off the reservation. That, or she'd been burned and abandoned.

Forgotten.

She stowed her rifle, then shoved her pack onto the floorboard behind the driver's seat.

"Let's go home, Will."

Let's go home.

There was something in the way she'd said it—the inclusiveness, the shared desire, the united goal—that set him at ease.

He didn't know what had brought her here.

But it didn't matter. Not yet. Because whatever else she wasn't saying, there were only two things that mattered. First, she'd saved his life—twice—and second, she said the word "home" with all the melancholy yearning of a desire long out of reach.

And that was enough for him.

For now.

Will stood, adjusted to the weight of shoes, then scavenged a handgun and an extra clip. "Hey, Coop?"

"Yeah?" Cooper asked.

"You were right," he whispered through a stress-roughened throat.

She glanced over her shoulder at him, and for a moment, he wondered if she knew what he meant.

Her mouth didn't so much as twitch, but her eyes crinkled with a little I-told-you-so smirk. "It's like I always said, Bennett." She held his gaze and he drank in a face he so desperately wanted to wipe clean and memorize. "Patience is a virtue. And meeting me? It's *always* worth the wait."

A laugh lodged in his throat and became a cough that had him doubling over and wheezing for air. But when a palm, tentative and warm, landed on his back, he calmed. Stood. And took his first true breath of freedom. Let himself believe it might not be the last.

"You always have to be right?" he asked.

She raised an eyebrow at him, which was answer enough.

"Let's get out of here, okay?" She stepped away, jerked open the passenger door on a creak of rusty hinges, and gestured him inside. "Ladies first," she offered with a smile.

He climbed in, forced himself to take a calm, steadying breath when the door slammed closed and locked him in. After a year in the pit—little more than a doublewide grave dug into the earth, covered by heavy steel bars—Will had a new appreciation for his sister's aversion to tight spaces.

He kept his hand on the door and his heart rate slowed. Cooper slid in behind the wheel and revved the engine, which had only come to life after she pumped the accelerator and grumbled a whole host of promises and threats.

A squeal cut through the night like the wail of a pissed off wraith, sharp and high and blessedly brief as they left the clearing.

"Subtle," Cooper grunted, forcing the stick to find third against the grinding protest of abused gears.

"Fan belt," Will offered, wincing as each bounce of the SUV echoed through his body like phantom fists. "Could hear this beast a mile out."

Cooper sighed. "We'll ditch the SUV a few miles outside town and walk the rest." She pitched a glance toward Will, her expression loud in the silence between them.

Sweat beaded on his brow and drenched the back of his neck. His breath rattled in his chest, and the cut along his ribs throbbed. Exhaustion poured into him, his limbs going limp and heavy.

They left the clearing behind them, trees rising on all sides, the canopy stretching across the road, obscuring the sky and casting them into a murky, rainy darkness. Cooper flicked on the headlights and tried the air conditioner.

"Optimist," Will accused with a laugh when the engine squealed but the vents only pushed warm air. He glanced into the sideview mirror as the road curved and watched as the jungle swallowed up the last year of his life.

He'd expected this place to swallow him, too. Consume him, piece by piece, until nothing remained but carrion for the birds and the bugs and the brutal efficiency of the jungle.

And even as the road passed beneath him and the pit disappeared behind him, he wasn't entirely sure it hadn't.

CHAPTER FOUR

The feeble cry of a new day, still weak and gray, tinged a horizon that would soon be bright blue and cloudless.

They'd made better time down the rough-cleared mountain road than Cooper had expected, and they'd managed to ditch the car where no one was likely to stumble upon it. But that had been the easy part.

They'd faced half of the five-mile walk into the outskirts of the small fishing village where she had a standing arrangement with the captain of a trawler. But they'd lost their window for slipping into town undetected.

And Will was dead on his feet, pain and exhaustion and the silent slide into sickness weighing him down.

They couldn't keep going. *He* couldn't keep going.

So she'd led them off the road and several hundred yards into the tree line.

"There," Cooper said, pointing toward the base of a ceiba tree that rose so far into the darkness that neither of their beams revealed the top. "We can shelter in the roots. Grab some food and some rest then get the hell out of here."

She took the flashlight from him, converted it to a lantern, and set it in the middle of a wide arc created by the base of a tree the size of New York City apartment. A beetle scuttled along the spine of a giant root and Will stepped away with a full-body shiver.

In less than a minute, she cleared the forest floor, nudging away the flotsam and jetsam of an environment caught in the throes of life, death, and rebirth. She dropped her pack, her spine sighing in relief, then opened the top and pulled out a waterproof cover. She spread it out, then gestured for Will to take up a seat against the base of the tree.

"Hungry?" she asked, sorting through her supplies and wishing she'd brought a little more in the way of cover.

"Starving." He sank gracelessly to the ground, almost as if he'd given his muscles permission to relax and they'd simply turned liquid. "Please tell me you got a bucket of fried chicken in there," he groaned, dropping his head back against the trunk of the tree.

"'Course I do."

"And coleslaw? Gotta have the coleslaw."

"Damn," Cooper said, withdrawing two of the MREs she'd brought. "Knew I forgot something."

"Can't have fried chicken without the slaw," he mumbled, his voice slow and thick with the sap of encroaching sleep. "And baked beans. And rolls. Big, fluffy, buttered rolls."

"Guess you'll have to make do with either chili mac or beef brisket."

"Mac works."

"You got it." She brought it to him, along with a bottle of Tylenol for the fever that clung to his cheeks.

He stared up at her, a bony sprawl of folded, too-thin limbs that reminded her of the spiders that used to lurk on her father's deck. He snatched the food from her hand like a cornered, feral thing, and tore the top off with his teeth.

"Oh wait, I've got . . ." She rooted through the pockets of her bag for the stainless-steel spork she carried. She turned to Will, then stumbled to a halt.

He'd already dug in, scooping out food with his fingers and shoving it into his mouth.

Cooper shrugged off the shock and went to hand him the spork, but he jerked away, hunching over the food and toward the tree, snarling at her like a vicious, starving dog that had long ago forgotten how to trust.

She didn't blame him.

She'd known gnawing hunger and the desperate relief of food —and the all-too-rational fear of having it taken away.

But before she could regroup, stow her pity, and hide her surprise, Will came back to himself. Caught her staring.

And dropped his head in shame.

He set the food next to his boot, glanced at his hands, flexed his fingers.

He went to wipe them against his pants, then stopped mid-movement, as if he'd remembered how dirty they were.

Caught somewhere between exhaustion and embarrassment, he glanced away, closed his eyes, and clenched his jaw as if he could rewind time or at least become invisible.

Cooper knelt next to him, took a wet cloth from the pack she'd set out earlier, and grasped his hand.

He jerked, his eyes snapping open, his gaze wary and confused and defensive, and tried to pull away.

"You hit the MREs the way I hit my dad's smoked ribs—all go, no quit, napkins are for pussies and forks are for stabbing people who get too close to your plate." When he didn't say anything, just stared at her between long, slow blinks, she grinned at him. "*Respect.*"

She pulled his arm forward, and when he only resisted a little, she gentled her touch, forced herself to slow down, to tackle something that should be quick and efficient with soft, soothing strokes. "Never could get used to the grime I'd pick up in the field," she admitted. "Always hated having my hands coated in dirt or gun oil or whatever. Made my skin dry out and crack; couldn't stand the way it changed the touch of my rifle, the feel of the trigger. Guys used to make *unmerciful* fun of me for carrying these around." She shrugged, turned his palm face up, and gently cleaned his hand from wrist to fingertip, revealing wide palms and long fingers.

It was her turn to push back a shiver and slide away from the thought of what those hands might feel like on her skin.

"Five or six days in, no shower, restricted water, baby wipes started to look pretty damn good." She reached for his other wrist, and he gave it to her willingly, sighing as she pulled out another wipe, then another and another, until his hands were clean of earth and sweat and food and blood. "At five bucks a wipe, I got the last laugh," she said with a wink.

"I bet you usually do," he whispered, staring at his fingers as if the memory of what clean and comfortable felt like was so damn distant it was practically déjà vu.

Clean skin was such a little thing. But a dignity—one he'd probably been denied for months—and one she could easily restore.

Kindness, as her mother would say, didn't cost a thing.

A lie, as it turned out. And one of the first a life on the run had stripped her of.

Kindness. Compassion. Empathy. They were all little more than currencies to be traded and used to purchase an advantage or seal a fate.

But reaching for Will had been instinctual and easy. Honest. She wasn't trying to trick or manipulate him.

She was losing her touch.

"It's not as good as a hot shower but does the job in a pinch."

"Thank you," Will whispered.

Coop pulled another wipe free—the package half gone already—and slid it across his forehead and beneath the tangled mass of hair they'd likely have to shave.

"Don't!" he barked, jerking away and grabbing her hands in an unyielding grip that wavered after only a few seconds, betraying his flagging strength. "Don't," he repeated on a whisper, tilting his head away, as if there were something to hide, something he couldn't bear for her to see.

She pulled away, pressed a few more wipes into his open palms, and didn't tell him she'd already seen the half-missing ear, or that the months of captivity were painted across his body in bold strokes and subtle lines. Some would fade. Others . . . well, those he'd learn to carry. In time, when exhaustion and depravation weren't riding him, he'd remember he was more than strong enough to face whatever scars were left behind. "Sorry. Didn't mean to go all Aunt Edna on you."

"W-wha—?" His cheeks hollowed, and his beard flexed, the lines around his eyes creasing.

"You know . . ." Cooper pretended to lick the edge of her thumb, then mimed swiping it across his cheek. "Aunt Edna. We all got one."

He laughed, the sound tight and strangled, as if at some point he'd outgrown it until he no longer knew how to wear it. "Not me. No aunts. No uncles."

Cooper raised an eyebrow as she pressed the stainless-steel spork into his hand.

"Okay, okay. No Aunt Edna. Just a cranky octogenarian who taught second grade."

"Everyone's got an Edna," Cooper said with a grin. "Sorry I brought her to the party."

"It's fine." Will pulled a wipe over his face and along the back of his neck, smearing months of layered dirt and sweat away until his skin began to show through. When the pack ran out, a tiny pile of discolored cloth next to him, he leaned his head back on a sigh.

"I know it's not fried chicken, but eat up, Bennett." She nudged his foot and set the last of her water near his hand. She'd have to source more later and use the purification tablets in her pack to make it drinkable.

Water that tasted vaguely of a public pool, yay.

"God, the things I'd do for an ice-cold cider." Sure would make this slop go down easier.

"Apple juice? Seriously?" he asked as he picked up his discarded meal and scooped out something that did *not* look like chili mac.

"Beer snob," she accused, opening her own pouch of barely edible dinner. "Should've known. You have the look about you."

"What look?"

"You know," she said, stroking her chin as if she had a beard and the gesture somehow increased her contemplative prowess. "The paper-towel-selling, beard-balm-buying, I-only-drink-craft-IPA hipster look."

Will scoffed. "I don't know what beard-balm is, paper towels aren't environmentally friendly—"

"*Hipster*," Cooper coughed into her hand.

"And I imagine I look more like Grizzly Adams or Robinson Crusoe—"

"Or *Chewbacca*—"

Will glared as Cooper pulled on her sweetest smile. It was the one she wore to church, the one that made her mother happy and her father scoff, her teachers sigh and CO scream—and it was one that had always made her spotter swear and reach for his helmet.

"You're gonna be trouble, aren't you, Coop?" Will asked, folding up the top of his empty MRE and licking the edge of the spork clean.

"Wouldn't be much fun if I wasn't." Though just how much trouble she was bringing into Will's life, she couldn't say. It hardly mattered. Even if she wanted to send him home, to write him off as a dead end or a man who'd paid enough for any sins of his past, the reality was, there was a price on his head and it *would* grow. Cooper hadn't invented whatever trouble was after Will.

She'd just brought it to his door.

His hands quivering, Will popped the cap on the Tylenol, shook out several pills, and washed them down with a huge swig of water. On a sigh, he leaned his head back against the tree and closed his eyes.

"Hey, Coop?" he asked, popping one lid open to stare at her.

She didn't answer. Nothing, and she meant *nothing*, good ever came of a sentence that began "Hey, Coop."

Shit like that was how she'd taken a joyride in her father's pickup at fifteen.

How she'd shattered Sid Paulson's nose at seventeen.

It was what had convinced her that outshooting her training officer was a good idea.

And it was what Will had whispered across a quiet phone line just before he'd taken their relationship—if she could call it that—from witty banter and bad jokes to sexually charged promises and a desire she could name but never taste.

"Hey, Coop," Will started again, his chest rattling with the warning of a coiled and ready-to-strike copperhead.

"Don't even *think* about it . . ."

"How'd the hipster burn his tongue?"

She stared into the open top of her meal and played along. "Ugh, your jokes make my brisket taste bad."

"He ate his food before it was cool."

She shook her head on a snort, then disposed of the packages they'd emptied. "I've always wanted to know; what's with the jokes, Bennett?" As long as she'd known him, Will had been full of two things—confidence and terrible jokes.

The corner of his beard twitched, as if a long-forgotten memory tugged at the edge of his mouth.

"Special Forces training—you spend a lot of time being uncomfortable, and a lot of that time focused on being uncomfortable. Different units handle it different ways. I know a SEAL whose unit used to sing their way through long nights tucked into the Pacific—we did that, too," he explained. "But turns out, we had this one guy—smartest damn fucker I ever knew, in the field anyway, I know a guy back home who could run caffeine-driven circles around Einstein—"

"Focus, Bennett."

"Right. Anyway, guy couldn't carry a tune to save his life. Sounded like a cat in heat trying to swallow sandpaper. Drove the rest of us nuts."

"So, no singing," Cooper supplied.

"No singing. But we had to have something to keep us up, keep us going, keep us talking."

"And *dad jokes* are what you came up with?"

"Man has his best ideas at two a.m. when he's freezin' his balls off and knows exactly what his CO will do if he nods off."

"But *dad* jokes."

"The worse they were, the better they worked. Kept us going and drove everyone else nuts." He shrugged. "Over the last few months . . . helped pass the time. Let me focus—or get a little lost. And I guess," he said with a tired sigh, "honoring the tradition feels like honoring Felix, too."

"The guy who couldn't sing?"

"Felix Harrigan—used to call him Felix the Cat, the way he always managed to turn trouble to luck."

Death itself sighed against the back of her neck and Cooper went still.

Will slid to the plastic mat, tucked his arm beneath his head, and mumbled, "Caught up to him though. Traded his ninth life for a sniper round in Afghanistan."

Cooper swallowed hard against the bile that tried to rise and looked away. Afghanistan wasn't something she ever wanted to think about, but though the words were thick and heavy, she forced them past a tight throat. "I'm sorry."

"Not your fault," he said.

No, it wasn't, she reminded herself.

Will blinked, long and slow, then finally let his eyes fall shut just to snap them open again.

He tightened his jaw and shifted to his back, staring up at the canopy.

Coop recognized the look. Less obstinate refusal to sleep and more desperate fear that *this* time he wouldn't wake. Freedom was *so close* he could taste it. He'd probably even let himself think about home. About hot showers, double cheeseburgers, and clean sheets. Thoughts that had been forbidden. Dreams that had felt unattainable.

But there they were. Just out of sight. His for the taking.

"I know the feeling," she whispered, keeping her voice steady as wants and wishes encroached like hungry, laughing hyenas, ready to tease her with thoughts of chili fries and barbecue, of cold cider and the gingham tablecloth her mother still used for every backyard crawfish boil. She heard the laughter and inhaled the smoke of cedar chips and charred meat.

She pushed all of it away.

"I know what it's like to be so damn close to the end you can practically taste it." Her sister's laugh rang in the back of her head. The ghostly touch of her mother's arms wrapped her tight. The deep timbre of her father's voice struck her bones like a bell. "To fight back the fear that if you stop, if you let yourself rest"— she swallowed hard but carried on—"it could all be snatched away in a heartbeat. That the road home could be lost forever if you stray even just a little."

He turned his head and studied her in the quiet way of a predator confronted with something that both confused and intrigued him. "Yeah?"

"Yeah."

He rolled to his side, carefully cradling the wound they'd done their best to clean and treat and bandage in the car. He needed antibiotics. Intravenous fluids and a shit ton of rest.

She could only offer him the rest.

"Sleep, Will. It's all going to be waiting for you tomorrow."

"Promise?" he asked.

She nodded and forced the word past dry lips. "Promise."

It was an oath she knew better than to make. And one she might not be able to keep.

But as his eyes closed and Will fell into sleep the way only the truly exhausted could, Cooper knew she'd move heaven and earth to try.

Will deserved to go home.

They *both* did.

CHAPTER FIVE

Fuck, he was cold.

He pulled his knees close and tucked his arms to his chest. A cramp hit his gut and he extended his legs, then pulled them back in, then extended them again. Nothing helped. Everything hurt. And though misery had become familiar, it certainly hadn't become comfortable.

"Bennett, you all right?"

He jerked and opened his eyes to find Cooper sitting across from him, a hazy vision he was half tempted to believe was nothing more than a mirage.

It wouldn't be the first time.

How many nights, lying at the bottom of that fucking pit, had he looked up and seen Georgia's scowling face just outside the bars?

How many times had he stared through sweat and grit and agony to see Ethan prowling the tree line?

How many times had he heard Cooper's voice, pressed to his ear, low and sexy and seductive even as she'd laughed at him?

In the early days, he'd taken strength from friends who weren't there, but were almost certainly looking for him.

But as time had worn on and hope had grown dim, he'd considered those hallucinations little more than specters of his old life there to escort him to the next.

But they never had; they'd left him behind to die, then worse, left him behind to live.

And every time a fever broke, or the agony stopped, and his mind loosened its stranglehold on fantasy and let reality intrude, Will had come back to find himself both disappointed and alone.

Forgotten.

Sometimes, when he was weak enough to be lonely, and hurt enough to be angry, he hated them for it.

He trembled, the cold going bone deep.

"Will?" Cooper prompted, sitting up from where she'd reclined against her bag.

"Got a Tauntaun in there?" he asked through clenched, chattering teeth.

"Keeping to the Star Wars jokes? Really?"

"Trekkie," he accused, his shoulders aching beneath the grip of tight, tense muscles he felt all the way up his neck.

"Don't be insulting."

He shivered as she stood, pulled the bottle of pills from her bag, and brought them to him with the water at her hip.

"Cold?" she asked, shaking two pills into the palm of her hand.

He jerked his head.

"It's the fever," she whispered, helping him sit up. "And the sweat." She handed him the pills, which he swallowed past a tight, dry throat. The metallic rim of a water bottle touched his lips. "Drink, Will. You need the water."

His hands shook, and his teeth clacked against steel before a warm hand settled on top of his and helped guide the water to his mouth. When it ran dry, he collapsed back to the ground, his skin pebbling, the cold spreading like an oil slick as he sweat through his shirt.

"You're getting worse," Cooper mumbled.

He was, but he knew from experience there was so much further still to go. It wasn't the first time his body had been besieged by fever. Wasn't the first time he'd exhausted muscles beneath the strain of full-body shivers.

Worse was what came next.

Severe dehydration.

Waking nightmares.

Hallucinations so real and vivid they became an agony all their own.

He'd been here before. Suffered as infection or disease ravaged him. Broken beneath his body's inability to keep going under the merciless strain of too much brutality and too little water.

It wasn't the first time he'd wondered if *this* time he'd fail to rally, fail to come out the other side of freezing fire.

But it *was* the first time he feared that sickness would prevail where cruelty and torture had not.

He was so damn *close*.

Will tucked his arms to his chest, pulled his knees in tight, and tried to focus on something, anything, that would keep him there.

"So close. So close," he mumbled, over and over and over again until the words became little more than the hiss of a river as they spilled past his lips.

He blinked and sweat slid into his eyes, stinging and burning and blurring the world around him.

Something rough and wet touched his face, wiping away the salt and water his body couldn't retain.

Cooper slid back into focus, her touch gentle as she worked her way across his skin with the edge of a soaked shirt.

"Try to sleep."

He stared into a face smeared with dirt and paint and carved with the hard lines of too much living and too little sleep. He'd know her voice anywhere, but would he recognize her on the street? At a bar? In his bed?

"Getting ahead of yourself there, Bennett."

"Sorry," he mumbled, realizing he must have said the part about having her in his bed out loud.

"I'm not a walk of shame kind of girl."

"Buy you dinner first." He grinned, or at least tried to. He was pretty sure his face moved. "S-send you off after a hot shower and my famous eggs on t-t-toast."

"Never happen," Cooper assured him, her words harsh, but her touch gentle. "I'd kick you out of *my* bed the second I was satisfied. You can take your own walk, wondering just where you'd lost *your* underwear, and make your famous eggs on toast for *one*."

"M-m-issing out," he chattered through lips too tired to smile.

"I guess you'll have to rest up. Bounce back." She stared down at him, a curve pulling at the corner of a mouth he dreamed about. "And earn the privilege to prove me wrong."

He wanted to laugh, but it escaped a sigh and he slid back into sleep, focused not on whether or not he'd wake, but instead on just what it would take to see what Coop looked like when *she* did.

They'd brought out the ants.

God, how he hated them. The way they scuttled across his skin, their tiny feet a dotted line *tap tap tapping* to the place they'd bite.

The back of his neck

Behind what was left of his ear.

In the curve of his armpit.

As bad as the bites were—and they were an agony he could not have imagined—the anticipation was so much worse.

Stripped and strapped to a chair, ankles bound at the bottom of the legs, hand secured behind his back, and blindfolded, he could do little more than track the dozens of insects as they marched across his skin.

To wait for the skittering to stop.

Each bite, an agony.

Each held in scream, a victory.

He could handle the pain. Pull it in and push it through his system like a determined tide that would eventually turn. He just had to wait it out.

No, the pain wasn't the problem.

His helplessness was.

Bound tight, sight gone, muscles immobilized to the point that a simple flinch was painful—that was the hard part. Of all the things that had been stolen from him over months of captivity —his flesh, his freedom, his honor—the loss of his ability to fight back had been the worst.

But he never stopped trying. Let the desire fester until it became something cold and unforgiving.

Vicious.

Something scuttled across his skin, and Will jerked, a yell caught in his throat, and struck out.

"Fuck, *calm down*," a voiced urged him.

Hands gripped his shoulders, pushing him back, holding him down, and Will realized he wasn't bound at all.

He threw a punch, caught someone across the chest, and rolled away to freedom.

Amidst a hail of cursing, he turned to his belly. Pushed to his hands and knees, drove his feet into the ground and his body forward . . . only to eat dirt when he tried to stand. His head swam, and his vision blurred, and Will trembled, his muscles like overcooked spaghetti and his head a beating drum.

Booted feet approached. "Jesus, Will. It's me. It's Cooper."

Cooper?

He knew that name. Recognized that voice. He couldn't quite pull together the pieces—hadn't even matched those two things together, but then he didn't really need to.

Because he knew who it wasn't.

Knew home when he heard it.

Knew kindness when it touched him.

No pain. No laughter. No lingering sense of humiliation.

Gentle fingers stroked along his shoulder and down his arm. "You with me, Bennett?" that soft voice asked.

He rolled to his back, let cool, malleable earth cradle his skull, and opened his eyes just to slam them shut again against harsh, piercing light that made his head throb and stomach turn.

"Coop?" he asked, tasting the name against his tongue. Smooth and crisp as fresh spring water, it lacked the bitter tang of a lie.

"Yeah." She put a palm to his forehead. Slid her hand along dry, gritty skin. "Jesus, you're getting worse."

The world tilted like a carnival ride when she helped him sit. "Keep your eyes closed until I get you back under the shade." She helped him scoot back until his hands touched plastic; something crinkled and cracked as he lay back down. Even beneath eyelids that felt thick and swollen, he could sense the change in light. He cracked open one eye, then the other, and stared into a gaze the color of still, deep-blue waters.

"Time is it?" he asked, pushing the words through a throat lined with barbed wire.

"Mid-afternoon," she answered.

He let his gaze roam from the olive-green tarp above his head to the periphery—so much green. Nothing but jungle vegetation as far as he could see.

"W-where . . ." This wasn't camp. Wasn't the pit or the mountainside . . . but it wasn't home, either.

Wasn't safe.

"You don't remember?" she asked on a slow drawl of cautious words.

He shook his head. Regretted the decision when his neck ached, and his head throbbed like a revved engine.

"S-s"—he licked his lips, his tongue swollen and mouth dry —"secure?" They wouldn't let him go. Wouldn't let him leave. Wouldn't let him live.

"Shhh," Cooper soothed him, pushing his shoulders back to the ground with an embarrassing amount of ease. "They're dead. They're all dead. Remember?"

Did he? He searched his mind, pushing through a heavy fog that refused to part but slowly turned to a persistent wash of rain.

A storm. A fight. Lightning had struck.

"Thunder," he whispered, the crack echoing through his confusion, and slicing through his questions. He remembered the rain. The death. The brutal pleasure.

He shivered.

"That's right. Now drink, Will," she said, holding more water to his lips. "And rest so we can get the fuck out of here when night falls."

That time, he heard it. The stumble of words. The indicative pause. The lie—though whether it was for her benefit, or his, he didn't know.

But he wouldn't be leaving. Not tonight. Maybe not ever.

And they both knew it.

She should leave him.

Probably *would* leave him when she realized there was no way he'd be able to get up, to walk out, to carry on.

He caught her wrist as she pulled away. "Don't . . ."

He couldn't say it. Couldn't do it. Even as fear clogged his throat and helplessness made his limbs thick and heavy and unco-ordinated. He couldn't beg.

But she didn't make him.

"I'm not leaving you, Will," she promised. "You're stuck with me."

Stuck with me.

A casual statement bolstered by a conviction he didn't understand from a woman he barely knew.

Fuck, he hated this. Only hours ago, he'd sworn he'd never again be at the mercy of another.

But here he was. Helpless. Broken. *Dying.*

"Sleep, Will. I've got the watch."

I've got the watch.

I've got your back.

A hand cupped his cheek, stroked back his hair. Her voice grew dim and far away, the words a tumble of stones he couldn't catch.

But he held on to that voice. It had come for him. Saved him.

He shouldn't trust it to do it again.

But as something cool and wet touched his forehead, stroked his skin, soothed him into a fevered sleep . . . he did.

CHAPTER SIX

Twelve hours. That was how long it had taken for everything to go to shit. A new record. Even for her.

Twelve hours since Cooper had pulled Will off that mountain.

Twelve hours since he'd taken his first breath of free air.

Twelve hours since she'd first let herself believe this nightmare might finally, finally end.

Damn fool; she should have known better. She'd set herself up for this. Courted disappointment from the moment she'd put any trust in hope or let herself forget, even for a second, that she couldn't afford to have any feelings. Will was *dying*.

And there wasn't a damn thing she could do to stop it.

Not here, not with limited water, over-the-counter drugs, and fast-disappearing rations.

She was out of time—they both were—and a betting man would wager every last dime he had on Will never seeing the light of another day.

It was all so goddamned unfair.

Unfair that Will had endured a year of captivity, only to die on this mountain the second he was free to walk away.

Unfair that, yet again, Cooper could feel hope slipping through her fingers like sand.

Unfair that, just for a moment, she'd felt as if she wasn't so fucking alone anymore. That maybe she'd found an ally, someone who'd understand how incredibly tired she was, even if he couldn't or wouldn't help.

Unfair that Will had reappeared in her life as abruptly as she'd once appeared in his, only for the universe to snatch him away.

Again.

Will had been a variety of things to her: a pleasant daydream, a fun "what if" scenario, a knowing, sometimes even intimate, voice on the other end of the phone. Someone who not only understood the job but thrived on it. Lived for it. In so many ways, and for so many reasons, she'd treasured those irregular phone calls.

Enjoyed the flirting and the trash talking.

The teasing and the understanding.

The friendship, uncomplicated by demands, expectations, or careers that drove them in different directions.

It was why she'd never pushed to meet him, though she'd certainly thought about it.

She'd always assumed there'd be time.

How wrong she'd been.

She'd lost her freedom, her career, her *life*. And she'd lost those late-night calls, random texts, and terrible, terrible jokes.

Silly, that she'd missed that contact, that sense of intimacy with another human being. Especially when she'd spent so much of her life alone. It was the nature of the job, and one she was usually okay with.

Until, like so much else, the choice had been stripped away and the isolation forced on her.

She sat on a sigh, checked the pulse at Will's wrist. Fast, too fast, a brutal rhythm his body couldn't keep running to.

Coop smothered a curse that felt like a goddamned sob caught in her chest.

So. Fucking. Unfair.

Will moaned. His eyelids fluttering, his pupils twitching. Nightmares had haunted him, prowling through his sleep like specters in the night. But as his back arched and the muscles along his neck bulged, Cooper longed for the kindness of a nightmare—and her ability to soothe it away.

She could do little more than watch as seizures wrung him dry and wore him out.

She turned him to his side, held him as his exhausted body twitched and spasmed and contorted.

Will turned, a moan passing through dry, cracked lips, and fisted a hand in the fabric of her shirt, his grip tight and desperate. A silent plea that needed neither voice nor interpreter.

Don't leave me here.

She pulled his hand free. Stood and brushed off the pieces of jungle that clung to her pants and retrieved the satellite phone she kept buried at the bottom of her pack.

As last resorts went, this one sucked. But she dialed anyway. Waited through the endless ringing. Hung up, braced herself for a fight, and dialed again.

"What?" Pierce drawled across the line, his voice thick and heavy with sleep or satisfaction or both.

"I need to change my itinerary," she offered, cautious over a line she didn't control and couldn't secure.

"What number are you calling me from?" Pierce swore, a bed creaking in the background. "You know what, don't answer that. I'll call you back."

It took less than a minute before the phone in her palm vibrated against her hand. She answered on the first ring.

"Hey—"

"You know better than to call from an unsecured line."

"I didn't have much choice," she muttered.

"I need some help."

"I thought you had an exit strategy in place."

"I did. I do," she explained. "But it won't work."

Silence, thin and taut as the line between friend and enemy, stretched between them.

"Then make an adjustment," Pierce grunted.

"I can't." Cooper swallowed and braced herself against the explosion she knew was coming. "Not for both of us."

The *swish click swish* of Pierce thumbing his lighter open, then closed, then open again, filtered down the line.

"What are you doing, love?" Pierce asked, his voice like honey-laced bourbon—a smooth sweetness meant to temper the sting but deliver the punch.

"I can't get him out. Not on my own."

"Then leave him."

Simple. Direct. Obvious. She wondered if it really was that easy for Pierce to make the practical decision. No emotion. No feelings. No loyalty. Had he always been that way? Or had time and practice cut the fabric of cold-hearted mercilessness closer and closer, until he wore it like a flawless second skin?

"I can't."

"Can't, or won't?"

"I need him, you know that—"

"You need his fingerprints, nothing more. You got a knife in your pack?"

"Yes, but I—"

"Then do what needs to be done and get the fuck out of there."

He hung up on her.

Do what needs to be done. No. Just no. Cooper couldn't even bring herself to consider it. Even if Will never woke, never knew, she couldn't stand the idea of carving away a piece of him. Of treating him like an object, a means to an end. He was more than that, damn it, and so the fuck was she.

She called Pierce back. Did it again and again and again until finally, her phone rang.

"I thought you'd learned this lesson already?" Pierce asked. "The hard way, no less."

Cooper closed her eyes, sagged with frustration, and let the sun bathe her face as it came up over the trees. "It's not the same."

"Isn't it, though? You let things get personal. You got attached. Even now you're acting out of emotion rather than logic. That nearly got you killed once. My mistake, I suppose, thinking you were smart enough to figure it out the first time."

She swallowed hard against the cold clutch of betrayal that surged up her throat like acid. He was right, and they both knew it. Faith had gotten her into this mess and loyalty, loyalty had given her a blind spot that had nearly gotten her killed.

"I don't want to hear it."

Experience told her she was making a mistake. She only hoped it was one she could live with.

"Oh, but you need to," Pierce assured her. "An extraction takes time you do not have. His location has been disclosed—I know of at least three mercs in the area who'd be all too happy to pull one job and get paid for two. Leave. Now."

"No," she snapped, her skin flushing hot then cold, her fingers trembling with nerves she refused to give in to.

Pierce sighed. "Get out of there, Cooper. Before it's too late."

"No," she repeated, stronger, more determined.

"Even if I were willing, what you're asking for takes time you *do not have*."

"I won't leave him here." Her mind set, Cooper said the only thing she knew would shut Pierce up and bring him to her side. "I'm calling in my favor. I need an extraction, a secure destination, and a medical team waiting for us when we get there."

Silence dropped, whistling through the air like a ten-ton bomb about to blow everything to shit.

"You're cashing in your favor for *this*? For a man you barely know?"

She'd shocked him, a feat she'd once thought impossible. If she'd ever wondered what it would sound like, she now had her answer. Ugly. Harsh. Judgmental.

"I can't get him out on my own, and I won't leave him behind." Cooper pushed a hand through her hair and gripped the phone. "A life for a life, that's what you said. Pay up, Pierce. Or break your word. Your choice."

But it was no choice at all, and they both knew it. All Pierce had was his word and his reputation. Whatever code he lived by, it would drive him straight to her.

"You're sure?" he asked quietly, carefully, as if giving her the chance to back out. "That favor was meant to save your life. This is a waste, and I'm not a generous man. I won't take your call again."

"My favor, my call." She sighed and prayed she'd never need Pierce again, that she'd never have cause to regret calling in the favor he owed her. The one she'd carried for months like a lethal ace up her sleeve.

He sighed. "Send me your coordinates. And Cooper?"

"Yeah?"

"I sincerely hope you live to regret this." He hung up, but his words, quiet and soft and genuine, lingered with her.

How often had he cautioned her to be smart, to be hard, to be merciless? To shoot first and die last.

And he was right. That mentality would keep her alive.

But she wondered if she could live with the choices Pierce so easily dismissed as beneath his time and consideration.

In so many ways, Pierce was just one of the destinations on the path beneath her feet. This life had pushed him, tormented him, imprisoned him, and in the end, taken damn near everything from him.

And Pierce had emerged, hardened and jaded, clinging to a life void of all the things Cooper missed the most.

Friends. Family. Trust. Intimacy.

Somewhere along the way, he'd made one tough call too many, crossed a line he could never come back from. Had he known it at the time? Understood that if he pulled that trigger, took that life, or turned his back, that he'd never be the same again? That no amount of answers or justice or vengeance would ever be enough to save him?

And when that line lay before her, stretched and thin and so very easy to step over, would Cooper know it for what it was?

Or would she cross it without a second thought . . . and never look back at all?

CHAPTER SEVEN

Panama City, Panama

The metronomic beat of a heart rate monitor drowned out the noise of early morning traffic . . . and was a greater comfort than Cooper wanted to admit.

The last forty-eight hours had been a hellish torture meted out in high-pitched bleeps and one single, heart-stopping note stretched and pulled and plied to the breaking point.

In reality, death had come and gone again in little more than ninety seconds.

A minute and a half of a world without hope. Without answers. Without salvation or redemption.

Without *Will*.

His heart had stopped, and in that moment, so had hers.

And fear had set in.

Cooper had tried to tell herself there'd be another opportunity. That all her hopes for answers, for freedom, for justice, weren't pinned squarely on Will's shoulders.

But they were. Because in the breathless moments where life had failed but death had not yet won, Cooper had understood that one way or another, Will was the end of the road.

She couldn't keep running. Wouldn't keep hiding. Her past was coming for her, and it was time to face it.

Rage, rather than hopelessness, had consumed her.

"Well, he's not much to look at, but he'll live," Pierce said as he went through the now-familiar routine of checking Will's vitals. Through it all, and despite his constant bitching and obvious disapproval, Pierce had been nothing short of a revelation.

A doctor in a former life.

Of all the professions Cooper might have imagined for him, medicine had never once entered her mind.

Do no harm.

Words she couldn't imagine Pierce had ever willingly uttered, let alone lived by.

And yet the experience, the confidence, the painstaking attention to detail was all there. From the moment he'd extracted them from Colombia, Pierce had been a man possessed. By power. By passion. And by the sheer egotistical certainty that when he stood toe-to-toe with death over a patient's bedside, that the outcome was a forgone conclusion. The fight to save a life little more than the pomp and circumstance death demanded before walking away empty-handed.

But then that was Pierce. A riot of conflicts and a mess of impressions. Frightening and miraculous. Devastation and salvation.

Mercenary and hero.

"How is he?" Cooper asked, turning her attention back to Will, her breath falling in sync with the easy rhythm of the steady rise and fall of his chest. She hadn't left his side. Hadn't let herself close her eyes for longer than a fifteen-minute stretch of sleep here and there. She'd been so certain that if she left the room or looked away, she'd come back to find him still and cold beneath that sunny yellow sheet.

Like so much else in her life, there one minute and gone the next.

Another failure. Another death.

So she'd kept her vigil.

"Alive, as promised," Pierce answered, checking the fluids suspended above Will's bed, then looking over the IV he'd placed at the crook of Will's elbow. Pierce's incessant bitching about dehydration, lack of nutrition, and the shitty state of Will's veins still echoed through her mind.

A lot of things did.

None of them pleasant.

But it was the seizures, the nightmares, and the screams that would linger with her.

Even now, Will's time in captivity, the starvation and neglect, the dehydration and abuse, the desperation and the fight, still rode him. She'd helped Pierce undress him. Revealed the harsh lines carved into long-starved limbs. Exposed skin mottled with a bouquet of bruises in greens and blues, yellows and purples, as if the colors had been painstakingly blended and layered. And she'd laid bare the scars—so many scars—that had been left by cruel instruments and crueler hands.

She'd touched some of them. Wondered how old they were. What had put them there.

And prayed to anyone listening that she'd shot each and every one of those bastards dead. That not one had lived. Not one had escaped.

That Will would never have to glance over his shoulder to find his past lurking in wait.

Ridiculous of course. Even if he found a way to put everything the cartel had done behind him, the past was still there, a familiar stranger in a darkened corner.

Watching.

Waiting.

A wraith that never left. Never forgot. And if it had its way, would never let him move on.

Not on my watch.

"All in all, he's come through the last year better than he should have," Pierce added.

Cooper followed Pierce's gaze, tracked the planes of Will's chest, the slope of his shoulders, the dip of his collarbone. He was thin, too thin, and though she'd taken the time to clean his skin with hot water and wrung-out washcloths, he needed a shower. A shave. To do something about that tangled mass of hair. But Pierce wasn't wrong. Will wore the evidence of his captivity, of the casual cruelty and harsh conditions, like the warrior he was.

"It's remarkable, really. He's underweight but hasn't lost all his muscle mass. Regular meals, clean water, plenty of rest—he should rebound quickly." Pierce stepped back, studied Will with the same expression he so often turned on Cooper. Critical and calculating, that look spoke volumes and even managed to *sound* annoyed without the benefit of so much as an accompanying *tsk* to break the silence.

Pierce, Cooper had learned, liked things neatly ordered and predictable. Obedient to the way he saw the world.

As he was so fond of saying, he didn't do sloppy seconds, suppressors, or surprises.

But Will *had* surprised him.

He'd surprised, Cooper, too.

For a guy who'd been on death's door, he looked good. Alive, if not whole. Rebounding, if not healthy.

Color, rather than fever, had returned to his face.

He dreamed—his eyes flickering back and forth beneath their lids—but didn't scream, or plead, or beg.

He slept.

And he snored. Just a little. Just enough to torture him over later.

It brought a smile to her lips that she'd have the opportunity.

"Everything looks good," Pierce said, snapping off his latex gloves as he headed out the door.

Cooper stood and followed Pierce out of the bedroom and into the tiny living area of the three room flat he'd brought them to. She'd been here two days, but it still felt like she was seeing it for the first time.

She hadn't missed much. A worn, but comfortable-looking sofa along the far wall, a tiny kitchenette. A little trifold, dropleaf table next to the door. The air conditioner rattled, the laminate floors were chipped, and a spider had made its home in the corner, his web spreading from wall to ceiling.

It was still the nicest place Cooper had stayed in over a year.

"He'll sleep for a while." Pierce strode into the kitchen, pulled a bottle of juice from a refrigerator that aspired toward greatness and a temperature below sixty. "I gave him several rounds of general antibiotics along with the fluids, and you'll need to follow up with a shot of penicillin, then the pills I've left for you." He chugged down half the bottle, the halogen lights amplifying the dark smudges beneath his eyes. "Given his condition, and the long-term exposure to the elements, I wouldn't skip any doses."

"Any idea when he'll be back up on his feet?" As much as Cooper wanted to give Will time to rest and recover, to eat three square meals and take a long, hot shower, the reality was that the longer he was down, the more dangerous it became to stay. She never lingered long in one place for a reason, and already her skin was itching with the urge to move on.

"At this point, he's just sleeping off the exhaustion and the fever—he should be up and around in the next twenty-four hours. But keep an eye on him. He'll tire easily, and relapse is a serious possibility." Pierce finished off his juice and set the bottle in the sink. "Ever administered penicillin before?"

She shook her head.

"Shot goes in the ass. You may be unfamiliar with the procedure"—he flashed a grin, the line near the top of his cheek deepening—"but you're well acquainted with the results. You'll be fine, I'm sure."

Well acquainted with the . . .?

"Wait, did you just call me a pain in the ass?" she asked, squishing a laugh between her tongue and the roof of her mouth.

"If the shoe fits, love." He braced his hands on the counter and rolled his shoulders, though if he were slipping off tension or bracing for a fight, she couldn't tell.

"Have you given any thought to what comes next?" he asked, his voice dropping and his gaze going toward the bedroom door.

Cooper shook her head, though that wasn't entirely true. As Will's fever had ebbed and his seizures disappeared, all of her thoughts had turned from if he would live, to what happened next if he did.

"What are you going to tell him?"

A deceptively complicated question. Will was no mark. No naive civilian she could manipulate with easy lies or half-formed truths. He'd have questions. He'd demand answers.

And she had to assume that above all else he'd want to go home.

She couldn't let him. Not yet.

"The truth, I guess." As much of it as she could stomach, anyway. A redacted and sanitized version that wouldn't end with Will walking out . . . or with his hands around her neck.

"The truth?" Pierce asked skeptically. "And what, you're just going to hope he feels like helping you?"

"I can't lie to him, Pierce." She sighed, resigned to the now-familiar fight between them. "He deserves to know what he's getting into. What's at stake." He deserved to know everything. Deserved to know not only what his role in all of this was, but hers as well. She'd tell him, if it came down to it, though she didn't want to. Didn't want to hear the words that rang through her head fall from his mouth.

Traitor. Coward. Murderer.

But if that was what it took, if that was what it cost to set things right, then she'd pay.

Cole deserved that much, at least.

"There are other ways, Cooper."

She shook her head. "I need him to access that safe deposit box—"

"You needed his fingerprints to access that box—a distinction you conveniently ignore."

"You can't be serious." Working to keep her voice down, Cooper shoved her hands into the pockets of her jeans and tamped down her irritation. "I told you that wasn't an option. I'm not like you, I can't just—"

"Just what? You think it was easy for me?" Pierce slapped the edge of the counter with an open palm. "That I just woke up one day, cold and ruthless? I didn't. And I paid for it. People died because of it." His tone lost its ragged edge, softening into something like melancholy. "This life, it pushes you, Cooper. It's a never-ending sequence of choices, and none of them are good. The sooner you accept that, the better shot you have of making it to the other side."

But at what cost? she wondered. If she lost that part of herself, buried it deep and walked away, could she ever get it back?

"You got what you wanted. Will's alive, and we're even." Disappointment and a vague sense of disgust rode him. "I hope it works out for you."

"Exactly. *My* choice. So what's your problem?" she asked, frustration thrumming through her veins and pounding at her temples.

"I don't have a problem," he grunted. "I just don't like wasting my time."

"You consider saving a man's life a waste of your time?"

He rounded on her. "What I consider *a waste of my time* is the not-insubstantial effort I've invested in keeping you alive."

"And here I thought you'd be grateful—"

He snorted. "For what, exactly?"

"To be out of my debt, for one. Lord knows you've bitched about it enough."

"Yes, well." He tugged down the crisp cotton sleeves that he'd rolled up when he'd walked in the door to check on Will. "You'll forgive me my disappointment—I never expected you to call in your chips over something so common as affection or banal as loyalty. My mistake, obviously."

"Common as aff—" She snapped off her angry retort. "He was *dying*, Pierce. I couldn't just leave him there."

"Of course you could have. And you damn well should have. I could have easily faked a set of fingerprints, Cooper. You know that." He stormed out of the kitchen, frustration stiffening his shoulders as if he'd forgotten to remove the hanger before sliding on his shirt. "Lie to me all you want, but for fuck's sake, don't lie to yourself. You didn't save that man's life because you had to. Calling me in wasn't a tactical decision or a calculated risk, and you know it. This was sentiment and friendship, pure and simple. The seduction of memories from a life that is *gone*." He shook his head. "It's a potent cocktail and your go-to drug of choice."

She snapped her mouth shut. She wanted to call him out. Accuse him of being a cold, uncompromising bastard.

But he wasn't wrong. And they both knew it.

Sweat itched along her palms and a shiver rose across her skin, all her mistakes and sins whispering reminders against still-sensitive flesh.

"Whatever else you've done, whatever you're trying to atone for, you're a good person, Cooper." Pierce stared at her, his expression guarded but his voice sad. "This life, it kills the good ones. Snuffs them out and carries on as if they never existed in the first place. I want to see you out and free before then."

"Why?" she asked, giving voice to the question that had haunted their strange friendship.

He didn't answer. Just studied her as if he wanted to know what button he had to push or cut he had to make before the wound finally went deep enough to scar.

He reached for her hand, ran his fingers along the raised line of skin on her palm. That cut, and the one that matched it on her other hand, *had* gone deep. *Had* scarred.

And had changed *everything*.

"What's it going to take before you realize the only person you can truly save is yourself?"

"I don't believe that." She swallowed hard and pushed back against the fatal current of fear and doubt and just managed to keep her head above the tide that threatened to drown her. "I can't believe it. I have to make this right, Pierce."

"And that's the problem. You're trying to fix something that cannot be mended. You've shouldered the blame for something that was never your fault to begin with. And you're trying to save a man who is *lost*, Cooper. For fuck's sake, let him go."

She turned away from him, walked toward the drop-leaf table and the curtain-covered window. "I didn't set things in motion," she agreed. "But I pulled the trigger. I killed those men."

"You followed orders," he corrected. "That's all. And they tried to kill you for it. Are *still* trying to kill you for it." He pulled her around to face him. "How do you know the man in that room won't do the same?"

"Will wasn't part of that—"

"Of course he was part of that." He gripped her by the shoulders, shook her once, twice, as if trying to strike what he was saying down to the very marrow in her bones. "If he wasn't part of it, then he wouldn't be here. There wouldn't be a hidden box in a private bank. You wouldn't have pulled him off that mountain and there wouldn't be a price on his head. Everyone has their own agenda, even him." He let her go, knocking her back a half-step with the force of his irritation. "Bennett is part of this, whether you like it or not."

"Then we're right back where we started," she said, thumbing her nail across the scar along her palm. "By your own admission, I need him."

"That doesn't mean you can trust him." Pierce grabbed a tin of a cigarettes from the table and slid one out of the case. "Quite the opposite, actually. You don't know how he plays into this. You don't know what he wants. And you definitely don't know what he's protecting. And each and every one of those things could get you killed."

"And each and every one of those things could get him killed, too," she levied at him. "Someone wants Will dead, and they're willing to pay for the privilege. Which makes him—"

"All the more dangerous," Pierce answered, flicking open his lighter and igniting the end of his hand-rolled tobacco. He breathed in, the ember flickering dark, then bright again as he exhaled. "Man's spent the last year of his life at the mercy of others. Beaten. Tortured. Starved. What do you think he'd do to go home?" he asked, raising a brow at her as he took another drag. "Who do you think he'd sell out to get there? His mother? His sister? His best friend?" he asked, his mouth turning harsh and ugly. "How about some woman he barely knows? How about the woman who *killed his friends?*"

Cooper sucked air, Pierce's one-two punch a physical blow that reverberated through her body and down to her toes. "You don't know him."

"Neither do you," Pierce reminded her. "How do you think your life stacks up against theirs? Against his own?" Pierce asked, his mouth a hard, tight line as he leaned over to flick some ash into the sink. "If the situation were reversed, if Will had pulled the trigger that day, if you'd watched Cole's life drain away, a hole where his head used to be, would you give one goddamned thought to anything other than punishing the person who'd stolen him from you?"

No, Cooper thought viciously. No, she wouldn't. She'd want justice. And if not that, then vengeance. Cole was her partner, her brother, her friend. She'd been his best friend and his wingman, and later, after she'd goaded him into hitting on the pretty brunette sitting lonely at the bar, she'd stood at his wedding.

No one touched him and got away with it.

No one hurt him and lived.

And no one destroyed him without Cooper laying their life to ruin.

"Do you really think it will be any different for Will?" Pierce asked.

Cooper swallowed against the doubt that surged like bile up her throat. "What choice do I have? I have to tell him something."

"Or you can tell him nothing," Pierce offered, unzipping the small leather bag that sat on the table. He pressed three capped syringes into her open palm.

Cooper stared at them, her mouth dry, questions like flocking birds in her head.

"Scopolamine. Laboratory refined for injections."

"No!" Horrified, Cooper shoved the syringes toward Pierce.

"Yes," he hissed, catching her wrist and pulling her close.

"It's *wrong*."

"It's *safe*," he argued, closing her fingers around the needles. "You don't know what you're walking into."

She shook her head and slapped the drugs on the table. "And you don't know what you're asking." Didn't know the horrors he was unleashing. To Pierce, this was little more than an unpleasant practicality. A situation in which it was better to ask forgiveness than permission.

But to Cooper?

To Cooper it was betrayal. Unconscionable and unforgivable.

"One injection will buy you eight to twelve hours, Cooper. He'll be open and impressionable. If you have questions, then ask him. He won't lie to you—it would never even occur to him to try," Pierce urged her. "Walk him into the bank. Access the box. Get your answers. And do it all with the absolute certainty of the control scopolamine will give." He pushed back his shock of brown hair and sighed. "It's been used for far less—and far worse."

To Pierce it was a Colombian legend. Derived from the borracherro tree, scopolamine was used by locals to carry out the perfect crime. A lost woman on the street. An open map. Someone kind enough to stop and help. All it took was a breath of air and a face full of powder. Twelve hours later and the victim's memory was as empty as their bank account.

But security footage would reveal the game.

The victim, walking in, alert and responsive. Emptying their accounts. Handing over the cash. And doing it all with a ready smile.

Completely open to suggestion and entirely at the mercy of their captor.

The crime as horrifying as it was non-violent.

And Pierce didn't know the half of it.

Didn't know the ways the CIA had used it.

Or maybe he did. As a truth serum that had been abandoned in the seventies, at least. But he didn't know about what came later. Didn't know how they'd coupled it with cutting edge software and state of the art medicine for something much, much worse.

Assassinations. Programming. Enslavement.

But Cooper knew. She'd seen it, even if she hadn't realized it at the time.

And she'd have no part of it. Not now. Not ever. Not for any reason or anything.

"No," she repeated, forcing all of her firm resolve into a single word. "It's a line I won't cross, Pierce."

He cursed. "Not even for Cole?" he asked.

She shut her eyes, pushed down the nagging sense of failure, and ignored the promise she'd made. "Not even for him."

"What then?" he asked, his voice harsh, his face slashed with frustrated lines. "Tell Bennett the truth and trust him to do the right thing?"

"I trusted *you* to do the right thing," she said, meeting his gaze. She'd expected to find amusement, surprise, or even that smug look of satisfaction he wore so well, but instead found only horrified shock.

He recovered fast and moved faster.

"Trust?" he asked the second he had his arm around her neck, his huge hands braced against her face and jaw. "Trust just got you killed." He jerked his hands but turned her loose instead of snapping her neck.

She stumbled away from him, only to find him at her back, one hand on her shoulder, his gun at the base of her skull.

"This is what trust feels like, Cooper." He dug the cold metal of the barrel into her head. "This is what it sounds like." He cocked the gun, the click deafening . . . and still not half as loud as the whispered warning against her ear.

He spun her, shoved her back against the wall, then holstered his gun.

Tired of his games, she struck out, landing a blow to his jaw, to his cheek, to that goddamned mouth. She smothered a scream and bit off a curse when he caught her hands, pried open her fingers, and held her palms up, his thumbs digging into the scars he found there.

"This is what trust gets you, Cooper." He dropped her hands and stepped away. "If you're lucky."

Tears burned at the back of her eyes. He wasn't right, but he wasn't wrong, either. And he'd known just where to hit her. Just how to make it hurt.

But it didn't matter. Because if she did as he suggested, if she crossed that line, then she'd become the very thing she hated.

And there'd be no coming back. No going home. Not for her. Not ever.

"It's not an option, Pierce. Not for me."

He nodded, the muscle in his jaw twitching. "Then God help you, Cooper." He strode for the door, pulled it open, and walked away.

Because I won't.

He didn't say it. But then, he didn't have to. She'd heard him anyway.

His debt was paid, and he was done.

She wondered if she'd ever see him again.

Probably not.

She closed the door and braced her palm against the wood.

It should be a relief, watching him go.

But it wasn't. Not really.

Just a hollow sense of understanding that sometimes, death

wasn't the worst thing a person faced. And not all who lived through trauma survived.

She turned away from Pierce. She couldn't help him. Couldn't save him.

But there was someone else she could.

CHAPTER EIGHT

Pain, both familiar and foreign, registered first.

Familiar, in that Will couldn't remember the last time he'd woken to anything else. The ache of bruises had become a ready, if not friendly, touch. The throb of infected skin as consistent as his own heartbeat. The pull of overtaxed or underworked muscles—extremes, always extremes—was little more than a tease and a torment. A lover's touch that promised a lot, delivered less, and always left him aching.

But this time, there was something new, too. The foreign warmth of unencumbered sunlight burned across his eyelids, urging him to wake, to rise, to face the new day.

It seemed an impossible and terrifying thing.

He didn't know where he was, but he was damn sure where he wasn't. Forgotten in the jungle. Trapped in a pit. At the mercy of another. He'd been so certain that place would become his grave. Had tried to make his peace with that. And toward the end, when he'd had enough, he'd let himself hope it would be.

He'd cursed himself a quitter and a coward but had let himself pray for the end anyway.

Knowing he was free, that he'd won, that he'd lived, and those bastards had died, should have been easy. Welcome.

Instead, it was the most frightening realization he'd had in over a year.

Now that he wasn't dying, he'd have to face the monumental task of living.

And he had no idea where to start.

"Are you trying to do that thing where you're not asleep, but you pretend to be anyway?" Cooper asked, her voice soft but amused. "You know, the whole regulate your breathing, tamp down your heart rate, and utterly fool the other person in the room?"

Will turned his head toward her voice, felt a smile tug at the edge of his mouth. "Maybe," he croaked, his mouth dry and his lips chapped.

"Then I regret to inform you that you've utterly failed." The bed near his hip dipped beneath her weight, and Will opened his eyes, wincing against the sunlight streaming through a gauzy curtain. Cooper smiled down at him. "You'd make a terrible spy— it's the first thing they teach you."

He sat up and she handed him a bottle of water, condensation seeping into his palm and running down the side. He chugged down half.

"I'd make an excellent spy," he assured her. The sheet slid down to bunch around his hips, and a thin cotton t-shirt, crisp and clean, clung to his shoulders. The neckline gaped a little and his arms didn't fill out the sleeves the way they once had, but he did his best not to focus on that. Time, food, and exercise would bring back a physique that had always required maintenance and devotion. His strength would return. It had to. "And a better ninja, which is frankly more impressive."

"They do have the better uniform," she agreed with a grin.

He lifted the bottle, ready to down the rest of it, but didn't get more than two huge mouthfuls.

"Easy on the food and fluids, okay?" Cooper said, pulling the water from his lips with a fingertip pressed to the end. "Lots more where that came from."

Will stole another swallow, then made himself stop. He couldn't really remember the last time he'd had clean, cold water. Thumbing the edge of a peeling label, he wondered what else would taste this good, feel this forbidden. Where to even start? He'd been denied and wished for so many things. The mundane —sex, a hot shower, a double cheeseburger and fries greasy enough to disintegrate the bottom of a paper bag. The well-earned indulgence—an aged steak, rare and the size of a plate, a day on Lake Champlain with silent friends and biting fish, sex with a woman who made the pursuit interesting, the foreplay fun, and the climax memorable.

So many things he wanted. Some of them far away and out of reach . . . and some an arm's length away.

As if she knew what he was thinking, Cooper arched and eyebrow and asked, "So? What's at the top of the list?"

And in the end, the answer was simple and came to him with a rueful grin.

Priorities.

"Water heater work?" he asked.

"Far better than the air conditioner." She stood and stretched, arms above her head, the hem of her shirt riding high and the waistband of her jeans sliding low. He wanted to touch the line of skin that showed between the two, brush his thumb back and forth, trail a finger along the curve above her hip.

Remind himself she was so much more than a fevered dream or distant memory.

He swung his legs over the edge of the bed, pushed himself to his feet, then sat right back down again when the blood rushed to his head and the room tilted to the left.

"Shit."

Cooper laughed, the sound warm and rich and not at all at his expense.

"You Delta boys." She shook her head. "Always in such a hurry. Take your time. I'll get the shower going."

She wandered toward the bathroom and the rusty squeal of ancient plumbing and the hissing gurgle of water pushing through pipes followed.

Will braced his hands on the edge of the mattress, took a deep breath, and pushed himself to his feet. Blood rushed from his head and his vision fizzed like it had gone carbonated, but the room remained steady.

Progress.

When everything settled, he followed his feet out of the bedroom door and around the corner, taking the time to catalogue the aches and pains that accompanied each step.

He felt surprisingly good. Sore, yes. But less like he'd been beaten to within an inch of his life—a state he'd become depressingly familiar with—and more like he'd slept for far too long and allowed his muscles to go loose and heavy, then achy and uncooperative.

He pushed open the bathroom door and a billow of steam rolled out to greet him, the heat and humidity a heavy, cloying reminder that reached with ghostly fingers to try to pull him back in time.

He pressed forward instead. He was done with all that.

"Towels," Cooper said, appearing behind him with a stack of stark-white cotton. She dropped them on the counter near the sink. "Soap and shampoo are in the shower, Grizzly Adams, and I managed to source a razor and a pair of scissors if you're feeling adventurous."

He tugged the ends of hair that had never been short. He'd spent enough time in the Middle East to grow an "in-country" look, but he doubted he'd be deploying anytime soon—hell, his military career was likely over; psych would never clear him for field work after a year in captivity—and he was ready for a fresh start.

He stood there, caught between the door and the shower, wondering when simple things had become so overwhelming.

As usual, Cooper seemed to have some idea of what was going through his head . . . even when he didn't.

"It's normal, you know," she offered when he didn't move. "That feeling that nothing's the same, that even daily chores we once did by rote are now foreign and overwhelming."

"We?" He didn't turn to face her but dipped his chin and tilted his head in her direction. He couldn't look at her. Not yet. Wasn't even sure he was ready to face himself. But neither could he deny the sleepy sliver of curiosity that lay beneath his skin like a splinter. Something easily overlooked, but noticeable when prodded. It would grow, too, he realized. As the fog of illness and too much sleep pulled back, questions would set in. Already, they circled the perimeter, curious as cats, hungry as wolves.

But they'd wait. For a little while longer, at least.

Cooper touched his back, her fingers light against his t-shirt, a cautious hello and a sad goodbye in one small gesture. "We," she confirmed. "Shower. I'll figure out food—"

Will turned, a laugh climbing his throat. "You cook?" He wasn't sure why he found the idea funny, but he did. Cooper had featured in a lot of fantasies over the years but dressed in an apron and tied to the stove had never been one of them.

"Not as well as I shoot," she said. "But then that's setting the bar very, *very* high."

Yes, it most certainly was.

"Bet a lot of things sail right under it."

She met his gaze, her clear-blue eyes dancing like open water on a cloudless day. "Most," she agreed. "But not all." She dipped her chin toward the shower. "Get to it, Bennett, and I'll see what's on the menu."

She walked away, pulling the door shut behind her and denying him the pleasure of watching her go.

He turned back to the shower, another familiar, yet foreign feeling stirring beneath his skin.

Priorities, he reminded himself.

It took nearly an hour, two tanks of hot water, half a bottle of shampoo, and two full bars of soap before the water ran clean and clear. Will's skin was pruned and his body tired as he stood at the sink, a towel around his hips and a straight razor in his hand.

An hour on his feet, and it felt like he'd been running on fumes for days.

It was damn depressing.

Cooper knocked on the door, though he'd left it mostly open to let the steam escape and the cool air in. "Brought you some clothes. You okay?" she asked, eyeing the way he clutched the razor in a fist on top of the chipped counter.

"Yeah." He swallowed, glanced into the sink and at the ragged scraps of hair he'd cut away from his face with the scissors she'd left him. It had been easy enough, long as it was. He wanted the rest gone, or at least cropped close, but . . .

He lifted his hand, watched the razor tremble, then set it back down in disgust.

"Food ready?" he asked, taking the clothes from her hands and ignoring the way her gaze skittered like a windblown leaf over the bare expanse of his chest.

What was left of it anyway.

He wasn't sure what he'd expected. He'd known, of course, that he'd lost weight. A lot of it, apparently. Had felt the weakness in his limbs. But that hadn't really prepared him to face the damage that had confronted him first in the shower and later in the mirror.

He'd barely recognized himself.

Fitting, then, that outside matched the inside.

Nothing felt the same. Nothing looked the same.

He wasn't the same. Of course not.

He just had no fucking clue what to do about it, or how to live with it.

He'd always been big. A weed at ten. A pole at fifteen. And then, when life got hard and he got mean, he'd filled out. Piled on a few more inches and packed on fifty more pounds. All of it muscle.

He'd made an imposing big brother, a decent athlete, and a helluva solider.

Being physical, being capable, being strong . . . it was just who he was. It always had been.

And now that identity had been stripped from him. But then, maybe he'd deserved it.

He'd never used that strength on someone else. Not until—

"I'm fine," he grunted.

"Sure you are."

And a shitty liar, apparently.

Will shook his head. He'd never shied away from a fight. Wasn't about to start now. So he sighed, clenched his teeth, and faced himself.

As a kid he'd spent endless days with action figures—pitting them against each other, blowing them up with leftover fireworks, burying the remains then digging them up to do it all again. And always, he sided with the heroes. Let G.I. Joe and He-Man save the day. And though he couldn't say he'd done it on purpose, he'd created a life in their image.

Strong. Fierce. Loyal.

Steadfast in the face of evil, brave in the face of weakness.

He hadn't been prepared to confront either of them in himself.

He shivered and turned away from the mirror.

What did she see when she looked at him? What would his friends see when he returned? What Georgia would see when she hugged him—or slugged him. It was a tough call, really. His sister had never handled her emotions well or predictably.

He'd been gone a long time. She'd probably moved on. Probably written him off as dead. When he turned up alive . . . Yeah, she was going to deck him.

The thought brought a forlorn smile to his mouth.

"They still go on the same way." Cooper's voice drew him back to the here and now. "One leg at a time, in case you're wondering."

"You just going to stand there and watch?" he asked, resisting the ridiculous urge to hold the clothes close to his chest.

"Is that an invitation?" She cocked her hip against the door and let her gaze roam where it liked.

"Can't imagine why you'd want one."

It was an odd sensation, being on the receiving end of that stare. Wondering if he'd measured up. Resisting the slow, determined crawl of insecurity and embarrassment that swept over him like a hungry tide. In his experience, women tended to step into the pitfalls of vanity and insecurity. Will couldn't remember a single one who hadn't gone still or quiet or reserved, even if only for a split second, just before or right after the clothes came off.

He'd never before wondered what that felt like. Hadn't cared, really. Naked was good. Naked and touching was better. Naked and sliding into a willing woman was the best. And it usually didn't take much to set aside those fears and move past those insecurities.

A smile. A touch. A whispered assurance.

Fuck, he'd been lazy.

Now here he was, tables turned, half naked and self-conscious with it . . . and battered by the sudden realization that Cooper would have no such reservations. All too easily he could picture her walking away from him, shedding clothes as she headed to the bed, glancing back to ensure he followed.

He would. Like a lamb to slaughter, he would.

"You've given me a number of invitations in the past, but I was never in a position to accept them." She stepped into the room and closed the scant distance between them. Slowly, she drew a fingertip along the edge of his towel, her nail brushing his still-damp skin.

"That was different." He caught her hand before she reached the fold at his hip. "I was different."

"In the mood, you mean?" she asked sweetly. "Or maybe you just enjoyed the game. The knowledge that you could say anything, promise anything, and never have to follow through."

Oh, he'd wanted to follow through, all right. Had wondered what it'd be like to carry out the promises he'd made. To put her on her knees or hold her against a wall. To pull her pants down her thighs and bury himself in her. To bite her shoulder and bruise her hips. He'd known from the moment Cooper had first saved his team that she was different in every way that mattered.

An enigma. A contradiction. A challenge.

He hadn't even needed to see her to know he wanted her.

He'd already drawn a picture in his head. Knew she'd be like the profession she'd chosen and the gun she carried. Tough. Competent. Dangerous.

Still and quiet one second, a riot of chaos the next.

And nothing less than one hundred percent confident.

He'd thought himself up to the task. Hell, he'd never even thought to question it.

When women came to Will's bed, it was for the thrill, the story. They liked his height, his muscles, his job.

He was the warrior they took to bed simply to say they had— all fine by him.

And always, he'd restrained himself. Understood that what they considered wild, he considered tame.

But with Cooper, restraint would be out of the question— he'd promised her as much. Told her where he'd wanted to put his hands, his mouth. Warned her that there'd be no romance, no seduction. That between them, foreplay would look like war games, and the winner would take all.

It'd be him, he'd promised. That stripped of her gun and her perch, she'd be at his mercy. Smaller. Weaker. Conquered.

She'd moaned. Fucking *moaned*. Then told him she'd like to see him try.

The very idea had made him feel like a man in a way little else ever had.

Cooper would cede no ground. Give no quarter. And when he had her, pinned and writhing, wet and ready, he'd ensure defeat felt like victory and surrender like triumph.

But now, standing before her in little more than a towel and a body that had betrayed him, he couldn't imagine what Cooper saw when she looked at him.

Whatever it was, it wasn't strength, and that, more than anything, felt like weakness. Tasted like shame.

"So that's it?" she goaded him with a huff. "Are you all talk, no follow through? Of course, you are." She rolled her eyes on a sigh. "I suppose it's easy, making promises in the dark you don't intend to keep. Like video games and virtual reality—half the thrill and none of the risk."

"I intended to keep them," he assured her, grasping her wrist when she drew her fingers along the harsh, sloping line of his collarbone.

"Ah. *Intended*. Past tense. So either I've disappointed you, or you no longer think you can. Is that it, Will? Am I a letdown?" She knew damn well she wasn't but tried to pull away all the same.

He didn't release her. Instead, he let himself revel in the feel of her wrist trapped in his hand, the bones tiny and fragile and so easy to rub together. To snap.

"Not even close."

He let go.

Backed away from the violence that was just there, simmering beneath his skin, ready to erupt. It had always been there. In school. In the field. In his bed. And he'd made his peace with that. Turned it toward something useful. Kept it leashed and harnessed and tamed.

But the last year had changed him. Brought forth darker, meaner urges. He'd been stripped of decency and restraint.

It was probably a good thing that the time had eaten away at him. That his strength had failed, and his body had withered.

"You think you're weak."

She traced her finger along the curve of a scar, one of the many Matías had carved into him.

"You're not," she promised when he flinched.

"How could you possibly know?" he asked, his voice gruff and unsure.

What was it about this woman that stirred passion to something else entirely? It wasn't violence, or malice, or cruelty. He didn't want to hurt her, not really, not in any way she wouldn't like. But he did want to take her, use her, wreck her and ruin her. Enough so that she'd come back for more. Come back to him and only him and beg him to do it all again.

Cruel, that now that he had her here, in his grasp and taunting him, he wasn't sure he could do any of those things.

"You must be joking." She wrapped her fingers in the towel and led him toward the toilet. She dropped the lid and pushed him to sit. "You've had a taste of weakness, Will. But you don't know what it is to live with it. Not really."

"Don't I?" he asked as she reached for a can of shaving cream and the blade he'd abandoned.

"No," she assured him, "you don't. How much do you want to lose?"

"What?" he asked, trying to keep up.

She drew a fingertip along his jaw and over the ragged ends of his beard. "I'm guessing mangy Wookiee was not the look you were going for, right?"

He swallowed hard. He'd hacked away haphazardly with scissors, assuming he'd clean it up or shave it off with the straight razor. But he hadn't counted on the tremors.

"Gone would probably be easier."

"For you, or for me?"

Either. Both. He wasn't sure what he'd find if he shaved it all away. But he wanted to feel human and well-kept more than he wanted a close-cropped beard.

"You know how to use that thing?" he asked, eyeing the glint of the blade beneath the bathroom lights.

"I do." She dropped a folded towel to the floor beneath his feet and stared down at him. "So, baby face? Neat and tidy? Or full lumberjack?"

"Neat and tidy."

She knelt between his legs, her knees cushioned by the folded towel she'd dropped to the floor, and moved in close.

She shook the can of foam, then dispensed a cloud of white into her hand. With a gentle touch, she smoothed it over his cheeks, then over his chin and down his neck.

And Will forgot to breathe.

Like this, Cooper kneeling between his legs, the heat of her body close and her scent as thick as the steam that had rolled out of the room, he didn't feel so damaged, so broken, so inadequate.

And Cooper didn't look so whole and strong. Face to face, tucked neatly into the space between his legs, the heat of her body pushing away an encroaching chill, she looked so damn small.

All an illusion, of course. She might be on her knees before him, staring up at him, her eyes wide and her mouth parted, but she held the knife. Pressed it to his face, worked across his skin in short, smooth strokes.

"It's temporary, you know," she said, wiping the blade clean on the towel he still had wrapped around his waist.

"What is?"

"The weakness. The tremors. The exhaustion." She brought the blade back to his face, angled his chin with her knuckles, and continued to work a line along his cheek. "They all fade. Faster than you think they will. And your strength will return."

He swallowed, his Adam's apple bobbing as he did.

"Already you're bouncing back. Five days ago you were barely on your feet. Three days ago you were suffering beneath a fever so high it was inducing seizures. Now here you are, freshly showered and—"

"And unable to do something as simple as shave myself."

"Lucky me." She wiped off the blade again with a smile. "Though I bet you'd do just fine after a hot meal and a little more sleep."

When he glanced away, she brought their faces close, her breath warm against his mouth. "Do you really think so little of me, Will?"

"What?" He pulled back, so he could stare into her eyes.

"How tall am I?" She trailed a finger across a smooth line of skin as if checking her work.

"I don't know. Five-six? Five-seven?" he guessed.

She grinned. "Flatterer. I'm five-five and as my grandfather used to say, I have the shape and tenacity of a weed. Thin," she explained, "and stubborn when I plant my feet." She gently grasped his chin and tilted his head to the left. "Now, ask me what that was like in boot camp." She moved the razor along his skin. "Ask me what that was like when I was the one selected for sniper school." She paused, curving the blade up his neck and beneath his jaw. "Ask me what that was like, Will, when I got recruited by the CIA."

He didn't have to. Could all too easily imagine the conde-scension, the slurs, the abuse. Cooper wasn't the sort of woman to back down from a fight, and she wore confidence like a favored outfit. To most men, it would have looked like a Texas-sized chip on her shoulder.

How many had tried to knock it off?

How many times had they succeeded?

How many times had she gotten up again anyway?

"No one wanted to work with me," she admitted, her voice firm and flat, which was how he knew it still bothered her. "One of the best shots in the country, and I very nearly didn't make the cut for sniper school."

"I find that hard to believe." He'd had her at his back more than once, now. Seen what happened when precision and destruction intertwined. When Cooper's rifle was at her shoul-der, a man would be damn stupid to give two fucks about what was between her legs.

"Men looked at me and saw a petite blonde who didn't fit their image of what a sniper ought to be. Small. Feminine. Weak." She cleaned her blade again, then inspected the line she'd made beneath his jaw and *hmmed* her approval. "Spotters have the hard job, you know?" She switched tracks as she tilted his head and began working on the other side of his face, but he had a pretty good idea of where she was going. "It's technical and tedious and more often than not, the difference between a wasted round and a positive outcome. Spotters do the work—"

"And snipers get the glory," he finished for her.

A smile touched her mouth, though her blade never stopped moving. "Everyone wants to pull the trigger, be the hero. Hard enough to realize that's not how it's going to go." She cleaned up an area by the corner of his mouth, then closed and set aside the razor. "Most didn't want to work with me. A few even outright sabotaged me." She stood, turned on the cold water, and tossed a hand towel into the sink. "I had to pass all the major qualifiers on my own—until Cole, anyway."

"I met him once, passing through an airport. He was coming. I was going. Nice guy."

"He told me." Fondness, like a warm drop of sunshine peeking through a sky full of clouds, entered her tone . . . and was gone just as quickly.

"Your strength *is* going to come back. Your muscles will return. Your stamina will improve. But I'm not ever going to get any taller. Or any bigger. I do my best to stay in shape, but let's be honest—I'm small."

She shut off the water and wrung out the towel.

"Without my rifle, I'm ordinary."

Bull. Shit.

"And without a gun, I'm vulnerable. Does that make me weak?" she asked, pressing the cool fabric to his face and wiping away what remained of the shaving cream.

"You're a field asset, Cooper, one of the best I've ever seen. I think we both know the answer to that."

She nodded. "I am. And I had to work damn hard to get there. Had to find my limitations, push them, exceed them, and when that didn't work, I had to find a way to live with them. Use them." Cold air slapped his skin when she pulled the towel away from his face. "But if it came down to a fight—" She shook her head, as if arguing with herself about what she was about to say. "Nine times out of ten, in a straight fight, both of us at our best, you'd win, Will. Simply because you're bigger. Stronger." She smiled down at him. "I'd make you hurt for it, but you'd win." She slid to her knees again, rubbed her thumb along his jaw. "But you're not at your best right now."

She tilted his chin down so he met her gaze. "Nine for ten . . . you'd still win. You're big and you're smart and you're exceptionally well trained." She swallowed hard, as if the admission itself had tried to choke her. "Even now, even like this, you still win. Does that make me weak?"

"No," he croaked and forced himself to remain still and silent beneath her touch when her fingers slipped up along his jaw and into his hair. She tucked the still-damp strands behind an ear that was only half there.

"Are you sure? I can't change it. I'll never get bigger or stronger or more capable than I am now."

He pressed a palm to her cheek, soaked in the heat of her skin, and nodded.

"This doesn't make you weak." She touched the ragged curl of cartilage that remained. "Neither do these." She trailed fingers over scars, so many scars. Some long-healed and decades old. Others still new and pink and puckering. "This," she said, running the flat of her palm along his chest to rest over his heart, "is the only strength that matters. Proof you survived. Proof you won," she whispered the benediction against his ear, brushed her knuckles along his beard, and pulled away. "Don't confuse weakness with vulnerability, or helplessness with trust."

For a moment, it sounded as if she were reminding herself, as much as him, that those things weren't the same.

Why she'd felt the urge, he didn't know. Had only started to wonder and question why she was here, what she was running from.

When she touched him like this, with words as much as hands, it didn't matter. He suspected she needed him, and that was enough.

He closed his eyes and caught her wrist, pressed a kiss to the pulse he found there. It was the only thank you he could muster, though God knew she deserved so much more.

"I just needed the reminder."

"And a good shave," she said with a grin.

"You plan to let me return the favor?"

"Are you accusing me of having a beard?" She laughed and went to stand.

He pulled her back down, boxed her in with his legs, and smiled.

"I'm prepared to make do." He brushed a thumb against the skin along her throat, reveled in the shiver it elicited. In the way her chin tipped up just enough to let him draw out the drag of his skin against hers.

Her eyes darkened, and she made a little *hmm* in the back of her throat. "Promises, promises," she whispered beneath her breath, throwing him back in time to late night calls and whispered thoughts. For a moment, everything grew close and quiet and dark.

Charged.

In a whoosh, the past rushed forward, invading and saturating the moment with every promise, every denial, and every single night they'd spent apart. Will had wondered if the time would ever be right, and later, if he'd ever get the chance.

And all of it had led him here.

He didn't know what day it was.

Didn't know what country he was in.

But none of that mattered.

Because Cooper was willingly on her knees before him.

Only an idiot would waste that opportunity.

"I missed you, Coop." He slid his fingers through her hair, a mid-toned brown that didn't suit her, but given the time would definitely grow out to something lighter, something longer. Something he could wrap around his fists, or thread between his fingers. "I'd never met you, not really, but I missed you all the same."

"Will, I—" She swallowed hard. "You don't know what I've done."

"I don't care." He clenched his fingers in her hair, gripped the back of her skull, and pulled her mouth to his. He swallowed down whatever she'd been about to say. He didn't care about any other word than "no" or "stop." Didn't give two shits about yesterday, or tomorrow. Just the here and the now and a moment that had eluded him for far too long.

He'd wondered what this kiss would taste like. If it would come as a first negotiation or the very last surrender. Either way he'd expected it to be a hard-fought concession.

But this was none of those things. It was softer, sweeter, slower. An indulgence, neither illicit nor forbidden, but rare as a warm afternoon, with a cool breeze and nothing to do but relax.

She slid both hands along his forearms, her greedy fingers spreading wide as if she needed to touch as much of him as possible, then opened her mouth and invited him in.

He'd missed a lot of things in the last year. Craved everything from fifty-cent wings to a fifty-dollar steak. Had even fantasized, a time or two, about what he'd eat first.

As he stroked his tongue along Cooper's, he doubted he'd crave anything else but her ever again. He released the tangle of her hair, cupped her cheeks, and pulled her lower lip between his teeth.

A promise for another time, another night.

He pulled away just enough to look at her, to flick his thumb against the flush in her cheeks, to swipe it along the corner of her mouth.

God, she was beautiful like this.

She didn't move, didn't sway, and didn't get up to leave. Just gripped his wrists, circling them with her fingers and holding on with everything she had as he cradled her face. Her eyes fell closed and her chest heaved as if she had to swallow down a sob . . . then she said the last thing he wanted to hear.

"We need to talk."

CHAPTER NINE

Half an hour and a solid meal later, and Cooper still had no idea where to start.

Or, she thought darkly, maybe she simply didn't want to. Avoidance had never really been her play, but she could certainly make a case for it now. She could still feel Will's hands in her hair. Still taste him on her mouth. Still hear the silent promises he'd made when he'd touched her, held her, kissed her.

She'd only meant to set him at ease. To drown out the voices in the back of his head, the ones that sounded like doubt and insecurity and guilt, with a truth that deep down he knew but didn't remember.

His body was healing but he'd been hurting all the same . . . and she'd wanted to make it stop.

He wasn't weak or broken or any of the myriad things he'd been contemplating as he'd stood at that sink and clutched that razor.

She just hadn't expected that reminding him of that simple truth would so ruthlessly remind her that *she* was both of those things.

Broken, in that she'd left little pieces of herself in so many different places, so many foreign countries, that she didn't think she'd ever be able to collect them all again.

Weak, in that she wanted to push everything aside, bury it deep and pretend it didn't exist so she could take every single thing Will had been offering.

Comfort. Solace. Forgiveness.

Except, that last one had to be earned. And she hadn't, not yet, maybe not ever.

Not from him, at least. Saving his life didn't erase the fact that she'd taken others.

It would be his right to hate her.

She could live with that. *Would* live with that, as she did so many other things.

So long as he didn't walk out on her.

Will watched her from the sofa, an empty bowl of chicken and rice on the coffee table. "Cooper," he said gently, his voice packed with patience that would soon dissipate like rain on a hot summer sidewalk, "why am I here?"

Right, okay. He'd given her the opening, told her to rip off the Band-Aid.

"Because I need your help."

"Anything." He went to stand, to come toward her, as if he couldn't fathom that she'd ask anything he wouldn't or couldn't give.

He had no idea.

"Three blocks from here, there's a bank with a safety deposit box in your name."

He sat, his face shuttering as if a trespasser had tripped a security gate.

So he knew. She'd wondered. Figured it was a fifty-fifty shot that he'd been told about that box. It might have been better if he hadn't known, if this was all new to him. He'd have been less wary, less reluctant. Curiosity, if nothing else, would have led him through the door. And Cooper could have saved her confession for after.

"I don't know what you're talking about."

A lie, and an obvious one. She wondered why he bothered. But then, people had died, and worse, because of the contents of that box. But no more. Not if she could help it.

Not unless they deserved it.

"Yes, you do."

He didn't deny it. Just propped his elbows on his knees and laced his fingers together. His expression remained neutral, but his shoulders bunched, and his eyes never left hers.

In a blink, she'd gone from friend to enemy.

She didn't give herself time to mourn the change.

"I need you to access it."

"How do you even know about it in the first place?" he asked, his voice going hard and stubborn and suspicious.

It was the one question she didn't want to answer. Knew that any explanation she could give would only enrage him.

"I need the contents to—"

"That's not what I asked."

She snapped her mouth shut.

"Fine. Why don't I start with what *I* know?" He looked up at her, his jaw set and his eyes fierce, determined.

But memories haunted that face. Guilt. Sorrow. She'd seen their shallow lines and subtle curves often enough to recognize them on someone else.

"Eighteen months ago, I was deployed to Afghanistan. An operation went bad, and my unit was called in for support." He cracked his knuckles, popping each finger in turn. "In the end, it didn't matter. Sniper took out six men that day. Could have just as easily been seven." He sighed, forcefully exhaling the grief and anger and guilt only survivors carried. "I got lucky."

No. Luck had never played a role in any of it. He simply hadn't been the target.

"Ever wonder what it's like on the other side, Coop?" he asked, though it didn't sound like an accusation, just an honest question he didn't expect her to have the answer to. "I've been in a lot of shitty situations in the field. But that one stands out." He stared through her, his mind in the past. "By the time you hear the shot, it's already too late. Another man's dead, and you're just glad it wasn't you. But then you wonder if the next one has your name on it. If you'll hear another round. See another man fall."

He brought himself back to the here and the now, and she wondered just how often he'd been in that position, waiting for the kill shot. Waiting to be next.

"I lived that day. Did my best to put it behind me. Told myself it was for a reason. But other men—some of them friends I'd known for years—didn't." His laugh was brittle and broken, with sharp edges and missing pieces. "Chalked it up to a bad day."

One of the worst, she'd imagine. It had been chaotic and brutal, and, in the end, people had died . . . and others had been left to live with it.

"It happens, you know? The rest of us pick up and move on. I would have—did, if I'm honest—but then five months later Felix Harrigan sends me a fucking letter from beyond the grave." He wiped his palms against the fabric of his sweats. "Tells me that his team was betrayed. That they'd stumbled across intel—something highly classified and highly illegal—and that if he or any other member of the team died, that I should assume the C-I-Fucking-A had killed them over it." He shook his head, his laugh still tinged with the incredulity he must have felt upon reading that letter. "He told me to watch my back. I might have dismissed it all out of hand—men die, soldiers more than most. But that day . . . that day stood out to me. Always had. Quiet one minute. Chaos the next. Between the explosions and the gunfire, everything had gone tits up . . . but the sniper—that felt personal. Precise. Patient." He reached for the glass of water on the coffee table, chugged down half, then sighed. "Kill count could have been higher. Probably *should* have been higher."

"But it wasn't," she offered.

"No. Which had always felt odd to me. Even so, I might have dismissed that letter as a bad prank or the stress of the job."

"Except for the box."

"Except for the box," he agreed. "It was all so damn surreal. Impossible to believe and impossible to ignore."

"But you did ignore it."

He shot her a withering look. "The hell I did. But I wasn't going to rush into anything, and I damn sure wasn't going to grab the first plane to Panama City. I didn't know what or who I was dealing with—if the information Felix said he'd left was still there, then it was still safe. I had time." He rubbed a hand over his chin, along his jaw. "And then—"

"And then Colombia," she said simply.

"Colombia," he agreed, the wound still fresh and raw and vicious. "Look, Cooper, I don't know what Felix found, or what's in that box. But if I believe what Felix wrote in that letter—and I don't have reason to doubt him—then six good men were murdered over what's inside it. By our own government. By your goddamned employer."

The accusation fell from his mouth like an anvil. Not that she'd killed them directly, that wasn't what he meant, but that her people had. That she was guilty—or at least suspect—by association.

He had no idea.

"I know," she admitted, the word little more than a breath of sound that carried the weight of a damning confession. Could he hear it, too?

"What do you know?"

"Everything." About that day, at least. But it still wasn't enough. Not by a long shot.

For a moment, he just stared at her. Didn't move. Didn't blink. Didn't say anything. Just looked at her as if he didn't know her, wasn't sure what to make of her.

"I think you better start at the beginning." He shoved a hand through his mop of damp, wavy hair. "The truth, Cooper. All of it. Or I swear to God I'll walk out that door."

He didn't trust her, and worse, he suspected what she was going to say. Had already braced himself—with coiled muscles and cold looks—to hear it. To hate her. By the end of the conversation, he would.

She just had to make him understand that *she* wasn't the enemy.

"You know that I enlisted in the army." She fell into a quick pace to the door, then the bedroom, then back again, the entire journey less than thirty steps.

"I don't see what that has to do—"

"You said start at the beginning," she cut him off with a raised palm and a frustrated grunt. "So let me just . . . just let me tell it, okay?"

"Okay."

She heaved out a breath. "You also know I was selected for sniper school."

"I do," Will offered quietly, tracking her as she moved across the room. "And that you were then recruited by the CIA."

She nodded jerkily. "Right. I wasn't a full agent, or anything —I spent most of my time deployed with my unit, but occasionally Cole and I—"

"Your spotter."

"Right." Her throat tried to close, but she forced words through it anyway. "We'd get a call, catch a helo . . ." She shrugged. "Might be gone a few days, a few months. We never knew." And had never asked. There'd been no reason. It was the nature of the job. Receive orders and go. And for a while, it had been a thrill. A challenge. A constantly changing landscape with always-moving targets.

She'd just never expected to become one of them.

"You know how it is."

"I do," he acknowledged.

"Then, eighteen months ago, Cole and I got orders. Job seemed pretty normal." Regrettable, but normal. She hadn't gloried in taking out that unit, but she hadn't questioned it, either. It wasn't her place or her job to parse through intel. She was just the final result. The period at the end of the sentence that judged a man guilty and condemned him to death.

"But it wasn't a typical assignment, was it?"

She stopped pacing. Shoved her fists into her pockets, then pulled them free again.

"I—" She searched for a lie or a half truth, something, anything that could fill the gaps without tipping the conversation in a direction she couldn't hope to control. It was pointless, and she knew it. "I wouldn't have any idea just how wrong it was until after. There weren't any red flags. Cole and I were stateside one minute, overseas forty-eight hours later." She tucked a chunk of hair behind her ear. "Intel was good. Comprehensive. Names. Photos. But there wasn't much time. The job had to be handled . . . quietly." Or at least as quietly as a sniper ever handled anything. Still, even that hadn't been unusual. Everything the CIA did was quiet. "You know how it is. All hurry up and wait, and wait, and wait and then everything happens in a rush and before you know it, you're stateside again, like you never left at all."

"Spent half my career on standby," he agreed.

Should she have seen something? Realized something was off? She'd looked back on that day often enough, and nothing ever stood out.

"Conditions were good on the ground," she remembered. Mid-morning. A calm, windless day. Endless blue skies. Great visibility. She'd goaded Cole about being obsolete and redundant. Like an appendix she was forced to carry around but didn't actually need. "Insertion was clean. I had direct line of sight, distance of two to three hundred meters. Easy." She should have known. More often than not, the easy jobs turned out to be anything but. Cole used to call them black ice. One second everything was good, and the next, it had all gone sideways and the road was sliding out from under you.

"What changed?" Will asked.

"Nothing. We did the job then pulled back to rendezvous at the extraction point and go home. In and out again in twelve hours." Had taking lives really been so easy for her? So clinical? She couldn't remember a time that she'd ever even hesitated. Ever even thought about the gravity of what she was doing. What she was good at. Took pride in.

It was her job. Her *calling*. And just what the hell did that say about her?

"I did what I was supposed to do, what we'd planned. Orders were to keep everything neat. Clean. Take out the targets in the field and make it look like an operation gone wrong." She swallowed back the rising tide of useless regret and forced herself to look him in the face as she finished. "Cole called out targets, and I took the shots. Worked my way through the mission systematically, efficiently." If she closed her eyes, she could still feel the recoil of the rifle into her shoulder. A love tap and a high five all rolled into one. "Six targets. Six traitors double dealing in classified information. Or so the story went."

"What were their names, Cooper?" Will ground out as he pieced it together, his face hardening and his fists clenching. "Do you even remember?"

She'd never forget, but she ignored him.

"Another team showed up to provide support."

Like a butterfly knife opening then locking into position, Will stood, unfolding in one smooth, polished movement, ready for use, ready for battle. "Did you know I was there? That I'd been sent in to help men pinned down between enemy combatants and a fucking sniper?"

"Not at first. But . . ."

"But you saw me."

"At a distance." She'd missed a shot because of the shock of it. Déjà vu had numbed her hands and stilled her heart. She'd seen him through her scope once before. Tracked him through an operation for very different reasons. If that had been the only time, she might not have recognized Will at all. But he'd contacted her. Texted her. Called her. Sent her pictures from faraway places he'd visited on leave. She'd stared at them enough, searing them into memory, that she'd have recognized him anywhere.

Even in the middle of an operation.

Even when her mind-set was impersonal, engaged, and deadly.

"Suppose I should thank you for not blowing my head off," he sneered at her.

"You weren't on the list," she said simply.

"Would it have mattered to you if I was?"

She wanted to say that yes, of course, it would have fucking mattered.

But she just couldn't bring herself to lie to him.

"I don't know," she admitted. Truthfully, had Will been one

of the named targets that day, it only could have gone two ways. Either there'd have been enough intel to bury him and she'd have done her damn job, or she'd have objected . . . and another team would have been called in to see it through.

Either way, Will would be dead.

"At least you have the decency to admit it." His body relaxed, but his next words were a blow all the same. "Not that it did Jason any good."

She sighed. Jason McCurdy—Cole had been forced to call the shot on him twice. Once as her scope had slid over Will's face and she'd hesitated, then again when she'd forced herself to move away from him. To reengage with the job at hand.

Thirty seconds later, Jason moved, Cole called the location, and Cooper finished the job on sheer force of will. It was the kill she struggled with the most, though she couldn't quite say why. Seeing Will hadn't changed anything, and she'd had a job to do.

The shock had lasted the space of a breath, five slow beats of her heart, which had been loud in her ears. But after that, she hadn't hesitated. Hadn't even blinked. But it hadn't been her best shot. Not by far. She'd caught McCurdy in the neck, rather than the head. It would have been fast, but not instant, and that kept her up at night.

"Jason was the last, wasn't he?"

"Yeah. Six confirmed kills. Clean sweep. We packed up and got out."

"Well, congratulations, Cooper. You got the job done, but you sure as fuck weren't clean about it," Will snapped. "Jason spent the last ninety seconds of his life staring at me from the ground as he choked on his own blood."

"I know!" She'd seen the spray, watched him go down, and she'd *known* she'd fucked up. "I know, and I'm *sorry*, okay?"

"For what? Killing him? Or making a mess of it?"

"I. Didn't. *Know*."

"And you didn't ask."

"You wouldn't have either!" she shouted. "People like us don't have the luxury of questioning orders and demanding facts. We don't need to know *why*." It was, perhaps, the greatest lie she'd ever told herself . . . and the easiest one she'd ever believed. That it was all bullshit had been the hardest truth she'd ever confronted . . . and the most difficult realization she'd ever had to live with. "I put my faith in the system. In the idea that when I was given a mission, an order, a target, at the end of the day I was doing the right thing. Are you really going to stand there and say anything different? That you were any better?"

He opened his mouth to argue, then snapped it shut again.

"Fine. Just . . ." He sighed and flipped a hand in her direction. "Just finish it. What changed? When did you realize you'd been played?"

"Cole and I were debriefed in Germany. We made our reports, sat through the interviews." She made a half-hearted attempt to lift a shoulder. "Flight out wasn't until the next morning, though, so the agency put us up for the night." Even after all this time, even with the scars embedded in her palms, it all seemed so surreal.

"I walked in and got my hands up a second after I saw the noose hanging from the beam that traversed the room. Caught the garrote against my palms." She raised a palm, showing him the thick, white line that would never fade. "They'd wanted it to look like I'd hung myself. The attention to detail probably saved my life—and my fingers. The garrote was thick, needed to be if the bruises were going to match the rope. It cut deep when I fought but didn't sever any nerves." She pressed her hands flat against her jeans and rubbed away the sweat that felt too much like the memory of blood. "I got lucky. Got a boot up against the island and shoved him into the wall hard enough to slip loose." Fear, remembered and distant, but potent all the same, slid through her. "All I could think was, 'God, where's Cole? Is he back yet? Already dead in the next room?' I never expected to turn around and find him staring back at me."

For a moment, Will went perfectly still. "He tried to kill you?"

"It was like he didn't even recognize me," she admitted. "There was nothing there. No acknowledgement. No remorse. Just this sort of blank determination to get the job done."

"I'm sure he had his orders."

She flinched as if he'd struck her, then responded in kind. "Low blow, Bennett, and fucking beneath you."

He glanced away, and at least had the good grace to look ashamed.

"But you're not wrong. I tried talking to Cole. Tried pleading with him. Nothing made a difference."

"He was determined."

"He was *possessed*." Even then, even amid the terror and the betrayal and the bone-deep disbelief that had very nearly gotten her killed, she'd known something had been terribly, horribly wrong. "He didn't say anything. Not one word. Not 'this isn't personal' not 'I'm sorry, Coop.' Nothing. When I realized he'd really do it, that he was committed, that he'd beat me to death with his own fists . . ." She had to stop. Had to breathe. Had to fight back the memory of what it had felt like when she'd realized that between her and Cole it was kill or be killed . . . and she hadn't wanted to die.

"I fought back." The second she'd realized that only one of them was going to walk out of that apartment alive, training had kicked in and instinct had taken over. "I wasn't armed and damn straight lucky he wasn't either. But I knew I couldn't beat him hand to hand. I grabbed the first thing I found—a marble rolling pin on one of the counters." The crack of his skull echoed through her mind. "Caught him across the head. He went down. Didn't move."

Then she'd sat there, breathing through the disbelief and the pain. "Didn't realize until later that Cole had broken my wrist, cracked four of my ribs, fractured my cheek." She'd healed, but the hurt had remained. Even now, a year and a half later, the betrayal still seared like a white-hot flame. She'd never forget what his fists, his boots, had felt like.

She'd taken hits before. Worn bruises of both victory and failure.

But they'd never been put there by a friend.

"You killed Cole?" Will asked, his voice sad but his face closed.

"I thought so at the time." She'd stood over him, every inch of her in agony, watched blood seep into the floor and held onto the shattered pieces of her sanity. Forced herself to act rather than fall apart. "I knew I couldn't stay, and I didn't dare report in."

"You ran."

"I did." It hadn't been easy. She hadn't been lying when she'd told Will she'd been attached, more than recruited, to the CIA. She and Cole had been put through extensive field training, of course, but all suited toward their specialties and the roles they'd play within the CIA.

"How can you be sure Cole didn't just turn on you? That they didn't have some sort of leverage—"

"No," she said viciously. "I know what our handler said. I know what happened in that room. And I *know* that Cole would cut his own hand off before he ever laid it against me."

"He wouldn't be the first guy to shut down emotionally to get the job done, Cooper—and you wouldn't be the first to rationalize a trauma."

"You don't know him. He was my *best* friend. My spotter. My partner. I stood at his wedding. Was there when he christened his daughter. Cole was loyal to a fucking fault—it had gotten him into trouble before." Which was how she knew, how she'd always known, that no matter what, Cole had her back. She'd just never expected the cost of that loyalty to be so goddamned high.

"I didn't know the first thing about falling—and staying—off the grid. The learning curve was exhausting. The lessons, brutal. But once I got the hang of it, I started looking for answers. Chasing rumors."

"What kinds of rumors?" he asked.

"Genome mapping. CRISPR. Genetic hacking." She swallowed hard and went all in. "Mind control."

"Bullshit."

She laughed, but the sound came out strangled and broken. "God, how I wish it was. It was all so outlandish and terrifying and utterly outside the scope of anything I could ever have dreamed up." Exhaustion weighed her down, rooting her to the spot when all she really wanted to do was pace. "And anyway, I knew I couldn't run forever, not from the CIA. I needed to know why they wanted me dead."

"And you found something?"

She nodded. "Curtis Strauss." Thanks to Pierce, though God only knew how he'd pulled it off.

"Am I supposed to know who that is?" Will scoffed.

"A program director with York Pharmaceuticals. Turns out, they have a number of classified contracts with the Department of Defense. He was in charge of one of them. He filled in a lot of the gaps."

Will snorted. "And you expect me to believe that you, what, took his word for it? Do you even hear yourself?"

"Of course not," she snapped. "He had files. Studies. A few names, though most were redacted." She sighed and shoved a sweaty hand through her hair. "But when it was all spelled out in black and white . . . it became less insane and more terrifying with every page. Genotyping. Using drugs and viruses to target specific genes. To make *changes*."

"What you're talking about—it's just not possible. Not on the individualized scale you're talking about. It would take years just to map a single person's genetic makeup, decades to manipulate more than a single gene."

Cooper shrugged. "The files referenced some kind of super advanced predictive analysis algorithm that was being used to analyze, enhance, and predict war games and black ops. If the DoD was already using it in one area, it's not a stretch to assume they were using it in another. That in the right hands it could be used to predict how someone's genetics would react to drug protocols."

Will went preternaturally still and silent. He watched her from the other side of the room, his face closed and his gaze calculating.

"Don't play me, Cooper."

"I'm not," she said, willing him to believe her. "I have the files—"

"I'd rather speak to Curtis."

She dropped her chin and shook her head. "You can't."

"Because he doesn't exist?"

"Because he's dead," she snapped out, frustrated with his attitude, even though she'd expected it. "Two days after he passed off the files, he died in a 'tragic' car accident."

"A hit?" he asked.

"He isn't the first lead to wind up dead . . . or the only one with a contract on his head."

"Who else?" he asked, though he had to at least suspect what she'd say.

"You. Me," she said, and wondered when it had all become so normal to her. "Felix Harrigan and the others discovered one of the trials. Compiled proof—"

"The bank."

"Yes," she confirmed. "Then I was used to clean up the mess. To prevent exposure—I wasn't meant to survive it."

Will looked away from her, his jaw set, and his fists clenched.

"I don't know what's in that bank, but Felix thought it was worth hiding and the CIA thinks it's worth killing for. I *need* that information. Names, dates, studies, results, tissue samples. I need patient records and the doctors involved. What I have right now . . . it's not enough."

"You want an insurance policy."

Cooper barked a laugh. "Please. I'm not that naive. The more information I find, the higher the price on my head grows. This wasn't some huge government program. This was the work of a few people. It was quietly managed, quietly orchestrated, and when shit started to go wrong, it was meant to be quietly shut down." Problem was, she didn't know who was behind it all, which meant as far as she was concerned, she had to move forward as if everyone was. "This is kill or be killed, and at the end of the day, I intend to make sure both Cole and I are still standing."

"Cole?"

"He's out there. Snared in the steel trap they created inside his own head. A prisoner. A plaything. A pawn on a board he isn't even aware of. I have to find the people who did this to him before . . ." She swallowed hard, afraid to voice just what lay at the end of that sentence. "He's a prisoner in all this."

Like you. Like me.

"I need to get into that bank, Will."

"Right." He let the silence stretch between them and push its way through the room, filling every corner like the wet, oppressive blanket of Southern summer humidity.

"Far as I can see, there's only two possible scenarios here, Cooper." Like a predator, he advanced on her.

She held her ground, refused to take a step back, and refused to forget that though the last year of his life had eaten at him, the skills, the muscle memory, the dogged efficiency and determination of a Special Forces soldier remained.

"Either you're desperate enough to tell me the truth, no matter how damning and outlandish it is," he said, pinning her with a look. "Or you're here on behalf of your employer, and once again, you're *just doing your job*. So which is it, Cooper? Are you in over your head? Or are you just like every other spy I've ever met—a mindless drone devoted to the job, and damn the consequences? I mean, what's six lives in the grand scheme of things anyway?"

"Mindless drone?" She bristled, his jab landing a little too close to home. "You were Delta how long again? Five years? And a solider before that." She snorted. "And I suppose you made a career out of arguing with COs and questioning orders. I'm sure you never went on an op you didn't agree with or deployed for reasons you didn't know." The very thought, the simple accusation that he hadn't made the same decisions, been put in the same positions, grated against her skin like wind-tossed sand. "But then, if that was true I'd never have had to pull you out of the Colombian jungle in the first place."

Shock, as effective as an open palm, slapped across his face.

"What are you talking about?" he asked.

"That little raid that landed you as a guest of the Vega cartel? Turns out it was bought and paid for by a private party. You were used, Will. For something so petty as war profiteering, apparently. And then left to *rot*." She clenched her fists. "So don't talk to me about mindless devotion to the job."

She forced her fingers open and worked on breathing through the anger. It wouldn't do her any good.

He set his jaw and stared at her with that condescending brown gaze.

"Christ," she swore on an exhale. "I never would have pegged you for a hypocritical asshole."

"And I never would have pegged you as manipulative bitch," he hissed, then reeled his anger back, tucked it away until it was simmering just beneath the surface. "It's a good story, Cooper, I'll give you that. Sympathetic. Neat."

"Nothing about that day or anything that came after it was neat."

He ignored her. "Hits all the right notes—looping in the program was a nice touch."

"The program?" she asked, but he ran right over the question.

"And you almost had me."

Almost. God. She was losing him and didn't know what to say or do to change that.

"You don't believe me."

"Oh, I believe you killed that team. I even believe you were following orders—"

"Then—"

"I might even have bought everything you told me about Cole, even the medical trials, impossible as they sound." He advanced on her, his body vibrating with a quiet kind of rage she didn't know how to subdue. "But you know where you lost me, Coop?" He stepped around the coffee table and she backpedaled toward the door. "When you tried to *play* me. 'He's a prisoner, too,'" he mimicked. "It was a gamble, and it tipped your hand."

"No, I—"

"It makes sense, I guess, why they'd send you. We have a history, and I bet your handlers thought I'd do *anything* for the woman who saved my life. Who *freed* me."

She retreated until her ass hit the drop-leaf table by the door, her hands going to the surface to keep it from tipping over. Something rolled into her hand, and her fingers curled around a syringe Pierce had left behind.

"But if you thought, for even a moment, that I could ever trust the woman who killed six of my friends, then you're as stupid as you are cold." He went to step around her and toward the door.

She slid to the side, blocking his exit.

"Move."

"No." She couldn't. Wouldn't. And may God forgive her for it.

"I'm leaving, Cooper, and you can't stop me."

She thumbed the cap off the syringe, desperation drowning out every protest screaming at the back of her mind. "You've got a price on your head, too, you know."

"Right." He snorted. "Except that as you said, I'm the only one who can access that bank, so what good am I dead?"

"You die, and that box gets buried with you, the contents lost and harmless—I can't let that happen."

"How do you propose to stop me? Nine out of ten, right?" he reminded her.

She sucked a breath and slid her thumb over the plunger, unsurprised but still hurt he'd use her own words against her.

"Move."

She shook her head, and he slid that cold brown gaze down her body. The second he saw the syringe, she moved, surprise her only real advantage.

She went for his thigh, but he was ready, and fast, so shockingly, violently fast.

Desperate, she managed to empty half the syringe to the floor at her feet before he turned it on her, forcing it into her arm, and pumped her system full of scopolamine.

And as the drug hit her system, pulled at her mind, all she could think of was how sorry she was.

Sorry that she'd taken those shots.

Sorry that Will would forever believe the worst of her.

And sorry that after everything, she'd failed the only person who really needed her.

So damn sorry.

CHAPTER TEN

"What was in the syringe, Cooper?" Gripping her by the arms, Will shoved her back against the door and held her there.

She did a long, slow blink. Like a spill of black ink, her pupils grew like a stain, eating away at rich blue irises until only tiny band of color remained.

He shook her, and her head snapped back against the wood. "What was it?" he demanded.

She stared at him as all the fight bled from her bones. The syringe she'd held clattered to the floor, forgotten.

The confession fell from her mouth like the smooth, unwavering swing of an executioner's ax. "Scopolamine."

Rage snapped through him, a living, breathing thing with teeth and claws and an animalistic determination to maul anything that threatened him.

She'd tried to stop him. Tried to hurt him. Tried to *control* him.

It was the last one that had him tightening his grip and digging his fingers into her biceps until she winced.

A voice, dark and ugly and vicious, told him to slide those fingers up. To wrap them around her throat.

To stop *her*. Hurt *her*. Control *her*.

Permanently.

Because he thought about it, because for a single, terrible moment he wanted to do it, he shoved her away and let go. Forced himself to step back. Then again. And again.

Until he was certain there was enough space between them that reason would override rage.

Every instinct he had said to deal with the threat in front of him. To strike first and strike last because there would be no second chances.

The jungle had taught him that.

Taught him to be relentless. Ruthless. Fearless in the face of his enemy . . . and in the face of death.

But Cooper wasn't there to kill him.

He pulled in a breath. Tasted the drier, temperature-controlled air of the apartment. Rubbed his fingers together, skin sliding against skin and clean of sweat and dirt and blood.

Will reminded himself where he was—and where he wasn't.

Focused on who he was—and who he never wanted to be again.

"Will . . ." she whispered his name, the sound distant and hollow, as if she'd said it from far away rather than the other side of the room. But she *was* far away, Will realized. Oh, she was fighting it, swimming hard against a riptide she couldn't see but was dragging her away all the same. It was there in her eyes, the way she constantly tried to focus on something, anything. Even him, a lighthouse on a jagged coast.

Too bad he felt more like the treacherous rocks, waiting to batter her. Destroy her.

He needed her *gone*.

"I won't *ever* be at someone else's mercy again. Not even yours, Cooper."

Her words came slowly, as if she had to push them up through layers and layers of cotton. "I'm sorry."

"I. Don't. Care." Each word carried him forward, closer and closer to something he couldn't take back. Something he'd never be able to live with. "Get. *Out*."

"Please . . ." she begged, fear, acrid and unmistakable, seizing her.

"Get out!" he raged, terrified of what he'd do if she stayed.

A tear slid down her cheek and the drugs took hold. She turned, pulled open the door, and disappeared from his life.

She just walked away. Didn't even bother to close the door.

He slammed it shut behind her.

Fuck. Just *fuck*.

Scopolamine. For a moment, he'd let himself believe the lives she'd taken were the worst of it. The worst of *her*.

He hadn't even been close.

He knew what that drug was. What it did. What she could have done to him.

What he could have done at her command.

Mindlessly. Remorselessly. Mercilessly.

He couldn't forgive her for it.

Didn't even know how to try.

He was so damn tired of being used.

To fight other people's wars.

To kill for the entertainment of men with too much time and too little power.

To open some goddamned box.

He plowed a fist into the wall. Plaster rained down and the skin around his knuckles split.

He did it again.

And again.

And when it didn't help, he pulled himself back and paced to the other side of the room.

The anger clung to him like a cloak, but worry followed like a starving, pathetic dog he didn't have the heart to send away.

He'd thrown Cooper out into the late-afternoon rush of Panama City. Drugged. Vulnerable. Alone.

Because he didn't want to give a damn and didn't know what the hell to do with the fact that he obviously did, he snatched his dish up off the coffee table. Stomped to the kitchen and washed it under water that was too hot and with movements that were too rough.

He shouldn't give two shits about what happened to her. She wasn't his problem or responsibility.

Too bad he couldn't get her face out of his mind.

Couldn't forget what she'd looked like as she'd told her story —devastated, wounded, desperate.

Or what she'd looked like when he'd accused her of being a manipulative bitch—hurt, but not shocked. Resigned, but determined to try all the same.

He might have been able to chalk up those reactions as the well-rehearsed emotions of a master manipulator.

Might have, except for the way her face had fallen, devoid of expression or emotion, as she'd lost the fight against the scopolamine, done exactly as he'd told her to, and walked out that door.

She would have just as agreeably walked into traffic.

Or over a cliff.

Or climbed into a car.

The possibilities of what could happen to her were endless, and all of them horrors he could all too easily imagine.

But he hadn't condemned her to them. She'd done that on her own the second she'd raised that needle against him.

He should hate her for it. A part of him *did* hate her for it.

He'd spent the last year of his life at the mercy of people who didn't understand the word. People who'd used him to kill. For sport. For pleasure. For the sheer satisfaction of knowing he would.

And every time he'd won those fights, taken another life, he'd wondered if he'd killed off another piece of his decency.

By the time Cooper had come for him, it had started to feel as if the only thing filling him, the only thing keeping him going, was a bleak and brutal fury. A determination to win—and make others suffer for trying to hurt him in the first place.

He'd hated himself a little more with every life he took.

Hated how it got just a little bit easier.

Hated how it bothered him just a little bit less.

Hated that he couldn't just let them kill him. Let them win.

But more than anything else, he hated that he'd looked at Cooper and seen Matías. That his *first* instinct had been a violent one.

Because regardless of her reasons, Cooper *had* come for him. And though her words were easy to discount as lies, her actions were much harder to ignore.

The way she'd fed him—as if she understood what it was to be that deprived, to be that hungry.

The way she'd cleaned his hands. Gently. Patiently. Wiping away the filth as if it didn't even register.

The way she'd shaved him. With a deft touch and a steady hand, she'd brought Will back to himself—and shorn away the shame that had tried to snare him.

Had all of that been a manipulation? A lie?

He didn't think so.

He closed his eyes and remembered what she'd looked like in the moment after he'd kissed her. Raw, passionate, open . . . and miserable as she'd pulled away.

She'd known, Will realized. That he wouldn't believe her. That he'd be furious when she told him the truth.

So why had she?

Why tell him about Afghanistan? Why take responsibility for an order she'd been trained to follow?

To gain his cooperation?

There were better ways, and she'd had all of them at her fingertips.

He'd certainly given her the opening. She could have taken advantage of his moment of weakness and insecurity. Sat him down, talked him through it, cleaned him up.

And shoved that syringe full of scopolamine into his thigh.

He'd never have seen it coming. Never have been able to stop her.

So why hadn't she?

Doubt, slick and insidious, slid through him.

He wandered to the window and gazed out on a city he'd never seen before and longed for a city he'd thought he'd never see again.

He could go home. One phone call, and Ethan would move heaven and earth. Will would be safe at the embassy in under an hour. Home in twenty-four.

He could deal with the bank another time. When he was rested. When he was ready.

When he had the full force of Ethan's team at his back.

He glanced down at the street below and scanned the sidewalks full of people. Even several blocks up, Cooper was easy to spot.

She wasn't moving quickly, but she wasn't stumbling as if she was drunk, either. But then, that wasn't how scopolamine worked. She wasn't likely to trip or slur or pass out on the street. She would, to most, seem normal, if not a little distracted. Tomorrow, though, tomorrow she'd have one hell of a hangover and no memory of what she'd done . . . or what had been done to her. And that would be its own sort of agonizing punishment.

He watched her as she made her way up the street and wondered what she'd do. Where she'd go.

Maybe she'd wander the city for the next several hours. Maybe she'd find a corner or an alley or a café and sleep it off.

Maybe the city would consume her.

Not my problem.

He should find a phone and make that call. Put the memory of this place, the memory of her, behind him.

But when he closed his eyes, he had to acknowledge a truth his head fought but his heart had already embraced.

Far too much had happened that he could never forget.

He had blood on his hands. The best he could hope for was that he'd learn to live with it. For the most part, he thought he could.

But could he live with condemning the woman who'd saved him?

Will opened his eyes and let himself find Cooper one more time.

Moving against the crowd at half the energetic pace of the city, she stood out.

And for the first time, so did the man following her.

On a curse, Will turned and sprinted for the door.

CHAPTER ELEVEN

He'd lost her.

He'd fucking *lost* her.

From the window of the fifth-floor walkup, Will had been able to track Cooper easily enough. But the second his feet had hit the pavement, he'd given up his bird's-eye view and the city had swallowed Cooper whole.

Panic pushing him, he jogged another block, weaving through the oncoming crowd of pedestrians and ignoring the urban din of too much traffic squeezed onto too-narrow streets.

Nothing.

He couldn't have passed her. She was easy enough to recognize and there was no way she was still ahead of him, not at the rate she'd been moving. So either she'd turned off on a side street, ducked into a store, or been pulled into a car.

Shit. Shit. Shit.

He turned and doubled back, glancing down busy blocks and into darkened alleys as he went. If Coop had flagged down a cab —unlikely, given the drugs—or been forced into a car—a possibility he couldn't bring himself to consider—then there was nothing he could do except hope she got herself out of whatever he'd so callously thrown her into.

Hope. Right. Because that had worked so well for him up until this point.

He could just kill Coop for this. For the drugs. For the lies. For the goddamned worry churning like a maelstrom in his gut.

But he'd have to find her first.

He slowed his pace to a jog and peered through shop windows and down alleyways, hoping like hell that he wouldn't have to live the rest of his life wondering what had happened to Cooper Reed.

If she was okay.

If he'd thrown her out of his life and into something much worse. Something she couldn't hope to handle on her own. Not when she was drugged and helpless and so fucking scared.

Because she *had* been scared. Terrified. It had flickered across her face, brief but so damn familiar that shame now crawled across his skin like a swarm of insects, biting and stinging and spreading a poison that grew like an aggressive rot.

Will *knew* what it was to be desperate.

Knew what it was to be beneath someone else's mercy.

And as Cooper had stood there, a tear slipping down her cheek as she tried to explain, tried to make him understand, Will had seen himself. Seen the last year of his life splayed across the face of another.

And like a selfish coward, he'd turned away.

Anger had been so much easier to embrace than compassion or understanding. It had kept him alive. Kept him going. When there'd been nothing else in that godforsaken pit, Will had clung to his rage. Fed off it. Embraced it.

But now he wasn't sure he knew how to let it go. Because even now that he was free, now that the men who'd hurt him were dead, the rage was *right there*. Just beneath the surface like a shark beneath the water. Ready and waiting, full of serrated teeth and a primal need to attack and destroy.

So he'd ignored Cooper's anguish, her desperation—partly because he'd *needed* to put space between them, needed to get her out of sight, out of mind, and out of danger . . . but also because anger and betrayal and the spiteful desire to hurt those who'd hurt him were so damn inviting.

So damn comfortable.

Somewhere along the way, anger had become easy.

And he *was* angry, furious even. But he didn't want to be.

Didn't *need* to be. Not anymore.

And as he'd forced back the rage, questions had begun to bubble to the surface.

Will wasn't sure he'd like the answers, but he'd figure out a way to deal with them.

But first he had to find Coop and fix this.

Please, God, let it not be too late to fix this.

He forced himself to slow down.

To study faces. To look through shadows and block out the noise of horns and music and the chatter of people on cell phones until the only thing he could hear was the echoing condemnation of his own desperate steps.

Like a ghost, Cooper had vanished.

Guilt twined with worry and regret as Will's options withered.

He was already more than halfway back to the apartment when a cry caught Will's attention. Thin and brief, it sounded as if it had been born of surprise rather than fear or pain or frustration. He glanced around, but there was nothing to see and nothing to find. Just an endless stretch of sidewalk and the determined throng of pedestrians.

Where had it come from?

He'd nearly dismissed it as a figment of his imagination when the clank and clatter of an overturned trash can caught his attention. Will backtracked a few paces and glanced to his left. He'd passed up this alley with little more than a dismissive look because of the huge, black, iron gate, heavily tagged with graffiti, that sealed it off from pedestrian and street traffic alike.

Will pushed against the right side of the gate, but it was firmly secured and did little more the rattle in protest. On a frustrated sigh, he tried the left, then put a little more of his weight behind it when it moved. Will turned and wedged his shoulders through the two-foot-wide opening—just far enough to glimpse down a narrow alley that stretched a full block between two towering buildings. Sunlight did little more than graze shadows. Dumpsters flanked the walls and smaller bins had been overturned, their contents spewed across pavement like a buffet for desperate scavengers.

It smelled like damp and warmed-over rot, but that wasn't what snared the breath in his lungs.

Ten yards down, on her knees and still as stone, Cooper faced the crumbling wall of a cinder-block building and waited quietly, patiently, obediently as Cole, her fucking spotter, the man who was supposed to have her back no matter what, attached a suppressor to the barrel of his pistol.

Seconds, that was all she had left.

A new, far more basic anger eclipsed the complicated and fading fury that had carried Will down sidewalks and across busy streets. The blowback of Cole's betrayal singed Will's skin and reignited the rage he'd worked so hard to smother.

Will hit the gate with his shoulder, forcing it open, the bottom corner of the iron frame dragging along beat-up asphalt with the irritated wail of a dying wraith. The screech of metal provided the split-second distraction Cooper so desperately needed.

Cole's head snapped up and around at the same time Will sprinted down the alley.

In the end, that damn suppressor saved both their lives. If it hadn't been attached to the gun, Will would have taken a half-dozen rounds to the chest. If it *had* been attached to the gun, same, slightly less noisy, outcome.

But Will had caught Cole mid-action and found Cooper in the breath between life and death that hung suspended and glinting like a guillotine in the sun.

And that shadow of space? That split second that existed between one heartbeat and the next, separated one lifetime from the next? Will *owned* that sliver of time. Had lived in it, fought in it, survived in it. He knew how it could stretch like an eternity—how it could be the difference between life and death.

And that bought him the advantage and the seconds he needed to enter the fight with all the weighted force of his Delta training at his back.

"Cooper, down!" he shouted, praying that the drugs would give weight and force to his words. But he didn't slow to see if she followed his orders.

He didn't think. Didn't strategize. Just went in hard and fast, relying on speed and strength and good old-fashioned muscle memory to do the job.

With his left hand, he caught Cole's wrist just behind the pistol, then slid to the outside as his right hand caught the barrel of the gun and forced it up into a vicious one-hundred-and-eighty-degree arc that forced all the pressure of the maneuver against Cole's thumb.

Because it hurt like a bitch, the bastard dropped the weapon on a pained grunt.

And because Will had caught more of the half-attached suppressor than the barrel, so did he.

Fuck.

He hadn't made a clean strip only to drop the damn weapon since his sister had come home a marine and summarily surprised the shit out of him.

One mind, any weapon.

Just one of the marine's mottos, it rang through Will's head with the smug sing-song cadence of Georgia's amusement.

As usual, his sister was right, damn her. And training was the best weapon of all.

He brought his hands up and blocked the first punch to his face. It glanced off his forearm, and Will rolled with the strike, then stepped to the left. A hook came next, but a quick retreat killed it dead. Then a combination—easily read and easily defended.

Will was either being teased or tested. The latter, if he had to guess. Cole, all six-foot-two of rangy, compact muscle, was lethal with a gun, probably dangerous with a knife, but only proficient in hand-to-hand combat.

Will snorted. That was the problem with specialties. Guys got a chubby for one thing—guns, explosives, rifles, whatever—and got sloppy with the rest of it.

But not Will. He liked his training like he liked his vacations and his women. Constant change and constant challenge.

So yeah, keeping hold of the gun would have made things easier, but he could manage without it.

He sidestepped, putting himself between Cole and Cooper, who was on her hands and knees, her shoulders trembling. If it was because she was hurt or scared or just fighting against the prison of drugs that had forced her out of the fight, Will didn't know.

"You even care that she trusted you?" He didn't wait for an answer. Instead, Will slung his weight into the fight behind a right hook that he generated from his hips and pushed through his fist like a freight train.

And came up empty.

With an elbow up and a hand behind his head, Cole stepped in close, blocked the shot with one arm, and drove an open palm into Will's face that he followed with a knee that mule-kicked the breath from Will's lungs.

Instinct, more than thought, had Will sliding away and back on the defensive.

Fuck. Cole kept his hands up and hips squared as he stepped to the right, circling as Will matched each movement with a step to his left.

Any hope this prick was all trigger and no real training died a fast, violent death.

Will attacked again, a combination this time, only for each move to be countered, parried, or blocked.

Shit.

He'd always, *always* gone in aggressively. Been the first—and last—to strike. Spec ops didn't train men in basic self-defense. It wasn't about avoiding a fight or creating the room to walk away. In combat it was win or go home, and Will had been trained to win. Brutally. Efficiently. No mercy and no remorse.

But aggression required *speed* and as Will backstepped, ceding both ground and the offensive position, he faced the truth he'd momentarily forgotten.

He was a half second too slow. A fraction too weak.

Still, his body took the abuse. Training merged with desperation, and he blocked what hits he could, took the rest on places that would bruise but not break. And with each step and every blow, he slowed. A hundredth of a second here. A tenth of a second there.

And each one of them marched him one step closer to the blow he wouldn't be able to block. The one he wouldn't see coming . . . at least not until it was far too late.

He got his arms up in a high guard just in time to block a fist aimed at his jaw—but left himself open to the brutal sidekick to the ribs.

He wheezed and slid to the side, refusing to be backed into a wall or boxed into a corner.

Shit, that fucking hurt.

He had to think. Had to rely on more than instinct—which hadn't lost its edge—and training—a long-stored promise his body remembered but couldn't deliver on fast enough.

Against an unskilled opponent, even in Will's current condition, he'd have won. Easily.

But Cole *wasn't* unskilled. He'd been trained, maybe not as thoroughly, or ruthlessly, but it was stamped across his actions all the same. He wasn't just versed in the basics, and he hadn't simply stopped at proficient.

And as they fought and moved, blocked and charged, Cole was slowly stamping that painful realization into Will's body, too.

And oh God, he was *losing*. Not because he was outmatched or outnumbered. But because he was slower. Because he was smaller.

Because he was *weaker*.

Will blocked a haymaker with a helmet guard but took a double blow to his exposed ribs. He stumbled, but recovered fast, his ribs singing and his breath coming in short, painful bursts. Already, his muscles were screaming with fatigue. Sheer aggression wouldn't work. But he couldn't afford to play this like Ethan, either. To be patient. Calculating. He couldn't win the long game. Wouldn't last long enough to wear Cole down until he was frustrated and tired and stupid enough to stumble into a mistake.

Will had to end this.

Fast.

But how?

He glanced around for the gun, but it had skittered out of sight and disappeared amongst the rest of the garbage in the alley.

He blocked half of another combination and managed to keep his footing even as the skin along his eyebrow split beneath a glancing blow that sure as fuck felt like a direct hit.

How the hell was he supposed to win this fight?

"Please," the plea left Cooper's lips like a prayer: quiet, reverent, as if she weren't even aware she'd given it voice. She struggled to her feet, one hand braced against the wall, and Will wondered if she had any idea where she was. What was happening around her.

What would happen if he failed.

He dodged a blow and landed one of his own that paid dividends with the satisfying *clack* of teeth.

The victory was short lived, and Cole came back twice as hard. Twice as fast. Twice as strong.

Shit.

Lean into what you are. Work with your weaknesses, make them strengths. Take his strengths and make them weaknesses.

He'd said the words before. To Georgia—who he'd taught to defend herself long before the marines had taken that training and honed it to a lethal edge. To Parker—who'd gotten sick and tired of Ethan knocking him on his ass day in and day out. To people who were smaller. Slower. Weaker. He'd taught them to fight. And taught them to win. Against people who were faster. People who were stronger. People who were better trained and better conditioned.

And only hours ago Cooper had said something similar. Reminded him that where some saw weakness, she'd cultivated strength.

Fight smart, Parker told him.

Fight like a girl, Georgia whispered.

Bring him in close and make him pay for the privilege, Cooper offered.

All good advice.

One good blow, and he could end this.

Just one.

Will needed an opening.

"*Cole, please . . .*" Cooper whispered, her voice hollow and thin, like the echo of thunder through a cloudless sky, the storm still harmlessly out of sight.

As if he was surprised to hear his own damn name, Cole paused, and Cooper gave Will his opening.

He struck.

He threw a straight-fingered jab to the left side of the face, aiming for the eye. On instinct, Cole turned, letting the blow slide past, taking his eyes off Will . . . and completely missed the fist Will drove against the soft target just beneath the ear and along the jaw.

For good measure, and because he was just that fucking pissed the man could kill his own partner, Will stepped in with a knee to the groin that took Cole to his knees.

The Georgia special. Half feint, half fearless follow-through and a hundred and ten percent brutal. It worked like a charm and hurt like a motherfucker.

Cole went down, and Will was on him, snaking his arm around the bastard's throat, his hands ready to finish the job and snap the neck of the fucking shit who could so easily shoot a friend in the back.

But it was too quick. Too clean. Too easy an end for a man who deserved so much worse.

"She trusted you, asshole," Will grunted, countering every move Cole made to slip his hold. "All so you could put a bullet in the back of her head like she was nothing and no one."

Cole didn't say anything, didn't argue, just fought against the hold that was slowly stealing the breath from his lungs and the blood from his brain.

"You'd have done it, no questions, no hesitation, wouldn't

you?" Will grated against his ear. "Shot her in the head and left her here to rot like she was *nothing* to you."

Left to die alone in some foreign pit. Discarded. Forgotten.

Rage had Will wishing for a knife. For a way to make it hurt. For the strength to beat his face in.

To make the end every bit as painful as the betrayal.

"*Don't* . . ." Cooper slid down the wall, her legs simply folding beneath her weight. But for the bruises, still fresh and blooming, her face was chalk white and smooth as the frozen surface of a lake, the drugs trapping her just out of reach. But Will could see her fighting to surface, trying to crack the ice and take a breath.

As if he'd forgotten Will had him pinned, Cole lurched toward her, and Cooper simply stopped breathing. Panic, Will realized, pulled at her every bit as hard as the drugs. Pumping her system full of adrenaline and bringing her consciousness closer and closer to the surface.

Will thought he'd seen every shade, variation, and combination of fear a man could wear. Had worn most of them himself.

Anger. Tears. Hostility. Disbelief. All of them ugly and all of them honest in their own unique ways. Because fear brought *everything* to the surface. Carved the truth onto faces with such ruthless efficiency that even the most skilled of liars had trouble concealing it.

But Cooper's expression didn't so much as flicker with a shadow of change. And somehow, somehow that was so much worse to witness.

Her face remained slack and open, vulnerable and honest as her gaze moved from Cole's to Will's.

God *damn* it.

"Will, please," she croaked as she struggled against the weight of everything keeping her down and out of this fight.

The drugs had stripped her of every lie and half-truth she

owned—even the ones she'd told herself so often she'd probably begun to believe them.

And when she looked at Will with that expression, forced his name past her lips in that flatly pleading tone, he understood.

She'd told him the truth.

All of it.

Cole had been sent to kill her . . . and for reasons Will still didn't entirely understand, she was more than willing to die to save him.

Even tucked away in some deep recess of her mind, she'd fought her way out just to beg for Cole's life. And though she couldn't muster the desperation across her face or into her tone, Will saw the fear, instinctual and predatory, that lived within her.

And he knew without question that killing Cole would surely destroy her, too.

Fuck.

He couldn't do it. Even if every instinct he had said they'd both be better for it, he couldn't hurt Cooper that way. Couldn't ignore the fact that she hadn't been able to fight for herself, hadn't found the strength to beg for *her* life, but had managed to beg for Cole's.

That alone told Will everything he needed to know in that moment. Whatever else she was, Cooper was *better*. Than Cole. Than the shitty hand she'd been dealt.

And better than Will, too. Because she still knew how to forgive. How to care about someone who'd so ruthlessly betrayed her.

In the face of it, Will could do no less.

"It's okay," he promised her, though even as he did he saw her begin to fade. "It's going to be okay." Will tightened his arm and cut off both blood and oxygen.

Held it, until Cole stopped fighting, stopped moving, and nearly stopped breathing.

Against every instinct he had, Will dropped Cole to the ground and forced himself to walk away—and headlong into the next set of problems.

Cole had found them; Will had to assume that the apartment wasn't safe. Not anymore. But they had to go back. Grab gear and resources, then run and regroup.

Cole wouldn't be out nearly long enough for that.

They had minutes but needed hours.

Searching the overturned bins, Will came up with a thick length of twine, hog-tied Cole, then dragged him none too gently into the narrow space between two dumpsters. He gagged him with the shredded sleeve of Cole's shirt, then turned back to where Cooper sat, her back against the wall, her eyes on something far away.

Will knelt in front of her and watched as that tiny sliver of personality that had surfaced just long enough to plead for Cole's life floated back down to the depths.

"Hey," he said, brushing a thumb across a smudge of dirt and wincing at the bruise he found pinking up beneath it. "We need to go."

Cooper stared at him, lost inside her own mind. He pulled her hair free from the tie that was barely doing its job and let it fall around her face. She wasn't too banged up—probably because she hadn't fought back—but Cole hadn't been gentle with her, either.

Because his fury was banked, but burning, just waiting for the tinder to set it off, Will forced himself to extend his hand and say, "Come on, sweetheart."

Obediently, she placed her hand in his, but didn't seem to notice that her palms were scraped to hell or that her knuckles were bleeding.

He locked her fingers in his, tucked her arm up under his

elbow, then wiped at the blood trickling down his face with the edge of his shirt.

Folding Cooper into his protection was easy, but walking away from the man who'd hurt her, betrayed her—no matter the reasons—was infinitely harder.

As always, the anger was right there, snapping and clawing and demanding justice or vengeance or just the sweet satisfaction of paying hurt with hurt.

For Cooper, Will realized as they left the alley and stepped back into the sun, he found the strength to walk away. To step back from the violence that had become so damn easy. From the cruel desires that had kept him alive.

She'd hurt him, yes.

But she'd given him something, too. His life, twice over, but more, she'd helped him take the first steps back toward the man he wanted to be.

The man he'd been—and the one he'd thought he'd buried in the muddy depths of that pit.

Cooper had brought him back to life, to himself, and he was damn well determined to return the favor.

No matter the cost.

CHAPTER TWELVE

Something had made a home in Cooper's mouth and proceeded to die there.

She sat up, her head pounding and the room spinning.

Oh God, she felt as if she'd just had the best, worst night of her life. How much had she had to drink?

Her pulse throbbing painfully behind her eyes, she swung her feet to the floor and realized two things simultaneously—she wasn't wearing anything other than her underwear and she had no fucking clue where she was.

Fragmented memories flashed through her brain like a strobe light—fractured and pulsing and painful.

Will. The truth. The fight.

The *drugs*.

And then . . . and then . . . Oh God, she couldn't remember.

Didn't know where she was or how she'd gotten here.

Didn't know if she'd gone to bed as she'd woken up—alone.

Fear flooded her mouth with saliva and the echo of poisonous choices. Cooper lurched for the open bathroom door at the other side of the room.

She tripped and flailed, her legs an uncooperative tangle of overtaxed muscles. She caught herself against the wall and her palms sang with pain, but she didn't stop to inspect the damage she knew she'd find. Just used the wall to keep herself upright long enough to make it to the bathroom and fall to the floor in front of the toilet as she lost her fight with the nausea.

She heaved, and humiliation burned through her, adding to the mix of dwindling drugs and rising wave of pain and panic.

She shook, her skin flushing hot, then cold, then hot again.

Sweat slicked across her skin, drawing up an oily sheen of illness she couldn't shake.

She heaved again, and tears burned her eyes until she could do little more than let them slide down her face.

She fought another wave of nausea and lost, emptying her stomach until cramps and exhaustion and a pitiful weakness finally settled in.

And still that cloying sickness and instinctual humiliation that accompanied retching couldn't compare to the fear that was just beneath the surface, waiting its turn to tear her to pieces.

How much time had passed? Hours? Days?

Where was she? Cooper lifted her head and glanced around the bathroom, but nothing about it looked familiar. A pedestal sink. A tiny shower. A chipped mirror and cracked white tile that was clean, if not new, and blessedly cool against her skin.

It was bland and basic and *definitely* nowhere she'd ever been before.

She could be anywhere, she realized, her stomach cramping all over again, though there wasn't much left to bring up.

Could be anywhere, with *anyone*.

She forced her way past the sound of her heart thundering in her ears. Nothing. Everything was quiet.

But then, she knew better than most that quiet didn't mean empty, and that alone didn't mean safe.

How many times had she taken a shot, shattered silence, and proven that the deadliest threats could be blocks away?

She sighed and let her head rest against the curve of her arm as her stomach cramped in protest but settled again. Alone or not, it didn't matter. She was in no shape to defend herself. Besides, of all the enemies she'd made, not one of them needed or wanted her alive. They'd have killed at the first opportunity. That she'd lived to wake with the worst hangover of her life told Cooper everything she needed to know.

She'd gotten lucky.

She flushed the toilet, then wiped the back of her mouth and winced when her fingers dragged against a split and swollen lip. As if that one small action had demanded a full report, Cooper's body lit up.

Her cheek throbbed and she gently fingered bruises she didn't remember.

Her palms burned, and a quick look revealed abraded skin, as if she'd braced herself for a rough fall against an unforgiving surface.

When she shifted, the skin at her knees pulled painfully tight, and Cooper knew they'd be just as torn up as her hands.

A hysterical laugh bubbled up like acid and escaped as a single, forlorn sob.

Lucky. To be alive, maybe. But at what cost?

Cooper swallowed back a wave of questions that churned like anxiety and dread and pushed her hair away from her face.

Another cramp, smaller but no less painful, wracked her.

A fresh wave of tears burned at the back of her eyes. They stung, not with the acidic shame of sickness, but with the sobering realization that something *bad* had happened.

Something that had left bruises.

Something that had put her on her hands and knees.

Something that she couldn't—and probably never would —remember.

She'd have to find a way to live with it, with the bruises and the fear and the questions, all the same. And really, it was a drop in the bucket of all the things she was learning to carry.

A sob caught in her throat, choked the air from her lungs, then burst free without her permission. Another followed, then another, and another, until she was heaving with emotions she couldn't name or place or repress a single second longer.

So was just so damn tired.

So much had happened over the last eighteen months. So much stress. So much fear. So many impossible obstacles, lined up one after the other until they loomed like a stack of dominos that were spaced just far enough apart that she couldn't possibly hope to topple them.

She'd held herself together and faced all of it.

But this . . . she didn't know how to deal with this. Didn't know what to do with lost time, a blank memory, and an endless string of questions she wasn't sure she wanted answers to.

As the sobs turned to steady tears, Cooper forced herself to breathe. To try to find some sense of calm as she knelt on the floor, her bruises singing and her knees burning.

Salt, coarse and plentiful, coated her skin and her limbs ached with dehydration and exhaustion . . . and what else? she wondered.

She'd thought the hardest thing she'd ever have to live with was the knowledge that she'd killed an entire team of innocent men.

But now she was faced with a new, more brutal reality.

She didn't *know* what she'd done or who she'd hurt.

And she didn't know what had been done to her, or who had hurt her.

The realization cauterized the flow of terror.

The questions, the fear, would never leave her. She'd always wonder. But she'd only lost hours—a day or two at the absolute worst. But Cole . . .

Cole had been under for eighteen *months*.

Even if Cooper found a way to save him, how would he come back from that?

Would he be able to live with always wondering what he'd done and who he'd hurt?

And if he did remember, would he be able to find a way to forgive himself?

For the first time, Cooper let herself wonder if she'd save Cole only to condemn him to something far, far worse.

She pushed the thought away. It didn't really matter.

Cole might very well hate himself for the things he'd done, but she knew damn well he'd rather die than remain a pawn in someone else's game.

Whatever the cost, Cooper had to find a way to free him.

He'd do the same for her.

She closed the lid of the toilet and tried to stand. Her head pounding and her legs trembling like a newborn giraffe's, she tipped to the side and tripped over the edge of bathtub.

She flailed, grabbed for the opaque glass door, then flinched when roughened hands grabbed her arms.

"Easy, it's just me," Will said, his voice lax with sleep and slow with patience as he helped her stand. When she swayed on her feet, he steadied her. "You okay?"

She nodded, if only because he expected her to. But no, no she wasn't okay at all.

Cooper cringed, her shoulders curling forward as she brought her arms up to cover her breasts. Will looked good. Tired, but rested. A sheet print clung to his cheek like the lingering touch of a lover the morning after. This close, she could smell him. Soap and sleep and the hint of sweat that came with tangled sheets, warm air, and a lazy morning.

Standing there, her body wrecked and the scent of sickness still clinging to her skin, Cooper could barely stand to look at him.

And she was ashamed of how badly she wanted to lean her forehead against his chest, close her eyes, and just breathe.

He tilted her chin up, and as if he knew exactly what she needed to hear most, he said, "You're okay, Cooper." He met her gaze, brushed his fingers gently across her face, carefully skirting the worst of the bruises and her split lip. "You're *okay*," he reassured her. "Nothing a little time and a handful of aspirin can't fix." He cupped the base of her skull, his fingers scratching gently at her scalp. "Nothing you can't handle, all right?"

She nodded. Exhausted, nauseated, and utterly stunned to find Will standing there, all sleep-mussed and worried and so *fucking* gentle it flooded her with a renewed sense of shame.

It was so much more than she deserved.

"Oh Jesus, don't do that."

Will pulled her close and tucked her head beneath his chin as an ugly sob made a break for freedom.

"Christ, Coop. I'm not trained for tears."

Yeah, well neither was she. But she was a raw nerve, flayed and exposed and reacting to absolutely everything. And through it all, Will held her, stroking her back and mumbling about how Delta had prepared him for interrogation and torture, when clearly, they should have set aside at least a day to cover a woman's emotions.

Stiff, his movements awkward, Will was obviously a little uncomfortable. But he held her anyway.

What had changed? Why was he here?

And how the hell could he stand to look at her, let alone hold her? Soothe her?

When Will had turned that syringe on her and thrown her out of his life, she hadn't expected to last an hour, let alone long enough for the drugs to run their course.

That she'd woken up at all, even with her head throbbing and her body aching, had been a shock to the system. Cooper figured she'd either crawled into some stranger's bed or been dumped in some cheap room after the fact.

It was the only way she knew how to explain the fact that she was still alive. It had certainly never crossed her mind that Will had found her. Helped her.

Pierce, maybe. Though he'd have been in the room, waiting to flog her with the strands of her own stupid choices.

But Will? He didn't owe her anything.

When questions finally overrode emotions, and Cooper could no longer bury her head in the warm sand of Will's arms, she pulled away and searched the room for a towel or robe or discarded t-shirt. Anything to provide a little sense of cover.

"Hang on," Will said. "Let me just . . ." He left, then quickly returned with a white button-down shirt, one of the things Pierce had picked up, draped over his arm.

Cooper reached for it, but Will didn't hand it to her. "Let me help you, Coop. I know you're sore."

Because she was, and because emotions churned like bile at the back of her throat, she let him pull it open and help her slip it on.

As he worked the buttons, she asked, "What happened?"

"What do you remember?" he asked, pushing the last button through the hole, then rolling the cuffs to her wrists.

"Fighting," she offered, shrinking into the comfort of cotton.

"In the alley?" he asked carefully.

Her head snapped up. "What alley?"

"You meant us," he realized aloud and gently squeezed her shoulders. "Anything after that?"

She shook her head, but quietly offered, "You told me to leave. I left."

His face softened, and his grip loosened. "I was angry."

"You had a right to be." She wouldn't apologize. Couldn't, not unless she meant it. Not unless she could say she never should have done it—that she'd never do it again.

The best she could offer was that she hadn't wanted to, that it shamed her that she had—but that wasn't anywhere near good enough.

Cooper hadn't planned to drug him, and she still didn't agree with Pierce, who'd have done it cleanly, preemptively, and without any sense of conscience or remorse.

But she'd been scared and desperate and, in the end, she'd chosen Cole over her own scruples.

Had chosen her partner over her . . . She didn't even know how to classify what Will was to her and she was too exhausted to try.

And the truth was, she'd probably do it all again.

So she wouldn't let a hollow sorry fall from her mouth, not even if it was the polite or decent thing to do.

Whatever else she was, Cooper wasn't a liar. She'd told Will the truth and for better or worse, she'd stay that course. He deserved that much, at least. So she kept her mouth shut and waited. For his anger. For his condemnation.

"I—" He swallowed hard against an emotion he wore like guilt and carried like sadness. "I needed you gone, Coop."

"I know."

"You don't," he assured her. "The thoughts that went through my head. The things I wanted to do . . ." He dropped his hands and stepped back, as if just the memory of what he'd considered doing scared him. "I would have hurt you."

"I don't believe that." She said it because Will looked devastated at the mere thought of it, and it was an expression she couldn't stand. Not on him. Not over her. Not when she'd started it. "It's not who you are, Will."

"It's not who I was," he corrected her. He ran his fingers through his hair and across the back of his neck. "A year ago, yeah, I'd have handled it differently. I'd have been pissed." He sighed and dropped his hand, his shoulders slumping as if an albatross had landed around his neck. "But I'd have controlled the anger. Now, though . . ." He trailed a thumb along the edge of her biceps. She couldn't see them, but she could feel the gentle ache of bruises that lingered there. Knew without looking that they were finger shaped. And though he couldn't see them through the shirt, Will couldn't seem to look away, either.

Jesus.

"I hurt you," he whispered, the sound of his voice tortured and broken. "I left marks."

"You let go," she reminded him gently and covered his hand with hers. "You were scared and cornered and betrayed. You lashed out, but only because I forced your hand to begin with." She put her other hand to his t-shirt-covered chest, let his warmth seep into her palm, and hoped her conviction would seep into his skin. "I trapped you there, Will. Refused to let you leave. After a year of imprisonment anyone, *anyone*," she repeated when he shook his head, "would have lost it. I don't blame you for being angry. Or for sending me away."

But into what? she wondered. Because there were bruises and scrapes and sore muscles she couldn't account for. And she didn't believe for even a single second that Will had put them there.

"No excuse—none—makes it okay for a man to put his hands on a woman. I hurt you, Cooper. Even if it was only a little, even if the marks will fade, I *hurt* you." He jerked away from her, as if he couldn't bear to let her touch him. "A part of me *enjoyed* it. That power. That knowledge that I wasn't helpless or weak or at someone else's mercy. I *liked* knowing I could hurt you back." He choked, as if the admission were something he had to purge like poison. "And a part of me wanted to do so much worse. What kind of man does that?" he asked, the question hollow and flat, as if he didn't believe it even had an answer.

But it did. She knew it did. And before they did anything else, she was determined he'd know it, too.

"The kind of man who spent the last year of his life in captivity. You were at their mercy, Will. Beaten and starved and tortured—"

"And they fucking broke me—"

"No," Cooper cut him off with all the harshness she could levy at a man who simply didn't deserve it. "A broken man would have done the things that instinct and imprisonment and the white-hot rage told him to. A *broken man* would have snapped my neck the second I raised a hand against him." She laced her fingers around his forearm and gently squeezed. "It's been *days*, Will. Days since I pulled you off that mountain. Days since you nearly *died*. You haven't had the time or opportunity to even begin to deal with what happened to you—I didn't give you the chance."

"You were desperate—I understand that a little better now," he admitted.

"How?" she asked, nudging the conversation back onto a safer track. For him, at least. "What happened after I left?"

She swallowed the little flutter of panic that said maybe she didn't want to know. That maybe nightmares were better left in the dark.

"You wandered for a few blocks." Will let his palm hover over the bruises he'd left, then ghosted it up her shoulder. His face twisted, as if he wanted to touch her. To comfort her? To remind himself she was still alive? She wasn't sure, but she didn't startle or flinch when he settled his huge palm at the curve of her neck and brushed his thumb over her collarbone. "I watched you from the window—I thought I could let you walk away. Figured you weren't my responsibility."

"I'm not."

The fingers against her skin flexed but didn't squeeze.

"But when I realized you were being followed . . ." He shrugged and pulled his hand away.

"You came after me," she finished for him.

"I was too late, though." Will sighed heavily, as if he'd expected more of himself. "I lost you in the crowd. When I finally found you, he had you on your knees, a gun to the back of your head." He shifted and bunched his fists at his sides. "You scared the shit out of me, Coop. I thought . . . I thought I was too late to save you, but just in time to watch you die. You were so . . . cooperative. Accepting—"

"It was the drugs, Will." Because no way would she have gracefully knelt to accept a bullet to the back of her head otherwise. She'd have fought. Maybe she wouldn't have won, but Cooper would have gone down fighting.

"Yeah. I think you'd have done just about anything anyone told you to." Anger, brief but hot, crossed his features. "I would have been completely at your mercy. Helpless. Thoughtless. A prisoner in my own mind."

"I couldn't let you leave—"

"You had no right to make me stay!" He stepped back, as if the outburst had caught him entirely off guard, then deflated.

"I know," she offered. "I know, okay? I didn't plan it, Will. Didn't even remember the syringe was there until it rolled into my palm—"

"I know." The admission dropped between them with the weight of a field pack after a thirty-mile hike. It wasn't a platitude or an agreement or just something he'd decided to take on faith. There was conviction behind those two words. And knowledge.

"You questioned me." She had no right to be angry, none. She knew that. And she wasn't, not really. But the realization that he'd felt the need to interrogate her still stung. That she'd never know what he'd asked her, what she'd told him, itched beneath her skin like a sliver of fiberglass. "At least now you can be sure I was telling you the truth." She sighed.

"I knew that before I asked you the first question—I just needed to be sure there wasn't anything else."

She jerked her chin up, caught him staring at her in a way she wasn't quite sure how to interpret. His gaze was steady and somber, but soft, too. As if he'd seen the very heart of who she was.

"How?"

"You went meekly to your death, Coop. But you fought like hell to beg me not to kill him."

Cole.

Oh God. She hadn't even asked who'd found her. And wasn't that a sad reality? When had she gotten so used to running for her life? When had it become *normal* for her to close her eyes and wonder if *this* time she'd wake? Somewhere between the CIA's betrayal and the mounting price on her head, Cooper had faced her own mortality and moved on.

But if Cole had been the one to find her . . .

Fear, and something that tasted a little like relief, flooded her mouth.

"Is he . . ." She was too afraid of the answer to finish asking the question. If Cole was gone, then she'd failed him. But a part of her, a weak, selfish part, wanted this nightmare to end. Wanted to stop worrying about what would happen if Cole caught up with her.

Wanted the thought of what she'd do if it came down to that one, brutal choice—his life, or hers—to stop haunting her steps.

"He's not dead, if that's what you're asking." Though he didn't exactly sound happy about it.

Not that she could blame him. He had fresh bruises, too. New marks and hurts and scrapes.

Because he'd come for her.

"I couldn't do it," he admitted.

"Why not?" It didn't make sense. Not coming from the man who'd just admitted how on edge he was.

Will shivered.

"You were out of it, Coop. Completely pliant—so much so that you'd have happily died in that alley." He gently brushed a thumb across a bruise she barely felt on her collarbone. "There was no fight left in you at all. Not until I had my arm around his neck. *Then* you fought. *Then* you surfaced. Just long enough to plead. For him."

"He's my best friend," she whispered.

"He hurt you, Cooper." Will brushed the tips of his fingers to the cut on her lip, to the bruise on her cheek, against the scrape on her brow. Then let his gaze travel over her body in a slow, saddened sweep. "Betrayed you. And still, when you were at your most vulnerable, you protected him."

He stepped back and propped his shoulders against the wall. "I wanted to kill him for touching you."

"But you didn't. Because you're stronger than that—"

"No," he snapped with a clipped shake of his head. "Because *you* were stronger than that. Because you could fight for him, forgive him . . . forgive *me*—" he whispered brokenly.

"There's nothing to—"

He cut her off with a shake of his head. "You're better than the both of us, Coop. Loyal, *clearly* to a fault." He tried to smile, but his face fell under the weight of a guilt and regret he couldn't seem to let go of. He gave up, and all the tension left his body in a sad, defeated rush. "You came for him. Fought for him. You won't stop . . . you won't give up on him, will you?"

She shook her head. "Cole wouldn't give up on me." That he'd hurt her, more than once, would devastate Cole. But he'd be here and whole and she'd help him through that, too.

"Then he's luckier than he knows." The sorrow of an unwelcome realization clung to him like a wound he couldn't let heal.

"You weren't forgotten, Will."

"A year, Cooper. A *fucking year.*" His body vibrated, and his voice shook. With rage. With agony. With a desperate loneliness that ate away at confidence and self-worth and the conviction that some foundations were unshakable.

But Will had lost faith in his friends, in his family, and in turn, he'd lost faith in the certainty that he was worth fighting for. Worth saving.

Cooper wished she didn't know exactly how that felt almost as much as she wished he'd never had cause to doubt himself in the first place.

But in this, she could give him at least a sliver of hope.

"Your friends and family didn't give up on you," she said gently, reaching for him, then running the back of her fingers up his t-shirt-covered abs when he tried to dodge her. He trembled, just a little, beneath her touch, but stilled when she settled her palm over his chest, met his gaze, and said, "They didn't forget you, Will. They *mourned* you. *Buried* you."

"I . . ." He swallowed hard. "I guess I understand that they'd stop. That they'd have to assume . . ."

"No." As if she could wipe away the shadow that clung to him, she brushed her thumb back and forth over his heart. "I don't have all the details," she explained. "Only the basics. But you were declared dead and a body was retrieved. Given full honors. No one gave up on you. No one forgot or abandoned you

—not your friends, at least. They didn't *know*, Will. No one did. Not until very recently."

"You're sure?" he asked, his voice raw with hope and relief.

"I'm sure. I wouldn't have been able to find you if people hadn't been making inquiries on your behalf. They were discreet, but inquiries drive questions and questions always have answers. If you know where to look. And who to pay." And if you had Pierce. But Cooper didn't bother to explain that.

"The second your family knew you were alive, they started looking." She stepped in close and was utterly humbled when he let his head fall forward and tucked his face into the curve of her shoulder. He shuddered, and she brought her arms around him, held him, and let him bury at least one of the demons haunting him.

"Thank you for that." He pulled away, his eyes dry and the lines of his face the most relaxed she'd seen them. "And for pulling me off that mountain, even if it was because you needed me."

"No matter what, I wouldn't have left you there."

"Because whatever else you've done, you're still a good person, Cooper. How the fuck that's possible given everything you've told me, I have no idea."

Regret and denial lodged in her throat like a sob and smothered the air in her lungs. She tried to pull away, but he bunched a fist in the front of her shirt. "I'm not," she whispered. But oh God, she wanted to be. Somehow, someway, Will had not only forgiven her, but found a way to see the best in her.

"You are, Cooper."

That he believed the words didn't make them true, but they humbled her all the same.

"I tried to *drug* you. It doesn't matter why, or that I panicked, or that I was desperate—I crossed a line." Her voice dropped, the next admission a jagged breath of air that hurt to voice. "I've crossed so many lines since I took those shots." She looked up at him, forced herself to hold his stare. "You're not the only one who's changed, Will. Some days, I don't even recognize myself. I've done so many things I'm not proud of. So many things I'll have to find a way to live with." She took a breath and spoke her shame. "But I don't regret them. I can't."

And there it was. The fear that kept her up at night and the one that greeted her every morning. She'd done terrible, brutal things. Taken contracts to earn the money to keep on running. Keep on searching. It didn't matter that she'd been selective. It didn't matter that she'd trusted Pierce to find her the worst humanity had to offer. She'd killed. For money. For Cole.

And she'd do it again.

"I've done so many things I *never* thought I'd do. How am I going to know?" she asked, praying Will had an answer for her. Lord knew she didn't.

"Know?" he asked, tilting his head to the side.

"When it's a step too far? How will I know that *this* line is the one that can't be uncrossed? Am I going to recognize it?"

Had she already crossed it? She told herself no price was too high to save Cole. That she had to find a way to free him and expose whoever had done this to him.

But what if she succeeded? What then?

"Every step I take to save him is one step closer to a woman I don't know." And one she didn't like but was becoming far too comfortable with. "I'm so afraid that in the end, I'll have crossed so many lines I'll never be able to find my way back."

Will let go of her shirt but tilted her chin up until she had no choice but to meet his gaze.

"You haven't crossed that line yet, Cooper."

"How do you know?"

"Because I *have*." The admission came out rough but determined. As if he'd cleaved off a part of himself that had been festering. "I moved past the point of no return a long time ago. Believe me, you know what it looks like. What it feels like. It killed a piece of me, Coop. Made me bitter and angry and cruel." He traced the pad of his thumb over the arch of her brow bone, his touch a gentle contradiction to his confession. "I *know* what that feels like." He pressed his lips to her temple, then moved his mouth next to her ear. "Just like I know what it feels like when someone brings that deadened part of you back to life."

He stepped away, but his warmth remained like a favored, well-worn blanket.

"You pulled me back from the edge, Cooper. Gave me something I thought I'd lost forever."

"What?" she asked, her fingers itching with the need to reach for him, to pull him back, to put his hands back on her skin.

"Decency. Forgiveness." He dropped a kiss to her parted lips, the briefest brush, the gentlest thanks. "Hope."

She squeezed her eyes shut and tried with every single thing she had to keep that same hope out of her mind and out of her heart.

It hurt too much to trust in it.

"I'll take you to the bank." Will headed for the door. "And, Cooper?" he asked, glancing over his shoulder. "If it comes down to it, if you get too close, I'll stand between you and that line."

Something tugged at the corner of his mouth. Nothing so simple as happiness or humor, but something warm and friendly that held just a touch of conviction.

"You're not alone anymore."

CHAPTER THIRTEEN

"What, no eggs on toast?" Cooper asked as she emerged from the bathroom, showered and dressed and looking far less vulnerable than she had just a half hour ago.

Will should have found it a marked improvement. He'd hated seeing her hurt. Loathed hearing her cry. But while he'd always had a soft spot for confident, bossy Cooper, he'd be lying if he said he hadn't enjoyed holding her. Comforting her.

"Reserved for special occasions." He set the plate of eggs and fried ham on the table.

"Special occasions?" she asked, the words rote, but humor tugging at the corners of her eyes all the same. "Or special *friends*?"

"Either, but preferably both."

"I'm hurt."

"There's coffee," he offered by way of an apology.

"You're forgiven." She accepted the cup he poured for her, then sat and drank half of it in three long swallows before finally reaching for the sugar.

"Feeling a little better?" It was as if the shower had washed away the exhaustion and the vulnerability along with the grime. She'd calmed, pulled herself together, and tucked away the parts of her that Will was surprised to find he very much wanted to explore.

"Yeah." She pushed wet hair behind her ear and glanced away. "Thanks for taking care of me."

"You took care of me, too, Cooper."

"Even?" she asked, her voice thick but her eyes hopeful.

"Not even close," he said, then flinched when her face fell, and her fingers clenched the handle of the mug.

"Okay." She nodded and focused on pushing her food around on her plate. "I get that."

His body tightened, and Will fought back conflicting urges he didn't fully understand. He wanted Cooper. Always had. Her sexy, sassy brand of confidence had always drawn him in. Tempted him. Challenged him. On more than one occasion, it had inspired thoughts of all the varied ways he could test it, taste it, provoke it.

None of that surprised him. He'd always known they'd be combustible. That when they finally came together it would be in a tangle of limbs and a battle of wills. There'd been a time when nothing would have made Will feel more like a man than putting Cooper on her knees, against a wall, or over a desk and laying waste to the woman's battle-hardened control. But that was before.

Before Colombia.

Before captivity.

Before the anger that simmered on low, waiting for the right moment to boil over.

And while he still wanted to do all of those things, what caught him off guard was how much he wanted to shelter her, too.

"Cooper," he said, watching as she stood, one arm tucked

across her stomach, the other clutching a cup of coffee she was doing her best to hide behind.

"It's fine. We should talk about what's next." She paced her way around the room, her shoulders tight and her expression carefully curated. "Where are we, anyway?" she asked, peeking through curtains he'd kept drawn shut, just in case. "Still in Panama City, right?"

"Cooper, come here." She didn't move from the window—and really, he hadn't expected her to, nothing about her had ever been easy or compliant, which was half the reason he liked her so damn much. But his words had hurt her, so Will stood and went to her.

"What time is it?" She huffed a little laugh that tinkled, high and hollow, like broken glass swept along a sidewalk. "Guess I should be asking what day it is."

Will plucked the mug of coffee from her fingers and set it on the windowsill. When she sighed, and her body went lax, she let him see another side of her. One he'd glimpsed in the bathroom.

One he didn't like.

This was the Cooper who'd gone to her knees in that alley. The one who'd accepted death as her due. But this time, there were no drugs to blame.

This was guilt. Undiluted and harsh as bleach, it scrubbed away everything dynamic and beautiful and fierce until all that remained was a meek acceptance of whatever accusation or condemnation he wanted to hurl.

He couldn't stand it. Vulnerability was one thing, a layer of Cooper he found oddly soft and compelling and worth exploring, but this . . . this he wouldn't accept. Not from her.

And certainly not because of him.

"Cooper," he whispered, trailing his fingers down the nape of her neck, following the curve of her spine all the way to the waistband of her jeans.

She went still beneath his touch. Desire? Confusion? A longing she couldn't name but that matched his own?

He intended to clear it up for her.

He curled his fingers in the back of her pants and pulled her flush against him, then wrapped both arms around her, trapping her in tight and close, surrounding her as he let his head drop to the curve of her shoulder.

Because the shirt she wore gaped, and her skin smelled soft and clean, he let himself taste and smiled at the shiver that wrought.

Following the column of her neck, Will pressed a kiss to the pulse point he found there, scraped his teeth over skin she exposed with a tilt of her neck, then put his mouth to her ear.

"By my count, you've saved my life *three times*."

She didn't say anything, but brought her hands up to grip his forearms, as if she was afraid he'd step back. Afraid he'd leave.

He wouldn't. Couldn't, if he were being honest with himself. And it wasn't because *she* needed *him*. It was because standing here, Cooper tucked up against him, waiting, wondering, hoping, Will felt more like himself than he had in almost a year. He couldn't give that up.

Cooper was his touchstone, the steady point on the horizon he saw when everything else shifted and whirled and raged.

Will would be damned if he'd be any less than that for her.

"Once, a very long time ago, a bossy, egotistical sniper got my entire team though a hostile operation that had gone to shit." Her cheek twitched beneath his mouth, as if a smile had risen to her face at the memory. "I liked her—even if she did call me a moron."

"You wouldn't *listen*," she said.

He silenced her with a none-too-gentle nip to her ear. "Then she pulled me out of a pit and off a mountain, saving my life *again*." He soothed the bite with a gentle brush of tongue, smiling when she shivered. "And *again* when I was too sick, too tired, too hurt to keep going." He let her go and turned her to face him, then pressed her back against the wall. "I saved your life *once* and it was only necessary because I threw you out to begin with. So no, we're not even *close* to even."

Her breath caught, then left her in a rush, taking her tension and fear and guilt right along with it. Good. Those weren't welcome, not between them, not going forward. And because he'd dreamed about this moment for fucking *years*, had wondered what it would be like to put his hands on her shoulders and press her back against the wall, he laid his mouth to hers.

Twice now, Will had tasted her. And both times had been nothing like what he'd expected. There was no clash of teeth or battle for control. No whispered promises or breathy moans. He didn't want to drag his mouth from hers just to put it somewhere hotter, somewhere darker.

Well, he did.

Of course, he did.

But not with any real sense of urgency.

There'd be time. For the fire. For the fight. Time to take and plunder, ravage and ruin. He'd make sure of it.

But this? This was soft and slow. Thorough—Will wasn't about to leave any corner of Cooper's mouth unexplored—but gentle, too.

He brushed his thumbs along her cheeks, threaded his fingers through her hair, and let himself enjoy the fact that this woman—this fierce, capable, stubborn woman—let him hold her. Comfort her. Touch her when she was utterly disarmed.

She'd saved him, seen some of the worst of him, and still, she'd forgiven him. Trusted him. And in her arms and on her lips, that tasted like home and freedom and a comfort he hadn't known he needed.

That she could take the same from him was an addiction he'd never overcome.

Reluctantly, because oh God he wanted to stay there, Will pulled away. Pushed the hair back from Cooper's face, brushed a finger across her full, lower lip.

When she tilted her chin up, went to her toes, and reached for him, he stepped back, but let a grin curl the edge of his mouth.

"We need to talk."

When she groaned, he laughed, and that felt *almost* as good as kissing her.

"So how do we do this?" Cooper asked from the corner of the couch where she sat with her feet tucked up and a fresh cup of coffee in her hand.

"I think we have to assume the bank is under surveillance." Will joined her in the tiny living area of the flat he'd paid for with the cash he'd found tucked away in Cooper's gear. Apparently, the going rate of anonymity was triple the list price these days. But staying off grid was essential. At least until they got through retrieving whatever Felix had left for him at the bank. "It's the only thing that explains how Cole found you so damn fast."

"Makes sense," she agreed, then took a sip of her coffee and let her gaze stray to the curtain-covered window. "We were only blocks from the bank. So when I turned right instead of left . . ." She shrugged. "Maybe it was subconscious on my part, I don't know. But I headed that direction and I guess Cole just got lucky."

"So did we," Will whispered and squeezed the top of her knee. "But going forward I'd rather not rely on luck."

"Right. So we assume the bank's being watched. We can't go in the front—now that there's a confirmed sighting, they'll have a sniper on site. They might let us walk in, but there's no way they'll let us walk out."

"Thank God Cole found you on the street—"

Cooper shook her head before he could finish the thought. "He won't do it at distance."

"I thought spotters and snipers had to function in both roles?"

"We do." She stood and stretched, her t-shirt riding up as her back popped and cracked. "But Cole's orders were specific. It has to be up close and personal."

"How do you know that?" he asked, suspicion winding through him.

She shrugged. "He kept mumbling it when we fought. Over and over and over again. 'Face-to-face,'" she recited.

Jesus.

Will started to stand, but Cooper waved him off with a flick of her wrist and a sad smile.

"It's fine," she assured him. "*I'm* fine."

"The fuck it is. Cooper, it's—"

"New to you. And horrifying, I know. But I've been living with this ax over my head for eighteen months now. I'm used to it."

Used to it. Used to running. Used to looking over her shoulder. Use to waiting for her best friend to come for her. Hurt her. Kill her.

Jesus, it stirred the rage in him. To be betrayed so thoroughly by those she'd trusted . . .

The darkness must have touched his face and curdled his expression, because Cooper sat next to Will on a heavy sigh. She pressed her leg against his, the touch firm and familiar.

"I don't know how you live with this, Coop. Let alone forgive it."

"Because it's not his fault," she said simply, then touched his arm and met his gaze. A sad smile changed her face to something soft, something tired. "You accused me of being loyal."

"To a fault," he agreed.

"Right. But the truth is, that was always Cole's default setting, not mine." She stretched out her legs, her bare toes curling in a way that pulled his thoughts in an entirely different direction.

"Cole, he was—is—one of the best. Stone-cold calm. Great at troubleshooting in the field. Super adaptable and the best to work with because he doesn't let the stress touch him. The harder things get, the better he performs. He could have worked with *anyone*. But he chose me," she said, her voice quiet but her tone reverent. "Did you know we went into the army at the same time?"

Will shook his head.

"Yeah. From basic on. We were always friendly but never close. That came later. Guess that's why it always surprised me." She shrugged off a little laugh.

"What did?"

"He knew I was a great shot," she said by way of explanation. "Maybe one of the best. But he also knew I was being pushed out. Bullied into failure or deliberately overlooked. When it came to marksman training, no one wanted to work with me."

"Except Cole," Will offered.

"Except Cole. He put his foot down. Forced the other guys to back off. Forced the brass to take notice. He was good that way— could command attention without getting haughty or combative. They kept trying to reassign him to someone else. Someone better."

"Better?" Will asked. He knew what she meant, but he wanted her to say it. Wanted her to know he'd believe it.

"Someone more suitable," she hedged, but then gave in. "I can't say I blame our training officer. Women don't get selected for sniper school. There was a very real risk I was going to hold him back, keep him from realizing his potential."

"But he wouldn't have it."

"Nope. Couldn't have been easy, either. He's a crack shot—partnered with anyone else, he could have taken the sniper position. But . . ." She shrugged.

"But he was loyal to you."

"Always." Her eyes watered, but she blinked way the emotion in the next second. "When it came down to it, Cole prioritized our partnership—me, really—over everything else." She tugged the sleeves of her shirt down, her fingers worrying the right cuff. "It started in the army, took us all the way through sniper school. But that's not where it ended." She swallowed and took her time with the next part. "We'd been working with the CIA maybe six months when an operation went bad. It was a two-parter." Her gaze went loose and distant, as if the memory had pulled her through a scope and far away. "Cole was on retrieval. I was on overwatch. One second everything's good, the next . . . Well, you know how it is."

"When shit goes bad, there's no warning, no sense of the situation slipping away from you. It just *goes*."

"Yeah. Anyway, Cole made it to the extraction point but I . . ." She swallowed hard, the ghostly touch of fear stroking her face. "I didn't, and orders were to complete mission."

"And leave you."

"Yes."

"Cole disobeyed."

She nodded, and it made Will want to kill the prick just a little bit less.

"We both walked away from that one, and *with* the data, but Cole was disciplined over it." She shook her head. "He didn't give a shit about the write-up."

"He didn't abandon you. Wouldn't quit on you." It was an

oversimplification of a complex relationship, but it was one Will understood.

"And I can't give up on him."

That kind of bond. That kind of loyalty. It was part of what made Special Forces so damn elite. It was all too easy to put himself in Cooper's shoes. To imagine the fear and denial and bone-deep conviction that Ethan wouldn't, couldn't, betray him. That there had to be a reason. An explanation.

If what had been done to Cole had been done to Ethan instead, Will would have gone to the ends of the Earth and back again to make it right.

So yeah, he understood *exactly* what drove Cooper.

"Then let's get into that safety deposit box." And pray it held the key to setting Cole free and taking down the people who'd done this to him.

"How? It's being watched."

"Turns out," Will said, squeezing her hand then letting go. "That's the easy part. I called the bank to confirm what forms of identification I'd need to gain access—"

"Shit." Cooper dropped her head into her hands. "I hadn't even thought about paperwork."

"Apparently, that's not necessary. Box is accessed with finger-prints—they were pretty fucking cagey about how they got mine on file, by the way—and then there's an additional authentication step, which they would not explain on the phone, but insisted would not require any form of ID."

"Great, but that doesn't get us into the bank itself."

"Right." He stood and stretched, wincing when the stitches in his side reminded him that, yeah, they were still there. "The woman I spoke to said security and anonymity is what they're known for. They have protocols in place for quietly accessing the vault. They'll send a car for us, then bring us in through a private garage. In and out. No one the wiser."

Beside him, Cooper went stiff and still. "It's too easy."

"Yeah," he agreed with a sigh. "I thought so, too. The second we climb into that car, we cede control."

"Is there another way?" she asked.

"Maybe. *If* we had time or money or a court-ordered transfer."

She looked at him, lines of stress changing the topography of her face.

"It's your decision to make, Cooper. Wherever you go next, I'm with you."

She stood, pressed a quick, chaste kiss to his mouth, and lingered just long enough to brush her thumb along the edge of his beard.

"Call for the car."

CHAPTER FOURTEEN

Cooper hadn't gotten this far by taking stupid, uncontrolled risks.
And despite what Pierce might think, she never put her life in the
hands of a someone she didn't know or couldn't predict. So when
the black Mercedes with heavily tinted windows had pulled to
the curb, Cooper thought sliding into the backseat would be the
hardest thing she'd do all day.

She'd been dead wrong.

Watching Will force himself to join her, seeing his face when
the driver had shut the door and sealed them into a darkened
interior, had been so much worse.

The car made a turn and came to a stop outside a heavy, steel
security gate that slowly rolled up after their driver entered a
passcode into the callbox.

"Where are we?" Cooper asked, leaning closer to Will to
glance through the windshield. Nerves danced beneath her skin
like angry wasps. "We're still blocks from the bank."

"Yes, ma'am," the driver said, glancing at Cooper in the
rearview mirror then pulling the car into a dimly lit, underground

garage. "Many of these buildings have private service tunnels. The bank makes use of them when necessary."

Will flinched as the gate rattled shut behind them, blocking out the heavy sun of mid-afternoon. He clenched his eyes shut, his jaw flexing, his hands balling into fists.

"Hey." Cooper touched his wrist, then pulled away when he jerked back against the door. "Will." Though she didn't feel it, she kept her voice steady and calm. "Look at me."

He kept his eyes shut. Sweat beaded on his forehead and slipped down his temple. "I'm fine," he ground out through clenched teeth.

"No, you're not," she whispered, the conversation something she didn't intend to share with their driver. "And that's okay." She wanted to reach for him. To lace their hands together or curl her fingers around his wrist. Instead, she slid her open palm from shoulder to wrist, reminding him she was there, that he wasn't alone, but careful not to hold him. Trap him.

"Hey, Bennett," she said, sitting back but keeping her eyes on him. When he tilted his chin her direction and cut her a look, she quirked her lips at him. "What do you call a fake noodle?"

Surprise pushed back against the fear and anxiety that had carved harsh, tired lines across his face.

"An impasta."

He choked on a laugh as the car pulled to a stop. "That was *terrible*."

Yeah, it was. But he'd smiled despite himself and Cooper found herself wondering just what she'd find beneath that beard. Dimples, she thought. Long and deep. Canyons carved by better days and happier memories. Someday, she hoped to see them.

Hoped to see him free of the beard and the hair that covered his half-missing ear. Free of the insecurity and shame that drove him to cover the proof of his strength and survival in the first place.

"If you'll follow me," their driver said as he held open the door for Cooper. "I'll escort you into the bank."

She slid out of the Mercedes and into the dimly lit quiet of a private garage. Will followed her out, put a hand to the small of her back and left it there as they followed their escort to the steel door.

"I'll wait for you here." The driver entered a code into the security pad next to the door, then pulled it open on silent hinges.

A woman in a neatly tailored suit and mid-height heels waited for them on the other side. "*Señor* Bennett?"

"Yes." Will extended his hand, which she shook before gesturing them inside.

"I'm Victoria Bustillo, regional vice president of investments," she said in the sort of crisply accented English that said though it wasn't her first language, she was far more than simply proficient. "I'm also the designated representative for your account."

"Thank you for meeting with us on such short notice, Ms. Bustillo."

The regional vice president of investments? What the hell were they walking into?

"Victoria, please," she offered as she badged through another security door and led them down a windowless but brightly lit hallway. "And it is the bank's pleasure to accommodate you upon request. If you'll follow me?"

Cooper stepped in closer to Will and let the heat of his presence buffer the adrenaline thrumming through her veins. The more she tried to talk herself down, convince herself that they were fine, and this was normal, the more her body pumped a warning through her blood.

She hated this. Hated being on the ground and in the mix. She was comfortable behind the scope. Deadly at a distance. When she had her rifle and her orders, she could see *everything*.

But up close, as the situation evolved second to second? She was disarmed and blind to everything but what was in front of her.

"Try to relax." Will bumped her shoulder with his. "This is what I do."

When she glanced up, the grin he wore bordered on arrogant. On anyone else, it would have grated on her nerves. Smug, male superiority had never done it for her and she'd had her fair share of fun subverting that sense of self-importance. But on Will? Maybe it was the fact that she knew damn well he could back up words with actions, or maybe it was because it was just so damn good to see him embrace a sense of confidence that only a year ago he'd have worn like second skin—either way, that cocky tilt to his lips looked good on him.

Which made her wonder what else she could do to stroke it to life.

Something to explore later.

"Are we far from the bank?" Will asked, acting for all the world as if accessing a hidden box in a foreign country through tunnels that amounted to secret passageways was a normal occurrence. At least the brightly lit hallways didn't seem to bother him in the way driving into the garage had.

"Top side, yes. We'd be several blocks away," Victoria explained as she badged through yet another security door. "The long way, if you will. But there are several establishments in the area that require additional security—banks, jewelry stores, that kind of thing—so we make use of the underground parking and service and delivery entrances." She swiped her badge again, and this time doors slid open and they stepped into a service elevator. "Standing outside the garage entrance, it would be nearly a two kilometer walk to the front of the bank. But through the service doors"—she cast a smile over her shoulder as the elevator stopped and the doors slid open—"five minutes."

Will and Cooper stepped out onto the high-shine of polished

marble floors, but they weren't in the front lobby. There were no doors or windows facing the street.

The sort of setup, security, and VIP treatment she might have expected in the Caymans or Switzerland. It heightened her nerves . . . and stoked her expectations.

"It's one of the reasons we hold a contract with Atlantic Insurance & Investments. Their standards are very strict, and we take great pride in meeting each one of them."

Atlantic Insurance & Investments? Another player. Another question. Another potential problem in a stack that blotted out the sun.

Will cast Cooper a careful look, but she didn't have any answers to give him. She'd assumed from the start that they'd be dealing with a standard safety deposit box setup. But between the hired car, private entrance, and VIP treatment, Cooper was beginning to understand that what they were walking into was anything but normal.

"This way, please." She led them to a security desk with two armed guards. "Just a quick thumbprint scan."

With a glance at Cooper, Will stepped forward and pressed his thumb to the scanner. "How is it you have my fingerprints on file?" he asked as the computer ran his biometrics. "The account was set up in my name, but without my knowledge."

"A process I'm unfamiliar with, I'm afraid," Victoria said, though her clipped, rehearsed words told a different story.

It hardly mattered. Just another dead end of missing information and though curious, Cooper couldn't bring herself to press for more. She didn't care how Felix had opened and set up the account. Didn't care what Victoria knew, or didn't. And didn't give a shit about another bank—or ten other banks. Cooper gave a damn about one thing and one thing only, and it was sitting in a box on the other side of the vault door.

The computer chimed and one of the security guards rose

with a nod. "Arms out," he instructed as he approached with a wand that looked similar to devices used at airports and special events.

Will lifted his arms as Victoria explained, "We have a strict no-electronics policy. If you have any cell phones or tablets, we'll store them for you here."

Will shook his head. "I don't have one with me." Security finished the scan and nodded in agreement.

"Will your friend be accompanying you into the vault?" Victoria asked.

"Yes."

Reluctantly, Cooper pulled her burner phone from her pocket, handed it over, then lifted her arms for the scan.

When security cleared her, Victoria turned toward the heavy steel doors of the vault. "Excellent. We can proceed." She stepped up to a control panel, then glanced toward security. When the man behind the desk nodded, she tilted her face toward the camera mounted in the far-left corner. A few seconds passed, and the panel came to life. "Victoria Bustillo, regional vice president of investments," she said, then repeated the same phrase in Spanish. There was a high-pitched beep and she placed her palm against the panel, then leaned closer for a retina scan.

"What kind of regional bank has this level of security?" Will asked quietly as they waited for the authentication to go through. "Dual-language voice recognition, multiple types of biometric screenings, and some sort of additional security that requires remote viewing—it seems extreme," he whispered. "What the hell is in that box?" he wondered aloud.

"We take our security protocols very seriously," Victoria said with a practiced smile as bolts disengaged with heavy *thunk thunk thunks*.

She pulled the door open and led them inside a room that finally met Cooper's expectations. The space was relatively small, no more than twelve by twelve, with a sturdy stainless-steel table bolted to the center of the floor, a single conference phone sitting on top. The walls were brassy and monochromatic, lined floor to ceiling with numbered boxes in multiple shapes and sizes, but instead of the expected keyholes, each box had a fingerprint scanner.

"If you'll follow me, Mr. Bennett?" Victoria led him toward the right corner, then knelt to access a small box three rows up from the ground. "I'll need your thumbprint one more time," she said, pressing her own thumb to the scanner and waiting for the beep of authentication.

Will followed her actions and the door popped open.

Cooper struggled to breathe. Finally. *Finally.* Eighteen months, and every single agonizing second had been leading her to this moment. To proof and answers. To freedom and justice.

Victoria removed the box and set it on the table. "I'll leave you here," she said. "You may use the bank's secured line." She tilted her head toward the conference phone that sat atop the table. "When you're done, just replace the box. I'll be waiting at security to escort you back to your car."

Cooper watched her go, Victoria pulling the vault door shut behind her. The locks didn't engage, but the questions that had been multiplying like viruses through her mind did. A glance at Will said he was as shocked and overwhelmed as she was.

"What the hell have you stumbled into, Coop?" he asked, running his fingers over the edge of the table as he approached the steel box.

She bristled. "Me? Account's not in my name, Bennett." Questions flocked and screeched like drunken birds, but one rose above the rest. "Why would we need a phone?" she wondered aloud.

"I don't know." He touched the edge of the box, fingering the hinged lid. "When you said there was a safety deposit box in my

name . . . I don't know. I guess I pictured something . . . simpler."
He glanced up at her, his face a roil of confusion. "This level of
security—did you know to expect this?"

She shook her head, her mouth dry and her palms sweaty.
"But maybe I should have. So many people have killed or been
killed over those damn trials."

"But how the hell did a guy like Felix set this up?" Will
wondered, his hands clenching into fists and his muscles
bunching beneath his shirt. "And what does Atlantic Insurance &
Investments have to do with it?"

"I don't know," Cooper whispered. "I've never heard of them
before today." Every time she got close to answers, questions
seemed to multiply, faster and faster, until they were all she
could see.

Except, this time was different. This time there *were* answers.
And they were sitting right there, on the table in front of her.

She stepped up next to Will. Ran a finger along the edge of
the box's lid.

As if he knew how long she'd waited, how hard she'd worked,
how much she'd suffered, and all to get here, Will dropped a
heavy palm against her shoulder, slid it along the back of her
neck, and squeezed her opposite shoulder.

"Go ahead, Coop."

On a deep breath and a silent prayer, Cooper opened
the box.

CHAPTER FIFTEEN

Hope died a bitter death, and betrayal, like a sharp knife she should have seen coming, slipped between her ribs and took aim for her heart.

Cooper choked back the bitter tang of disappointment, both with herself, for being stupid enough to get her hopes up in the first place, and with the contents of the box.

She shoved away from the table on a curse, her eyes stinging, her fingernails biting into her palms.

"Cooper." Will reached for her, but she walked away, putting the table between them.

She didn't want him to touch her, soothe her, comfort her. It would be a lie, and temporary at best. And for once, because she was safe behind thick walls and steel doors, she wanted to indulge in the weakness of emotions she'd been beating back for months.

Disappointment. Exhaustion. Frustration.

And most of all the rising tide of faithlessness that threatened to drown her. How much longer could she do this? How many more questions would she have to find before she finally faced the reality that maybe there weren't answers. Not for her. And not for Cole.

"I can't keep doing this," she whispered, the truth bland and boring and tasteless. Lies were sweeter, though they carried the tang of something manufactured and processed and false. God knew she'd grown accustomed to the flavor with every single one she'd told.

It's not my fault.

No cost is too high.

I can save him.

"You can. You will. People like us?" Will said, his words firm and solid, comforting in their inability to yield or soften or compromise. "We don't know how to quit. Even when we should. Even when it's easier."

She'd retreated so he couldn't reach her. Couldn't touch her. Couldn't calm or comfort her.

She should have known better.

His voice stroked over her with the determination and strength of a steady palm down her back. She couldn't ignore it. Or what came next. Because he was right. She couldn't quit.

Even when she wanted to.

Cooper turned and came back to the box, eyeing the contents with disdain.

"I'm so fucking sick of surprises."

Will cut a grin in half when she glared at him. "Fair enough. But let's see what we're dealing with."

He pulled the two items out of the box—a large coin and a matte white business card with a phone number embossed in black across the front.

"Guess that's why we need the phone," he said, turning the card over in his palm.

"And the coin? What is it, anyway? A silver dollar?"

"Nope." He flicked it off his thumb, let it turn end over end, then tossed it over.

Heavy, and thicker than an average coin, it was silver with a gold halo surrounding the center with script along the rim.

Limited Edition Ten Dollar Gaming Token Bellagio

"Las Vegas? Seriously?" Cooper asked, turning the coin over in her palm and inspecting the details for anything that might explain why the hell it should matter to her. "I thought they stopped using coins twenty years ago?"

"They did," Will agreed, taking it back and running his thumb along the edge in a gesture that was distinctly familiar. "This was Felix's lucky charm—we used to trade it back and forth a lot."

"Why?"

"He won it in a drunken game of poker—he was too wasted to realize it wasn't actually worth anything." A memory stretched Will's mouth in a sad smile. "Called it his favorite challenge coin."

Cooper rolled her eyes. "Last I checked, challenge coins were reserved for special accomplishments or military readiness."

"As far as Felix was concerned, sneaking back onto base drunk off his ass and naked from the waist down was the definition of military readiness." Will spun the coin on the surface of the desk, then slapped it flat with a *thunk*. "He'd issue challenges —usually stupid, sometimes dangerous—but complete it, and you got possession of the coin and the right to issue the next challenge. We passed that thing back and forth like weed at a frat party."

At a bar and over a beer, Cooper would have pumped Will for the stories that were so clearly attached to that coin. Memories that sketched his face with humor and regret and shadows of the man he used to be. But that was an indulgence for another day.

"Why would Felix leave it for you?"

"I don't know," Will said, "but I've got a feeling whoever's on the other end of that phone number does."

He came to the other side of the desk and set the business card next to the phone. "Ready to do this?"

Like there was a choice. "Yeah."

Will hit the button for speakerphone, waited for the dial tone, then keyed in the number on the card. The phone rang twice.

"Mr. Bennett." A deep, accent-less American voice, the sort high-end news personalities spent years perfecting, resonated over the line. "I've been expecting your call."

"Who is this?" Will asked, his fingers curling against the edge of the table until his knuckles turned white.

"I'm an account manager with Atlantic Insurance & Investments."

Cooper clenched her teeth against a curse. Goddamn it, couldn't anything be simple?

"That doesn't answer my question."

"And is irrelevant, as that's not the question you've called to ask."

"Wait just a second—" Will started, anger bunching his shoulders and leaking through his voice.

"You're wasting time, Mr. Bennett." The words were clipped and impatient, as if the speaker had far better things to do with his time. "Listen carefully, and I'll walk you through the authentication sequence, and deliver the information Mr. Harrigan entrusted to our care."

"But I—"

"Please describe the item Mr. Harrigan deposited for you."

"The coin?" Will asked, his confusion matching Cooper's own.

"Yes, Mr. Bennett, the coin."

Will sighed and shot the phone a look that said he had some

choice words for the person on the other end. "It's a ten-dollar Bellagio chip. Silver at the center, gold rim."

"Anything else?"

"It's got the initials F.H. carved onto the face."

"Thank you. Now if you'll please describe the circumstances that led to the last time the coin was in your possession—"

"I don't see what that has to do with anything," Will snapped, banging his fist against the table.

"Nor do you need to, Mr. Bennett. Your only concern is providing the key. I turn the lock," the man said, and though his voice was smooth and without inflection, condescension dripped from each syllable as if smug superiority, rather than English, were the speaker's native tongue.

"I really hate this guy," Cooper mumbled.

"Also an irrelevant detail, Miss Reed."

So they knew Will wasn't alone and who was with him. Cooper didn't have the energy to claim surprise on either count.

On a sigh, Will said, "Two years ago, on leave in New York City. Felix challenged me to the three-pound, thirty-minute pancake problem. I won."

"Please hold for authentication."

The line breathed with the sort of pregnant silence that lingered, thick and heavy, until something else replaced it.

"Three pounds of pancakes?" Cooper asked, her stomach rumbling. "Sounds like a great way to ruin a good breakfast."

Will lifted a shoulder. "I won. Got the t-shirt and the free breakfast to prove it."

He looked proud, but she studied his face for the tell that had to be there. No one downed three pounds of pancakes in thirty minutes without repercussions. "And at what cost?"

"A brutal betrayal, a nasty divorce, and a monogamous relationship with the always loyal waffle."

"Gross."

"You've no idea. I nearly got ticketed in Central Park for public intoxication at ten a.m." He grinned. "Thank God I had the t-shirt to explain things."

Before she could reply, the voice came back on the line.

"Thank you for holding—"

"Like you gave us a choice," Cooper grumbled, but was neatly ignored.

"Listen very carefully, Mr. Bennett, because I'm going to give you coordinates, you're going to repeat them back to me, and then I'm going to hang up."

"Wait—"

"The business card will be confiscated, this line will be permanently disconnected, and you will be escorted back to your car. We will not speak again."

"I don't understand—"

"It's really quite simple. Your identity has been confirmed, your key authenticated. I'm going to pass on the information we've held for you, and this conversation will be over. Now, the numbers—"

"What's at the location you're giving me?"

"Not what, Mr. Bennett. Who. Specifically, one Dr. Jerome Mitchell."

Cooper swallowed back a gasp, but not before Will jerked his head to face her. "He's the physician who oversaw several of the trials—I thought he was dead."

"As you were meant to," the voice on the line supplied. "Now, the location—"

"Wait, I don't have anything to write on," Will said, glancing around the room.

"No, you don't, so I suggest you pay attention."

As promised, he read off the coordinates, then waited for Will to repeat them back to him. When it was done, the voice said, "Be at that location in thirty-six hours. Not twenty-four. Not forty-eight. Thirty-six," he stressed. "Dr. Mitchell will be waiting. Arrive with more than the two of you, we cancel. Arrive too soon and we cancel. Arrive too late—"

"You cancel?" Will snapped but was ignored with little more than a beat of a dismissive silence.

"Your window closes and, for the safety of our client, he, along with all of his information and documentation, will be moved."

The line went dead.

"What a prick," Will said, shoving a hand through his hair.

Cooper reached for him, curling her fingers into the fabric of his shirt, and waited for the ground to stop shifting beneath her feet. More and more she felt as if she were staring through her scope, lining up the shot, only to wonder if she had the right target in her crosshairs.

"What do we do?" Her voice was small, but the vault bounced it back twice as hard anyway.

Will turned to her, one hand smoothing across his beard-covered jaw.

"Only two choices, really." He pocketed the casino coin and set the business card back in the box. "Move forward or quit."

God, he made it sound so easy. So simple.

"How much information do you think Mitchell really has?"

"All of it," she said, her voice flayed by the double-edged blade of hope and yet another setback. Another mystery. "He was the man in charge of the clinical trials. He would know *every-thing*. Patients. The pharmaceutical companies, the officials who gave the green light. Medical records. Names and files. Tests and outcomes. The drugs and the side effects and . . ."

She swallowed back the flood of words before she could utter the one she most wanted to hear and was most afraid to say.

"And a way to reverse it all," Will finished for her. "A way to free Cole."

Cooper closed her eyes against just how much it meant to hear someone else say it, out loud, like it was more than a pipe dream or fragile possibility. "Yes."

"We'd be going in blind, Cooper." Will sighed and let his gaze wander over the boxes lining the walls. "I don't know where these coordinates lead, but based on that call? On the security measures we had to go through just to make a damn phone call? We won't be able to do any kind of recon. Can't plan or prepare or call in support. They'll have done all of those things, but us? We'll have to take it on faith." He released a frustrated breath. "So, I'll ask you—do you think we can trust these guys?"

"Honest answer?"

He nodded.

"I think they'll do exactly what that guy said. In thirty-six hours, they'll move Dr. Mitchell and I'll be right back to square one." Cooper drummed her fingers along the tabletop. "But do I trust them not to turn on us?" She shivered, and words of warning that sounded suspiciously like Pierce filtered through the buzz of racing thoughts. "No, no I don't."

"Neither do I."

"What about you?"

"Me?" he asked, surprise pulling his attention back to her face.

"How much do you trust Felix? Because he left this box for *you*. Made sure that you were the only one who'd know that story, who could unlock that location. I'm here by accident, but you— you were always meant to walk this road." She met his gaze and asked a question she knew would hurt. "Would he betray you?"

Will's mouth dropped open, his first instinct, just as hers would have been, to bite off a quick and harsh denial. Instead, he snapped his mouth shut and forced his reply through jaded experiences and a new, more suspicious outlook. Another wound, another scar left by twelve months of captivity and torture. And one Cooper couldn't hope to erase or soothe or heal. Betrayal burned deep, and the brand would last forever.

But hopefully it would fade over time.

"I trust him," Will finally said. "There's a reason he chose the coin. It's always been a series of escalating challenges between us. That ten-dollar token is the reason I applied for Delta. The reason he made a pass at an admiral's son . . . and the reason Felix took him home to meet his parents," Will explained, and Cooper tried to ignore the way it cut, deep and painful, knowing that *she'd* been the end of that relationship.

That she'd been the end of this tradition.

"It wasn't all pancakes and pickup lines—it was a promise. That there were always more adventures. More challenges. More *life*. He'd have no reason to set me up . . . but even if he did, he wouldn't use this. Wouldn't trade on it that way."

Cooper wanted to argue, wanted to insist that *of course* he'd trade on that coin and the history it carried. That loyalty and friendship and the memories those things created were, in the right hands, the deadliest of weapons. But because the words were jaded and bitter and Pierce's, she bit them back.

"Then I have to go," she said.

"*We* have to go," he corrected. "We're in this together."

Copper barely felt the smile she forced to her face. Will meant every word. Even now, even after everything, he was so damn loyal. So damn willing to stand by a friend.

And as badly as she wanted to cling to his hand and walk by his side and face the rest of what would come with the added strength of someone else's support, she simply couldn't bring herself to be that damn selfish.

She'd needed Will to access the vault. But now his job was done. He could go home. He *deserved* to go home. Deserved to rest and recover and find the parts of himself he'd buried deep but hadn't lost.

And Cooper could give that to him. *Would* give that to him.

This man, she thought, with bittersweet clarity, she *could* free. He'd hate her for it, but she could do it.

She just had to be strong enough to leave him behind.

CHAPTER SIXTEEN

Cooper Reed was a lot of things. Sexy. Smart. A sharp shot and a loyal friend. But subtle?

Not even a little bit.

From a perch or in a hide, she was probably used to being just shy of invisible.

But being still and silent enough to disappear was one thing. Going unnoticed while trying to sneak past a spec ops guy in the middle of the night was another skillset entirely.

And one Cooper definitely did not possess.

Will had known almost from the jump that *something* had changed. Cooper had been quiet, subdued even as they'd left the bank and made their way back. At first, he'd thought it disappointment.

That much, he could understand.

She didn't have to tell him how much it had hurt to open that box and find questions where she'd expected answers instead.

It had been written across her face. Crushing defeat. Hollowed-out exhaustion. And the terrifying realization that it *still* wasn't over.

So her quiet reflection in the car hadn't surprised him.

Neither had her resigned reaction to mapping the coordinates—a desolate stretch of Costa Rican coastline, accessible by a single, narrow and winding road that would require a four-wheel drive.

What had surprised him was her lack of interest in planning what came next. Getting a truck—which they'd done that afternoon—planning the route, accounting for travel time, packing their gear.

She'd been quiet through all of it, responding to questions with one- or two-word answers.

It had taken him longer than he'd like to realize she wasn't tired or despondent or just plain used to this sort of constant change.

She'd been up in her head. Making plans. Looking through rations of food and ammunition. More than once, he'd caught her mumbling her way through well-used checklists. He hated that it all came so easily to her.

That she was so used to thinking on her feet, planning out her steps, moving quickly and efficiently. There was no second guessing. Not where Cooper was concerned.

It was the sort of utilitarian discipline spec ops trained for. But in Cooper it was next level. Tested and hardened under brutal, unrelenting conditions.

And she was used to doing it by herself. Without support or backup or the simple comfort of knowing she wasn't alone. That there was someone else, equally trained and just as competent, beside or behind her.

The loneliness that realization wrought ached in Will like an ulcer that would never heal. He understood it, had lived with it, and hated seeing the mark it had left on Cooper.

But because he knew what it was to get on with things, to keep moving—because really, what other choice was there?—he recognized just what was happening when she'd set her gear by the door and her boots by her bed.

They might have agreed to leave at the break of dawn, but when that sun came up, Cooper planned to be long gone.

That she thought she could sneak past him amused him.

That she planned to leave him behind enraged him.

She made her way across the floor, her boots in one hand, the keys to the truck in the other.

She was good, he'd give her that. Quiet. Organized. Light on her feet.

But he was better.

Will rose from the couch, slipped silently into her wake, and closed the distance.

When her hand touched the knob and she reached for her pack, he reached past her in the dark and flicked the switch for the single, recessed bulb that lit the kitchenette.

"Fuck!" She jumped, and her boots clattered to the floor. "Christ, you scared me," she said, her breathing hard and fast, her eyes darting everywhere but his face.

"Going somewhere?"

She swallowed and looked up at him, her irises a slowly expanding pool of blue as her eyes adjusted to the light.

"I—"

"Be very careful with what you say next, Cooper." He braced a palm against the door and leaned in close, trapping her against the wall. "And do *not* lie to me."

She shut her mouth, swallowing back whatever excuse she had poised on the tip of her tongue. She closed her eyes, and her muscles went loose and tired.

"I have to do this," she whispered, lines of sadness and resolution changing the contours of her face. "But you don't."

She opened her eyes, tilted her chin, and met his gaze head-on. "You can go home, Will. In thirty-six hours you could be

stateside. With friends and family and the people who love you."
She put her hand to his chest when he shook his head. "You
deserve to go home. To rest and heal and recover." She trailed her
hand down the front of his t-shirt, let her fingers trace the row of
stitches along his side that he never forgot but mostly ignored.
"So much has happened in such a short time. It feels like I found
you on that mountain weeks ago. But it was *days.*"

He flinched when her thumb pressed against the wound.

"You're still hurting, still healing. And I've asked more of you
than was ever right or fair." Her hand dropped away. "I had to.
Getting those coordinates would have been impossible without
you. But the rest . . . I can do this on my own."

He'd thought she was walking out on him. As he'd lain awake
on that couch, every conceivable thought had run through his
head. That she'd lied to him. That she didn't trust him or just
didn't need him.

That she'd played him.

But it was so much worse.

"Go home, Will."

She was trying to *save* him. Protect him. By sending him
home and going forward alone.

Like hell.

"Get healthy. Be happy." She actually had the damn nerve to
smile at him. "I'll be okay from here."

And this from the woman who was worried about losing
herself. About crossing a line she could never come back from.

There were a thousand things he wanted to say and a million
ways to say them. He went with the simplest.

"No." He dropped his chin, let his forehead touch hers, and
breathed her in. There was nothing fancy about the way Cooper
smelled. No French perfumes or high-end lotions. Just the simple
scent of soap and skin and the lingering mark of a recent shower.

It was honest and fresh, and he knew if he led her back to bed and climbed in next to her that the same scent would be there to greet him, surround him, and lull him into a sleep he chased but rarely achieved on his own.

Maybe it had happened when she'd left Matías alive and let him take his vengeance. Maybe it happened when she'd found him, weak and trembling and unable to do something as basic as shave, yet seen only a survivor's strength. Maybe it had been the culmination of a hundred little moments over a handful of days. Or maybe it stretched back over years and texts and unfulfilled promises; a seed that had been planted and waited for the right conditions to grow.

Ultimately, it didn't matter where it had begun, because it all ended in the same place. Somewhere along the line, Cooper Reed had become synonymous with home.

Which meant Will couldn't go back without her.

Because she was there, the heat of her body close and comforting, her face turned up and her mouth a hard line of frustration, he leaned in to kiss her.

She turned her head away, but a tiny, agonized noise escaped her throat.

She ducked beneath his arm and reached for the knob.

"Don't walk out that door, Coop," he warned.

She stiffened, the order stripping back the vulnerability that had been riding her and leaving behind the woman he was far more familiar with.

"Or what?" she snapped, bristling like an indignant cat that had been backed into a corner but didn't intend to stay there. "You going to keep me here? We both know how that plays out."

"Nope."

At his casual tone, she shot a look over her shoulder.

He shoved his hands into the pockets of his sweats. "You're free to leave." He grinned. "And I'm free to follow. I know where you're going, Coop. How you plan to get there. When you have to be there. How long do you really think it'll take me to catch up?"

"You don't have a car, or the money to get one."

"Like that'll stop me."

She turned on him, her eyes flashing and her fists curling. "You have the chance to go home!" she yelled. "Do you know what I'd do for that? How much I dream about it? How scared I am that I'll never have it?"

"Cooper..."

"No," she snapped, and shoved him back when he stepped forward. "No, you don't get to do that. I don't need you to make it better."

He ignored her words and focused on her tone. Listened to the way each syllable climbed in pitch. The way she rushed out each word, as if she had to get it out in a single breath or not all.

"And I don't need you to protect me," he said, walking straight into her personal space and crowding her between his body and the door she couldn't seem to open. "I can't go home, Coop. Not without you."

On instinct, or frustration, or just because she was plain pissed off, she put both her hands on his chest and *shoved*.

He didn't so much as take a step back.

"What's stopping you?" she demanded with another shove. "You've got no reason to stay."

When she shoved him again, with both words and fists, his patience snapped. He grabbed her wrists, forced them against the door and above her head, and claimed that frustrating, demanding mouth with his.

As if he'd caught her entirely off guard, her hips jerked, but then her mouth dropped open and her tongue met his and finally, *finally* he kissed her the way he'd always wanted to. With teeth and tongue. Fire and ice. With bold strokes and ruthless maneuvers.

And like the worthy adversary she was, Cooper met each tactic with a gambit of her own.

Invaded as often as she retreated.

Bucked as much as she succumbed.

When she tugged at her wrists, he tightened his grip, and she sucked his bottom lip into her mouth and bit—hard enough to hurt, fast enough to get away with it—then let him go with a grin he tasted on his tongue and felt in his dick.

When he shoved a knee between her legs, she wrenched her mouth from his and lost control of a moan—an agony and an invitation and a promise—and turned her head to the side, exposing the long column of her throat.

He scraped his teeth along the corded tendons, licked a path over a pulsing vein, dragged his beard over soft, sensitive flesh. And this time when she opened her mouth, it wasn't to moan or demand or tell him to go home.

It was to *beg.*

"Will, *please.*" She jerked her hips, searching for the friction his knee promised but his own long-held desires denied. When he finally allowed her to come, it would be under his hands and at his mercy. If he had his way, she'd be out of control and out of her mind. There'd be no thoughts. No countermeasures. No demands.

Just the final confrontation and the surrender he knew she'd fight but ultimately embrace.

But not yet.

He let her go and stepped back, his cock aching and his heart racing.

But it was worth it for the single second she stood there, suspended against the door, her wrists above her head, her legs splayed and her breathing hard. As if he'd never let her go. Never stepped away.

"Now, tell me again," he said, watching as her arms slid down the door and a pretty pink flush slipped up her neck. "Tell me again that I should go." He shifted, his t-shirt a constant itch against skin that had gone hot with anticipation. "Tell me again that I've got no reason to stay."

She set her jaw and clenched her fists, her mouth swollen and her hair a mess.

"Tell me that *you* want me to go home, Cooper. Say it and mean it, and I'll go."

It would kill him, but he would. He'd walk away. If that was really what she wanted. Really what she needed.

But it wasn't, and now they both knew it.

She licked her lips, glanced away, and he watched as the lie she'd prepared to protect him died in her mouth.

"No matter what this is, we're in it together," he said.

She swallowed hard but nodded. "Together."

"Now," he said, stalking close but stopping just short of touching her. He looped a finger in the gap between the top two buttons of her shirt. "Tell me *no*." He pulled, and the first button gave way with little more than a whisper of protest. "Tell me to stop." The second button let go, exposing the top of bra-covered breasts he'd seen, but not yet had the chance to appreciate. "Tell me you don't want this." He stared into her eyes. "Tell me you don't want my hands on your skin, my tongue in your mouth, or my cock in your body." The next two buttons slid free and he let his fingers trace across soft skin that pebbled in welcome. "Tell me now, Cooper, and I swear I'll go straight back to bed and see you at dawn."

She swallowed hard, but her words were still raspy and dry when she said, "I want it."

"Which part?" he asked, trailing a finger along the curving cup of her bra.

"All of it."

He brushed a thumb over a cotton-covered nipple and stole a shiver.

"I've always wanted all of it." She reached for the waistband of his sweats, cupped the long, firm length of him.

He let her tease him once, her grip loose and her stroke slow —the woman turned comfortable sweats into a prison and a torment she could wield against him. But when he hissed out a breath, and smug triumph curled her mouth, he grabbed her wrist and pulled her hand away.

"It's been a long time coming." A slow-burning desire stoked over long, unfulfilled months that had stretched to years. A promise built, piece by piece, over late-night text messages and stolen moments. "*Someone* always had a reason we couldn't meet."

"We were never in the same place—"

"That's what leave is for. We could have found the time, could have made it work."

She pulled at her wrist, but he jerked her in close.

"You enjoyed teasing me," he whispered against her mouth. "Didn't you, Coop?"

"Yes," she hissed as he tangled his fingers in her hair, scratching at the base of her skull.

"I warned you about that, didn't I?" He pulled the hair he'd caught in his fist, jerking her head back so he could stare into her eyes. "Promised I'd make you pay for it."

Her stare was defiant, her mouth full and fierce and challenging. "You promised me a lot of things. So far, it's all been talk."

With the hand he had wrapped in her hair, he pulled her close, slid his other hand down the gentle curve of her spine, splayed his fingers wide as he continued over the curve of her ass. He wanted to linger and explore and promised himself he would— eventually—but kept going until his fingers slid beneath her ass and between her thighs. He stroked back and forth, pressing his middle finger firmly against the denim seam, just enough to tease, to torment, to bring her to her toes and pull a gasp from her mouth.

When she shifted her hips, rocking against his hand, he held her still and forced her to look at him.

"Tell me how bad you want it, Coop." He pressed a kiss to her mouth, tasted her desperation on his tongue. She was so goddamned intoxicating he pulled away. "Tell me what I can do to you."

"Anything. *Everything.*"

"Bold promises," he said, letting her go and pushing her back a step. "Let's see if you can live up to them." Her eyes flashed, and her fists curled as she stood there, waiting for him to throw the gauntlet. "Take off your shirt."

He backed up until his hands hit the back of the sofa, then braced himself against it, partly so he could enjoy watching as she met each and every one of his demands, and partly to keep himself from taking everything he wanted, everything she was offering, in a single, frenzied rush that he'd enjoy, but knew he'd never quite remember.

"Now," he ordered, when she didn't move.

Her fingers trembled as she undid the buttons, but she didn't protest and didn't look away. When the fabric pooled at her feet, he said, "Step forward."

She did as he asked, stepping into the center of the spill of light from the kitchenette. If it bothered her that she was fully exposed, while he lounged in the shadows, she didn't show it.

But then, she didn't have any reason to worry. Cooper Reed was one long, lean stretch of muscle. Life on the run had whittled back everything but what was most essential. Small breasts. A flat stomach. A shadowed valley at her hip that disappeared into her pants.

A warrior's body in a survivor's skin, and though he wanted

to see what she looked like safe and content and just a little bit soft, this, *this* was compelling in its own way.

"Now the bra," he said, his voice rough and wanting and straining against a control he couldn't hope to keep hold of.

She undid the clasp and slid the plain cotton material from her shoulders. A flush spread across her chest and her nipples hardened without a touch. God, he wanted to touch. To suck. To pinch.

She caught him staring and her smile spread like a slow spill of ink, staining her face with amusement at the power she held just *standing* there. And because she was the sort of woman who loved nothing more than a challenge—and meeting it with one of her own—she brushed her thumb over the tight tip of her breast, closed her eyes, and sucked her bottom lip between her teeth on a *hmmm*.

He'd make her pay for that. Soon, he promised himself, his fingers itching with the need.

"Are you wet, Cooper?"

She opened her eyes. "Come find out." She slid the button on her jeans free, and drew down the zipper, exposing the top V of her matching underwear. When she reached for the waistband, he stopped her.

"That's enough."

She froze and waited, anticipation stealing the breath from her lungs in ragged gasps until she visibly forced herself to calm, to settle. The second she did, he said, "Touch yourself, Cooper. Touch yourself and tell me how wet you are. Tell me how much your body wants me." When she slid her fingers beneath her underwear on a sigh, he said, "Tell me how bad you wish you had my cock instead of just my commands."

Her hand moved, just out of sight, and somehow the action was all the dirtier for it.

She rolled her hips, bit her lip, and defied him. "No."

"No?" he asked, straightening from the sofa, his control fraying strand by strand.

"Always knew you were all talk," she said, her hand moving faster. "It gets the job done." Her shoulders dropped, and a tiny, desperate sound caught at the back of her throat. "But I can take it from here." She smiled, then let that deep blue stare travel down his body and below his waist in a caress he felt to his bones. "Don't think I'm missing out on much anyway."

Will was moving before he thought about it. Had his hands on her at the same second it occurred to him that she'd baited him. Toyed with him. And won.

It didn't matter. He caught her wrist and pulled her hand from her pants. In one swift move he spun her, pulling that wrist up behind her back and pinning her chest against the door. She turned her head, stared over her shoulder, and reached back for him with her free hand.

He caught her before she could grab his cock, slapped her palm against the door, then leaned down and sucked the wet, greedy fingers he held trapped between her shoulder blades into his mouth.

If there was a woman alive who could steal his orgasm without a single touch, it was the one writhing beneath him. The sound she made when he sucked—half squeal, half moan—was all sex and pleasure and need. It wrapped around his cock and stroked him to the very edge of sanity.

Fucking hell, the things this woman did to him without even trying.

He loosened his grip and pulled her arm down, then pressed her palm flat against the door. "God, I need to be inside you. Tell me I can come inside you, Coop. Tell me it's safe."

She turned her head just enough to smile at him. "Tell me how hard you are," she mocked him. "Tell me how much you wish you had the warm heat of my body wrapped around your cock. Tell me how bad you want it, Will, and maybe I'll give it to you."

He rubbed himself against her ass and laid his mouth to the curve of her shoulder. Sucking up a mark, he admitted, "Bad enough to have spent months dreaming what it'd feel like, wondering what you'd taste like. Let me fuck you, Cooper. Right here. Right now. Then let me take you to bed so I can do it again. Taste you again. Have you again." And again and again and again until she'd crave him for the rest of her damn life.

"Then do it."

Possessed, he tore his mouth from her neck and his hands from hers. He shoved his sweats low, then yanked her pants and underwear halfway down her thighs. When she went to wiggle out of them, he stopped her. "No. I want you like this. Desperate and needy and so fucking ready that you can't even get your clothes off."

"God, *yes*," she moaned, then bit back a gasp when he slid his cock back and forth across her folds.

When she reached for her clit, he caught her hand and brought it back to the door. "No," he bit out. "At my touch, on my cock . . . or not at all." Covering her body with his, he nudged her opening, grabbed her biceps for leverage, and froze when she jerked and hissed—pain, not pleasure, stealing her breath.

He tore his hands from her and wrenched himself away, cold replacing heat. Regret replacing desire.

"I'm sorry," he said, his hands trembling, his eyes fixed on the bruises he'd left on her arms not two days ago. "I—I got a little carried away."

She didn't turn, didn't say anything, just slid her palm across the door and dropped her forehead into the crook of her arm. She took a deep breath, and Will forced himself to look at what he'd done, how he'd treated her.

Naked from the waist up, her hair a riot over her shoulders, her jeans around her knees.

Her right hand was still pressed against the door beside her head, her wrist red from where he'd manhandled her.

"Tell me," she said, mumbling into her arm. "Which part of this are you sorry about?" She shifted to glance at him over her shoulder. "The part where you ripped off my clothes? Oh wait. I did that. How about the part where you shoved my fingers between my legs? Oh no, that was me, too—"

"Cooper," he warned, trying stay in front of her temper and focus on the issue.

"How about the part where you threatened to fuck me against the door—oh, no, that can't be it because *I asked you* to do that, too." She turned, propping her back against the door, but didn't bother to pull her jeans up her legs.

Fuck, she looked wanton and ready to spit fire at his feet.

"So what, exactly, are you so damn sorry about?"

"I shouldn't have been so rough," he whispered. "You're hurt, and I—"

"So are you!" she snapped at him.

He shook his head. "It's not the same. I hurt you. Bruised you. If I'm not careful, I'll do it again—"

"This guilt-ridden hero bullshit stops right now." She jerked her pants up and stormed toward him.

He didn't move, couldn't, as she had him pinned up against the couch.

Topless and furious, she looked like some sort of gorgeous and unstoppable Greek goddess or Amazonian warrior.

"You're not bringing that shit into bed with us, Will—"

"But I—"

"No. You were hurt and cornered and scared and *I* attacked *you*. I didn't plan it, and I didn't mean it, and I *hate* that you felt like you had defend yourself against me. That you had to get away from me. That for even one single second *I* was as bad as *them*." Her face softened, and she put a palm to his cheek. "I will *always* hate that I pushed you. That I trapped you. But this?" She brought his hand to her chest, let his fingers cup the warm weight of her breast and touch the steady beat of her heart. "It doesn't have a damn thing to do with that."

"I left marks," he whispered, brushing a thumb across the ring of bruises that circled her biceps, and wondered how he'd ever forgotten about them in the first place.

"And if I had it my way, you'd be halfway through littering my body with more."

That statement wrapped itself around his dick and pulled twice. God, the things that came out of that mouth.

"When I wake up tomorrow, I want to *feel* it." She brushed her thumb along his collarbone. "I want your fingerprints on my hips. Your marks on my neck." She stared up at him. "And every single time I rub my thighs together I want to feel the whisper of your beard between my legs. I don't *need* you to be gentle or careful with me, Will."

"I don't want to hurt you."

"And I'm not asking you to," she said, clenching a fist in his shirt. "And I am *definitely* not asking you for anything you don't want to give, okay?" She looped an arm around his neck and brushed his mouth with a kiss. "If you don't want to do this, we won't. If you just want to take this to bed, we can. But if you *want* to shove me against that door, if you *want* to fuck me like it's the only chance you'll ever get, if you *want* to grab my hips or hold my wrists, then I am telling you I want that, too."

"This isn't smart, Cooper."

"Smart?" she asked, pulling far enough away to stare into his face. "Who the fuck gives two shits about smart? I'm not looking to master linear equations or launch a rocket—"

He couldn't help the chuckle that rose in his chest.

"Shut up, you know what I mean! Fucking smart," she grumbled. "No one wants smart sex, Will."

"I can think of a guy who might take that as a personal challenge," he said, brushing her hair away from her face with his thumb.

"Is he in this room?"

"No."

"Then smart sex is off the table. Wild, rough, filthy, and entirely ill-advised sex remains on offer—if you want still want it," she said, then, more softly, followed it with, "still want *me*."

He stroked his fingers through her hair, brought her mouth to his for a kiss. "I don't think there's ever gonna be a time I don't want you, Coop. You see every part of me—sometimes I think you see me better than anyone ever has, better than I ever will." He pulled her close, held her tight. "You found me, Coop. And every time I get a little lost, you find me again. Don't stop, okay?"

"I won't," she promised, her words soft and sweet against his neck.

He let her go and pushed her back and missed her the second she was out of reach.

"So," she said, shifting from foot to foot, self-conscious nerves getting the best of her for the first time all night. "Bed?"

"Yes," he said, then watched as her face fell and she mustered a smile and extended her hand.

He took it, laced their fingers together, then jerked her toward him. He stepped aside and set the hand he held on the couch. Stepping behind her, he put her other hand where he wanted it, then settled his palms on the waist of her jeans.

"You'll tell me if you don't like something," he whispered roughly against the back of her neck. "Tell me to stop if I go too far?"

"Always," she breathed.

He pushed her pants down her thighs and slipped a hand

between her legs to find her still wet, still ready, still wanting. It was enough to take him right back to the edge, as if he'd never stepped back at all.

"Your hands don't move," he reminded her, stroking his index finger against her clit.

"Then don't make me." She shifted restlessly against his hand and whined deep in her throat when he pulled away.

"You've got a gorgeous ass, Cooper Reed." He grabbed her hips and jerked her toward him. "I think I need to see more of it." He pressed a palm between her shoulders and pushed. "Bend over, show me how much you want it. How much you crave it."

She did him one better, gripped the cushions of the sofa, spread her legs, and arched her back, presenting her ass for his appreciation.

"Fuck, you're beautiful."

"Compliments don't count when your dick's in your hand, Bennett. But feel free to tell me again tomorrow."

Because he couldn't think of a better way to shut her up, he positioned his cock and slid home in one smooth, wicked thrust that took her to her toes.

"*Ugh,*" she grunted.

He settled a hand against her shoulder, brought her feet back to the ground, and met her with another vicious plunge.

"Oh God."

He grasped her hips and set a brutal pace, all too aware of the fact that he wouldn't, couldn't last. Not like this. Not with her writhing and pleading and cursing beneath him.

And definitely not when she matched every thrust and every demand with one of her own.

He may have had Cooper Reed half naked and bent over the sofa, every inch of her body at the mercy of his, but there was no mistake—*she'd* conquered *him*. Mastered *him*. Ruined *him* for anything or anyone else.

Because good God who could possibly measure up to this?

"Will, please. *Please, please, please,* I need . . ."

He pulled her hand away from the cushion and, though the angle was awkward, brought her fingers to his mouth, sucking them deep. When they were wet, and he was ready—so, so fucking ready it hurt—he guided her fingers down, settled them against her clit, and controlled every flick, every nudge, every thrust her hand made until she came spectacularly undone, her orgasm rolling through her and over his cock in pulsing powerful waves.

She went limp and loose and willing and tried to pull her hand away.

No chance. No mercy. No relenting.

He moved her fingers faster, brought her right back to the edge, her cries sharper, her agony sweeter, as he stole a second, more violent orgasm with the tips of her own fingers.

This time, he toppled over the edge right along with her, emptying everything he had on one last, brutal thrust.

Will laced their fingers together and set her hand back on the edge of the couch. They came down together, breathing hard and still connected, sweat slicking their skin everywhere they touched.

Slowly, because damn, there was a part of him that didn't want to, he slipped free then went to his knees, gently working her jeans down her legs and helping her step out of them.

With a firm grip and gentle hands, he turned her, scraped his beard up along the length of one leg and pressed an open-mouthed kiss to the inside of her thigh.

He stood and let himself stare at the devastated perfection of her body. The hard nipples, the sex-mussed hair. The way her chest flushed, and her legs trembled.

"I don't think I'll ever see anything so beautiful as you,

wrecked and ruined, as you try to catch your breath while my come slides down your thighs."

She straightened, then turned her back on him and headed toward the bedroom.

For a second, he thought he'd gone too far, said too much, been too crass.

But when she reached the door, she glanced over her shoulder and her lips turned up in something wicked and wild and welcoming. "You lack imagination, Bennett—you've never seen me on my knees."

Helpless to do anything else, he followed her into the bedroom and willingly into her trap. "That, I'd like to see."

She sat at the edge of the bed, leaned back, and braced her weight on her elbows. Spreading her legs as wide as her smile, she said, "You first."

CHAPTER SEVENTEEN

Dappled sunlight danced across her eyes, pulling Cooper from the warmth of a nap. The truck shifted as Will made a sharp right turn, then shimmied as it left smooth pavement and churned over a rough-cleared road.

They were getting close, then.

Cooper stretched, her back arching and toes curling, and sighed.

"I like the sounds you make." Will settled a palm against the top of her jean-covered knee, then slid it up her thigh. The gesture was warm and familiar and as friendly as it was intimate.

"Do you?" She turned her head and opened her eyes, staring at his profile as their little 4X4—an ancient Toyota pickup that guzzled gas and belched exhaust—bounced along a road.

"Satisfaction looks good on you." Afternoon sunlight punched through the canopy like Morse code. He shifted gears, and the tires churned and spat, eating through ground softened by recent rain.

She grinned. Though his words were all ego, she couldn't quite muster the energy to bust his balls over it. As far as she was concerned, he'd earned that cocky tone and smug smile. She'd told him she wanted to feel him the next day, on her skin and in her body, and once he'd set himself to the task, he'd been single-minded and creative in his devotion.

And then some.

Eventually, they'd slept, but only in quick, rejuvenating snatches, before they were giving in and consuming each other again. As a result, they'd had to trade off driving duty to get caught up and rest. Thank God they were both accustomed to grabbing sleep when and where they could find it. Still, as satisfied as she was—and she was very, very satisfied—she did wonder what it'd be like to simply lie in bed with him, wrapped in the knowledge that there was time. That they had more than a single night to explore everything that lay between them.

Ironic. She'd never wanted more than a night with anyone else. Yet with Will, she wanted weeks, months, years. *Time.* To explore and conquer. Escape and surrender. Fuck and sleep.

God, she wanted to sleep with him.

A long, lazy lie-in after a rough and tumble night—the ultimate indulgence.

And one they couldn't afford.

"How far out are we?" Cooper turned her attention back to the here and the now and searched through her bag for a protein bar and a bottle of water.

"About fifteen miles." He waved off the bar she offered him. "Hey, Coop?"

"Ugh, nothing good follows that sentence."

He shot her a grin. "We're good, right?"

When she just looked at him, he elaborated. "I mean, I know you said I could . . . *you know* . . . without a condom."

"'You know'?" she repeated, complete with finger quotes. "Really? *Now* you're shy?" She snorted. "After the things that came out of your mouth—hell, after where you put your mouth—

you're seriously going to get all conservative on me now that the sun's up?"

He huffed. "I just want to make sure everything's covered."

She laughed. "*Nothing* was covered, or we wouldn't be having this conversation." When he shot her a frustrated look, she rolled her eyes. "I got an IUD—long-term birth control—the last time I was on leave. I've got another two years before I even need to worry about replacing it. So if you're worried about accidentally creating little Bennetts, don't. We're good."

"Okay." He sighed, relief relaxing his hands on the wheel. "Okay, good."

The silence didn't last thirty seconds. "My last tests were clear, too. In case you were wondering. I hadn't been with anyone since my last round of labs and then . . ."

And then Colombia. And then captivity. And then he'd had things other than sex on his mind. She got it, and she didn't need him to say it.

"Never even crossed my mind to worry about that." When he didn't say anything, she put her hand on his forearm. "I'm not a reckless person, Will. This job, it kinda weeds that out."

"Then why'd you let me—"

"Because I *know* you. Know the kind of man you are. If you'd thought for even a second that there might be a reason to wait, you'd have said so." She gently scratched her nails along his skin. "You'd never put me at risk like that."

The tires caught and spun. He downshifted, jabbed the accelerator, then looked at her as they shot forward. "No, I wouldn't." He moved his arm, then picked up her hand and kissed the back of her knuckles.

A breathy laugh escaped her.

"What?" he asked.

"You're a constant contradiction, Bennett."

"Am not," he grumbled.

"Domineering and filthy one minute, total gentleman the next." She shrugged. "The contradiction suits you. The straight-laced soldier without the clean-cut look." She leaned across the narrow cab, scraped her teeth along the edge of his jaw. "The beard looks good," she admitted, deliberately putting her lips against the ear he worked so hard to hide. "But I wanna see you without it, too." She licked the lobe, traced her tongue along the edge, pressed her lips to the ragged curl that was left. He shivered —she'd discovered just how sensitive that ear was last night—then went very, very still, but didn't pull away.

"Why?" he asked, and she sat back before she started something there would be no time to finish.

"Why what?"

"Why would you want to see . . . that?"

With her index finger, she brushed the hair back and tucked it behind the back of his half-missing ear. "I like the beard." *A lot*, she thought, rubbing her thighs together. "But I have this image I can't seem to get out of my head. You all neat and tidy, with a clean shave and a fresh cut." She grinned. "I can see it all—the dress uniform, fresh pressed and fitted. Buttons shined. Shoes gleaming. Captain America come to life. A man who comes across that clean-cut can inspire a woman to do some seriously dirty things," she said, watching out of the corner of her eye as his jaw flexed and his weight shifted. She shrugged and propped her elbow against the window. "Personally, I'd like to do them with you."

"Yeah?" he asked, his voice thick and dry.

"Any time you're ready, Bennett." She grinned. "I've still got that razor . . ."

"And I still need to return the favor."

Heat pooled low and heavy at the image those words elicited.

Climbing a sharp hill, they rounded a corner, and dipped straight into a washed-out gulch.

"Shit." The truck bottomed out hard, then fishtailed when he hit the accelerator. Mud sprayed, and the back end shimmied. He tried reverse, but the wheels just squealed and whirred and turned and the truck sank farther into the mud.

"Damn it."

Cooper let out a heavy sigh. "How far out are we?"

Will checked the trip odometer. "Ten miles—might as well be fifty with the ground this saturated." He slapped his hand on the steering wheel. "It's gonna be a hell of a hike and approaching the rendezvous on foot isn't ideal."

"Never was." She zipped her pack shut as an engine revved out of sight and over the hill ahead of them.

"Locals?" he asked but turned the engine over and shoved the truck into first.

"Oh God, that's not a truck." High-pitched and frenzied, the noise of multiple engines cut through the surrounding jungle. "ATVs," she said, just as four of them appeared at the top of the rise in front of them.

"Ah, shit we're being flanked," Will said, glancing into the rearview mirror.

Cooper turned to look out the window, and sure enough, three more ATVs appeared behind them, approaching fast.

"God damn it, they knew we'd bottom out here. That the road would be impassable."

Dread coiled, tight and angry, like a cottonmouth in her gut. Pumping adrenaline instead of poison through her veins.

"What do we do?" she asked, though she damn well knew the answer. Nothing. There was *nothing* they could do. "Bail?"

"And go where? Jungle's too dense to outrun them. You've got your rifle, but there's no room to maneuver in the cab, and the second you step out with a weapon, it's over." He nodded toward the semiautomatic rifles strapped across the chests of the approaching men. "We're outgunned and outnumbered." He reached for her hand, squeezed it once. "We're gonna have to cooperate and hope this doesn't all go straight to shit. Don't panic. And don't fight unless you have to. Could just be another security protocol."

Something heavy hit the driver's side door with a *thwack* and a second later, the doors locked down and the dashboard electronics died.

"Shit. Shit, shit, *shit.*" Will yanked the handle of his door, then tried to manually raise the lock.

"Will!" she yelled at the same time she saw the lead driver bring a weapon to his shoulder and fire.

Something hurtled through the windshield, the glass cracking and splintering from corner to corner.

Smoke filled the cab, stinging her eyes and clogging her lungs.

"Try to hold your breath," he said on a hacking cough.

Tears streamed down her face and she gagged but got her boots up on the dash and tried to kick out the windshield. No dice. The dash was too high, and she couldn't get the leverage. With the steering wheel in the way, Will fared no better.

Smoke filled her lungs as Cooper gasped, her need for air outweighing her fear of whatever was filling the cab.

"Try the window," Cooper said, her thoughts fuzzy and her vision narrowing to a painful point. She coughed and wheezed and tried not to focus on the fear clawing its way through her.

"Fuck." He turned, and Cooper braced his back as he kicked at the window. Once, and it cracked. Twice, and it shattered.

But it was too late.

"Cooper . . ." Will coughed, the smoke so thick and heavy she could barely see him.

He collapsed into a hacking, coughing fit, then went still and silent against her.

She reached for him, got a fistful of his shirt, and toppled back when the passenger door was jerked open.

She was out before she hit the ground.

Her head throbbed.

Her tongue stuck to the roof of her mouth.

Something coarse rubbed against her cheek.

Cooper pried open her eyes, blinked back against the sunlight that intensified the pounding in her head until it sounded like waves beating against rocks.

She took a deep breath, forced back the nausea, and tasted salt.

"Coop?" Will whispered, his voice thin and tight and low. "You awake?"

She nodded, then regretted it.

What the hell had happened?

A gull cried and some of the fog receded. She sat up and stared out over an endless blue ocean.

"Where are we?" she asked as the world settled and the memories began to piece themselves together. When Will didn't answer, she glanced around. She wasn't sure what she'd expected. Death? Yeah, it had occurred to her, though if that had been the end goal, it would have been better to just shoot them in the car and be done with it.

But whatever her expectations had been, waking up on a sprawling veranda overlooking the ocean hadn't been one of them. Six stone arches spanned the width of the room, and white curtains restlessly undulated in the breeze.

She stood on wobbly legs, unpolished travertine beneath her feet. Cooper put her hand down for balance and realized she'd been left on a canvas-covered daybed.

"Coop?"

Confused and still getting her bearings, she scanned the room and spotted Will, hands and ankles bound to a sturdy wood chair in the corner. "Untie me," he rasped out, pulling against the restraints.

"You okay?" She unsteadily worked her way toward him and came back to herself a little more with each lungful of salty ocean air. "Will?" she asked when he didn't answer.

He jerked against his restraints, the chair scraping heavily against the floor. "G-get me out of these." Sweat slicked his brow and saturated his shirt, the fabric clinging to his chest. He clenched his eyes shut and she watched as he fought, face pale and gray, to control his breathing. "Untie me," he mumbled.

Shit.

Life came hurtling back at full volume and with high-def clarity.

He was panicking.

Of course he was.

She moved fast. "I'm coming, hang on." She reached him in three determined strides, settled her hand on his shoulder, and ignored the way he flinched. "Just hold on, let me find something to cut the ties."

"That won't be necessary," a voice said from across the room.

Cooper glanced up to find a man standing in the open French doors, two bottles of water in hand. Mid-fifties and fit, he was tan, and his hair and beard were a salt-and-pepper set. None of this made any sense—the house, the man. None of it felt threatening and all of it set her nerves on edge.

"As I told Mr. Bennett, we'll remove the restraints if he'll simply calm down."

Cooper slid her gaze from the middle-aged man to the one lingering in the corner. Compact—he couldn't have been over five ten—but densely built, he stood near the door in tactical pants and a t-shirt, a gun at one hip and a radio at the other.

"Cut me loose, you fuck, and I'll show you calm," Will wheezed.

"I'm Dr. Mitchell," the middle-aged man started, "and this is Vargas. If you'll just—"

"He's not going to calm down while he's tied to the damn chair," Cooper snapped.

On an aggrieved sigh, Dr. Mitchell set down the water bottles. "This isn't productive," he told Vargas. "He's one man. I assume you can manage that."

"Fine." Vargas pulled a folded knife from his pocket and Cooper put herself between him and Will.

"There's no need for that." Vargas extended the knife to her, still folded and handle out. "But do see to it that Mr. Bennett doesn't do anything drastic."

Cooper didn't hesitate. Just snatched the knife from his hand and hurried back to Will.

"Hold still, okay?" She braced her hand on his knee and slipped the blade between the ties and his ankles, freeing his legs. "Two more. Just breathe."

He shuddered beneath the palm she settled on his shoulder.

"Just hang on." His hands were red and angry, the zip ties brutally tight, but she carefully worked her blade between skin and plastic. When the last one gave way, Will sprang from the chair, knocking it over with a heavy *thunk*.

"Who are you?" he snarled, pushing Cooper behind him and backing them toward the open arches.

Cooper glanced over the rail. Fifty feet up. Jagged rocks below. If Will wanted out of here, they weren't going that way. "Hey," she said, softly settling the flat of her palm between his shoulders.

He glanced back at her. "You okay?"

"I'm fine." *And so are you.* She didn't say it, didn't want to call any more attention to just how hard this had been on him, how much it had stressed him. Instead, she rubbed her hand up and down his back and waited for him to settle.

When he took his first full, slow breath, she stepped out from behind him and settled in next to him.

"How did we get here?" she asked Dr. Mitchell but kept her eyes on Vargas.

Mitchell sighed. "Atlantic I & I is very . . . diligent in their security protocols, I'm afraid. They insisted on the ambush and the knockout gas. For my protection," he added, as if that helped.

"You couldn't have just black-bagged us or, I don't know, asked politely?" Cooper snapped, watching as Will rubbed circulation back into his wrists. Though to be fair, that wouldn't have been any less stressful for him. "Was all of this really necessary? Atlantic *gave* us your coordinates."

"Yes, we did," Vargas said. "Over the phone. Without oversight—"

"But after multiple levels of authentication!" Will stepped forward on a snarl, and Vargas snapped to attention, his hand hovering over his pistol.

"We don't take chances with our clients, Mr. Bennett. We had no way to ensure you wouldn't be compromised or followed." Vargas widened his stance but didn't move from the corner of the room. "Our methods, while uncomfortable for you, were necessary for Dr. Mitchell's safety."

"Where are we?" Cooper asked. "It's not the coordinates you gave us—I checked satellite imagery of that stretch of coastline. An estate this size would have shown up."

"Not in any database you'd have had access to," Vargas assured her. "But you aren't far."

"Why the blind arrival? Our instructions indicated Mitchell would be moved anyway—"

"Mitchell will be relocated, but this estate will not. Maintaining its secrecy maintains its usefulness. But that's not what you came here to discuss," Vargas said, what little patience he'd had for her questions hardening like cold tree sap. "Your pickup has been removed and your things collected—when you've got what you came for, we'll deliver you safely to Puerto Limón."

"Where's my pack?" It hadn't been her first concern, but now that things began to settle, and adrenaline began to ebb, Cooper felt the loss of her rifle.

"Safe, as are you," Vargas explained.

"Yeah, I feel real fuckin' safe." Will jerked his head toward the pistol at Vargas's side.

"Your *feelings* are inconsequential. You are safe—Mr. Harrigan's contract with Atlantic Insurance & Investments guarantees it. As I've said, we will leave you at your truck when our business is concluded."

Will's body went tight, and he clenched his fists. Cooper slipped her fingers over the back of his hand, lacing them with his when he relaxed. She got it. Fear and adrenaline and bad memories were riding him to the edge of panic and anger was an easier emotion.

But one he couldn't indulge in. Not right now.

"Fine," Will said, loosening his stance. "Let's start there. How'd a guy like Felix Harrigan manage to set up all of this?"

"Mr. Harrigan inherited his grandfather's account with our firm—we were only too happy to accommodate his request."

Will shook his head. "That doesn't square up. Felix was from the bad side of Boston—"

Vargas barked out a laugh. "Is that what he told you?"

"He had the accent to prove it."

"Mr. Harrigan's father was, indeed, from South Boston. His mother, however, was Rebecca Gershwin."

"And?" Will asked.

"*General* Gershwin's daughter."

"Wait—as in the former vice chairman of the Joint Chiefs of Staff? *That* General Gershwin?" Cooper asked.

"The same," Vargas confirmed. "The Gershwins are an old family, and they've had an account with us for a number of years."

Yeah, the guy said years, but Cooper heard decades. But she tamped down on the questions. AI&I wasn't what had brought her here.

Next to her, Will shifted and rubbed a hand over his beard. "He led me to believe he was poor. Used to tell me stories about the old neighborhood . . ." Hurt added depth to toneless words and Cooper reminded herself that this man, this brave, selfless, resilient man, couldn't take any more lies or betrayals.

"Not untrue," Vargas admitted. "His mother was disowned for the marriage. It wasn't until General Gershwin passed several years ago that Mr. Harrigan would have received his inheritance —and his grandfather's account with us."

Will visibly relaxed, even as Vargas stepped away from the wall. "But again, it appears we've gotten off track. Come inside. Sit down and ask your questions."

She glanced at Will, who shrugged, then followed her toward the door.

"Please, have some water," Mitchell said, gesturing to the bottles he'd set on a side table. "I know the knockout gas must have left you dehydrated."

Cooper picked up a bottle, handed it back to Will, then screwed off the top of her own. She followed Mitchell into a sprawling living area and through to a dining room and a table laden with food.

"Help yourself," Mitchell said, taking a seat on the other side. He sipped from a glass of orange juice, condensation beading and slipping down the side, then asked, "Where would you like to start?"

"I . . ." It should have been an easy question. Everything, *everything* had led to this moment. Cole's attack. Eighteen months on the run. Every contract hit she'd accepted just so she could keep going, keep searching. For this. For answers. A laugh that tasted like bile bubbled up her throat and with it, one question rose above the rest.

"Why?"

Mitchell set his glass down with a chuckle. "How banal—money, of course. And power, I suppose, though really those are often one and the same."

"No." Cooper cut him off with a quick jerk of her head. "Why *Cole*?" She'd always wondered—of all the teams in the CIA, why them? Had it just been their shit luck that they'd been singled out? Or had Cole volunteered for something she hadn't known about?

"I'm afraid you'll need to be more specific."

"Why was Cole selected—"

"I'm afraid I don't remember most names—far too many to keep track of—and my files are stripped of identifying details like names and social security numbers. I'll need you to be specific—which testing group was your friend a part of?"

Cooper gripped the back of a heavy, carved chair. "There was more than one?"

Mitchell had the audacity to laugh. "Dozens. Endless applications meant endless studies—your friend Cole is merely the tip of the iceberg." He speared a piece of melon as if he hadn't just admitted to large-scale illegal medical testing. "But I'm curious if he, like your friend there," he said, tipping his head toward Will, "was one of mine."

"One of yours?" she asked, her voice distant and hollow as she slowly turned her head toward Will, her brain whirring to keep pace.

"What are you talking about?" Will asked, the blood draining from his face.

Mitchell laughed. "I don't know why, but I expected you two would have put more of this together." He turned his dark brown gaze on Will. "Didn't you wonder why Harrigan was killed? Why Miss Reed was ordered to take out an entire team?"

"I was told they were selling state secrets," Cooper said quietly. "But they'd actually discovered what you were doing. They were going to expose the experiments."

"Yes, and you were used to prevent that from happening." Mitchell paused, his eyes studying her as if he were waiting for a question or realization. When it didn't come, he continued. "Killing that team was neatly done—the CIA prevented the leak and destroyed the evidence in one fell swoop."

"What evidence?" Will ground out. "And what does that have to do with me?"

"Blood work, obviously. Living tissue samples." Mitchell waved his hand dismissively. "Oh, nothing that would appear on a standard test, but if someone was *looking* for something? A single vial of blood from any of those men could have exposed everything." Mitchell studied Will, ran his assessing gaze over every inch of his face, then down his body. "You were part of a different testing group, and so far as the CIA knew, ignorant of the trials." Mitchell shrugged. "At the outset, the CIA took a more conservative approach to cleaning up that mess. It wasn't until later that the program was ordered fully shut down and dismantled, all participants either placed under surveillance or scrubbed entirely."

"Conservative?" Cooper choked out. "I was used to kill an entire team of men and you call that conservative?"

"A half-dozen people versus nearly fourteen hundred program participants? Yes. I'd call that conservative." He rolled his eyes. "Not all of them were ordered destroyed—"

"You're not talking about tissue samples and test results," Cooper snarled. "You're talking about people."

"All the same." Mitchell inclined his head. "Once the CIA realized their program had been compromised, they went about systematically destroying the evidence—and ensuring that people like me couldn't blow the whistle. When I ran, I never expected to get another program update, let alone see the results of three years of study. Yet here you are, Mr. Bennett. I'd recognize my work anywhere."

"What did you do?" he asked, his voice so cold and sharp that Vargas moved farther into the room.

"Nothing you shouldn't be thanking me for." He chuckled. "Did you really believe that you survived a year in captivity on strength of will alone?" Mitchell shook his head.

"How did you—"

"Please." Mitchell waved him off. "Vargas was very thorough —not much slips past AI&I, as I'm sure you've realized. I know a great deal about you, Mr. Bennett, though there was less to find on you, Miss Reed, outside of your indiscretion in Afghanistan, of course." He grinned at her, as if that were some sort of accomplishment, then turned back to Will. "How many times were you tortured? Beaten? How many times did infection set in and fever take over?"

A muscle ticked in Will's jaw, and Cooper could practically hear him grind his teeth.

"Once or twice."

A smile curled the edge of Mitchell's mouth. "More than that, I'd bet. Based on what I've heard, exposure alone should have killed you. Jungle rot should have taken more than that ear," he said, nodding toward the side of Will's head. "How many times were you at death's door? How many times did a fever sweep through your body?" His voice turned serious. "It burned hotter, didn't it? Longer."

"You did that," Will realized aloud.

"Yes. We delivered a genetically modified serum as part of a standard round of vaccines. A relatively simple modification to your immune system, at the end of the day. You recover quickly and can subsist on less." Again, Mitchell ran an assessing gaze over Will's body. "A year in captivity—you should be more than half starved. But already you're bouncing back. Putting on muscle. When was the last fever?" he asked, his tone pure scientific curiosity. When Will didn't answer, he guessed. "Days, I'd bet. A week or two at most. Quite remarkable, even if it is self-congratulatory to say."

"You had no right!" Will shouted.

"And yet, here you are. Alive and healthy because of it. Any tedious questions you have about the trial itself are in the files I'll provide you. So let's move on, shall we?" As if entirely oblivious to Will's seething rage, Mitchell turned to Cooper. "I only oversaw a handful of the trials—which program was Cole a part of?"

Cooper glanced at Will, but when he just jerked his head in a nod, she said, "I only know the basics. It involved scopolamine and—"

"Ah, yes." He pulled a laptop from the seat next to him and opened the lid. "One of the obedience studies."

"He's not a dog," Will snapped, jerking a chair away from the table and then collapsing into it. "Or some beast for you to train and command at will."

Mitchell's gaze never left the screen. "Of course he was. You all are," he corrected, his fingers flying over the keys. "The military's elite. Their dogs of war—something I believe your kind take pride in." He stopped typing and a slick, oily smile cut a line through his face. "Tell me, Mr. Bennett. How many men and women do you think *volunteered* for our trials? Fifty percent? Sixty?"

"You had volunteers?" Cooper whispered.

Mitchell shot her a strange look. "Of course, though they all thought the program was sanctioned and classified. And who could blame them? It's what we all want, isn't it? To be special, exceptional even. To be the very best at what we do—" he cut his gaze to Will—"isn't that what drove you into Delta? Or Miss Reed into sniper school? Everyone wants an edge, and most are willing to gamble to get it. Even with their lives."

Mitchell grinned. "Now, give me the details on your friend Cole. These files are redacted for personal information, but of the few dozen participants in this particular study, we should be able to narrow it down. Blood type?" he asked.

"O negative," Cooper supplied, and Mitchell narrowed the search.

"Height?"

"Six-one."

"Hair and eye color?"

"Brown and brown." It hurt, summing Cole up in body parts and blood type. As if he were nothing more than a lab rat, barely distinguishable from all the rest.

He was so much more. To her. To his friends. To his family— a wife who loved him and a daughter who probably didn't remember him.

"Age?"

"Thirty-two."

"And voila," Mitchell said with a final keystroke. "Patient A-46971. Part of our cognitive programing trial."

"She asked you a question," Will reminded him on a snarl. "Why was Cole chosen?"

Mitchell glanced up from the computer. "I'm reviewing the patient history—"

"He wasn't a patient! Or your personal fucking science project!" *Is. Present tense*, she reminded herself. Cole wasn't dead or gone or forgotten. He still had a life and a future. "He's a person and he didn't ask for this."

"No," Dr. Mitchell agreed. "He didn't."

Coop let out a ragged sigh. Will reached for her, lacing their fingers together beneath the table.

"The goal for this particular trial was to decrease distractions in the field," Mitchell explained.

"Distractions," Cooper repeated woodenly.

"Too often missions are compromised by personal feelings or morals. Even loyalty between team members can become detrimental to the overall objective—"

"That's crap," Will said. "Spec ops teams rely on loyalty to get the job done. Knowing the guy in front of you would take a bullet, that the guy behind you would fall on a grenade—it's everything."

"A strength to be sure," Mitchell agreed. "And a hindrance, too. Tell me, Mr. Bennett, how, exactly, did you end up a captive of one Colombia's most infamous cartels?"

Beside her, Will went stock-still, anger hardening every muscle.

"You were captured on a mission, were you not? A raid against a Vega compound, if I have my facts right."

A muscle jumped in his neck, but Will nodded.

"Let me guess—altruism, loyalty, *brotherhood*," Mitchell all but sneered the words. "A gambling man would lay odds that at least one of those things led to your capture."

Cooper glanced at Will, rubbed her thumb over the back of his hand.

"We had a man down."

"And you stayed behind," Mitchell crowed. "Compromising both yourself and the mission. Now tell me, Mr. Bennett, do you have any idea what it costs to train a man such as yourself? No? How about a SEAL? Or a sniper?" He nodded at Cooper. "Millions, in case you were wondering. Which makes men and women like you one of our military's most valuable commodities. Expensive to train. Devastating to lose. And do you know why?" He sat back, his finger stroking the edge of his laptop. "Because men like you are *rare*. Not every recruit will qualify for specialized training. Even fewer will make it through the course itself." He turned his gaze to Cooper. "How many people were in your class at sniper school?"

"Forty-three," she admitted.

"And how many graduated?"

"Five," she whispered. It was a number she'd once been so damn proud of. Now it tasted like ash in her mouth.

"The trials aimed to triple that. To take the people who had the raw potential for greatness and refine them into something *more*."

"But Cole had already graduated sniper school. He already *was* on the cutting edge of our profession."

"And yet, he had a history of disobeying orders, didn't he?"

Air went thick and heavy and poisonous in her lungs. *No.*

"The goal for this particular trial was always two-fold. First, to increase the number of Special Forces candidates and ultimately broaden the pool of assets—"

"People, you son of a bitch," Will snarled. "They are people."

"To you, maybe, but to the men in Washington making minute-to-minute decisions? You're just names on a list and pawns on a board. Assets and weapons to be leveraged in the war against whichever backwater nation is uppity this week." Mitchell tittered, as if she and Will were painfully naive. "A valuable asset, to be sure, as all rare things are."

"And the second goal of the trial?" Cooper asked, though she suspected she already knew.

"Obedience," Mitchell said on a shrug. "Single-minded devotion to the mission. No guilt or remorse or inconvenient sense of conscience." He met her gaze head-on. "Tell me—how many times did you hesitate before pulling that trigger? How many times did you wonder if the person at the other end of your scope *deserved* the fate you were meting out?"

Cooper glanced away from his assessing gaze and pulled her hand, which had gone cold and slick with sweat, from Will's.

She'd wondered. But rarely, and only after she'd pulled the trigger and completed the mission. For so long she'd considered her ability to compartmentalize a strength. But maybe if she'd courted doubt, maybe if she'd had a fucking conscience, maybe, just maybe, a team of good, decent men wouldn't be dead.

She turned her gaze back to Mitchell and found him studying her with a small smile. "Don't let it bother you, Miss Reed. Your devotion to the job does you credit and makes for a fascinating psychological profile. It was, however, a trait your partner didn't share."

"What are you saying?" Will asked. "That you chose Cole because of the occasional misgiving? We all have those. We all work around them." As if he'd read her mind, Will glanced at her. "Before the kill or after, we *all* wonder if we did the right thing, Cooper."

"And how much easier would your job be if you never had to?" Mitchell asked. "You've seen the darker side of progress, Miss Reed, and for that, I'm sorry. But what about all of the positive implications?"

She choked on a laugh. "There's no upside to *mind control*."

"Then you lack imagination." Mitchell speared another piece of melon, chewed, then said, "Human genome mapping isn't new. The last two decades have been nothing short of groundbreaking when it comes to identifying genetic markers, isolating the diseases and disabilities they cause, and finding new ways of treating them. But very little of that science has been applied to the brain."

"For good reason," Will ground out. "You're playing with people's identities. And for what?"

"How about a cure for PTSD?" Mitchell asked, raising an eyebrow. "Or simply the ability to prevent it in the first place?"

Will sat back as if he'd been shoved.

"How many of your friends have struggled post-deployment? With guilt. With depression. With anxiety. How many have contemplated suicide?" Mitchell asked. "Those are your *brothers*, Mr. Bennett. So I ask you—how far does your loyalty extend to *them*? What price would you pay to see them happy, whole, and healthy?" He smiled as if he'd caught Will in a trap of his own principles.

"These trials? They could provide the answers to all of that and more. Dementia? Gone. Alzheimer's? Eliminated. Traumatic brain injuries? Cured."

Mitchell sighed as if he were explaining something very simple to someone very stupid.

"It won't be the first advancement, medical or otherwise, funded through black-market channels. Profit drives progress, and altruism comes last. Always has, always will."

Mitchell put his fork down and sat back. "According to Cole's file and the case history, there was a commercial buyer lined up to license the technology. But they wanted proof of concept." He stared at Cooper. "You're a smart woman, Miss Reed. Tell me, why, out of all the program candidates, was your partner singled out?"

She didn't need to think it through. From the moment Mitchell had referenced Cole's disobedience in the field, she'd *known*.

"Because of me," she whispered, her voice rough and broken.

Will snapped his head around to stare at her. He hadn't pieced it together yet, but he would.

"They wanted to prove the technology would work on

anyone," Cooper continued. "That even the most loyal, the most independent, could be brought to heel," she said, her voice trailing off. She took a breath and forced herself to voice the truth. "Because Cole was formally written up for disobeying orders and saving my life."

"Yes," Mitchell agreed. "He was. His actions, while heroic, made him a target."

Tears stung the back of her eyes and her nails bit into the flesh of her palms. Not once had it occurred to Cooper that it might be *her* fault. She couldn't force anything else past her lips, but Mitchell stepped in to finish it.

"If Cole could be ordered to kill you—his best friend, his partner, the person on this planet he was *most* loyal to—well, I'd say that amounted to far more than just proof of concept, wouldn't you?"

"You're a smug son of a bitch, you know that?" Will raged. "You stripped away every good, decent thing about that man and you're *proud* of it."

"I did no such thing—I wasn't even assigned to this trial." Mitchell reviewed his notes. "According to records, Cole was a phase-one participant. There were . . . complications with that testing pool."

Cooper didn't want to hear another word about trials or test subjects or the costs and benefits of results.

"How do I fix it?" she asked, her voice hot and her anger building.

"Fix it?" Mitchell cocked his head to the side, as if the question had completely caught him off guard.

"Cole was ordered to kill me. As you can clearly see," she hissed, "I'm not dead and he hasn't stopped trying."

"Nor will he. Phase one, while a success on paper, resulted in setbacks. Subjects became too single-minded, too adhered to their orders. There was no room for real-time problem-solving or flexibility in the field. Attempts to course correct failed rather spec-tacularly, I'm afraid."

"What does that mean?" Will snapped.

"Once programed and given a mission, subjects failed to thrive unless they were able to complete their assignment. If their purpose was frustrated long enough or rendered impossible, depression set in and suicide inevitably followed. Lost causes, I'm afraid," Mitchell said, a frown crossing his face as he reviewed the files. "A terrible blow to the study, but one that was corrected for phase two."

"And the subjects who completed their mission?"

Will snapped his gaze back to her. "That's not a goddamned option, Cooper!"

He reached for her, but she pulled away. She couldn't let him touch her. Not now. Not when she had to steel herself against the very real possibility that this was her fault . . . and that saving Cole might mean sacrificing herself.

Mitchell shrugged. "Fifty-fifty outcomes for phase-one partic-ipants. Half successfully reacclimated to everyday life."

"And the other half?" she asked.

"Failed to thrive."

"Cooper, whatever you're thinking, stop it. This isn't your fault—"

"It is." She stood and pushed away from the table, her mind racing with answers she'd been so desperate to have and only now realized she didn't want. "I'm the reason they chose him. He disobeyed orders and risked his life to save mine. Do you really expect me to do anything less?"

"It's not the same thing!" Will stood and stalked toward her. When she went to turn away, he gripped her by the shoulders. "He risked his life for you, yes. But you're talking about trading your life for his—it's not even close to the same," he repeated and brushed his thumb across her cheek, then cupped her face in his hands. "Cooper. He wouldn't want this. And he'd never, never find a way to live with it. Not without hating you. Not without hating himself."

Will was right, and Cooper knew it. Cole would never expect this of her, and even if it set him free, even if he lived a long life, he'd go to his grave hating them both.

It was just one shitty choice after another. When would it all end?

"There has to be something else," Will said, turning back to stare at Mitchell. "You said phase two was a success—"

"Because the protocol was changed. The drugs, the genetic modification and mapping—all different from the outset, none of which helps Cole."

Will reached for her, and this time, Cooper let him pull her close. What could the weakness hurt when everything else was an agony?

"There has to be something."

Mitchell shrugged. "Perhaps. But you'd need far more than what's in these files."

Hope, like a determined weed, pushed through the cracks of Cooper's grief.

"What?" she asked, her voice raw and desperate. "What else?"

"Extensive lab work. Blood work and tissue samples that pre-date the trials. A complete genetic mapping of both before and after the tests. Heart bypass and multiple transfusions to cleanse his blood and keep his body from replicating the same altered cells. And you'd need someone with the ability to reverse engineer both the delivery system—genetically typed and modified scopolamine—and the target-specific mapping they used on your partner."

"Then it's possible."

"Miracles are *possible*, Mr. Bennett. As is winning the lottery. And both are more likely than what you're proposing."

"Because of the pre-trial lab work."

Mitchell laughed. "My dear, that's simply the hill before the mountain. Everything is stored in a lab in Mexico City. Blood work, biopsies, tissue samples, genetic mapping, and personalized, coded trials for every single program participant. It's a treasure trove of proof and a literal, step-by-step map of what was done to each subject."

"Then what's the issue? Access?" Cooper asked.

"Please. Easily solved if you're willing to get your hands dirty."

"What the fuck does that mean?" Will snarled.

"Blackmail, Mr. Bennett. I can promise you, all it will take is the threat of exposure and the laboratory director will be falling all over himself to assist you." Mitchell's smile turned condescending. "Human experimentation is quite illegal—violates a number of international treaties, I believe. The mere implication of knowledge let alone involvement could ruin the most pristine of reputations. I know the man in charge of that lab—trust me when I say that after greed, his greatest strength lies in his sense of self preservation."

"I want contact details," Cooper snapped.

Mitchell nodded, scribbled something on a notepad. "The laboratory in Mexico City and my contact there," he said as he handed over the sheet of paper. He shut the lid of his laptop.

"What else do we need?" Cooper asked.

"The original geneticist and access to the computer program she used to build out the mapping algorithm she developed. Without her, you cannot hope to reverse engineer the delivery system or walk back the genetic modifications."

"Where do we find her?" Cooper asked, determination settling deep in her bones.

"And there's the mountain—Dr. Olivia York disappeared nearly eight months ago while on a mission trip in the Sudan."

"Ransom?" Will asked.

"You're certainly meant to think so, but no. The CIA had her picked up and dropped into a black site."

"Why?"

"It was Dr. York's brilliant research that set all of this into motion," Mitchell explained. "An MD at twenty-two, a doctorate in genetics from MIT at twenty-five. A brilliant mind—the two of you would like her."

"I doubt it." As far as Cooper was concerned, Dr. York was as guilty as anyone.

Mitchell chuckled. "You don't know her, but I worked with her on a number of occasions. Like you, she's altruistic. More concerned with the greater good than the bottom line. And she had friends in high places—access to technology that would make your head spin."

"You'd be surprised," Will countered.

Mitchell grinned as if someone had just tipped their hand in a game they hadn't know they'd been playing. "I didn't think it would shock you, Mr. Bennett. You're well acquainted with this particular algorithm. The brain child of one Parker Livingston, if I'm not mistaken."

"Will?" Cooper turned to him.

"How do you know about that?" Will asked, ignoring Cooper's question. "That program is classified."

"And it was that secrecy that allowed Charles Brandt to turn a profit."

"Who?" Cooper asked again, confusion swirling her thoughts.

"I'm Delta," Will explained. "But I was also attached to a special task force headed up by the DoD and more specifically, Charles Brandt." He turned to her. "Black ops, Cooper. Not just classified, but completely off book. Missions backed by cutting-edge technology—a predictive program that could identify emerging threats, run complex risk assessments—"

"Or topple governments, start wars, incite riots—something Charles understood. And something he leveraged to great effect. Turned a nice little profit selling those outcomes to every warlord or corporation with deep enough pockets." Mitchell shrugged. "Before he was caught, anyway."

"It's why I was in Colombia in the first place," Will said, swallowing hard.

"And Brandt is the one who covered up your captivity," Cooper said, piecing together the pieces he'd given her with the ones she already had. "You were never supposed to be in Colombia at all."

Will jerked his head once. "But I don't see what that has to do Cole?"

"Really?" Mitchell cracked a grin. "And what if I told you that Parker Livingston and Olivia York were at MIT together?"

"They knew each other." Will ran a hand through his hair.

"Good friends, as it happens. And both brilliant minds."

"Parker gave Olivia access to his program, let her leverage the technology for her genome research," Cooper finished.

"The sharp shot has a sharper mind." Mitchell raised an eyebrow. "Dr. York used that program to redefine the landscape of modern pharmacology—her breakthroughs took her from startup to billionaire in under two years."

"If that's true then why the illegal experiments?" Will asked. "She already had more money than most people could spend in ten lifetimes."

Mitchell shook his head. "Dr. York is nothing if not committed to healing humanity's ills. She'd never contemplate, let alone authorize, human experimentation. Every dollar she earned went back into research or low-cost vaccines or simplified

AIDs tests. Profit never drove her." Mitchell sighed and shook his head as if he simply couldn't understand someone who wasn't motivated by profit margins. "Members of her board of directors, on the other hand, were far more invested in York Pharmaceutical's bottom line. How long do you think it took for one of them to figure out the source of her success?"

"How did the CIA get involved?" Cooper asked on a resigned sigh.

Mitchell shrugged. "People with money and power all tend to run in the same circles."

"You'd never get something like this past the Department of Defense. There's too many regulations. Too many laws that prevent shit like this from happening," Will said.

"True enough where the cognitive trials are concerned," Mitchell agreed. "Though how quickly do you think a defense contract could be authorized if another country—say China or Russia—deployed the technology first? The US has never been left behind in an arms race—that's not about to change. With the right motivation? Everything would have been quickly and quietly legitimized."

"Then why grab Olivia?" Cooper asked.

Mitchell rolled his eyes. "Trial data was stored on York infrastructure. It makes sense, I suppose, keeping it off government servers." He waved a hand dismissively. "Plausible deniability and all that. This country already hates corporate interests, and big pharma?" He shook his head. "I'd challenge you to find a better ready-made villain. And anyway, a company that large, it should have been easy to hide everything, but it seems Dr. York is much more hands on than anyone expected."

"She found out," Will said.

Mitchell nodded. "Redacted and encrypted *everything* and launched a thorough internal investigation. She made it quite impossible for her company to deliver on deals already struck with a number of parties." Mitchell grinned. "Those are not the sort of people you want as enemies, I can assure you."

"I want a name," Will demanded.

"Within the CIA, I don't have one to give you." Mitchell speared another piece of fruit, chewed and swallowed. "Within York Pharmaceuticals? I dealt exclusively with Gerald Reeves. He, in turn, liaised with his contact at the CIA. They had quite the lucrative arrangement going . . . until people started to piece it all together, of course." He sighed heavily, as if the loss of all those studies weighed on him. "Reeve's contact at the CIA might have been able to clean up after Mr. Harrigan and his friends relatively easily, but once Olivia became involved." He shook his head. "Another matter entirely, I'm afraid. Revoking everyone's access to those files was bold, but stupid, and it put a target on her back."

"And now Reeves is trying to force her to cooperate," Cooper finished for him. Which meant he'd hidden her well. It had taken her nearly eighteen months to get this far, how much longer would it take to find York?

"And the CIA is wiping the slate clean in the meantime—no more risks. No more leaks. No more loose ends." Mitchell stood and stretched, his back popping with the movement. "I knew when my colleagues began dying—suicides, car accidents, heart attacks—that the game was up. So when Mr. Harrigan approached me with a proposal, I agreed to disappear."

"What proposal?" Will asked.

"In exchange for answering your questions and providing all the proof you'd ever need to take down the studies, Reeves and every man in the CIA who tried to cover it up, he would use his account with AI&I to ensure I disappeared and lived out my days in the boredom that money and luxury and a new identity can provide." Mitchell glanced around the villa, as if he couldn't quite believe his luck. "I can only imagine how my disappearance has frustrated Reeves. The man never did like a job half done."

Mitchell pushed the laptop across the table. "Now, I've kept up my end of the bargain and you have all your answers."

A gunshot cracked through the room, the boom bouncing off stone and tile. Vargas hit the wall behind him with a thump, dead before his body hit the ground.

"You get what you needed?"

Cooper spun, her heart hammering in her throat, but put a hand on Will's arm when he tried to step in front of her.

Pierce strode in, his gun out and his face set. His gaze strayed from Vargas's body to Cooper's face.

"Did you get what you came for, love?" he asked.

"Yes."

"My turn, then." He pulled the trigger a second time, and a bullet tore a hole through Mitchell's face and painted the sunny yellow wall with the back of his head.

CHAPTER EIGHTEEN

"Good lord, I thought he'd never shut up," Pierce said, striding toward Vargas's prone form.

Her heart in her throat, her skin tingling with adrenaline, Cooper reminded herself to breathe. Hard to do when the echoes of the shots still rang in her ears. "Give a girl some warning, would you?"

Fucking Pierce.

It wasn't the first time he'd appeared in her life like a vengeful wraith. The fact that somewhere along the line it had become easy for her to simply ignore the dead guy on the floor said something about her and what her life had become.

She didn't plan to examine that too closely anytime soon.

"And where would be the fun in that?" Pierce asked, checking Vargas for a pulse.

She had no idea why he bothered. Pierce was an excellent shot—no way he'd miss at that distance. But he was methodical and a damn stickler for what he considered protocol.

"What are you doing here?" she asked, ignoring the way her pulse still fluttered in her neck. She knew she'd done a piss-poor job of getting her nerves under control when she jumped as Will grasped her by the elbow and guided her closer. He tried to tuck her behind him, his gaze locked on Pierce and the gun he still had in his hand.

"Soothe your gorilla, love, he looks agitated." Pierce stepped away from Vargas and holstered his weapon.

"Surprise murders have a way of doing that to people!" she snarled, then squeezed Will's arm, which was tense beneath her touch. "It's all right. I know him."

"Well I don't." He pivoted to keep her behind him.

On a huff, she gestured between them. "Will, Pierce. Pierce, Will."

"Seriously?" Will glanced back at her, his expression annoyed. "You're just going to introduce us like we're having brunch? Mimosas and a side of murder?"

She stepped away from the heat of Will's back and the protection she was grateful for but ultimately didn't need. Pierce was a lot of things—intimidating, dangerous, deadly when he wanted to be. That he'd never truly succeeded in keeping her at a distance was one of the reasons she liked him . . . and felt sorry for him. As lonely as she'd been the last eighteen months, God only knew what it was like for Pierce. Or how long he'd been on his own.

Long enough that at some point, he'd convinced himself that friends were unnecessary, loneliness comfortable, and ruthlessness a currency on which he could trade.

It would amuse him, and he'd call her a fool, but Cooper wasn't afraid of him.

"He just killed two people, Cooper," Will said.

"A great loss, I'm sure." Pierce sneered. "A doctor who uses people as lab rats and a man employed by a company that does far worse."

She sighed and rubbed her temples. She felt like she'd been

tossed in the dryer with a dozen rocks and been left to tumble dry. She didn't have it in her to take any more hits. And she didn't have the energy to go two rounds with Pierce.

"I trust him," she told Will.

"You shouldn't," Pierce offered, the warning familiar and the delivery easy. Between them, it practically passed for hello and goodbye. "And I killed nine men on this property—but who's counting?" He grinned, his deep dimples the parentheses around a mouth predisposed to stirring up trouble.

"Hello, love." He grasped her by the shoulders, pressed a quick kiss to her forehead, then leaned back and shot Will a grin. "Glad you're keeping better company these days, though I see you're still clinging to that stubborn streak." He brushed a thumb across her cheek like he was removing a smudge of soot. "It's going to get you killed one of these days."

"That a threat?" Will barked.

Pierce chuckled. "Seems you inspire what you so freely give," he said on a whisper meant only for her. "I'm rather glad. I worried, leaving you with him." That, of course, he said loud enough for Will to hear.

Cooper shrugged him off. God, he was a pain in the ass.

"I'm no threat to her," Will snarled. "Can you say the same?"

"As I continually remind your better half, everyone's a threat, Mr. Bennett—even you."

"The hell I am."

"No?" Pierce asked, and Cooper's temples turned the dial up from throbbing beat to war drum.

Great. The merc and the operative were getting ready to whip 'em out and measure.

Pierce pulled his gun and had it aimed at Will in the same breath it took Cooper to slide between them.

"Pierce," she snapped.

"See?" he said, pulling the barrel down and tucking the

Glock away again. "Dangerous. Because she cares about you. Insisted on pulling you out of Colombia when I told her to cut her losses"—he smirked—"and cut off your fingers. We'd have managed at the bank with just your prints, but oh no, she wouldn't hear of it. Ever wonder what that cost her?" Pierce asked.

Cooper cringed when Will settled both hands on her shoulders. "What's he talking about?"

She shrugged him off. "Pierce arranged an extraction—"

"She asked so nicely." He smiled.

"He's the one who treated you. He's a doctor, apparently—"

"Surgeon," Pierce corrected.

"Certainly has the ego for it," Will muttered, then turned to Pierce. "Why help her at all? You could have just said no."

"True." Pierce inclined his head. "And under different circumstances, I might have simply cut my losses. But she refused to leave you and she was still useful. So. Here we are."

"Useful?" Cooper asked woodenly, trying to force the edges of the puzzle together. She'd contacted Pierce, not the other way around. Called in her favor and finally let him off the hook.

But that didn't make her *useful.*

The tropical breeze blowing off the water turned cold. What was he doing here? What was she missing?

"Feel free to thank me." Pierce rolled his neck, the vertebrae cracking. "Saving your life was no easy thing. Not a true test of my abilities, but a welcome challenge." He tilted his chin and stared at Will. "You do look *remarkably* improved since I last saw you. Suppose that means the good doctor over there was telling the truth."

"How much did you hear?" Cooper asked.

"Enough to ensure we both got what we came for," Pierce said with a shrug. "I could afford to allow Dr. Mitchell a final confession."

"How gracious of you," Will said, his voice hard and judgmental. "It doesn't bother you at all, does it?"

"Not really," Pierce said and pulled his phone from his pocket.

"Just another day. Another kill," Will said. "How many is that? Do you even know?"

Something in Pierce changed. The muscle at his jaw flexed and his fingers twitched. He stilled, calm and cold and calculating locking over him like armor. For the first time, Cooper saw Pierce as everyone else did. Frigid. Uncompromising. *Ruthless.*

But she saw something else, too. Something that made her think he'd hardened to the point of breaking.

That one good strike to the right place would shatter him. Whether it'd set him free or tear him apart for good, she couldn't be sure.

"I remember every life I lost on my table," Pierce grudgingly admitted, his voice scalpel sharp. "And I remember the face or name of every single person I've killed since then, including the eight thugs Atlantic Insurance hired to guard Mitchell. Can you say the same?"

Behind her, Will tensed, but didn't say anything. He couldn't, and everyone in the room knew it. It was the nature of their jobs—sometimes he and Cooper had solid, detailed intelligence. And other times shit went sideways, decisions were made in seconds, and lives were lost—or saved—in heartbeats.

"The kills I made were in service of *my* goals," Pierce said, his gaze pointed. "No one else's. When I pull the trigger or bury the knife, I *know* what it's all for. If you could say the same, she'd never have had to rescue you in the first place."

"That's enough," Cooper snapped, glaring at Pierce. "And just for the record, you pompous prick, there were multiple layers of authentication at the bank. Fingerprints alone would have gotten us through the door . . . and either shot in the vault or arrested."

"What layers?" Open curiosity, there and gone just as fast, hobbled Pierce. Cooper couldn't remember a time she'd ever seen him openly *want* something. It added a dimension to him she'd sensed, but never seen the depth of.

"A token," she explained, "something we had to specifically describe and identify. Once that was authenticated, there was a story—one only Will would know—that went with it. Verification was done over the phone, but it was complex. It would have been impossible to fake."

Pierce considered her for a long moment, as if he were working out a puzzle in his head, fitting tougher pieces she'd given him with others he already had.

Nerves that had only just begun to settle flared to life again. Instinct said she was standing at the precipice of a drop into deep, still waters. She just couldn't see the edge.

"Interesting," Pierce said slowly. "Do you still have the phone number you used?"

Cooper shook her head. "Why are you here, Pierce?"

"Completing the contract I accepted on Dr. Mitchell, of course." He stepped over to Mitchell's corpse, knelt and snapped several photos at an angle that was sure to capture the man's face.

"I'd cut you in for the assistance," Pierce added as he stood, his gazed fixed on his phone, "but I'm afraid he's of little monetary value." Pierce stepped over Mitchell's corpse, then wiped the toe of his shoe against the edge of the rug, smearing it with a streak of red. "I suppose a thank you will have to suffice."

"What are you talking about?" Cooper asked, watching with no small amount of disgust as Pierce palmed a handful of grapes from the tray of fruit on the table, as if there weren't two dead men on the floor.

Pierce shot her an amused look. "You really have no idea, do you?"

"Obviously not." Cooper set her jaw and folded her arms.

"I've been searching for Mitchell for well over a year."

"To kill him."

"Yes."

"Why? You said the contract on his life wasn't worth much."

"I said it didn't have any monetary value—at least not to me." Pierce didn't do anything so common as smile or grin, but something smug and self-righteous tugged at his mouth and added depth to a face that had weathered beyond its years. "I haven't killed for anything so common as money in *years*. A three-million-dollar bounty doesn't interest me."

Jesus. No wonder security had been so tight around Mitchell. Million-dollar contracts were rare. It would be more than enough to entice the very best contractors . . . and the very worst. The sort of men who took hits for more than money. The ones who built their reputations on difficulty—or depravity.

"How long has his contract been open?" Cooper asked, because no way had the hit on Mitchell started out that high.

"Nearly two years," Pierce said. "Your friends at the CIA were rather desperate to shut him up, but I think they hoped to do so discreetly."

Which meant AI&I hadn't just hidden Mitchell, they'd practically made him disappear, and in the process elevated him to a career-making hit. Whoever made that kill would become a legend. In that world, it was a reputation that could invite challenge, but also provide a degree of protection.

Except, the man who'd made the hit was already legendary in his own right. Pierce had a Teflon-coated reputation for efficiency, accuracy, and brutal honesty. If he said he was going to do something, he did it. And he damn well expected the same of the party backing the contract.

None of which explained why he'd taken this job.

"I do hope whatever's on that computer is compelling, Cooper. Now that Mitchell's gone, focus will shift."

"What are you saying?" Will asked.

Pierce raised an eyebrow. "I should think it's obvious—Mitchell was the CIA's number one loose end. With him gone, they'll move on to number two . . ." He pinned Cooper with a hard stare. "You were merely an inconvenience, love. An annoyance, but one to be dealt with when time and resources allowed. You knew little and could prove less. You weren't a threat." He slid his gaze from her to the computer and back again. "Until now."

"I've been living under a contract for over a year. Maybe it's not worth three million dollars—"

Pierce shook his head, a laugh, low and vicious, rumbling out of his throat like a warning.

"It always amazes me, Cooper, that even after everything, you could remain so naive." His laughter died, and his expression turned sober. "It's one of the reasons I like you," he admitted, his voice edging toward something sad and resigned and layered with experience, "even though I know better. Affection only ever leads to grief, and I *would* grieve for you, Cooper, for whatever that's worth to you."

Cooper went still, and for the first time since she met him, Pierce felt every inch the lethal assassin she knew him to be. She stepped back and straight into Will, who stood behind her like a sentinel.

"I'm not here for *you*, Cooper." Pierce's eyes softened, and a line appeared between his brows.

He'd warned her, over and over and over again, not to trust him. Not to trust *anyone*. But he looked both hurt and surprised —with himself, she imagined—that for even a moment, she'd been afraid of him.

Cooper reached for Will's hand and loosely linked her fingers with his.

"I'm not here for him either," Pierce promised.

Cooper swallowed past the fear that had risen in her throat. She believed him, and yet, the anxiety remained.

"Then why are you here?" she asked.

Pierce's phone chimed, and he pulled it from his pocket. "For what I was promised," he said, staring at the screen. "For this information. For *her*."

Given his general predilection for gloating, Cooper expected a smug smile or a smart remark. Instead, Pierce's face went soft and open, his expression almost reverent, and for a split second, Cooper looked back in time. Saw the man Pierce had once been, before his life, and the cost of living it, had caught up with him.

He locked the screen, put his phone back in his pocket, and stepped right back into the role he'd carved for himself.

"As I said, thank you. I couldn't have found Mitchell without you."

"How did you find us?" Will asked, giving voice to just one of her questions.

"Tracker in her boot," Pierce said, nodding toward her left leg. "Another in your pack. One in the base of your rifle. I'm nothing if not thorough." His grin was for her, but his words were most definitely for Will. "Aren't I, love?"

The son of a bitch wore smug like a teenager who'd just discovered cologne.

"Ignore him," she told Will. "Pierce enjoys the sound of his own voice, but his ego withers without attention."

"You wound me." Pierce brought a hand to his heart.

"I doubt it," she snapped. "When did you start tracking me?"

"From the beginning, of course," he explained. "I like to keep a ready eye on my investments."

"Investments," she repeatedly hollowly, as the truth, one he'd told her often, but she'd never quite believed, crashed over her in waves. "You used me. For what? To find Mitchell? You could have done that yourself."

He laughed. "You flatter me. Atlantic Insurance hid him far too well. I could have searched for *years* and come up with nothing more than rumors and ghosts."

"But you thought I could find him?" Cooper asked. "Why? I didn't even know I was *looking* for him."

"You were my dark horse, to be sure," Pierce agreed. "It was always a long shot, but you were angry, and determined, and more than anything else, you were motivated."

Of course. Because with Pierce it *always* came back to motivation.

"I knew if I got you enough information to keep you angry, to keep you hungry, that it was possible you'd find him."

"It was a real win-win for you, wasn't it?" Will snarled. "If Cooper didn't find Mitchell, you were no worse off. And if she did, you got what you wanted without having to spend valuable time and resources looking for him yourself."

"You should keep that one," Pierce said, shooting Cooper a grin. "Lethal and smart—there are so few of us."

"You said 'got' me enough information," Cooper said, her thoughts racing as she sorted through her entire history with Pierce. "So every time you brought me a rumor or a tip, or some file you procured—"

"All thanks to your friends at the CIA. It wasn't easy, but I was able to convince my contact you were more asset than threat. It took some work—they preferred I simply put a bullet in the back of your head—but they came around. Gave me enough information to keep you going. Keep you—"

"Motivated," she finished for him.

"Yes."

"Jesus. Why didn't you just offer her up on a silver platter and save yourself the trouble?" Will stepped around Cooper, his body tense and vibrating, as if one more word, one more confession would send him over the edge.

When she glanced at Pierce, she took another step closer to that cliff herself. "Oh God—you did, didn't you?" She searched his face for a lie or regret or shame or simple shock that she'd accuse him of such a thing. Instead, she found nothing at all. "Why?"

"Did you presume to be the only one in this game who'd *lost* something?" Pierce asked, his voice tight and angry. "The only one who'd been betrayed?" He took a step toward her and stopped when Will put his arm out. "Look at how far you've gone to save a man who wants to kill you."

"He's—"

"Your friend," Pierce agreed with a nod. "I know. Now imagine he was something more. Imagine he was *everything*." Pierce stalked closer, and this time, he ignored Will's warning to stop. "Now imagine, Cooper, that someone took him from you. Permanently. Irrevocably. Brutally." He stared at her, his green eyes hardened chips of jade. "Consider everything you've done to save Cole," Pierce whispered. "And ask yourself how far you'd go to *avenge* him."

Though her heart hurt for him, she shook her head. "There are lines I won't cross, Pierce. I can't."

"I thought so, too," he said softly. "Until I'd crossed them. Until what lay beyond them was more important that what lay behind."

"I'm not you," she whispered and willed herself to believe it. That when the time came, she'd step back instead of plow forward.

"No, love," he said with a sad smile. "You're not. Go home, Cooper," he said, turning away from her. "You heard Mitchell; your friend is beyond help. Whatever's on that computer—it's enough to take down every single person responsible for what happened to Cole. What happened to you. This is your ticket home. Don't waste it."

"Would it really have been so easy for you?" she asked when he started to walk away.

Pierce turned to look at her. "Once, it would have. And that's the difference between us. If the CIA had been willing to trade this information"—he held up his phone—"for your life, I'd have struck that deal." Pierce smiled. "Lucky for us both, they simply didn't think you worth it."

"Just like that? My life for information. Like it was easy. Like I was *nothing*."

"Yes—and push come to shove, you'd have done the same."

"That's bullshit."

"Is it?" Pierce slid the phone back into his pocket. "Look at everything you've done up to this point. Every contract you accepted, every life you took—you made compromises, too. And if you don't stop, if you don't go home, you're going to keep making them." Pierce caught her gaze and held it. "Ask yourself now, while you have the time and the space to truly consider it— what are you willing to risk? What price you're willing to pay. Is it worth your life?"

Cooper set her jaw and tilted her chin. She wasn't about to answer that. Not when she didn't know herself.

And not with Will standing behind her, silent as the grave as he held his breath.

"Your life?" Pierce pushed. "I imagine you would, under the right circumstances. But that's an easy decision."

"Easier then betraying a friend."

"Is that what we are?" he asked, throwing her own words back in her face. "Then as your friend, let me ask you this: if it comes down to a choice—sacrifice one and save the other—who will you choose, Cooper?" His gaze slid from her to Will.

Cooper's blood turned to ice in her veins. Pierce wasn't talking about a choice between her life and Cole's. Oh no. He was talking about something so much worse.

"He's devoted already," Pierce whispered. "You could send him away—"

When she winced, he grinned.

"You've already tried. I wondered. He was so sick, and you were so very worried. And yet there he is." Pierce cut a glance in Will's direction but kept his words between them. "The way he looks at you . . . I'd be happy for you, if I wasn't so damn worried it'll destroy you," Pierce said, searching her face, though for what, Cooper wasn't sure. "He's going to follow you into the very depths of hell, love. You can't stop him. So the question is—can you protect him?"

Because terror had gripped her by the throat and stolen the declarations and denials she so desperately reached for, she fell back on anger instead.

"I hope you find what you're looking for," she snapped. "And I hope it's worth every price you pay along the way."

"Judgmental isn't a shade you wear well, love." If the words struck him or hurt him, it didn't show. "I've made my choices. I'll find a way to live with them." He stroked his thumb across her cheek. "I'd have found a way to live with killing you, too. I'd have been sorry—more than you'll ever know—but I'd have done it."

"I don't believe you."

"No, I can see that you don't." His smile was sad and resigned. "I don't know why, but I find myself glad." He turned to Will and handed over two sets of keys. "Take one of the ATVs into town—just turn right when you exit the property. It's ten miles. You'll find your truck parked near the marina."

Will nodded, his jaw set against anything he might have said.

"What will you do next?" she asked as she grabbed the laptop from the table.

"Me? I'm going to send my regards to Atlantic Insurance and burn this place to the ground."

He grinned, mischief and pleasure bringing forth a man Cooper wished she'd have known. "Keep an eye on this one," he told Will as they headed out the door. "She's prone to bouts of altruism." He paused, and Cooper heard the farewell Pierce didn't say. "I should know—it saved my life."

CHAPTER NINETEEN

The truth, laid out in black and white, was stark. Uncompromising. Brutal.

Mitchell's words had hit Will like a sucker punch.

I'd recognize my work anywhere.

Will had believed him, if only because Mitchell had been so fucking nonchalant about the admission. But in the moment, it had felt like little more than a glancing blow. A cheap shot designed less for impact and more to keep him off balance. And it had worked. Will's head had spun with implications before sliding right into the next horrifying realization.

And there'd been so many.

The depth and breadth of the testing.

Why Cole had been chosen in the first place.

Their best shot at saving him, though as far as Will was concerned it wasn't an option—good, bad, or otherwise.

Then Pierce had walked in with a muddled accent and too-familiar stares and disposed of Mitchell.

Will wasn't sure what rankled more—that Pierce had so casually done what Will had itched to do, or that Pierce had taken such glee in ensuring Will understood just how well he knew Cooper. There'd been intimacy between them and, as a result, he'd watched as Cooper had struggled with both hurt and betrayal.

All while Will had struggled with something so petty as possessive jealousy.

It had made for an exhausting day and a silent drive into town. That silence, charged and thick and unwelcome, had been an invisible but immovable barrier between Will and Cooper.

And it had kept him from thinking too long or too hard about what Mitchell had revealed about *him*.

But now, tucked away in a tiny villa that hugged the rocky coast, ocean breeze sliding through screened-in windows, a half-finished beer at his elbow, Will couldn't avoid it anymore.

I'd recognize my work anywhere.

He snapped the laptop shut, eliminating the glow of the screen and throwing the room into darkness. He'd read through file after file. He knew what they said. What had been done. Why he'd lived.

And for the first time, he had an idea of how many others had *not*.

In the distance, waves rolled ashore in time with the roar of the blood in his ears.

Cooper pushed away from the door that led to the veranda and the still night air.

"Want to talk about it?" she asked as she joined him at the table.

He shook his head and watched as she palmed his beer and took a long drink.

She sat on a sigh, her fingers mindlessly picking at the label he'd half peeled away an hour ago and stared at him with that guarded blue gaze. "Might help."

A thousand thoughts fought for dominance and a hundred

emotions plucked at his insides. He didn't know what to say. Or at least, didn't know how to say it to *her*. If everything Mitchell had said was true, and everything in the files he'd read was right, then that secret clinical trial was the only reason he'd made it this far.

"I should have died," he offered up as he thought back to the half-dozen times he'd been sure he would. What he'd been told was a simple round of vaccines—common to soldiers deploying overseas—had actually been so much more. They'd heightened his immune system. Strengthened his ability to recover. Enabled him to bounce back faster and stronger.

But for every file that confirmed his salvation, there'd been two more that painted a picture of destruction. He'd gotten lucky.

"Only reason I'm here is because—"

"Because you fought," Cooper finished for him. "Because you didn't quit. Because you refused to break. Maybe the drugs helped, maybe they made you more resilient, less susceptible to infection. And yeah, maybe they saved your life. But to say they are the *only* reason you're here?" She sat back on a shrug. "It's bullshit and you know it. Surviving what you did—that's a testament to strength and endurance that goes so far beyond the physical."

"Maybe," he hedged, dipping his head in agreement.

And what right did he have to complain when it could have been so much worse? When he could have been part of the cognitive reprograming trials. The one that had snared Cole had been the worst, the most invasive and debilitating, but hardly the only.

Felix had been a part of another—one that lowered inhibitions and obliterated caution. They'd wanted fearless soldiers, but in dozens of cases had ended up with men addicted to adrenaline and thrill seeking. And that testing pool had been huge. Big enough that when men started dying in pursuit of that rush, people noticed. Tried to help.

Reckless and unnecessary deaths—one guy had even tossed his chute out of a plane and followed after it—had led to questions. And those questions had, eventually, led to answers.

Answers that had sent Cooper to kill six good men, and all because they cared.

Answers that he didn't want to believe. He might have clung to that, too. Dismissed words like CRISPR and genetic modifications and bio-hacking as the stuff of science fiction. Implausible, if he were feeling generous.

Except, this wasn't Will's first brush with advanced technology. And though Parker's name wasn't anywhere in these files, his fingerprints were all over them.

Predictive analytics indicate a ninety percent success rate with group B.

After running the gene sequence and drug protocol through the predictive analysis . . .

When patient histories were filtered through the algorithm, failure to thrive was the predicted outcome for seventy-five percent of patients weaned off . . .

It wasn't the first time Parker's program had come up, either. Cooper had mentioned it before they ever even made it to the bank. And Mitchell had known about it—well enough to taunt Will with it.

So no, he couldn't dismiss any of this. Which meant he had one more thing he had to find a way to live with.

Will clenched his fist and fought back at the urge to send the computer flying. To pluck that bottle from Cooper's hand and send it sailing toward the wall.

Gentle fingers touched his.

"You can talk to me," Cooper assured him, her touch light and her gaze heavy.

"Not sure what to say," he admitted on a sigh. "Not really even sure how I feel."

"Angry?" she asked, sitting back in her chair.

He shook his head, then paused and really thought about it. "Maybe a little. Betrayed, too. That this was done *to* me. Without my knowledge or consent." That someone he trusted, someone he'd counted as friend, had done this to him. Inadvertently or otherwise. "I thought I was done with all that," he whispered.

"What do you mean?" she asked, the gentle hum, buzz, pop of tropical insects filling the silence that stretched between them.

"Done being at someone else's mercy. Done with wondering 'what next.' Just . . . done." He sighed, exhaustion catching up with him and stretching his muscles like sun-warm taffy. "I know that it happened long before Colombia, but . . ."

"But it doesn't feel that way."

"No."

"It feels like another nightmare. Another 'thing' that's behind you, but still there, still lurking. Just one more thing that someone else did to you, and that you now have to learn to live with. It isn't fair," she whispered, squeezing his hand. "And you have every right to be angry."

The kindness in her touch, the compassion in her eyes, and the conviction in her words cut to the very heart of it all.

"Do I?" He stood and paced away from the table and toward the door, fresh air, and the endless expanse of ocean that lay beyond fifty yards of sand. He glanced over his shoulder, found Cooper where he'd left her, beer bottle in hand, shadows blurring her just enough that the words came easily. "That drug trial saved my life."

"It didn't give them the right," she snapped out.

"How can I be angry when—" When it could have been so much worse. When it could have been his mind, instead of his body, that they'd fucked with.

What right did he have to be angry or bitter or betrayed when his friends had *died*? When Cole was still out there somewhere, fighting to complete a mission he hadn't chosen and wouldn't believe in?

Will glanced down when Cooper's warm heat appeared at his side. She didn't touch him, didn't reach for him, just settled in next to him, a steady, uncompromising presence he could so easily come to rely on. Had she been naked, her arms around his waist, her body plastered to his, it could not have been more intimate.

Or more comforting.

"Why did they choose Cole, instead of me?" she asked, her voice small and thin. "Of the two of us, I was the more stubborn, the more likely to question orders, the more likely to improvise in the field. So why not me?"

Will sucked in a breath of a fragrant air. The very idea was nauseating. He'd seen Cole. Looked him in the eye as they'd fought. There'd been *nothing* there. No rage. No determination. No cocksure arrogance. Just a bland sense of resolve. Lifeless, even as he'd put a gun to his best friend's head.

Will hadn't thought anything could make that image worse. But picturing Cooper in Cole's role—that did it.

He slid his hand down her forearm, let his fingers wrap around her wrist, pressed his thumb to the pulse he found there, and counted in time with the beat of her heart.

Cooper was so very much alive. Aggressively. Unapologetically. Enthusiastic in every single thing she did. The idea that someone could take that from her, take her smiles—the ones that cut him down and built him up—or promises—the ones that guaranteed painful retribution or lazy pleasure—Will couldn't, wouldn't fathom it. Didn't want any version of her that wasn't completely compelling in its complexity.

"I'm glad it wasn't you, Coop." And if that made him a selfish bastard then he'd find a way to live with that, too.

"So am I," she said, turning her wrist so she could lace their fingers together. "Does that make me terrible?"

Will turned, his free hand automatically coming to her cheek to caress, to comfort. When he gazed down into that upturned face, he expected to find sorrow or guilt or fear. Instead, he found wide eyes that sparkled and a mouth that threatened to smile.

She'd led him straight into her crosshairs, and as he was beginning to suspect he always would, he'd gone readily. Willingly.

"I'm glad it wasn't *you*, too," she said, her free hand coming up to grip his wrist the way he held hers, her thumb brushing against his pulse. "I hate what happened to Cole." Her voice bottomed out into something slow and deep, her drawl tinging the ends of her words. "I don't think . . ." She swallowed and tried again. "It's so much worse than I—"

Will pulled her close and hushed her. Cole was already gone, and all that was left was for Cooper to grieve the loss of her friend and shoulder the weight of her failure. If she let him, he'd help her carry that weight for as long as it took to simply become part of her.

"I'm angry. So, so angry," she admitted then pulled away to stare up at him. "But I'm so *fucking* grateful, too. Because you're here." She dragged her knuckles up the length of his abs. "You make me think about after. About what comes next. About family barbecues and lazy days at the lake. I haven't let myself think like that in a long damn time."

"Those the only thoughts I inspire?" he asked, a wry grin tugging at his mouth.

"The only ones worth mentioning."

"I'll have to work on that." He dragged the pad of his thumb across her bottom lip and watched when her mouth dropped open on a sigh. She closed her eyes and took a breath. When she opened them again, the indulgence was gone, and that strength he admired so damn much was back.

"My life would have been so much less without you in it," she said. "But I wouldn't wish you alive at Cole's expense, Will. I couldn't."

She shook her head when he went to assure her, to say that he understood, that he'd never ask.

"But neither would I wish him here and whole and healthy if it meant that you'd died, tired and alone and hurting." She squeezed his hand. "I'm angry, but I'm so goddamned grateful, too. One does not cancel out the other." She pulled away, taking her heat but leaving her conviction. "You can be furious that you were used, but thankful it helped you survive. Just like you can grieve your friends and be glad it wasn't you." She rocked back on her heels and shoved her hands in the back pockets of her jeans. "The bad doesn't have to taint the good, okay?"

"Okay," he agreed, surprised to find that yeah, it was. That he could feel all of it and not drown. Not when Cooper stood there, bright and steady, a personal lighthouse leading him home.

He followed her as she wandered back to the table and was struck with the realization that he could spend the rest of his life trailing in her wake.

"Did you find anything else?" she asked, diverting his thoughts before they could disappear entirely off the beaten path.

He shook his head and sat. "It's like Mitchell said. Tons of records, but they're all redacted. And the files that Felix passed on—those are encrypted."

"Any chance you speak computer?"

"Russian, yes. French, sure. Spanish and Arabic conversationally. But computers? I can turn them on and—"

"Search for porn?" she asked sweetly.

"Among other things."

"But Russian and French, those are more than just salad dressings to you, huh?"

"I think I'm hurt," he said, leaning back until his chair balanced on the rear two legs and waited for his moment. When she lifted the bottle to her lips, he said, "You thought I was all beard, brawn, and bedroom eyes?"

She snorted, then cursed, beer coming out her nose. "I hate you," she said, choking on a laugh and wiping the back of her hand across her mouth. "You did that on purpose."

"Yep," he agreed. "I do, in fact, have more than two brain cells to rub together."

"Believe it or not, you aren't the first Delta man to brag about the language component of Q Course."

"Airborne throws themselves out of planes, SEALs hold their breath, snipers pull triggers, and spotters do *math*," he said with a grin. "The minute a gorgeous girl walks in they're all squabbling, bragging, and posturing, but the guy fluent in another language? He takes her home. Every. Single. Time."

"Every time?" she asked, quirking an eyebrow.

"It's like you said—you're not looking to launch a rocket." His mouth stretched, both at the memory of her indignant rant, and the knowledge that the joke would linger between them for a long time to come.

She shrugged and took another sip of her beer, her lips quirking around the rim. "I don't know . . . I can think of at least one use for a guy who can hold his breath for minutes on end."

"You're a cruel woman, Cooper Reed."

"I took you for a man who liked a challenge, William Bennett."

"I do," he agreed, his thoughts trying to race in far more pleasant directions. He reined them in. For now.

"I can't crack the encryption, but I know a guy who can."

If he'd expected that statement to be met with enthusiastic relief, he was sorely disappointed.

"It's too dangerous." All the relaxed humor that had lit her face only moments ago flickered and died.

"He's a friend, practically a brother," Will offered when she stood, her movements mechanical and stiff as she dropped the empty bottle in the trash. "I trust him."

"You trust him," she repeated, as if the concept was something both foreign and bitter. "With your life? Because that's what we're talking about," she said, staring out the open window.

"With mine. With yours." Will stood, but when Cooper stiffened, he held his ground. She'd put another wall up, though why, he wasn't yet sure.

"We shouldn't involve anyone else—definitely not anyone we know."

"We can't do it all, Coop."

"I've come this far," she argued. "I can find someone to break the encryption. Pierce—"

"No."

"He helped me—"

"He helped himself," Will ground out. "And he betrayed you in the process. Would have done worse if it had suited his purposes."

"He wouldn't have gone through with it."

"Maybe. Maybe not. But he thought about it. And that's more than enough for me to hate him."

She turned, her expression calm but curious, and too late Will realized he'd shown his hand, in tone if not in words.

"You're jealous," Cooper realized aloud. "Of *Pierce*. For the love of God, why?"

He scowled and looked away. This wasn't a conversation they needed to have. Ever. Will knew when he'd been provoked. And there was no question in his mind that Pierce had been goading him from the first uttered "love" to the last. Will had resisted the bait then, he'd damn well resist it now. Because whatever Cooper's relationship had been with the man, Will was happy to leave it in the realm of the hypothetical.

"Not the point."

"You think I slept with him." She laughed. "And you are *jealous*," she repeated, as if it were the funniest thing she'd heard in a long time. She chuckled, and though it was entirely at his expense, he liked the things that little laugh did to her face. Liked the way it deepened the lines around her eyes and pulled that bottom lip taut.

"Pierce and me? Never a thing."

"Not my business if you were." He shrugged like he hadn't spent a solid half hour wondering just how Pierce had gotten access to her boots to plant that tracker.

She closed the distance between them, bunched her fist in his shirt, and smiled. "You are *so* good for my ego, Bennett. And while I like the way jealousy makes your jaw tick and your fists clench, let me assure you—there's no need. Not over Pierce. Not ever."

"I didn't like the way he looked at you. The way he spoke to you." He dropped a hand to her shoulder, let his thumb slip into the groove above her collarbone. "The way he touched you. Like he knew you'd let him. Like he had the *fucking* right."

"Pierce likes provoking people. Winding them up just to see what they'll do."

"I know," he admitted. "Doesn't mean it wasn't true."

"It wasn't."

"I'm glad." He slid his hand to the back of her neck, let his fingers card through her hair.

"I'm sorry," she said, stepping back with a laugh. "Were you under the impression I was a virgin? That you'd boldly gone where no man had gone before?"

"See? Trekkie."

She huffed at him.

"You're not the first, Bennett."

Yeah, he'd figured. She was too damn confident, too damn self-aware, too damn pleased with herself when he'd fallen to his knees before her. He wasn't the first, and that didn't bother him, but *fuck* he wanted to be the last. To be everything she wanted and more than she could handle. In bed and out.

He wanted to ruin her . . . but he wanted to worship her, too. And any man who wouldn't do both? He didn't get to touch Cooper Reed. Not if Will had anything to say about it.

"He isn't good enough for you," he ground out through a jaw tight with fury. "You trusted him, and he betrayed you. Used you. Treated you like an asset and a commodity. He saw you as disposable, Cooper. If I knew nothing else about him, that would be enough," he assured her. "I don't like him and I sure as shit don't trust him." He squeezed the back of her neck, his fingers sliding against her scalp. "Not with my life, and *definitely* not with yours."

"Okay," she said, the word little more than a breath of startled air, her face as close to awestruck as he'd ever seen it. "Okay. No Pierce."

"Parker's good, Cooper. The best when it comes to computers and code and encryption."

"He'll have questions," she said, stepping back and slipping away.

"And because he trusts me, he won't ask them. Not if I tell him not to. But Cooper, you should know that he'll have answers. I don't know when he gave Dr. York access, or if he has any idea what it was used for, but the algorithm Mitchell was talking about is his *baby*."

"Then how can you possibly trust him?"

"Because I *know* him. He's going to be furious, Cooper. And

he's going to be on our side. Let's get him the files. He can handle
the decryption and once we have a name, my team—my family—
can take down the people who did this."

"He's going to want you to come home," she whispered, her
voice rough with a fear he only now saw lurking beneath that
calm exterior.

"And he'll understand when I tell him I won't. Not until I
can be sure you'll go with me."

She glanced away from him, her shoulders bunching, her
hands flexing as if she needed something to keep them busy. "I
have to go to Mexico City."

"I know." Had known from the second that Mitchell had
dangled that carrot that she'd have to pursue it. "I'm going with
you. Don't," he said, interrupting her when she went to argue
with him. "Just don't. We're in this together. I left that mountain
with you. I'm going home with *you*. End of story."

"I wouldn't ask you to stay, Will."

"But I fucking wish you would, Coop." He dropped his forehead to hers and relaxed when she took a breath and leaned
into him.

"Let me make the call."

She brushed her mouth against his and nodded. Stepping
away from her when she was warm and soft and leaning on him
like he was the very pillar on which she built her strength was an
agony, but he did it.

"You got a satellite phone, right?"

"You're going to call him now?" she asked, her fingers sliding
up beneath the hem of his t-shirt to explore the skin above his
jeans. "It's the middle of the night."

He pulled away, laughing when she let out an indignant huff.
"Mid-afternoon Parker time. Trust me."

She caught him square in that deep blue gaze and said, "I do.
More than anyone. Maybe even more than myself." She walked

away before he could say anything. Before he could reach for her, drag his mouth over hers. She came back with the phone in her hand as if she hadn't just fused so many of his fractured pieces back together with a single sentence.

Because he didn't know what else to do and didn't have any reply that was worthy of her, Will accepted the phone and dialed a number he and the rest of the team had memorized a lifetime ago.

And his heart stopped in his chest when a sleep-roughened voice answered, "It is three o'clock in the *fucking* morning, that better be you, William Bennett, or I swear to God someone's about to die."

Will choked on a laugh tinged with the salt of a sob. "Georgie?" Two seconds after the warmth of her voice slid over him, reality caught up. "Wait. Better question. Why are you answering Parker's phone *in the middle of the night?*"

And as if desperate to prove that some things *never* changed, his baby sister laughed at him.

CHAPTER TWENTY

Cooper envied the smile Will wore, and worse, the woman who'd put it there.

She'd figured out early on that Will's sister had been the one who'd answered the phone. The one to dodge his questions and blast him with her own, and though Cooper wasn't privy to the back and forth, she could guess well enough.

Where are you?

When are you coming home?

What do you mean "soon"?

And once, when Will had demanded for the *third* time that his sister explain why she was answering one of his best friend's phones in the dead of night, Cooper could have sworn she'd heard a barked *"Because I like the way he fucks me, okay?"*

Cooper had laughed, and Will had sworn and cut her a look that said agreeing with—never mind defending—his sister would be a very bad call.

Still, Cooper liked what little she'd gleaned of Georgia. Loved the smile she'd brought to Will's face. Something warm and comfortable and familiar, like a faded, threadbare t-shirt; the colors muted but the memories attached to it still vivid. It was a good look on him. Wiped away so much of the hurt and fear that lingered, even when he wasn't aware of it.

So yeah, Cooper liked the woman who'd put that look on his face. And hated that she'd accomplished what Cooper could not.

She stood and stretched, her back popping and her muscles aching. Pink wasn't yet tinging the horizon, but it would be soon, the darkness already less inky black and intense.

She grabbed another beer from the fridge, wandered out onto the deck, popped the cap on the edge of one of the wood chairs, and watched as a bright green lizard scurried toward the railing.

She sat and sipped and wondered how hard it would be to convince Will to go home. Easier now that he'd had a taste of it. She envied him that first, brief taste of familiarity if only because he could take another. She, on the other hand?

She couldn't risk a phone call or a letter or even a brief peek at Facebook to see how everyone was doing. She'd learned the hard way that it hurt too much to see her family at a distance. She'd caved once in an Internet cafe in Istanbul. Five minutes of weakness only to face the brutal reality that they'd grieved—and slowly begun to build a life that didn't include her.

But that had been over a year ago and she'd learned her lesson. No sense wishing for things she wasn't sure she could ever have.

Her family deserved to move on, and she deserved to let them.

And he, Cooper thought, as Will stepped through the screen door, phone gone, his own beer clutched in his fist, deserved to go home.

But she didn't say anything as he joined her.

Couldn't find her voice when he sat.

Bit back the words she knew she should say when he reached for hand.

"You're quiet," he said, lacing their fingers together and taking a pull from the bottle. "Nothing to say?"

Did he expect her to say it? To give him an easy out and send him home with a sweet smile?

Probably. She'd tried, more than once already. But this time, she just couldn't do it. Didn't have the strength or the courage or the grace.

She wanted him *here*. With her. And if that made her selfish, well then so be it.

"It's late." She stood, tried to shake her hand free from his. "Or early, I guess. We should get some sleep."

"In a minute." He pulled her back until she stood between his knees, then down to sit on the footstool in front of him. "Want to make sure you're not going to disappear on me in the middle of the night in a not-so-subtle demand that I go home."

She shook her head, her hair brushing the back of her neck. "You should, though. I can see that you want to."

"Yeah," he agreed. "I do."

"Then what's stopping you?"

He grinned around his beer. "Fishing for compliments is beneath you, Coop. Especially when all you gotta do is ask."

She huffed and tried to stand, only for him to curl his fingers in the waistband of her cotton pants and yank her back down.

"I want to make sure we're clear on this point." He set the bottle on the table next to him. "I want to go home—and I want to take you with me."

When she tried to pull away, he wrapped his free hand around the base of her neck and pulled her face close to his. "Come home with me, Coop."

Temptation had never been so terrible, so real, so potent. "I can't," she whispered, breaking beneath the weight of her loyalty. "Not yet. I have to try."

"I know that." He pressed his forehead to hers, his breath

ghosting across her lips as he spoke. "You have to exhaust every option, because that's what he would do for you."

Biting her lip, she nodded.

"Parker's working on decrypting the files, but he's also looking into Alonzo Pérez —"

Cooper opened eyes she hadn't realized she'd allowed to fall shut. "I thought we had everything we needed to blackmail the lab director into helping us?"

"More can't hurt, and Parker is a pro when it comes to digging up dirt. When we make the call, we'll do it knowing that Pérez *has* to meet with us."

"Us?" she asked.

"Us. I told you once, Cooper. I'm not going home until you can, too."

She leaned away, putting space between them before his heat could sink all the way into her bones. But with his hand at the back of her neck, he didn't let her go far.

"We'll go to Mexico. And then we're going home. Together."

She shook her head.

"Yes," he argued. "One way or another, this is the end of the road, honey. You'll have done everything possible. Everything Cole would have done and far more than he'd have ever asked you to. It's time to let others help."

"There's still a price on my head—"

"Mine too," he countered. "But at some point, we have to stop running. Once Parker can access those files, we're going to have names and then things are going to move fast. It's time."

"I can't. Not until it's done. Not until it's safe. Even if we can eliminate the contracts, I can't risk drawing Cole to my family. My sister, my parents, they're innocent. Defenseless."

"But my family *isn't*." He pulled her close, pressed his mouth to hers in a promise she could taste. "My sister's a marine. Her— ugh, I can't believe I'm saying this—but her *boyfriend* is a tech genius with more government contacts than IQ points, and trust me, that's saying something. My best friend? Navy SEAL. They can protect themselves, Coop. And they want to protect us, too."

"Why are you pushing this?" she asked.

"Why are you fighting it?"

She didn't have a good answer for that. Just a vague sense of dread that things were racing toward a conclusion she couldn't see or predict or control. Going home . . . it meant that she'd arrived at the end of the line. That she'd exhausted all her options and resources. That she had to find a way to let go.

And suddenly, that thought was damn terrifying.

She sucked in a breath, her chest hitching with a rush of anxiety she hadn't expected. Even if things worked out, even if she and Will exposed the traitors within the CIA and by some miracle brought Cole home, what then?

"I'm scared," she whispered, the realization fresh and new and throbbing like a bruise she couldn't remember getting. "I can't just . . ." Get on with it. Go back to normal. Resume life as if the last eighteen months had never happened.

"So am I."

"Why?" He'd face a hero's welcome. He'd survived, and that was all anyone would care about.

But Cooper . . .

Cooper had done things. Made compromises and decisions that she'd live with, but never be proud of. "The things I've done . . ."

"Will stay with you," he agreed. Will tucked her hair behind an ear, let his fingers trace across the arc of her cheek, skirting faded bruises she'd nearly forgotten about. So much had happened in so little time. It set her mind spinning and made it hard to keep her feet. "They'll hurt, and they'll haunt and sometimes, sometimes they'll make it hard to stomach normal and ordinary and *life*."

She looked into his denim-blue eyes. "How . . .?"

"Survival comes at a price, Cooper. You know that better than anyone." He sighed and stroked his fingers through her hair as if that alone had the power to soothe him. "And I wasn't a saint."

"No one would blame you for anything you did on that mountain." She grabbed his hand and turned her head to kiss his wrist. "They'd understand."

"Would they though?" he asked, his voice roughened by a question that stiffened his shoulders. "I killed people, Coop. That was the choice they gave me. Fight to live. Fight to eat. Fight to keep going one more day." This time, he tried to pull away from her. To retreat into himself.

And as he'd so readily done for her, she kept him close, held him still, and offered what support she could. "They didn't give you a choice."

"There's always a choice." He sighed, his tension leaving his body as his confession left his lips. "It was a game to them. Make the Special Ops guy fight. See how many men he could take. See how much pain he could handle—"

"Then they fucking deserved it."

He grinned at her, his beard flexing with the effort. "You're a little bit ruthless, you know that, Coop? I like it."

"They started those fights, Will. No one could blame you for finishing them."

"Maybe," he agreed. "And maybe those kills were justified. But there was an innocent, too. And that . . . that I don't know how to live with."

"What do you mean?"

"Six months in, a few new guys joined the camp. With them was a fifteen-year-old kid."

Cooper sucked in a ragged breath. She'd spent enough time

in the South American slums to know how that story started—
and where it ended.

"He was poor. No family. No support." Will shrugged. "Just
looking for something better, you know?"

"And the cartels do a great sales job. Family. Security.
Money."

Will nodded. "But this kid, he wasn't cut out for it. Didn't
have a cruel streak. Life hadn't hardened him yet. Hadn't
ruined him."

Cooper tilted her head, felt her stomach drop, and linked her
fingers with his. "He tried to help you."

Will slid a hand up her cotton-covered leg, his fingers tracing
idle patterns over the denim. He didn't meet her eyes. "Yeah."

"And they caught him."

"Caught us both halfway down the mountain."

Cooper closed her eyes against all the ways that statement
hurt her heart. To know that he'd tried to get away. That he'd
almost succeeded. That they'd dragged him back to face what she
knew would be a brutal punishment.

"One way, or another, the kid was dead." A sob rose with the
words, but he choked it back down. "I didn't even know his name.
Wouldn't tell me."

Cooper squeezed his hand. She didn't want to hear the rest.
Didn't need to. But Will needed to tell it and that was all that
mattered.

"They gave me a choice. I could snap his neck . . . or they
could torture him to death."

"You snapped his neck."

He shuddered. "Not at first. Not until the screaming started.
Not until—"

"Not until you were sure they would do it."

"Yeah," he admitted. "I couldn't listen to it. I knew what they
were capable of. That it could last *days*."

"You ended it."

"I ended it," he echoed hollowly. "And killed a fifteen-year-old kid."

"It was the right thing to do, Will."

"How can you say that? How can anyone say that?" he raged, his voice a jagged blade. "All he'd tried to do was help me."

"And they would have *tortured* him for it." She pulled their faces close, pressed her forehead to his, let her fingers scratch along his jaw. "They were going to kill him either way. What you did was a mercy." She pulled back just far enough to meet his gaze. "For *him*. But not for you. For *you* it was just another torment. Another layer of degradation that they forced on you. No one in your life will think less of you or judge you or condemn you for that."

"Why do you find it so easy to see the best of me, but find it so damn impossible to see the best of yourself?"

She sat back on a sigh. "It's not the same, Will. The things you did, they were decisions made in the moment. Under the pressure of captivity and torture. But my choices were more complex. Premeditated. You shouldn't confuse the two."

"Tell me." It came out like a demand, but she received it like the invitation it was. And she couldn't refuse it. Not when he'd been so brutally open and honest with her.

"When I ran, I had nothing. No resources. No friends. No money. Running isn't easy—or cheap. I might have been able to get lost, take under the table jobs in bars or . . ." She swallowed hard, thinking about what few choices that desperate women had.

"Coop . . ."

She glanced up to find Will staring at her, his expression wrecked and his jaw tight. Like he'd personally failed her. It should have rankled, the idea that he thought she'd needed saving. Two years ago, it would have. But now? Now it slid through her like a hot chocolate on a cold day. A comfort she could so easily come to rely on. She didn't have to ask, and he didn't have to say it—he'd never let her face anything alone again. And that made the confession easier, if no less bitter.

"I was lucky. Had a few things I could pawn." She stared into his eyes. "And one thing I could trade for money or information."

"You took jobs."

"Hits," she said, refusing to soften just what she'd done. "I was picky. Didn't go after the more lucrative work—women, children. There was plenty to sustain me, and believe me when I say that no one will miss them. Arms dealers. Human traffickers. Cartel leaders. Not all that different from what the CIA and army paid me to do. But . . ."

"But this time you selected the target."

"And I did it for personal gain. So that I could afford a bribe or a room or a new identity."

"And so you could try to save Cole," Will finished for her.

"Yeah. So I could try to save Cole. So I could find a way home."

"You did what you had to, Coop."

"Did I?" she asked, her voice raw with doubt. "Or did I just do what I wanted to?" There'd been other choices. That she hadn't made them, hadn't wanted to live with them, didn't erase them. "At the end of the day, I killed people for personal, selfish reasons. How can I go home, how can I face my family, when I know everything I did to get there?"

"I don't know, honey. But I know they'd want you to come home anyway. I know that they'd rather have the exhausted, imperfect, slightly broken version of you than nothing at all." He tightened his grip on her thigh, his thumb digging into the seam of her pants. "I know you don't have to give them details you don't want to. And I know that you don't have to do *any* of that alone."

"What?"

"Come home with me, Cooper. Come home and let me introduce you to my family. Let them meet the woman who saved my life, who brought me *back* to them. And then, when you're ready, take me home to meet yours." He grinned at her. "Even if you don't know what to say to them, I do."

"Oh yeah?" She quirked an eyebrow at him and didn't fight the grin those words elicited.

"Yeah. Like how their daughter saved me when I was convinced I couldn't save myself. How when I was dying, she fought for me, when anyone half as ruthless or selfish as she thinks she is would have cut and run."

Her eyes stung, and his thumb rubbed away a stray tear.

"Or how she sees right through to the heart of me. Understands me in a way no one else ever could." He grasped her elbows and pulled her off the stool and onto his lap, settling her so that she straddled him, a knee on either side of his hips. He tilted his head, so he could look up at her. "You do, you know. See the best of me. The goodness and decency and strength I thought I'd lost." He slid his hand beneath the back of her tank top and spread his fingers across her lower back. "But that's not the reason I'm going to fall in love with you, Coop."

Her heart stuttered as if he'd reached right into her chest to touch it. The single, gentle nudge changing its rhythm forever.

"I'm going to fall in love you with because you see the darkness, too." He pulled her down, pressed his mouth to hers once, twice. "But you don't flinch from it. You're not afraid of it. Of *me*."

"No, I'm not." She shifted closer, laced her fingers in his hair, tucked a strand behind his half-missing ear.

"You could have killed every last man on that mountain, Cooper. But you didn't. Because you saw. Because you knew.

Because you understood what I needed. Not just closure or justice or revenge."

"You needed to take back what was yours," she said, brushing a finger along the edge of his ear.

He shivered. "Yes. And you understood that—I don't think anyone else could have. So please, Cooper, when all of this is done, let me take you home."

She smiled down at him. "On two conditions."

"Name them."

She brushed her mouth gently against his. "First Sunday of every month my dad hosts a family barbeque, rain or shine. Promise you'll take me. Promise you'll be by my side when I explain."

"Done. The second condition?" he asked.

"Before you take me to meet your family, or go with me to meet mine, take me to bed."

He stood in a rush, his hands gripping her ass and her legs circling his waist. God, he was strong. Even as his body mended and healed and glued itself back together. It made her wonder what it would be like in a month, in *six* months. When his frame had filled out and his confidence had returned. When he no longer worried about accidentally hurting her. When he knew her well enough to know he'd never go too far because she'd never let him.

Anticipation for what was to come, both now and in the months ahead, wound through her, heightening everything.

And slowing it down, too.

But instead of taking her inside, taking her to the queen-size bed tucked into the corner of the tiny villa, he walked her across the veranda and to the sprawling, extra-deep daybed at the other end. He set her down on the edge, the bed swaying gently beneath her. She glanced up and realized that what had looked like simple furniture was actually built more like a swing. Rope secured the platform to the ceiling and mosquito nets fell around the outer edge like a private cloud. Cooper sat back, and the bed rocked—inches, at most—but still enough to add a layer of sexy indulgence.

It made her feel relaxed and lazy. Like they had time and nothing better to do than touch and kiss and stroke.

Will stepped back and just stared, his gaze a slow meander that only made her long for his hands. For his mouth. His skin against hers.

"You're such a beautiful surprise, Coop."

She cocked her head to the side. She was oddly touched by that compliment, though she didn't quite understand it.

"What part of me surprises you?"

He shook his head. "Nothing really. In so many ways you're exactly how I imagined you . . . just more. More concentrated. More beautiful. More fearless. But my reaction to you?" he said, toeing off his shoes. "That never ceases to surprise me."

"Come 'ere." She grasped him by the belt and pulled him close, then slid the leather free of the buckle and opened his pants.

"I like putting my hands on you, Coop. Like holding you down and holding you close. I like that you don't just take it, you *want* it."

"Crave it," she agreed. Because hell yeah, she did. Loved it when he got a little wild, a little rough. When he treated her like something he had to conquer rather than coddle. "And I love making you work for it, too." She shucked his jeans down his thighs and took his underwear with them for good measure.

He laughed. "There's not a shy or submissive bone in your body, Cooper." He stepped out of his pants, drew his shirt up and over his head.

"You'd have zero interest in pushing me to my knees if there was." She wanted to reach for him. To trail a finger from his belly button up between his pecs. To grasp his cock, long and full and thick, and stroke him to the very edge. She could do it fast, have him desperate and wild in a blink. But he seemed to have something else in mind, so she resisted.

"True. And I guess that's where the surprise comes in."

She raised her arms when he grasped the edge of her tank. He drew it up slowly, the cotton a gentle stroke against her too-sensitive skin. When he discarded it, she stood, bare chested in just the pants she'd slipped on after a shower.

He touched her nipple with a thumb, his caress gentle. Curious. A soft hello rather than a promise of things to come.

"It never occurred to me I'd want to take my time," he whispered, his thumb moving slowly back and forth. "That I'd want to be gentle. That I'd want to worship as much as I'd want to conquer." He dropped a palm, warm and heavy, to her shoulder, then let his hand slide down the full length of her arm. "The need you inspire in me—that's the surprise, Coop."

Heat flared beneath her skin until it felt too tight, too warm. Like she'd napped too long in the sun and it had left its mark. Because oh God, she wanted those things too. Wanted slow and deep and careful. Wanted him to hold her close as much as she wanted him to hold her down.

"Will you let me love you like that?" he asked, pulling her pants down her legs.

"Yes."

"As slow as I want? As long as I want?" he asked when he stood.

She reached for him, the longing a deep and building ache. "Anything."

"I can love you here?" He pressed a finger to her lips, his smile just to the outside of wicked when she sucked it in her mouth and nodded.

"Here?" he asked again, sliding that same wet finger deep inside on a single, plunging stroke that took her to her toes.

"Yes, for fuck's sake, *yes*."

He left his finger where it was, stroking gently, and placed his other hand over her heart. "And here?"

He nudged her clit with his thumb and she came on a sob. His touch, his words, his presence sending her over the edge as easily as if he'd grabbed her hair and spread her legs. Fuck, the things this man did to her.

The things he was promising—she didn't know how she'd survive them. Or how she'd ever live without them.

"Good." He added another finger, pressed his thumb more firmly against her clit, and drove her right back to the edge.

She grasped his shoulders, her hips rocking, her nerves singing. "Oh God, I can't. I can't."

"You can," he assured her, using one large hand against her shoulder to push her feet flat to the floor, to make her take his fingers—three of them now—deeper. "You will. As much as I want. For as long as I want. Until every part of you weeps with need. For me to stop. For me to keep going. Until you're limp and loose and exhausted. Tell me to stop, Coop. But if you don't, I'm going to push you until you can't come even one more time but need it, beg for it anyway. Until I'm sure you'll always *crave* it."

"Damn you," she said, sobbing as she came, her orgasm longer, more intense, and just as he'd promised, the need for the next one was already building within her. "Please, please, *please*."

He pulled his fingers free and with impossibly gentle hands turned her to face the suspended daybed.

Will pulled her hair, already damp with sweat, away from her neck and twisted it over her left shoulder. He set his mouth to work on the side he'd exposed, sucking up a mark as he slid a hand over a breast and down her belly, his fingers skimming, teasing, testing. When he brushed her clit she shuddered but rocked her hips. He smiled against her skin. Kissed the mark she'd carry for days. Then said, "Bend over, honey."

With a firm touch he guided her down, one hand splayed between her shoulders blades, the other gripping her elbow as he bent her forward and pressed her to the mattress.

"Spread your legs," he said, nudging her knee with one of his. She shuffled her feet until they were shoulder width apart. "Wider." His hands, warm and rough and unyielding, parted her thighs and set her feet where he wanted them. When he was satisfied, he stepped in close, his cock brushing the back of her legs, the back of her ass. Will settled between her legs, draped himself over her back, and grasped her wrists, pulling her hands away from where they'd clutched the canvas cover on the daybed.

Slowly, he pulled her arms down, trapped her hands on the bed by her hips, and then slowly—so damn slowly, slid into her.

He withdrew on a long, agonizing slide, then pushed back in, the bed swaying just enough to heighten his movements, to make it feel as if everything were slower, deeper, longer.

He set a pace she didn't believe he'd ever be able to maintain. It was too slow, too gentle, too thorough. But he held her there. Trapped in a slow spiral of pleasure that wound tighter and tighter and tighter but never let up. Never released.

He withdrew on a curse and as he began to slide back in, she planted her feet and shoved. He laughed, let go of her wrists and grabbed her left leg, bending her knee until her leg was folded and pinned to the mattress. She wiggled, but he pushed her up on the bed until her toes only barely brushed the ground.

He slid out, then plunged in, going deeper, taking advantage of the better, wider access she'd granted him.

The orgasm built, slower, but no less powerful, then rolled through her like a lazy tide.

"One more, I think," he said, and finally, finally she heard the strain, felt him fight against the urge to plant his feet and snap his hips.

"I can't." Her eyes stung, and her nipples throbbed with every drag against the canvas-covered bed. And still, he maintained that infuriating pace. "Please."

"You know what I want. Give it to me, Cooper. Give it to me because I asked you to. Because I want it. Because you want it every bit as badly. Come again, coat my cock, and I'll finish this."

"Please, please just touch me. Make me."

"No. You'll do it yourself. Touch yourself. Torture yourself."

She shook her head but even as she did, the hand he'd let go to trap her leg slid beneath her hips.

She bit off a cry when the edge of her nail caught her clit, the tiny sensation too much, too big, too good.

"Do it again, Cooper. Do it now."

She did. God help her, she stroked herself until the blood roared in her ears, her vision turned to black, and all she could feel was Will as he moved insider her, her fingers rushing to match his pace.

On a wail, she came one final time as he snapped his hips and shouted his victory.

The bed creaked, and the night air buzzed, and Will pulled her onto the mattress, tucked her head on his shoulder, and placed her palm flat over his heart.

She fell asleep to the skip and skim of idle fingers and the beat of a heart that was every bit as sure, every bit as strong as the man who owned it.

CHAPTER TWENTY-ONE

"Whaddup, Laz?" Parker answered, his voice artificially chipper and laced with the staying power of caffeine.

Will seriously doubted the guy had gotten so much as a second of sleep in the last twenty-four hours.

"Laz?" Will asked, then immediately regretted it. He'd been gone a year, but he knew better. You *never* asked. It only encouraged him.

"As in Lazarus. As in rising from the dead. That wasn't obvious?" His tone easily conveyed his expression—half disgust, half smug self-importance.

"So sorry." Will grinned. He liked the kid. Always had. 'Course, that was before Parker had started sleeping with his sister. Now he liked him and kinda wanted to break his arms at the same time. "You're probably a few cups of coffee ahead of me. And anyway, not the reference I thought you'd go for and definitely not the one I prefer."

The other end of the line went silent with anticipation. Will let it hang there as he set a plate of breakfast in front of Cooper.

"Really?" she asked. "Eggs on toast?"

He tucked the sat phone into his shoulder and pressed a kiss to her head. "Eat. You need the protein."

"So bossy," she grumbled, but dug into her food.

"You love it."

"Having fun south of the border, are we?" Parker asked, his smile as clear as the mark on Cooper's neck.

"You sure you want to pull at this thread, Livingston? 'Cause if I talk about my sex life, you're going to talk about yours. That sound healthy to you?"

"Nope."

"Good call."

"So what reference did I miss?" Parker asked.

"Not really why I called."

"You brought it up and you know I'm not going to let it go."

Will shook his head and took a seat at the table with Cooper. "Ra's al Ghul. Obviously."

Stunned silence filled the line. "A Batman reference? No, wait, a *classic* Batman reference? You're my new favorite Bennett."

"I heard that," Georgia shouted in the background.

"She hears *everything*," Parker whispered, then got himself back on track. "So I repeat, whaddup, Ra's?"

"Looking for an update. Maybe a little good news?"

"How about a lot of good news and just a sprinkle of bad?" Parker asked.

"Works for me."

"Okay, so I managed to de-encrypt all of the files, and man, oh man, your friend Felix must have had some major pull because he was *thorough*."

"Apparently Felix had some family connections I didn't know about," Will offered, though the idea still felt off to him. Nothing about Felix had ever come across as blue-blooded or old money. But then, he supposed that made sense if he hadn't been raised that way. But it still made Will feel like they were talking about two different people. The guy who'd cursed like a sailor, sang like a dying cat, and issued challenges the way most people issued compliments. But then there'd been the guy who was a legacy. Part of a very old naval family. Wealthy. Connected.

A stranger.

"That makes sense," Parker said, the sound of his keyboard clicking in the background. "No way was he able to piece all of this together on his own. He'd have needed contacts in the DoD, the CIA." Parker sighed. "Truth is, I don't think even Felix understood what he was dealing with here. These documents are all redacted and classified."

"I thought you said you got through the encryption?"

"I did," he confirmed.

"But you said the files are all redacted."

Parker scoffed. "It's a good thing you know your comics, because you don't know computers. Or code. And your vocabulary is depressingly basic—"

"If you're done insulting me, explain."

"Encryption made everything difficult to *access*. Once I got past that, I found classified file after classified file. All of which are redacted—that means edited for content, by the way."

"I thought you said you had good news?"

"Well, yeah. Because even though everything's been sanitized, it was still enough for me to know what to look for. And that made the hack itself much easier."

What to look for . . .? Jesus. The more things changed. "How many government servers did you compromise this time?"

"Hmmm?" Something high-pitched and noisy droned on in the background. "Sorry. Out of fresh ground. And I don't know. Two or three?"

"Parker."

"Yeah, yeah. Save the lecture. I don't want to hear it twice and Ethan's on his way over to deliver it in person."

Will just shook his head. "So long as someone's got it covered."

"*Anyway*, it made it easier to find the full files. On the surface, everything looks legit. Smart, really."

"How so?" Will asked and snagged a slice of toast off Cooper's plate.

"Well, as it turns out some of these studies were legitimate. Olivia—"

"Dr. York?"

"Right. She's a big-time rule follower. High compliance, process driven, a hundred and ten percent by the book—but for God's sake, don't play poker with her, you'll end up fleeced of your quarters, your clothes, and your tech."

"You lost the program to her in a *poker game?*"

"Well, I gave her an exclusive license to use it in the medical field due to a poker game—which was totally unnecessary, by the way. I'd have just given it to her if she'd asked. But anyway, focus. You're worse than I am."

"Excuse me—"

"So anyway," Parker said, talking right over Will's indignant objection. "Olivia had already nailed down a few government contracts. She was working on multiple classified studies in the lab, and a few had even been green-lit by the FDA for human testing in the field."

"And the ones that hadn't? She just tacked those on for shits and giggles?"

Parker grew quiet for a beat. "You're mad," he realized aloud.

"Of course, I'm fucking mad, Parker. This is some Dr. Frankenstein-level shit and people *died* because of it. You get that, right?" Cooper dropped a hand on his forearm, stroked her fingers along the corded muscles, but didn't say anything.

"Hey," Parker said quietly. "I'm not the bad guy here. And neither is Olivia."

Will sat back on a surprised grunt. "Sorry. I know that. I do. It's just a lot's happened and I—"

"I know. Just don't shoot the messenger, 'kay?"

Will shoved a hand through his hair. "Parker two point oh, huh? When did you learn to start putting people in their places?"

"Batman, Frankenstein—and you didn't even confuse the doctor and the monster—and now a version two reference?" Parker laughed. "I'm not the only one who's changed."

"Maybe you just didn't know me very well."

"It's a possibility," Parker agreed. "And anyway, it's Georgia's influence, I'm afraid. Apparently, I've gotten mouthier."

"God help us all."

"You'll learn to love me," he promised. "All the Bennetts do."

"Get back on track, Parker." Will wasn't ready to think about that. Not because he didn't want his sister to be happy—of course he did. And not because Parker wasn't good enough—he was, and anyway, that was his sister's call to make. She'd put Will's balls in a vise before she let her big brother dictate who she could or couldn't date. But if Georgia was in a serious, committed relationship—and it sounded like she was—then a lot had changed. *She* had changed. They hadn't talked long, but she'd sounded happy. Confident. Comfortable in a way he'd only ever glimpsed here and there.

It hurt, a little, that she'd grown so much without him. That she no longer needed him to be the steady touchstone he'd always been. He'd heard it in her voice. In the way she'd talked about Parker. Her home was somewhere, some*one*, else now. Will was happy for her, but that joy was tinged with a sadness he barely understood.

"Right. So as I was saying, York Pharmaceuticals already had several government contracts and as is typical, all of those studies were classified," Parker said, cutting into Will's thoughts. "Adding in additional studies wasn't hard."

"What are you saying?"

"I'm saying that on paper, *all* of these programs were authorized, which was a smart move. Most of the time when people get caught committing these kinds of crimes, it's because of what's not there. Funds allocated to things that don't exist, missing paperwork, stuff like that. But all of this was documented and accounted for, then authorized and redacted," he explained. "Olivia was working on four different studies, it was easy enough to expand beneath each of them and run rogue trials that tied back to the originals. Everything on York's servers *looks* like it's part of one of the approved and classified trials."

"You just let yourself into their systems, huh?"

"Olivia wouldn't mind," Parker assured him.

"And you're sure she didn't know what was happening?" Will asked.

"Definitely not."

"But how? It's her tech, her research, her company."

"A company that employs *thousands*. She can't be everywhere and oversee everything. I know her, Will. Putting aside the fact that she totally cheats at cards, she's one of the kindest people I've ever met. Generous to a fault. The studies she authorized? All geared toward helping combat veterans. She was doing some really exciting stuff applying my program to brain mapping. Early results in treating things like PTSD and traumatic brain injury are really promising." Parker sighed. "She's one of us and she's *missing*. Has been for months and I didn't even know it."

"How has her disappearance gone unnoticed? She's a billionaire, for fuck's sake."

"Because she's always remained out of the public spotlight, and because her board of directors is hiding it."

"Why on earth would they agree to that?" Will asked. One

person, maybe two, could be manipulated into lying. But an entire board?

"The official story is that Olivia is doing outreach and patient advocacy in Africa. Since she's always preferred to keep her charitable efforts from becoming PR talking points, it's not a hard sell."

"That doesn't explain why her board would go along with it. Surely they aren't all in on it?"

"No. Just one of them."

"Let me guess. Gerald Reeves," Will ground out.

"Got it in one. He's vice president in charge of research and development and from what I can tell, *he* informed the executive team that Olivia was taken hostage by local warlords while helping with an Ebola outbreak in central Africa. From the emails I pulled from York's servers, it looks like he's convinced the board that the kidnapping and rescue specialist they contracted with has insisted that everything be kept quiet for Olivia's safety."

"But there is no K and R team, is there?"

"There is and there isn't. It's a CIA shell. So everything looks legit—"

"But nothing is actually being done."

"Right. Turns out Gerald Reeves and a high-ranking CIA official named Pruett Davis—and what the fuck kind of name is *Pruett* anyway?—thought they could turn a profit selling the results of these studies. When Olivia caught on and restricted access to York's servers, Davis had her picked up and dropped into a CIA black site."

"Do you know which one?"

"No." Parker sighed. "And searching for it is taking hacking to a whole new level. It's risky, not just for me and the rest of the team, but for Olivia, too. There are only two reasons she's still alive—one, because so far, this has all been contained to a handful of leaks and two—"

"She has something Reeves and Davis want."

"Yeah," Parker agreed. "But now we have enough leverage to bury Reeves and Davis. The crimes we can prove? They'll deal. And they'll give up Olivia's location in the process."

"And all of this will be over," Will said quietly. "What about the contracts on me and Cooper?" he asked, reaching for Cooper's hand.

"Best guess is Davis is behind that—he'll either cancel the hits when we bring him in, or I will."

"Can you do it now? I don't want this hanging over Cooper's head anymore."

"I can, but are you sure that's the best idea?" Parker asked. "The second I cancel them, we'll be tipping our hand."

Cooper squeezed his arm and shook her head.

"Isaac—"

"Flores?" Will asked.

"Yeah."

"He still an attorney with the Justice Department?"

"And a consultant with Somerton Security. He's going to get everything in order and secure arrest warrants, but it's still going to take a few days to locate, isolate, and pick up quietly. Can you lay low a little longer?"

"Yeah." Will sighed. "We can."

"Great. And I've got something to keep you busy in the meantime," Parker said.

"That little bit of bad news, I'm guessing."

"Can't be all dessert all the time," Parker confirmed. "I looked into laboratory director in Mexico City."

"Alonzo Pérez."

"Right. And he's a real gem. His name is all over these files, but he's also got a major gambling problem and he's in debt to the wrong people. I'm sending you everything I've got on him. Mitchell was right, he'll be easy to flip."

"That doesn't sound like bad news, Parker."

"So the bad news is that Davis can sense the noose closing in. Between you accessing the vault in Panama City and Pierce completing the hit on Mitchell, things are escalating. He's activated a contract on Pérez."

"Shit." That complicated things. "Has he disappeared yet?"

"No. Contract went active early this morning and there's no reason Pérez would know about it—kinda defeats the purpose."

"Okay, hang on." Will lowered the phone and quickly filled Cooper in. "How long does that give us?" he asked when he was finished.

"Days, maybe a week at the outside."

"That much time?" Will asked, surprise coloring his voice.

"Professional hits take time. A guy like Davis, he's not hiring some thug off the street to spray the back of a car with bullets." She shrugged and took a sip of her coffee. "Well, it *might* go down that way, it is Mexico after all. But just because it'll look like a cartel hit doesn't mean it'll be planned like one. Whoever picks up the contract will need time to assess his habits, his schedule. To do it right, this stuff, it takes planning."

"So we can get to him first?" Will asked.

"No guarantees, but yeah, probably." Cooper nodded, and Will pulled the phone back up to his mouth.

"Okay, send us everything you've got on the guy. We'll arrange a meet."

"You might consider bribes over blackmail," Parker offered. "The guy's in serious debt—he doesn't have the resources to run. It'll be easier—and faster—to buy him off."

"Yeah, but we don't have those kinds of resources either, Parker." Will knew that Cooper had some money stashed, but not nearly enough.

"Yeah, but I do. I'll set up the transfer. Think a million will do it?"

Will choked. "Parker, I—"

"It's just money, Will," he said quietly. "And not even a fraction of what I'd pay to get you home. Let's end this. As quickly as possible. For Georgia's sake," he said, his voice soft and quiet. "She needs you back."

Will sighed and fought back the pride that demanded he say no. "Okay. And, Parker?"

"Yeah?"

"Thanks for this."

"Yeah, well you just remember this warm fuzzy feeling when you get home and start feeling homicidal, 'kay?"

"What's that supposed to mean?" Will barked. But it didn't matter. Parker had hung up on him.

And in any case, he'd be back on American soil in a matter of days.

He turned to Cooper, put a hand on her knee, and set about constructing a plan.

Finally, the end had begun.

CHAPTER TWENTY-TWO

Tepito, Mexico City

On a street corner, beneath a royal-blue awning, Cooper nursed a paper cup of coffee that had been liberally laced with cinnamon and did her best to let the city ebb and surge and breathe around her. She'd been here before.

Was used to the thrumming, pulsing chaos.

Will, clearly, was not.

"Drink your coffee," she told him from beneath a baseball hat she wore low on her head.

"Why here, of all places?" Will asked, watching as crowds disappeared into Mexico City's oldest market. A claim to fame, for sure. But *not* what this area was known for.

"His mother's family is from the neighborhood," Cooper said. "He was lucky. She was beautiful, and he got out. But a place like this? You leave it, but it doesn't leave you. Not really."

And Cooper would know. Tepito was so much more than a series of streets or coordinates. It was a lifestyle. A community and in a lot of ways, a country unto itself, with its own commerce, its own rules, and its own militant presence policing a sense of right and wrong that could only be found in a neighbored that existed firmly in the gray.

Nothing here was black and white.

And nothing here was all good or all evil.

Nothing in the criminal underworld was.

"I feel like a fucking outsider," Will grumbled, scratching at the edge of his beard.

"Because you are."

"But not you?" he asked, bumping her hip with his.

She passed him small smile. She was an outsider, too, though not in the way he meant. And not in the way that mattered. Cooper might not have been born here, but she understood the market in a way Will never could. Over the last eighteen months she'd passed through a dozen of these markets in China, in Turkey, in Buenos Aires, and yes, even here. She had the contacts and spoke the language—not Spanish, but money. Desperation. A willingness to do what most people would never even consider.

That Will didn't know this place—or one like it—was a comfort against the sad realization that she did, and worse, that knowledge had left its mark.

It would never leave her, as it clearly had not left Alonzo Pérez.

Because she knew he was nervous, Cooper glanced up to Will. "Walk me through it again."

The words had barely left her mouth and already he settled into his stance, his gaze turning serious and focused. Operational readiness he knew. Walking into hostile territory he was used to. She just had to remind him.

"We enter the market separately and with an escort," he recited. "You're sure you can trust this guy?"

"Trust? No." She shook her head and ignored the way

Pierce's lessons whispered against the back of her mind. "But I trust that he can be bought. And anyway, I've worked with Fernando before. His entire business is connecting outsiders with the right people inside the market. His reputation is his every-thing—if he betrays us, his business dies. His business dies and . . ." She shrugged.

"Why were you here, Coop?" Will asked again. She'd dodged the question the first time, though she wasn't sure why. Maybe she just didn't want him to picture her here. But with nothing better to do than wait and watch, he'd press her for an actual answer this time.

"I needed things I couldn't get anywhere else." She studied the market. It looked the same to her, though she knew it had changed. It was always changing, and in that way, it remained the same.

Tarps in every color hung suspended over stalls and vendors called out goods and foods and sales. Even from a block up, Cooper could smell the food, taste the smoke of an old, well-worked grill. People sped past on foot, on bikes and mopeds, and even in cars, threading their way through the chaos.

"What things?"

"A scope. A handgun—something small and easily concealed —and ID. Passports, that kind of thing." Passports. Plural. Because she'd burned through identities as fast as she'd burned through countries.

"Guess that makes sense." Will shoved his hands in his pock-ets, shifted his weight back and forth. "That's why Pérez is here. Hard to run under your own name."

"The fact that Parker could front the cash for the IDs made this meeting possible."

"Yeah, I know," he agreed. "I just wish we could have done the exchange somewhere else."

"Cheer up, Bennett. I'll buy you a churro when we're done."

She grinned up at him. "Best in the city. Now, keep going. What happens after we enter the market."

"Fernando takes me to the meet and I transfer the money Parker is holding for us, he gives me the data and the tissue samples." He turned to her. "I don't like leaving you."

"Fernando will have me escorted to one of the hidden rooms above the market. I'll track your progress." And provide cover with the rifle that Fernando would have waiting for her. "In and out. Shouldn't take more than a half hour, tops."

"I still don't like separating."

Cooper sighed. "Neither do I. But it's too dangerous to go in together. The three of us have prices on our heads. Pérez will blend in and you're nearly unrecognizable with the beard. But I'm easier to identify. And anyway, Davis knows we're together. They'll be looking for a couple." Her palm itched with sweat she wanted to blame on the coffee. "It's safer this way."

"I know," Will agreed. "Doesn't mean I gotta like it."

"What happens after the exchange?" Cooper pressed him.

"Fernando escorts me out of the market and into a cab. We meet back up at the flat."

Cooper straightened as she spotted Fernando emerge from the market. She turned to look up at Will. "An hour. Two at most, and we're together again and heading for the airfield." She tugged the edge of his beard until he looked down at her. "Get this done and take me home, Bennett. It's time."

His smile unfurled, slow and lazy as a summer river.

"*Hola*," Fernando said, and Cooper turned to greet him.

"Hey. Thanks for taking my call."

"Sure. Sure. You remember Jorge?"

"Yes of course." Cooper nodded toward the man—a boy really, he couldn't have been more than sixteen—standing behind him. "This is the friend I told you about."

Will shook Fernando's hand, but didn't offer his name and Fernando didn't request it.

"Jorge will take you to wait," he told Cooper. "And I'll take your friend to the market. If you're ready?"

Cooper glanced back at Will, who nodded once.

"Let's do this."

Three stories above the market, in a windowless, cinderblock room, Cooper inventoried the promised scope and rifle.

"Here." Jorge beckoned her with a hand as he stepped off a metal ladder attached to the wall, over three feet of open air, and onto a ledge that couldn't be more than three feet deep and six feet wide.

It wouldn't be comfortable, but it didn't matter. Cooper had dealt with worse terrain.

Jorge withdrew a butterfly knife from his pocket, then used it to pry free one of the cinderblocks, one row up from the bottom. "*Venga.* Come." He nodded toward the missing brick and stepped back over the open space. Within a minute, Cooper was stretched out, her feet propped up against the wall across the gap, her rifle pointing out over the market. Because of the angle, she'd have to wait for Will and Fernando to make their way five or six hundred feet into the market. From there, she'd be able to track their progress through to the other side. She'd have neither a clean view or a clean shot, but hopefully she'd need neither.

Set and settled, she tucked an earbud into her ear and dialed the number of the burner phone she'd picked up for Will.

"Ready?" he asked, his voice steady and confident now that the op had started.

"Yeah, we're good," she said. "Market's busy. Lots of tarps, tons of umbrellas."

"It's just a precaution," Will reminded her. "You should be used to this, Coop," he teased. She picked him up as he followed Fernando's winding path through the crowds, Will's blue-and-orange Bronco's hat—and yeah, he'd complained about *that*—making him easy to spot.

"Used to what?" she asked.

"Being relegated to the sidelines. Backup. A glorified oh-shit bar in case things get a little bumpy."

"You're such a jerk," she complained.

"You love it," he countered.

And because there was really nothing she could say to that, she shifted, searching the crowd ahead for anything that felt off or out of the ordinary.

A thousand different things pinged that particular radar. The stand that held fifty-thousand dollars in counterfeit Nikes. The guy on the corner who had his smartphone out, so a customer could scroll through merchandise. Drugs, maybe. But guns, most likely. It was, after all, how she'd sourced her own weapon. And later, how she'd searched through vendors and inventories and cobbled together her rifle, which she'd had to leave at the flat they'd rented. Even concealed in her backpack, it drew too much attention, caused too much curiosity.

She'd had to rely on Fernando to have something ready for her. And he'd come through with a well-worn but well-serviced Remington M 700. Bolt action and an older model, it wasn't what she was used to, but it was what she'd grown up with. It would do.

"We're heading in," Will said quietly as he lingered outside a stand stacked floor to ceiling with counterfeit Louis Vuitton. "I'll call you when it's done," he said, then pulled the headphones out of his ear and shoved them into his pocket with the phone, leaving Cooper to settle in and wait.

Though the language and location were different, Tepito

wasn't so different from the urban landscapes and markets she'd covered while deployed or attached to the CIA. She'd long ago become skilled at tracking a target through a crowded street, beneath overhangs and past crowded storefronts. Cooper blinked, and they were there. Blinked again and gone. But as she settled into the rhythm of shoppers and vendors, street traffic and noise, it became easy to predict where and when her target would appear next.

Somewhere along the line, she'd lost the challenge, the thrill, that she'd so long associated with this job.

She couldn't say she'd miss it.

Maybe because she was tired. Maybe because it had been tarnished—by other people's decisions and her own. Or maybe it was because for the first time she was really looking forward to what came next.

With Will.

Ten minutes after Will stepped into the back of the booth and out of view, Pérez appeared, a backpack slung over one shoulder as he threaded his way through throngs of people and beneath tarps and umbrellas, disappearing one second, reappearing the next. Within minutes, he disappeared into the same booth that Will had, and Cooper was left to wait, left to watch.

She stiffened, pushing her elbows into the ground and focusing on the here and now as Pérez reappeared on the street, followed closely by Fernando, then Will, who had the small backpack Pérez had arrived with draped over his shoulder.

Fernando and Pérez shook hands, and Cooper watched as Will and Fernando turned to begin picking their way through the crowded market and toward the road at the opposite end, congested with cars and flanked with taxis. The walk was maybe a thousand yards, but it would feel like a thousand miles as they worked through all the people and vendors and mopeds that zipped between the chaos.

Will's hand came up to touch his ear, then her phone buzzed, and his voice filtered down the line. "It's done."

"You got it all?" she asked, her breath tight in her lungs.

"Labs. Tissues samples on ice—everything he promised. It's *done*, Cooper. We're going home." Something light and new and hopeful entered his voice.

Another shade of Will Bennett. Another facet to explore. Soon, she reminded herself, pushing down the joy that tried to bubble up.

Movement, fast and abrupt, caught Cooper's eye and she shifted her scope, checking, searching, and landed on Pérez, looking over his shoulder and moving fast toward the far side of the market.

Cooper followed his line of sight and found three men closing in fast.

"We've got a problem," she said into the mic on her headphones.

"What's up?" Will answered.

"Guys on Pérez's six. Closing in quick." She watched as Pérez broke into a run, pushing past people and stumbling over his feet. The guys behind him pulled weapons and followed.

"He's been made," Cooper mumbled. "Hit's going down now. Get the fuck out of there, Will."

She shifted her scope—Pérez wasn't her priority—as the first shots cut through the marketplace din, screams and chaos following.

"Is he down?" Will asked as Cooper searched for him, scanning crowds that were surging like a tsunami that had finally reached shore.

"If he's not, he will be soon. Two more guys were waiting at the end of the street." Which made *five* total. Shit. "Call out markers, I've lost you, damn it," she barked, but forced herself to work calmly, methodically as she tried to catch up.

"Plantain stand on the left," Will shouted over the pandemonium. "Blue tarp fifty feet ahead then a gap in cover. You'll pick us up there."

She moved her scope, her finger on the trigger, searching, scanning. She found the tarp and the gap. "You there yet?"

"Thirty feet," Will called, his breathing labored.

Screams erupted a couple hundred yards ahead of him and Cooper shifted her view forward.

"Shit."

"What is it?" Will asked, his voice nearly drowned out beneath the screaming stampede of people.

"Fire. Eight hundred yards up. Looks like one of the grills tipped and a stall went up. It's spreading fast and belching smoke." With the easiest exit cut off, Cooper immediately slid into finding him a new path out.

"Okay, I've got you," she said when his blue-and-orange hat appeared on the other side of the tarp he'd called out for her. "Go two hundred feet—you'll clear the opening in my line of sight, pass under a red umbrella, then just before you get to the yellow overhang, make a right. There's an alley, it'll take you two streets over."

"Got it," he replied.

"Move fast, Will. I don't like this."

The hit on Pérez was one thing. Unfortunate, but not entirely unexpected. But the fire . . .

That felt convenient. Planned. The sort of mass casualty event that could hide a number of sins. And the sort of thing that CIA *excelled at.*

"Making the right now," Will shouted and Cooper moved her scope, waiting for him to pop out the other side of the narrow passage she'd marked for him.

"I'm through," he said, coughing against smoke that was rapidly pushing through the market. Though it was open air, it was densely packed and strung with tarps and umbrellas, littered with flammable goods and jutting overhangs. It would burn, and it would be as bad as if the people inside had been caught in a warehouse.

"I've got you," she said, picking him up as he and Fernando emerged two streets over. "You're clear to the exit. Move, Will, this place is going up."

"Get out of there, Cooper," he urged her. "It's not safe for you either."

"I'm fine," she assured him.

"Go!" he ordered. "Now. We'll meet up as planned."

"Not until you're clear," she said, tracking his progress as he and Fernando bounced like pinballs through a screaming, desperate crowd.

The crowd that, up until now, had concealed the threat she'd sensed, but hadn't seen.

Cole.

"Down!" she shouted and thank God Will could follow a command. He dropped like a stone and the bullet that had been meant for him tore through Fernando's head instead.

Fresh screams erupted, and people scattered. Will stood, tried to turn, to run. But there was nowhere to go.

The crowd parted around the threat.

Cole appeared, gun in hand, face set, aim steady, Will already in his sights again.

Noise turned to a distant buzz in Cooper's ears.

Her vision tunneled, filtering out everything but the danger. The mark.

"Cooper, don't!" Will shouted at the same time Cooper did what she'd been trained to do.

She pulled the trigger.

Took a punch to the shoulder.

Felt as much as she heard the .300 Winchester Magnum round leave the gun.

And shot her best friend in the chest.

The bullet caught Cole, high and center, knocking him off his feet and hurtling him to the ground.

And though she knew that people were still running, still screaming, there wasn't room for any of it in her head.

Just silence, and the deafening realization that she hadn't even hesitated. Hadn't given it a second thought.

She'd saved Will . . . and killed Cole.

She'd chosen, when she'd said she wouldn't.

Couldn't.

Numbness spread like heated brandy through her veins.

"Cooper!" Will shouted. "Cooper, talk to me, God damn it!"

He'd been yelling for a while, she realized, her finger still poised, her gaze still searching for threats. Thank God for training. For strict adherence to discipline. It would see her through this.

"I'm here," she said through a thick throat and found him through her scope. She still had to see him out, see him safe. Then she could give into the nausea, to the guilt, the realization that it had all been for *nothing*.

"Baby, talk to me," Will said, the raw, ragged edge of his voice cutting through her. "Talk to me, Cooper," he repeated as he finally, finally cleared the market.

"Turn right," she said, shutting down the emotions surging within her. She couldn't fall apart. Not yet. "Taxis are idling four blocks up and to the left. The chaos hasn't hit them yet."

"I don't give two fucks about the cabs, Cooper. I'm coming to you."

"No!" she shouted, then repeated more firmly. "No. Too dangerous. Stick to the plan. Get somewhere safe. It's time to go home."

"Together," he confirmed, the noise of traffic beginning to overtake the screaming and the sirens and the chaos that was just three stories beneath her.

"You're coming to meet me, Cooper. Say it."

She set aside the gun. Wiped her palms on her jeans, then made her way down the narrow, metal stairs. And with every step, her agony turned to rage, and her failure to determination.

Davis had done this. *He'd* sent her partner, her best friend, the man she trusted most in the world, to *kill* her.

And in the process, he'd forced her hand. Made her choose. Kill Cole to save Will.

"Cooper, honey, talk to me," Will pleaded. "We go home together. You promised."

"I promised," she agreed.

"Then you'll meet me as planned?" he asked, his voice cautious and sad and hopeful all at once. "Come home to me. Let me help you. Let me hold you."

She wanted to. Oh, how she wanted to. He'd make it okay. He'd tell her it wasn't her fault.

But it was. She'd made the choice. Pulled the trigger. How could she go to Will, take comfort in his words and his arms, knowing what that comfort had cost?

She didn't deserve him. And she *would* miss him.

And for the first time since she'd rescued him, she *lied* to him. "I'll be there."

She hung up as she planted her feet on new, bleaker ground. She'd hit the point of no return, crossed the line she'd been so damn afraid of, the one she could never step back from. But it wasn't done. Not yet.

But it would be.

Soon.

CHAPTER TWENTY-THREE

The realization that Cooper wasn't coming came in seconds parsed out over minutes that lasted hours, each and every one of them an agony.

A part of him had known when he'd walked in the door of the single-room flat they were crashing in. Hell, a part of him had known long before that.

Had heard it in her voice. Had felt the lie even as she'd forced it over the phone.

He wanted to be mad. Furious, really. She'd promised him when she had no intention of following through. But he just couldn't force an emotion past the thick layer of sorrow.

Will would never have asked this of her. Had tried to stop her in the split second before a trigger was pulled and a life ended. She hadn't hesitated. There'd been no room, no time, no space for second thoughts or alternative plans. The choice had been simple to see, if not simple to make.

It should have been him, Will thought. Not because Cole could have been saved—Will had never clung to that belief as fiercely as Cooper had. And not because Cole was somehow more deserving of a second chance.

But because Cooper *didn't* deserve any of this.

Will propped his elbows on his knees and dropped his head in his hands.

Cooper had been so damn afraid that the last year and a half had changed her. Hardened her. Ruined her.

And in some ways, it had. Of course it had. A life on the run wasn't easy and the choices she'd made had scarred her in myriad, invisible ways. But she'd worn them well. And no matter what she thought, she hadn't lost her decency. Her kindness or her compassion.

Not for Will, who she'd saved more times than he could count. And not for Cole, who she'd both forgiven and championed.

She wouldn't be half as kind to herself. Or half as forgiving.

Cooper had told him how afraid she was of crossing that final line. Of going too far. Of losing herself to dark and desperate choices.

Of never finding her way back.

She'd view killing Cole as an unforgivable sin she could never wash clean and never learn to live with.

The point of no return.

If Will let her go now, Cooper would be lost. To rage. To remorse. To revenge. Because, oh yes, she'd want revenge. Cooper had been grievously wounded, and she wasn't the sort to slink off and lick her wounds. She'd lash out. In hurt. In anger. In grief.

She'd want revenge and she was more than capable of exacting it.

In so many ways, Reeves and Davis deserved her wrath. Deserved death.

And in a way that maybe only Will could understand, Cooper deserved to pull the trigger. To end this, once and for all.

A part of him wanted to step back. To do for her as she'd done for him on that mountain.

Except, this time an innocent life hung in the balance. If Cooper killed Davis before he gave up Olivia's location, she'd be lost. To captivity. To torment. Forgotten in some pit and left to die as if she'd never existed at all.

That choice was a selfish, if understandable, one. But it would mean Cooper would put revenge before all else. Sacrifice an innocent for her own, selfish goals.

And yeah, Will knew damn well she thought she'd already done that. But taking one life to save another was not the same as condemning an innocent woman for the sake of revenge, no matter how well deserved it might be. No matter how good it might feel.

And in time, Cooper would come to realize that. It might take days or weeks or months, but once that rush had worn off and the grief set in, she'd recognize that she'd crossed a line. That she'd become Pierce. Ruthless and vengeful and uncaring about costs or collateral damage.

And unlike Pierce, Cooper would wither, rather than harden.

The choice would destroy her—if Will let her make it.

He stood, shouldered his backpack and headed for the door.

Cooper might have broken her promise to meet him.

But Will had made promises of his own.

If it comes down to it, if you get too close, I'll stand between you and that line.

It was a promise he intended to keep.

The sun was high in a blue, cloudless sky when Will stepped off the private plane and onto the tarmac of a small airfield an hour outside Washington DC.

Funny, that in all the times he'd imagined being home, he'd never given much thought to the *arriving* part of it. He'd thought of beers and ballgames, of soft sheets and hot showers. He'd thought of endless days at the lake, spent in a quiet solitude he'd wanted to share with Cooper. And he'd thought of greasy burgers and endless buffets. Bad Chinese and boxed brownies.

And once or twice, he'd thought about what his sister would say when she saw him for the first time. But other than that? No. He hadn't given much thought to the reunion. To what it would be like to stare across pavement at people who knew him, loved him, missed him.

Nerves, unfamiliar and unwelcome, buzzed like ants beneath his skin.

He rolled his shoulders, adjusted the backpack he had slung over his shoulder, and forced himself forward.

There were four of them, and for that, he was grateful. Much as he wanted to see the whole team, there'd be time for that. The people who mattered most, they were here. All but one, anyway, and Will planned to fix that soon enough.

Georgia stood, her face neutral and her feet firm, Parker just behind her, his forearm draped across her chest. She leaned back, the movement subtle, and pressed her head to his shoulder but her gaze never left Will.

Next to them, Ethan waited, his fists shoved into his front pockets, his jaw set. A woman lingered next to him. When she went to back away, Ethan snagged the edge of her shirt and pulled her close to his side. She bit her lip and he dropped his head, whispering something against her ear then pressing a kiss to her temple.

Fucking hell, had *everyone* gone and fallen in love while he was away?

Figured.

Ten feet to go. The roar of the jet engines died, and blood pounded in his ears.

Parker moved his arm, whispered something in Georgia's ear, then none too gently pushed her forward. She cut Parker a look that promised retribution, then straightened and stepped toward Will, her face pale and her eyes fierce.

Oh hell, she was *pissed.*

"Hey, Georgie," he said, pulling a fond smile to his face as the wind caught her curly hair. "Miss me?"

"Miss you?" she spat, her voice clogged with rage and what he sure as fuck hoped weren't tears. Because, Christ, he'd learned to deal with just about every emotion his sister carried, but tears? No. Just no. He didn't have the field experience or the game plan.

"*Miss* you!" she screeched, clenching her fists at her sides.

Anger. Much better.

"Not gonna hit me, are you, Georgie?" he teased.

She opened her mouth to yell . . . and puked on his shoes instead.

"Oh Christ," Parker muttered, jumping forward and guiding Georgia away as Will stared down at his boots, trying to figure out what the fuck had just happened.

"I . . . what?" he asked, taking a few steps toward his sister, who was still heaving like she'd just completed her first post-deployment bender.

"Give us a second, huh?" Parker said, dismissing Will with a wave. "She's fine."

"She's clearly *not* fine," Will said, but stopped when Georgia shoved back her hair and shot him a look he hadn't seen in years and *really* hadn't missed.

Much.

"Take a walk," she mumbled, then heaved again.

"Not the welcome home you were expecting, huh?" Ethan asked, his smile small but amused when Will glanced at him.

"I—no, not really." He laughed and scratched the back of his neck. "I mean, I kinda thought she'd hit me."

Georgia threw him a middle finger over her shoulder and made a sound that had Will stepping back several paces.

"She okay?" he asked, turning to face Ethan.

"Yeah. Nothing time won't cure." Ethan cocked his head, and an awkward beat passed as he studied Will from head to toe then just cursed—creatively, in German—and pulled Will into a hug.

"I'm so fucking sorry," Ethan said, his voice tight with guilt. "We thought . . . I thought—"

"I know," Will whispered, squeezing him back then letting go.

"You look . . ." Ethan held him by the shoulders and looked him over again.

"Pretty good for a dead guy?" Will asked.

"Yeah," Ethan agreed with a chuckle, then sobered. "If we'd known . . ."

"You think I don't know that?" Will snarled. Because no matter what doubts, what anger had plagued him in darkness and in pain, he *did* know. And it didn't need to be said. "We're good."

"All right," Ethan agreed, and just like that, as it always had, their friendship snapped into place. Easily. Seamlessly. As it always did when deployments and commitments and captivity took up temporary space between them.

"I want you to meet someone," Ethan said, his tone telling a slow, cautious tale. "Keep an open mind, okay? She's important to me and she's nervous."

"About meeting *me*?" Will asked, utterly confused.

"Hey—" Ethan started, but the woman with him stepped forward and said, "I'm Natalia."

"Nice to meet you," Will said, shaking her hand as Ethan blew out a frustrated breath.

"He'll understand, honey."

Honey? So it was pet-name serious? Jesus.

"William Bennett," Ethan said, pulling the brunette closer to his side, "meet Natalia Vega."

It took a second and Will was blaming that on jet lag, airplane food, and a barfing sister, but his mind snapped into gear.

"Vega?" he asked, turning to Ethan.

"It's a long story," he replied. "But Natalia is the reason we were able to locate you," he explained. "Would have been the reason we brought you home, too, if you'd just stayed put a few more days."

Will scoffed. "So sorry to check out early and ruin your plans."

"Apology accepted," Ethan said smoothly. "You're here now, and that's all that matters."

"I'm here *now*?" Will repeated, feeling more and more like he'd stubbled down the rabbit hole. This was *so* not how he'd pictured this reunion going. He'd figured on hugs and manly claps on the back. Some cursing, mostly from Georgia. And questions. So many questions.

Instead, his best friend was sleeping with the enemy and his sister was shacked up with Poindexter.

"My head hurts," Will complained.

"You'll live," Georgia said softly.

Will turned, ready to try this all over again. She was pale, and her eyes were watery, but thank God she'd stopped puking.

"Here," Parker said, pulling a cranberry juice box and a pack of Sour Patch Kids from his jacket pocket. He fleeced the wrapper from the straw, popped it into the top of the box, and passed it over, trading it for the bottle of water she held.

"You okay?" Will asked carefully.

"Are you?" she asked and to his abject horror, Georgia burst into tears.

"Oh geez, not that," he said, pulling her into a hug. "You can't *cry*, Georgie." But when she didn't stop, just hiccupped a sob, he looked helplessly up at Parker who was trying *desperately* not to laugh.

"Why is she crying?" Will asked.

"Maybe 'cause she owes me ten bucks?" Parker snickered. "Told her it would happen."

"Why didn't I get a part of that action?" Ethan asked, pulling Natalia closer and dropping an arm over her shoulders.

With a shove, Georgia pushed away from his chest and rounded on both Parker and Ethan, her hair flying and tears streaming down her cheeks.

"This is funny to you?" she snarled.

"A little," Parker said at the same time Ethan said, "Nope."

Natalia rolled her eyes. "She's going to hurt you," she informed Ethan. "I'm going to let her."

"All right, all right." Ethan held his hands up. "I'd offer you a tissue but—"

"Are you okay?" Will asked, reaching for her elbow then pulling her back around.

"I'm fine," she snapped. "Why?"

"Why?" Will felt like he'd drunkenly stumbled onto a Tilt-A-Whirl and couldn't find his feet. Couldn't even find a steady point on the horizon. "Georgie, you're *crying*." He tried to wipe the tears that had not stopped falling down her cheeks, but she jerked away from him and rounded on Parker, who backed up a step, then held out the bag of candy.

"Tell him!" She snatched the pack from his hand and tore into it with her teeth.

With a sigh, Parker explained as if he'd done it a hundred times that day. "We don't comment on the tears. Much like the stick up Ethan's ass—"

"Hey!"

"We know they're there, but we pretend ignorance."

Georgia grunted something that sounded like a cross between a laugh and a "hell yeah you do."

"Yes, okay, fine," Will said, his head spinning with possibilities. "But *why* are you crying in the first place?" He'd love to believe she was just that damn relieved to see him. But Will knew his sister way too well for that.

Georgia just heaved a sigh, poured half the bag of candy into her mouth, and gestured to Parker.

"Why do I have to tell him? He won't kill you," Parker whined.

"Tell me *what*?" Will's confusion was crumbling away beneath the weight of his suspicions. *Surely* not.

"It's the hormones," Parker offered.

"Hormones?" Will echoed.

"Because of the pregnancy. That wasn't obvious?" Parker asked, his eyebrows climbing toward his hairline.

Will snapped his head back to his sister. "H-how long was I fucking *gone*?"

Georgia shrugged and sucked on a mouth full of candy. "Long enough for me to get knocked up, not long enough to become an uncle." She passed him the pack of Sour Patch Kids. "Brat likes sour stuff, by the way, just like his father."

"I don't understand," Will said, staring down at the package she'd shoved into his hand, then fishing out a green one. "How did this happen?"

She turned and started walking away. "Glow-in-the-dark condoms from China are faulty—did you know?"

"Oh Jesus."

"Don't ask questions you don't want answers to," she called back over her shoulder at the same time Parker shouted, "*His*! It's a boy?"

Will took a few stumbling steps forward and Ethan fell in beside him, a Vega under his arm and a smug grin on his mouth.

"I think I need to sit down."

"You'll get used to the idea. The rest of us have," Ethan said, clapping him on the back. "Welcome home, Will. Shit's about to get interesting."

And then his bastard of a best friend *laughed*.

CHAPTER TWENTY-FOUR

"I still don't like this," Georgia said, a hand smoothing down the front of her shirt. It was a gesture that looked oddly natural on her, though it drew Will's eyes every single time.

His baby sister was pregnant.

Probably with an evil genius.

Crazy.

"What if she shoots you?" she asked as he tugged on his boots.

"She's not going to shoot me, Georgia." He stood, beyond grateful to finally be in shoes and clothes that were his. Thank God, Georgia hadn't gotten rid of all his stuff.

"You're awfully confident," his sister continued as she followed him into the kitchen. "Have you met you? You can be a real pain in the ass, you know. It'd be tempting."

"So what you're saying is you missed me." Will shot her a grin and stepped around Parker, who was turning over what was frankly an impressive-looking omelet on the stove.

"Yeah, a little," Georgia snapped out, her tone fierce but her face sad. "I'd prefer it if your *friend* doesn't put a bullet in your chest."

Will reached for her, then tugged her close when she tried to plant her feet and avoid the hug. "Missed you, too, Georgie." He kissed the top of her head just to hear her complain then let her go. "And I'll wear Kevlar if it'll make you feel better."

"Won't stop a high-velocity round and you know it," she said mulishly.

"Or a headshot," Parker helpfully added.

"Thanks for that." Will pulled open a door, scanned the dozens of coffee pods he found there, and selected the one marked bold and dark. He pulled open the lid of the Keurig, but Parker intercepted him, taking the pod and tossing it into another drawer.

"She doesn't like the way that one smells," he offered by way of explanation.

Will sighed and selected another, then discarded it when Parker snorted and shook his head. Then another, and another. When he realized that Parker's collection of coffee rivaled Will's childhood baseball card collection, he gave up. "Just point to one that's safe."

"Here you go," Parker plucked one out of the drawer and handed it over.

"Creme brûlée donut? Are you kidding?"

Georgia shrugged. "Kid doesn't object to the sugary shit and I like keeping my breakfast down, so . . ."

"Good enough for me," Will grumbled, shoving the pod into the coffee maker. "Mugs?"

"Cabinet on the left," Parker said, and a split second later Georgia snorted and said, "He means the right."

"Killjoy, he'd appreciate my eclectic taste in mugs," Parker teased, plating the omelet and sliding it in front of Georgia, who took a seat on a barstool. "You want one?" he asked Will.

"Sure." Coffee made, Will took the chair next to Georgia and snagged a slice of toast off her plate.

"Jerk." She smiled at him and normalcy, like the hoodie he'd bought on base a zillion years ago, settled warm and comfortable around his shoulders. He'd missed this. Missed his sister and home-cooked meals. Snarky smiles and shared coffee. Over the past few days, Georgia had worked hard to make things feel normal. Easy.

But every time they shared a meal or a laugh or an insult, a part of Will focused on what was missing. Cooper, taking cheap shots at his eggs on toast. Taking his sister's side. Taking his coffee and his focus and his edge. Because, God, did she keep him off-center and on his toes.

He missed her.

In the waking moments when she was sleep mussed and soft, before life and fear and stress caught up with her.

In the shower, when he had cleaned up the line she'd created along his cheek and jaw, her mark still there, but fading every day.

In the quiet, restful moments when Parker worked, and Georgia napped, and all Will wanted to do was look at Cooper one more time. Memorize her profile. Lean into her warmth. Trace his fingers against her skin.

And at night, when he tossed and turned on Parker's monstrous modern sofa that was perfectly comfortable but still cold. He'd gotten used to having Cooper there. To waking from a nightmare with her hand on his heart and her face in his neck. And to waking up with her smile somewhere else, somewhere wicked and wonderful.

He missed her, God damn it. And it only made him angrier. And more determined to bring her home safe. Healing, if not whole.

He wanted to see what came next, and he was bound and determined to do it with her.

"She worth it?" Georgia asked softly.

Will swallowed his coffee and passed Parker a grateful look when he set a plate in front of him. "Yeah," Will said. "She's worth it."

Georgia studied him for a couple of long, slow blinks, as if she were piecing him together, merging what she'd known with what he'd become.

"You'll like her," he offered with a smile. "Busts my balls almost as much as you do."

"Well then," Georgia said, turning back to her food with a grin, "guess you better explain why putting yourself on the wrong side of her rifle is the best way of getting her attention."

"Yeah, man," Parker said, leaning over the sink to snag Georgia's other triangle of toast. "Can't you just call or send flowers or explosives or something."

"Explosives?" Will choked.

"Sniper," Georgia offered.

"Oh." Parker pushed away from the counter and tilted his head. "Ammunition then? A fancy scope thingy?"

"All fine ideas," Will said slowly. "But impractical as I don't know where she is."

"Just where she's going to be," Georgia grumbled around a mouthful of egg, goat cheese, and spinach. "And what makes you so sure of that, anyway?"

"Because I know her." Will sighed and when he sensed that such a simple statement wasn't going to be enough to sell it, he confessed, "And because it's what I would do."

Georgia laid her fingers on his forearm, a warm, welcome weight that didn't carry even a hint of judgement. But it was the wrong hand. The grip too light, too careful.

"Ethan had Gerald Reeves picked up outside his New York

brownstone and tossed into a cell. He's not going anywhere but he's not talking, either. He's rich and smug and egotistical enough to believe he can keep his mouth shut and ride this out."

"He'll break when reality sets in," Georgia said. "Bargain when he realizes he's not leaving that cell until he starts talking."

Will nodded. "But that will take time, and even then, he might not know where Olivia is. For that, we need to pick up Pruett Davis and play him against Reeves."

"First to talk gets the deal," Georgia said, spearing another forkful. "They should both rot."

"But Olivia shouldn't," Parker whispered.

Georgia's head snapped up and her face softened. "Of course not. We'll bring her home, Parker."

"What are the odds she's even still alive?" Parker asked.

"Good." Will couldn't bring himself to say the rest of what he was thinking. That there were worse things than death. That she'd been in captivity for six months. Holding out for six months. Holding on for *six months*. She wasn't walking away unscathed.

"Davis doesn't know that Reeves was picked up, so thanks to Parker"—Will tipped his fork in his direction—"we were able to access Reeves' line, contact Davis and setup a meeting."

"How's Cooper going to know where the meeting is?" Georgia asked, picking some spinach out of her omelet and dropping it on Will's plate with a sneer.

"Because Parker found the site Reeves and Davis were using to pass messages back and forth. I told Cooper about it while we were in Costa Rica. Guaranteed, she's monitoring that board, just in case one of them sends a message to arrange a face-to-face."

"Why are you so sure she'll show?" Parker asked.

"Cooper's been running on fumes for a while now and the only thing that kept her going was her loyalty to Cole. She would have gone to the ends of the Earth to try to save him." An ache opened deep in Will's chest, a wound that thrummed with a desperate agony every time he let his thoughts stray to Mexico City. "Reeves and Davis treated Cole like a lab rat, then used him to try to kill Cooper. But in the end . . ."

"In the end," Georgia picked up where Will left off, "she chose *you*. Saved you."

"Yeah." Will swallowed thickly. "And paid for my life with Cole's. She won't forgive herself. Worse, she'll consider it a betrayal. The *ultimate* betrayal." The line she could never uncross. The sin that could never be forgiven.

But she was *wrong* and Will would go to the very ends of the Earth and back again to make her see that.

"She's hurting and grieving and shutting out everything but the anger. It's keeping her going." *For now*. But the crash was coming and the grief would have it's day. But when it all finally caught up with her, and Cooper finally fell apart, he'd make damn sure she could do it in the safety of his arms.

"She wants revenge," Parker offered quietly. "So would I." He met Georgia's gaze, heat and loyalty and something Will couldn't name but was so damn happy to see passing between them.

"Me too." Georgie smiled softly.

Parker leaned across the bar and pressed a quick kiss to Georgia's mouth. "As I don't plan to get kidnapped and tortured *ever* again I think we can say your vengeance quota is full."

Georgia snorted and took a sip of the decaf coffee she'd complained loudly about.

A few days ago, the idea of this relationship, of his sister's new-found independence, had felt raw and wrong and threatening. He'd been afraid Georgia didn't need him anymore. That too much time had passed and too many things had changed. The idea had hurt.

But every time Will saw the way Parker looked at her,

touched her, teased her . . . Every time Will witnessed the way Georgia let Parker close, took a breath when he touched her, put a hand to her belly when she glanced at him . . .

Happiness unfurled like a full sail on an open ocean open. Will couldn't make room for anything other than the warmth that filled him for the way Parker treated Georgia.

Well, warmth, and a little bit of jealousy. Because he knew what it was for someone to act as the sun, a bright, steady center of gravity that kept everything stable.

Will's world had gone dark, but sunrise was coming. Even if he had to give it a little nudge.

"Cooper will show. The promise of catching Davis and Reeves together will be too much to resist."

"What makes you so sure she won't kill him the second she sees him?"

"Because I'll be in the way." Right between her and the line she'd never be able to uncross, just liked he'd promised. "No matter how much she wants to take that shot, she won't risk me." Will understood that it sounded insane. That he was essentially planning to be a human shield for a guy who didn't deserve it. But Cooper *did*. If she pulled that trigger out of rage, out of hate, she'd never get that part of herself back.

It would die as surely as Davis.

And Will wasn't about to let that happen.

"If she shoots you, I swear the last thing you hear will be my voice saying, 'I told you so.'" Georgia graced him with a grin that didn't quite make it past a grimace.

Will dropped a hand to her shoulder and squeezed.

"I'd expect nothing less."

CHAPTER TWENTY-FIVE

The sky was an inky, cloudless black when Cooper hefted her backpack up one shoulder, left Rock Creek Park Trail and picked her way through dense woods with nothing more than a pen light and a quarter moon to show the way. The quiet and the terrain—wooded and rolling with hills—reminded her of home.

She doubted she'd ever see it again. Would ever walk those trails again. Hear her father laugh or see her sister smile.

She found her spot and settled in. The hours passed and the cold bite of night gave way to a clear-blue and cloudless morning. Birdsong, then distant traffic ate away at the steady quiet. Soon cyclists and joggers and hikers would fill the trail behind her—one of Washington DC's most popular.

Getting in unseen had been easy. Getting out would be infinitely more difficult.

Cooper didn't care. Everything felt cold and distant, her sights set and focused on the target. She finished off a protein bar and a bottle of water, stowed both back in her bag, then slipped behind her rifle, already set and waiting. She stared through the scope, through the trees and straight into the Smithsonian National Zoo.

As she waited, everything became sharp and clear. The big cat enclosure. The bend in the walking path. The small bench where Davis and Reeves had met, more than once, for a cup of coffee before work and a walk through the zoo.

In this national park, they'd plotted and planned. Sold out their country, treated good men like science experiments, then sentenced those same men to death.

And they'd used her to pull the trigger and clean up their mess. Twice.

And whether they knew it or not, they'd set her on the path to a third—and final—job. In this pretty park, on the far side of the lion exhibit, Cooper was going end this, once and for all.

Could they feel it? she wondered.

Could Davis and Reeves sense that their time on this earth had nearly run out? She checked her watch then peered through her scope, waiting, watching.

They were down to minutes now, instead of hours.

Cooper stilled, filtering out everything around her . . . and let herself wonder what would come next. What would happen after.

This wasn't the end she'd wanted.

Wasn't the future she'd planned.

Eighteen months ago, all she'd wanted was to go home. To get back to normal. To go back to her life and her partner and her job.

It hadn't taken long for her to realize how naive that was.

For her to settle into her new reality. To realize there was no going back, only a bleak path forward.

She'd contented herself with chasing answers and looking for cures. Saving Cole had kept her focused, kept her going.

That singular goal had both consumed and distracted her, driven her to focus on the next step, the next obstacle or mark or country. Thinking about what came next, what came after, had been left to dark nights and vague dreams.

A thin, cold comfort when loneliness and despair threatened to encroach.

Until Will.

From the moment she'd stared down at him in that clearing, he'd lit up her world like a flare, bright and bold and determined.

He'd stood by her. Forgiven her. Encouraged her.

He'd touched her in ways he'd promised, ways she'd longed for, and ways she'd never expected.

And would never forget.

Even now, she carried him with her. His warm, rough voice. A rumble in the back of her head telling her to come home. That it was okay, that he was waiting, that life would work itself out.

Because her eyes stung and her fingers trembled beneath the weight of wanting him, of missing him, she tried to fall into her training, shut out the ancillary, and focused on what was in front of her.

Tried, and *failed*.

The longing wouldn't leave her. Understandable, she supposed, as his touch still lingered.

But it would fade. It would have to.

She didn't deserve a warm, bright future. She didn't deserve to feel his breath at the back of her neck or catch his smile from across the room or hear the rolling rumble of his laugh.

She didn't deserve to be happy. Not with him. Not when she'd bought and paid for that happiness with her best friend's life.

And definitely not when she didn't regret it, not even for a second. Not when she'd do it all over again.

She'd choose Will. Every time. Ruthlessly. Remorselessly. Without thought or hesitation.

Cole deserved more loyalty than that. More loyalty from *her*.

So no, she didn't get to be happy.

But she did have a job to finish.

Two joggers appeared, both men, each fit and trim, one dark haired, one ginger.

Cooper let them go. They weren't who she was looking for.

She glanced at her watch. Five past eight. The zoo had just opened and any second now, Reeves and Davis would meet and talk and die.

And finally, this nightmare would be over.

Another man appeared, his pace clipped and sharp, as if he had so many better, more important things to do. Cooper followed him, waiting for him to pass through sight-lines obscured by trees and buildings, and sucked in a breath when he strode to the open bench . . . and straight into her crosshairs.

Pruett Davis.

Cooper had spent the last several days studying the man. His face. His habits. Scouring every single detail that Parker had provided after unlocking the files. She knew Davis was an only child. That he'd attended a state school but graduated with a perfect GPA. That he'd served in the military, and later been recruited by the CIA. He was in his late forties, but ruthlessly devoted to both diet and exercise. It showed in his face—cut and tight where most men his age had begun to succumb to time and age, their jaws and chins and cheeks going soft or round or full. And it showed in his physique, a compact but commanding frame that made up in muscle what it lacked in height. This wasn't a man who planned to quietly succumb to the pull of time or allow himself to age with disinterest or grace.

But his efforts were all for nothing.

Cooper had no intention of letting him age more than a few more minutes. Just enough time for Reeves to arrive.

She shifted, tilting her head a fraction and letting her finger rest on the trigger.

She'd take out Davis first, she decided. By the time Reeves realized what was happening, the second shot would already be on the way.

Davis would never see it coming and Reeves wouldn't have more than a split second of fear.

It was a better end than either one of them deserved.

Another jogger appeared at the top of the path, his build too tall, too trim to be Reeves.

The hair on the back of her neck stood on end and her gut clenched.

Cooper adjusted the scope, watched as the two men who'd jogged past minutes ago reappeared and this time, she saw what she'd missed the first time.

Ear pieces. The bulge of guns at the smalls of their backs.

Shit. Shit. Shit.

They were here for Davis.

It all happened in a flash and a flurry of movement. Weapons were drawn. Orders were shouted. Davis went to the ground, and his hands were secured behind his back.

It had all been a setup, she realized with a dawning sense of frustrated rage. A ploy to get Davis out in the open.

Cooper ground her teeth.

Will.

He had done this. Had used his friends and his connections to set the meet and spring the trap.

Cooper bit back a curse. They'd probably caught Reeves *days* ago. And now they had Davis, too.

But they couldn't keep him. Couldn't take him. Couldn't throw him in some cell or cut him some deal.

He was *hers* goddamn it.

Davis didn't get to walk away from this. Didn't get to trade information for a lighter sentence.

She shifted. It wasn't over. Not yet. When they pulled the bastard to his feet she'd have a short window and a clean shot.

It was all she'd need.

Two men gripped Davis by the elbows and pulled him to his feet, but as he stood, another stepped directly in front of him, obscuring her shot. Rage, white hot and vicious, slammed through her.

Move. Move. Move.

As if he'd heard her, the man turned, pulling the hoodie from his head as he did.

Will.

He stood directly in front of Davis, his stance loose but his feet planted, his taller, broader body blocking her target. His brow furrowed, he panned his gaze, looking for something.

No, she realized, pulling her finger away from the trigger, someone. He stopped, his gaze fixed, and Cooper knew he'd worked out where she was most likely to be.

He was off, but not by much.

Move.

But he didn't. Just set his jaw and held up the shitty little phone they'd bought in Mexico and used in the market. She'd ditched hers the second she'd walked away from him. Common sense said he should have done the same.

That he hadn't sent a rush of unwanted warmth through her. There was only one reason for him to hold onto that piece of crap.

So she could reach him. God, how she wanted to reach for him.

Behind Will, Davis shifted, but the two men holding him didn't move. Just said something Cooper couldn't hope to hear. Will shook his head but kept his gaze steady and on the woods. On her hide.

A long moment passed and a smile, something grim and

determined and fierce crept to his face. He wiggled the phone and though he didn't know exactly where she was, he stared her down all the same.

Arrogant prick.

Minutes ticked by, and outside a single, sharp gesture he made to one of the other men, Will didn't move. Not one step.

Fine.

She hardened her thumping heart and dialed the number she'd memorized before they'd split up in Tepito.

When he picked up, she didn't give him a chance to speak. "Move," she ordered.

"No."

"*Move*," she ground out.

"I can't do that, Coop," he said, his voice soft and warm and patient. "I made you a promise. I intend to keep it."

Ignoring him, she ground out, "He's the reason your friends are dead. He orchestrated that hit in Afghanistan. He gave the order to take those men out. *He's* the reason"—she choked out, emotion clogging her throat and gripping her frame so hard she had to ease her grip on her gun—"he's the reason Cole is dead."

"I know—"

"Then why are you protecting him?" she shouted through the line, every emotion she hadn't wanted to deal with or acknowledge bubbling to the surface.

"Oh, Cooper," Will said with a fond, sad sigh, "I'm not protecting *him*."

She closed her eyes against the implication, but it slipped beneath her skin and settled her heart. She breathed and relaxed and wanted to resent Will for the simple power he had over her.

"Then move," she pleaded, "and let me end this."

"I promised you, do you remember? I told you if the day came and you were too close to that line, that I'd stand in front of you. I don't break my promises."

"I crossed that line in Mexico City."

"No," he assured her, his voice steady and sure. "You didn't. You took that shot to *save* me. But this is different. This is bitter and angry and vengeful."

"None of that stopped *you*," she snapped off. "I let you finish things. Let you have the final say."

"It's different, Coop, and you know it. Killing Matías didn't condemn another. There was no collateral damage."

"What are you talking about?"

"Olivia York is still missing," Will said. "I know you're mad, and I know it's easy to blame her for this. But she's an innocent, Cooper. She didn't know what Reeves was up to behind her back, but once she did, she tried to stop it."

"You'll find her," Cooper said, working hard to convince herself that York was not her problem. "Reeves—"

"Doesn't know where she is. He doesn't have those kinds of resources. But Davis *does*."

"I don't care," she forced out through clenched teeth, but the words lacked the ruthless conviction she tried to infuse them with.

"Will it make it better?" he asked quietly, his gaze still fixed on the trees. "Tell me that killing him will make you feel better, Cooper. Tell me that you'll stop hurting. That you'll stop blaming yourself. Tell me that doing this will erase a single ounce of the guilt you've shouldered for Cole's death. Tell me that taking this shot won't destroy you. Tell me it's what you need to move on, to move forward. Tell me it will bring you peace and closure and I will *move*. I will give you what you gave me. Tell me it will *save* you, Cooper, and I will step aside."

She wanted to, oh God, how she wanted to. But she couldn't lie to him. Not ever again. "It's my fault." The confession was easy but raw and sharp as it left her throat all the same. "I pulled that trigger. It was my choice—"

"Is that what you think? That you made a calculated, measured decision? That you chose who lived and who died?"

"He had a gun and you were defenseless and I-I—" She took a deep breath, forced back the memory that was sharp and vivid and cruel. Would it always be this way? Would she always remember Cole as the man in the market? The one she'd barely recognized, he was so cold and hard and devoid of every single thing she'd loved about him. Would he ever be more to her than the guy who'd tried to kill Will? "I shot him. I *killed* him. That's on me. I could have—"

"Could have what? If you hadn't taken that shot, he would have killed me, Coop."

"You don't know that."

"Yeah, honey, I do. And so did you." He shifted a little from foot to foot, but otherwise didn't move. "But it wasn't a *choice*, Cooper. You weren't judge, jury and executioner that day."

"I—"

"You did what you are *trained to do*," he stressed. "We both know that when it comes to threat assessment in the field that sometimes decisions are made in seconds. Heartbeats. There was no choice, honey. Your *job* was to protect your assets on the ground. To provide cover." He sighed and his voice went deep and rough, like he wanted to reach for her, touch her, hold her, and was beyond frustrated with the fact that he couldn't.

"How can you be so sure?"

"Let me ask you this," he said, his voice a steady thrum in her ear. "Same situation. Same setup. Except this time, Pierce was there, instead of me. Does it turn out any different?"

She hesitated for a long moment. She wanted to say yes, yes it would, and yet . . . the truth was she couldn't be entirely sure. Because Will was right, from an operational standpoint, she'd acted on instinct, identified and neutralized the threat.

"What if the roles had been reversed?" he asked, pushing her.

"What if you were working with Cole to try to save me? Pretend I'd made you eggs on toast *years* ago, Cooper." A smile, small but warm, entered his voice and graced his face. "Pretend it was me that had gone through that cognitive trial. You would have fought for me. Come for me. Done everything you could to save me."

He wasn't questioning it, she realized with a warm sense of pride. He just knew. How she felt about him. How far she'd go for him. Will might still be struggling, might still feel unsteady and unsure, but not about her. And for reasons she didn't examine, that *mattered*.

"Would you have let me kill Cole?" he asked.

"No," she said, and though doubt tried to thread its way through the hypothetical, she knew, down to her bones, that she'd have taken the shot. Covered her asset on the ground. It didn't matter who it was.

But it didn't *change* anything. Will was still alive and Cole was still dead, and Cooper had been the one to kill him. Maybe the action itself hadn't been selfish, but how could she ever look at Will, touch him, hold him, love him, and not hate herself for the price she'd paid for the privilege?

"You didn't choose me over Cole, honey," Will continued, a soft comfort in her ear. "You didn't choose love over loyalty. You didn't choose what you wanted over what he needed. You're not that selfish, Cooper, and your sense of loyalty is not that shallow."

She closed her eyes. "I'm not sorry," she whispered.

Will barked out a startled laugh. "That I'm not dead? Gotta admit, I'm damn glad to hear it, Coop."

"But I should be. I should want to do it all over again. Want to do it differently. How can I be so, so grateful that you're alive, when Cole isn't?"

The laughter died and Will went still. "Do you remember what you told me in Costa Rica? That I could be grateful that I lived, even though so many others had died. Grief and happiness are not mutually exclusive, Cooper. You can come home to me, wake up with me, be *happy* with me, and that will in no way diminish your loyalty to Cole. You *can* grieve for him and move on with your life. Cole would want that for you. Would be pissed as all hell if his death destroyed your life."

Will wasn't wrong, and she wouldn't argue with him. Cole would expect her to move on. To be happy. It wasn't something they'd talked about, but it was something they'd lived with. Their jobs were dangerous, and they lived and worked with the knowledge that they might not always be partners.

But they'd always be friends.

"He'd expect me to finish this, Will," she said, settling back in behind the rifle. "He'd want me to make sure it could never happen again."

"And we will," he assured her. "But not today. Not like this."

"He deserves to die."

"But Olivia doesn't. Please," he whispered, his tone going rough with a plea she'd never be able to deny, "help me bring her home. It's been *six months*. I know what that's like, and—"

"Okay." She sighed, already halfway through disassembling her rifle.

"What?" he asked, startled into stepping forward.

"*Okay*," she repeated on a huff. She'd heard him beg her once, just once, and never again. She couldn't stand it. Wouldn't hear it. Not under these circumstances. "Just . . . just promise you won't let him get away with this. Don't let him cut some deal he doesn't deserve."

"I promise. Now get down here—"

She shook her head and shouldered her bag. She wasn't ready. Going to Will, it meant moving on, moving forward, and it was just . . . too much, too soon. "I can't."

"Cooper—"

This time, the plea was hers. "Please don't ask me to. I—" she swallowed hard. "There are things I need to do."

"Let me do them with you, Coop. You don't have to do any of this on your own anymore," he reminded her. "Not if you don't want to."

"If I come to you now—it's the easy thing."

"That doesn't mean it's wrong."

No, no it didn't. But she couldn't be sure. Not yet. Not without some time and space. "I can't trust myself right now. If I come to you," she started and willed him to understand what she barely grasped herself, "I won't know if it's because everything's broken and hard and scary, or . . ."

"Or if you really want *me*," he finished for her.

"I just need to find my feet."

"How much time do you need?"

She picked her way through the woods and back toward the trail. She didn't know. Wasn't even sure why she wanted it or what to do with it. But she knew she needed it. "I don't know."

"You're free to go, Coop," he said, repeating something he'd told her not that long ago. "And I'm free to follow."

"Will—"

"I'm giving you a head start—and the time you're asking me for—but I'm not letting you go, Cooper Reed. Because even if you're not sure what you want, *I* am. You're my home, Coop. And I'm always going to come back to you."

A smile, small and fragile and real, touched her mouth. "Pretty sure of yourself, Bennett."

"I know you, Cooper. How long do you really think it'll take me to catch up?"

"Guess we'll find out."

"I'll see you soon." And just like that, promise made, he hung up on her.

See you soon.

She'd be lying if she said she wasn't looking forward to it.

CHAPTER TWENTY-SIX

The scent of burning cedar chips and charred meat greeted Cooper when she pulled to the curb outside her parents' carefully restored two-story craftsman.

Strange, the way some things never changed. The paint still looked fresh and new—her mother's doing, no doubt—and the lawn was still bright green and neatly trimmed, not a stray weed or overgrown patch to be found—her father's doing, as he liked the lawn the way he liked his hair, close cut and tightly regimented. The woods still sprawled in the back, and the same ancient pickup still sat in the drive.

And even with the car doors shut and windows up, she could hear children shouting and music playing. The first Sunday of the month and the family barbecue was in full swing.

Her hands went damp with sweat. She'd called ahead, of course, because the last thing she'd wanted was to rise from the dead just to send her parents to their graves with shock. There'd been tears and questions—so many questions—most of which she'd been able to evade or smother under her parents' heady sense of relief.

But now, she'd have to face them. Face the changes that time and grief had wrought.

She climbed out of the car and snapped the door shut behind her. How was it possible that after all of the places she'd been and all the challenges she'd faced, this was the one that felt the most intimidating?

She started up the walk and was halfway up the steps when the screen door creaked and her mom stepped out onto the shaded porch. "Cooper?"

Cooper froze, but her mother didn't, rushing forward on a noise that launched like a sob but flew through the air like a laugh.

"Hey, Mom," she said before her arms were full and her mother, who still smelled the same—like lemon-iced sugar cookies—had her arms around her.

Her mom squeezed her twice, then forced her back a step. "You're tan," she said, running a critical eye from the top of Cooper's freshly dyed hair—back to natural, which also felt strangely weird—to the bottom of her tried and true sneakers, which had, thank God, followed her around the world and kept her footing firm, even when everything else was shifting. "And you're too thin by half. Come on," she said, linking her arm through Cooper's and leading her through the house. "Your dad started grumbling about overcooking the ribs twenty minutes ago, but he wouldn't let anyone eat until you got here."

When they reached the back door, propped open with a heavy brick, her mother stopped her and pulled her into another hug. "We're just so, *so* glad to have you home."

"I know you must have a ton of questions." In all honestly, Cooper had expected to be greeted either with emotional hysterics or thousands of questions. This . . . this was on par with every time she'd returned home on leave, even if her mother did hug a little tighter or hold her a little longer.

"We do, of course, we do. But right now, we just want you here and home. There will be time enough for all that later." She brushed her fingers beneath her eyes and tucked her hair behind her ears, then stepped out on the back deck. "Besides, he said it would be best if we didn't pester you for the details."

"Who said?" Cooper asked as her sister took the back steps up the deck two at a time and grabbed her in a fierce, tight hug.

"You're here!" Kayla squealed, then shoved Cooper back a step. "You're so tan! And *blonde*."

Cooper tugged a bit self-consciously at the ends of her hair. "Had to go lighter to get all the dye out."

"Bet Mom said you were too thin, though."

Cooper pulled a smile to her mouth. Kayla hadn't changed a bit. Still tall and loud and full of life.

"Now," her sister said, leading her down the back steps. "We've been told to give you some space and let it all settle back to normal and blah blah *blah*—like this family has ever done normal!—but you know I'm not great with the rules. So, can I have just *one* question?"

"Sure."

"Where on God's good green earth did you find *him*?"

"What?" Cooper asked, following Kayla's gaze to the barbecue pit and the man standing next to her father.

Son of a bitch.

He'd remembered. And honestly, as she stood there watching as Will and her father studied the insides of the huge, black smoker, Cooper couldn't imagine why she'd ever doubted him.

As her feet hit the grass, Will straightened, giving her a full view of his uniform-clad backside.

Full uniform? The man wasn't playing fair.

As if he'd sensed her, Will turned, and stopped Cooper dead in her tracks.

Good. God.

"Yeah," her mother said, patting her on the arm as Will approached. "He does seem to have that effect on people."

Cooper swallowed hard and reminded herself that she was at her *family's barbecue*. Climbing the man like a tree would be inappropriate. "When did he get here?" she asked.

"This morning," Kayla offered, her tone smug and satisfied. "Seems pretty damn protective of you, Coop."

"He certainly had a lot to say," her mother agreed. "And a lot to ask. Wanted to be sure we didn't crowd you, or ask too many questions, or overwhelm you with too many people. Said coming home can be stressful and that we should give you some room. Isn't that right?" her mother said, all smiles for Will as he approached.

"Sometimes people need a little time to settle," he agreed, his words and gaze all for Cooper. "But not too much."

"Well," her mother rubbed her hand across her shoulders, "I'll leave you two to say your hellos and see if I can't go wrangle that baster from your father. Don't take too long, though, you know how he gets when he's hungry."

She left, dragging Kayla away by her wrist even as her sister looked over her shoulder, pointed at Will and mouthed, *yum-my!*

"Hey Coop," he said, his mouth stretching into a wide, clean-shaven smile.

And yeah, she'd been right. Dimples. Two of them, deep and curving, on either side of his mouth.

And because she was feeling a lot off balance and a little bit dazzled, she said the first thing that came to mind. "Nothing good ever starts with the words 'hey Coop.'"

"No?" he asked, his grin turning wild and wicked. The wind caught his hair, tugging at strands he'd left long on top, but cut close at the sides and the nape. God. She'd known he'd be beautiful. Had known that once he found his feet and his confidence that he'd wear his scars like medals and his survival with pride.

She just hadn't fully expected the effect it would have on *her*. That he'd dressed up the clean shave and fresh haircut with a full uniform and a wide grin told her that he'd begun the campaign to capture her heart and that he was *so* not above playing dirty.

"I can think of a *few* good things that start with the phrase, 'hey Coop.'"

"Like what?" she asked, because if the man was going to work this hard to prove just where his home was, she wasn't about to stop him.

"How about," he stepped in close and ran a hand down her arm, "hey Coop, it's good to see you."

She shrugged. "Not bad, I guess, but nothing noteworthy, either."

"Let me try again." He grinned, and twined their fingers together. "Hey Coop, I missed you." He pressed a kiss to the back of her knuckles.

She rolled her eyes. "Better, but hardly memorable."

He leaned in close, rubbed his smooth cheek against hers, and whispered against her ear, "Hey Coop, wanna defile Captain America?"

She couldn't help it, she broke into fits of laughter that rose from her belly, spilled out her lips, and stung at her eyes. She couldn't breathe, but Will didn't seem to care, he wrapped an arm around her waist, a hand around her nape, and pulled her mouth to his.

How? she wondered. How had she ever thought she could walk away from him? And how had she ever thought that standing in his arms, beneath his warmth, under his lips, could be anything other than a joy? She'd been so worried that she'd resent him. That every ounce of joy would be tempered with an equal sense of loss.

But Will was and always had been, brighter than the darkness.

He was her happiness. Her home. Her future.

She'd miss Cole. Would make time to mourn him, and then honor him. But she'd do it as she so desperately wanted to do everything else—with Will.

When he pulled away, he pressed his forehead to hers and stared into her eyes. "Wait. I have one more," he said, his words a warm puff of air against her mouth. "Hey Coop, I love you."

She pulled back just enough to watch his face as she said, "I know."

"Oh no," he said, his expression descending into a scowl, "you do *not* get to be the Han Solo of this relationship."

She pulled away and started across the lawn. Glancing over her shoulder, she grinned. "Come on, Chewy, I'll introduce you to the family."

Will grabbed her hand and jerked her back, pulling her close and kissing her breathless. When he was done, he said, "You're gonna be trouble, aren't you Coop?"

"Yeah," she agreed, "but you're gonna love it." She smiled, pressed her lips to his, then moved her mouth to the sensitive part of his ear. "But only *half* as much as I love you."

He shivered and pulled away. "Come on." He tugged her toward the barbecue pit. "Sooner we eat, sooner you can keep some of those *marvel*-ous promises you made."

"First the jokes and now the puns. God save me." Her hand clasped in his and a laugh lodged in her throat, Cooper did as she suspected she always would and followed Will home.

The End

THANK YOU

Thank you for reading FEARLESS! I hope you enjoyed Will and Cooper's story as much as I enjoyed bringing it to you. BREATHLESS, Liam and Olivia's story, will be out in 2019! To receive an alert when BREATHLESS becomes available for pre-order or goes live in Kindle Unlimited, please sign-up for my NEWSLETTER.

If you enjoyed this book, please consider leaving an honest REVIEW at the outlet of your choice. Reviews are wonderfully helpful to every author, big or small, and are both welcome and very much appreciated.

For the latest news, sales, and special offers for all of my current and upcoming novels (including Pierce's book!) sign up for my NEWSLETTER or like & follow my FACEBOOK PAGE.

For more information on all things Somerton Security and Elizabeth Dyer head to my WEBSITE.

If you're interested in receiving advanced review copies in exchange for an honest review? Sign-up to express interest in joining my READER TEAM.

ABOUT THE AUTHOR

Elizabeth Dyer likes her heroines smart and snarky, and her heroes strong and sexy. A recovering attorney and a recent coffee devotee, Elizabeth spends the majority of her time tucked into a corner table at Starbucks or pinned beneath her (overly affectionate) bullmastiff. When she isn't working or wrestling the dog, you can usually find her writing the types of sexy, suspenseful books she most loves to read.

A born-and-bred Texan, Elizabeth resides in Dallas, where she indulges in Netflix marathons, Instagramming her dog, and brunch. *Definitely* brunch. Elizabeth hates the phone as much as she loves all the social-media things and hearing from her readers.

DEFENSELESS

How far will she go to protect the sexiest guy in tech?

When ex-marine Georgia Bennett left the military for high-end private security, it was supposed to soften her snarky attitude. Instead, her short fuse just earned her a punishment of an assignment: protect too-smart-for-his-own-good tech genius and Department of Defense contractor Parker Livingston. It should have been easy--only no one warned Georgia that Parker was one seriously drop-dead-gorgeous geek.

The last thing Parker needs is a bodyguard, especially not one with killer curves and a sassy mouth who tempts him to do something incredibly stupid. He's too busy investigating whoever is turning his technology against him and threatening his team of covert operatives. But when an assassin sends Georgia and Parker running for their lives, it might just be the explosive sexual chemistry and the trust that's building between them that saves their necks. Because the only thing more dangerous than the combination of Parker's intellect and Georgia's aim is their steadfast desire to protect each other, no matter the cost.

RELENTLESS

A mission worth killing for. A love worth dying for.

Ethan Somerton doesn't do safe or easy. He's all about the challenge. The *risk*. In order to rescue one of his agents, Ethan must infiltrate the ruthless Vega cartel. One tiny error—just one—and he's dead. Which means he needs Natalia Vega. Bright, beautiful, and cut sharper than the most lethal blade, she's finally reached her breaking point. Now Ethan must find a way to make her *surrender*.

Caught between desperate choices and no-win situations, Natalia has survived the unthinkable by becoming dangerous, relentless, and feared. When it comes to protecting her sister, there's no line Natalia won't cross. But when Ethan storms into her life with his cocksure arrogance, stone-cold competence, and seductive promises, Natalia wonders if she's finally found a way out. But discovering whether Ethan is salvation or destruction is going to require the one thing Natalia doesn't have—trust.

As the cartel implodes and loved ones are threatened, Ethan and Natalia are going to have to choose between love, loyalty, and the lies they cling to. They could run, knowing they'll never be safe. They could fight, knowing they'll probably die. Or they can trust in each other...and do something *far* more dangerous.

Made in the USA
Las Vegas, NV
17 February 2021